ELECTRIC BLUE

Books by Nancy Bush

CANDY APPLE RED

ELECTRIC BLUE

Published by Kensington Publishing Corporation

ELECTRIC BLUE

NANCY BUSH

KENSINGTON BOOKS
www.kensingtonbooks.com

Library of Congress Card Catalog Number: 2006928695
0-7582-0907-X

First Printing: October 2006
10 9 8 7 6 5 4 3 2 1

Printed in the United States of America

Chapter One

Mental illness runs in the Purcell family.
I'd diligently typed this conclusion at the top of the report written on my word-processing program. I'd been so full of myself, so pleased with my thorough research and keen detecting skills that I'd smiled a Cheshire Cat smile for weeks on end. That smug grin hung around just like the cat's. It was on my face when I woke in the morning and it was there on my lips as I closed my eyes at night.

I spent hours in self-congratulation:

Oh, Jane Kelly, private investigator extraordinaire. *How easy it is for you to be a detective. How good you are at your job. How exceptional you are in your field!*

However . . .

I wasn't smiling now.

Directly in front of me was a knife-wielding, delusional, growling, schizophrenic—the situation a direct result of my investigation into the Purcells. In disbelief I danced left and right, frantic to avoid serious injury. I looked into the rolling eyes of my attacker and felt doomed. Doomed and downright *FURIOUS* at Dwayne Durbin. It was his fault I was here! It was his ridiculous belief in my abilities that had put me in harm's way! Hadn't I told him I'm no good at confrontation? Hadn't I made it clear that I'm damn near a chicken-heart? Doesn't he *ever* listen to me?

His fervent belief in me was going to get me killed!

Gritting my teeth, I thought: *I hope I live long enough to kill Dwayne first. . . .*

I was deep into the grunt work necessary to earn my license as a private investigator. Dwayne Durbin, my mentor, had finally convinced me I would be good at the job. His cheerleading on my behalf was not entirely altruistic: he wanted me to come and work for him.

I'd resisted for a while but circumstances had arisen over the summer that had persuaded me Dwayne just might be right. So, in September I became Dwayne Durbin's apprentice—and then I became his slave, spending my time putting in the hours, digging through records, doing all his dog work—which really irritates me, more at myself than him, because I'd *known* this was going to happen.

And though I resented all the crap-work thrown my way, Dwayne wasn't really around enough for me to work up a head of steam and vent my feelings. He was embroiled in a messy divorce case for Camellia "Cammie" Purcell Denton. His association with the Purcell family was why I'd delved into the Purcell family history in the first place. I admit this was more for my own edification than any true need on Dwayne's part, but I figured it couldn't hurt.

That particular September afternoon—the afternoon I wrote my conclusion on the report—was sunny and warm and lazy. It was a pleasure to sit on Dwayne's couch, a piece of furniture I'd angled toward his sliding glass door for a view of the shining waters of Lake Chinook. I could look over the top of my laptop as I wirelessly searched databases and historical archives and catch a glimpse of sunlight bouncing like diamonds against green water.

Resentment faded. Contentment returned. After all, it's difficult to hold a grudge when, apart from some tedium, life was pretty darn good. My rent was paid, my mother's impending visit had yet to materialize, my brother was too involved with his fiancée to pay me much attention, and I had a dog who thought I was . . . well . . . the cat's meow.

I finished the report and typed my name on the first page, mentally patting myself on the back for a job well done. Reluctantly, I climbed to my feet and went to check out Dwayne's refrigerator. If he possessed anything more than beer and a suspect jar of half-eaten, orange-colored chili con queso dip, life would pass from pretty darn good to sublime. My gaze settled on a lone can of diet A&W root beer. Not bad. Popping the top, I returned to the couch and my laptop.

Intending to concentrate, my eyes kept wandering to the scene outside the sliding glass door. Dwayne, who'd been lounging in a deck chair, was now making desultory calls on his cell phone. He stepped in and out of my line of vision as I hit the print button, wirelessly sending information to Dwayne's printer. Nirvana. I'm technologically challenged, but Dwayne has a knack for keeping things running smoothly and efficiently despite my best efforts. Since I'd acquired my newest laptop—a gift from an ex-boyfriend—I'd slowly weaned myself from my old grinder of a desktop. This new, eager slimmed-down version had leapfrogged me into a new era of computers. It fired up and slammed me onto the Internet faster than you can say, "Olly olly Oxenfree." (I have no idea what this means but it was a favorite taunt from my brother Booth who was always crowing it when we were kids, gloating and laughing and skipping away, delighted that he'd somehow "got" me. Which, when I think about it, still has the power to piss me off.)

The new laptop untethered me from my old computer's roosting spot on the desk in my bedroom. Now, I'm mobile. I bring my work over to Dwayne's, which he highly encourages. I'm fairly certain Dwayne hopes I'll suddenly whirl into a female frenzy of cleaning and make his place spotlessly clean. Like, oh, sure, *that's* going to happen.

Still, I enjoy my newfound freedom and so Dwayne's cabana has become a sort of office for me. I claimed my spot on his well-used but extremely comfortable one-time blue, now dusty gray, sofa early. Being more of a phone guy, Dwayne spends his time on his back deck/dock and conducts business outdoors as long as it isn't raining or hailing and sometimes even if it is.

Feeling absurdly content (always a bad sign for me, one I choose to ignore) I checked my e-mail. Nothing besides a note from someone named Trixie which I instantly deleted. One day I made the mistake of opening one of those spam e-mails about super hot sex and ever since I've been blessed with a barrage of Viagra, Cialis and penis enlargement ads and/or promises. If I didn't have penis envy before, I sure as hell do now. Eighteen inches? Where would you park that thing on a daily basis? There are a lot of hours when it's not in use . . . unless you count the fact that it functions as some guys' brains. I have met these sorts, but I try not to date them. Makes for uncomfortable dinners out where I talk and they just stare at my breasts. If I had serious cleavage I could almost understand, but my fear is that it simply means my conversation is really boring.

My cell phone rang with a whiny, persistent ring. I am going to have to figure out how to change it. A James Bond theme would be nice. I snatched it up without looking at Caller ID. An error. Marta Cornell, one of Portland's most voracious divorce lawyers, was on the line.

"Jane!" Marta's voice shouted into my ear. Her voice lies at sonic-boom level. I feared this time she may have shot one of my inner ear bones—the hammer, the anvil or the stirrup—into the center of my brain. Who names those things, anyway?

"You know Dwayne was working for Cammie Purcell," Marta charged ahead without waiting for my response. "Jane? Are you there?"

"Yes." I was cautious. Marta was Cammie's divorce lawyer and Dwayne had been following Cammie's husband Chris around for several weeks, intent on obtaining proof that he possessed a second family. Said family was apparently sucking up some Purcell money. Chris Denton wasn't exactly a bigamist. He'd never actually married his other "wife." But he had children with her and he divided his time between them and Cammie. Stunted as he was maturity-wise, I was impressed he could juggle two relationships. Sometimes I find it difficult just taking care of my dog.

"That job's pretty much finished, isn't it?" Marta asked.

"I think so." Actually, I wasn't completely sure. Cases like Cammie's seemed to undulate: sometimes the work lasted days on end; other times it nearly died. When Dwayne had first discovered the dirt on Chris, he'd disclosed it to Cammie and Marta. With divorce in the offing, Marta must have seen greenbacks floating around her head, but weirdly, Cammie's only remark had been a question: "What are the childrens' names?"

Later I'd learned this query had some merit after all: Chris's two girls—with his almost wife—were Jasmine and Blossom. When Dwayne told Cammie their names her face crumpled as if she were going to cry. But then she fought off the tears and went into a quiet rage instead.

"Her eyes looked like they were going to bug out of her head," Dwayne told me later. "I took a step backward. Her hands were clenching and unclenching. She wanted to kill me for telling her. A part of my brain was searching the room for a weapon. But then she kinda pulled herself together." Dwayne gave me a long look. "I don't ever want to be in a room alone with her again. No wonder the bastard left her."

Camellia's strange behavior was explained when it surfaced that many of the female members of the Purcell family were named after flowers. Apparently Chris's non-Purcell "wife" had fallen for this weird obsession as well, and since it was a decidedly Purcell quirk, Cammie appeared ready to kill over it.

This was about the time I decided to indulge in some Purcell family history. Hence, my report.

"Jasper Purcell would like to meet with you," Marta said, bringing me back to the present with a bang. "He needs a P.I."

"You mean, meet with Dwayne?" I asked, puzzled. I was the research person, not the A-list investigator.

"Nope." Her voice sounded as if she were trying to tamp down her excitement. Must be more money involved. "He called this morning and asked me for the name of a private investigator. It's something of a personal nature, to do with his family."

"This is Dwayne's case," I reminded her. I didn't add that Dwayne wanted to wash his hands of the whole thing.

"Jasper wants someone else to tackle this one. Says it's sensitive."

I glanced through the sliding glass door to where Dwayne, who'd removed his shirt in the unseasonably hot, early October sunshine, was standing on the dock. His back was hard, tan and smooth. Someone who knew him drove by in a speedboat and shouted good-natured obscenities. Dwayne turned his head, grinned and gave the guy the finger.

"How sensitive?" I asked.

"He said he wants a woman."

I wasn't sure what I thought of that. Just how many private investigators did the Purcell family need? "I'll have to make sure this is okay with Dwayne."

"I talked to Dwayne this morning," Marta revealed. "He said he's had his fill of the Purcells but if you wanted to step in, he was all for it."

Nice of Marta to keep that tidbit of information back while she felt me out on the subject. I didn't like being manipulated, and I was pretty sure that was what she was doing.

Also, I knew Dwayne's feelings about Cammie, but this sounded suspicious. Dwayne likes to cherry-pick assignments. That's why I'd been relegated to grinding research and drudge work. I narrowed my eyes at his back until he glanced around. His brows lifted at my dark look and he stuck his head inside the gap in the sliding glass door. "What?"

"I'm talking to Marta Cornell about the Purcells."

"They pay well, darlin', and that's the only goddamn good thing about 'em." He went back to the sunshine, turning his face skyward like a sybarite.

Marta persisted, "Our client wants you to meet him at Foster's around four. Get a table. He'll buy dinner."

Free food. I'm a sucker for it and Marta knows my weakness.

And Foster's On The Lake is just about my favorite restaurant in the whole world. I seesawed, thinking I might be getting into something I really shouldn't. In the end, I agreed to go. How bad could the Purcells be?

Two hours later I found a parking spot about a block from Foster's On The Lake—no small feat—then walked through the restaurant to the back patio, snagging a table beneath one of the plastic, faux-grass umbrellas that sported a commanding view of Lake Chinook. Most of the umbrellas are green canvas, but sometimes Jeff Foster, owner and manager of Foster's On The Lake, adds a bit of fun to the mix, hence the plastic-party-ones. He didn't notice my arrival or he would have steered me toward a less well-placed table. He knows how cheap I am and tries to give the paying customers the best seats. I was all ready to explain that I was being treated by one of the Purcells but a member of the wait staff I didn't know let me choose my table. Maybe it was because I'd taken a little extra care with my appearance. I'd unsnapped my ponytail, brushed and briefly hot-curled my hair, tossed on a tan, loosely flowing skirt and black tank top. I'd even done the mascara/eyeliner bit, topping the whole look off with some frosted lip gloss.

The Binkster, my pug, had cocked her head at me and slowly wagged her tail. I took this to mean I looked hot.

I'd forgotten to ask Marta what Jasper looked like. He was a Purcell and the Purcells were wealthy and notorious, so apparently that was supposed to be enough. From my research I knew he was in his mid-thirties. I settled back and ordered a Sparkling Cyanide, my new favorite drink, a bright blue martini that draws envious eyes from the people who've ordered your basic rum and Cokes.

I was sipping away when a man in the right age bracket strode onto the patio. He stopped short to look around. I nearly dropped my cocktail. I say nearly, because I'd paid a whopping eight bucks for it and I wasn't going to lose one drop unless Mt. St. Helen's erupted again and spewed ash and lava to rain down on

Foster's patio, sending us all diving for cover. Even then I might be able to balance it.

I felt my lips part. Marta must have guessed what my reaction would be when I clapped eyes on him. She probably was fighting back a huge *hardy-har-har* all the while we were on the phone. This guy was flat-out gorgeous. Women seated around me took notice: smoothing their hair, sitting up straighter, looking interested and attentive. His gaze settled on me. I gulped against a dry throat. He had it all. Movie star good looks. Electric blue eyes and thick lashes. Chiseled jaw. Smooth, naturally dark skin and blinding white teeth. And a strong physique—taut and muscular with that kind of sinewy grace that belongs to jungle cats. I should have known this was going to turn out badly. I should have heard the "too handsome" alarm clang in my brain. But, honestly, I just stared.

He flashed me a smile, then scraped back the chair opposite me. The sun's rays sent a shaft of gold light over his left arm. His gray shirt was one of those suede-ish fabrics that moves like a second skin.

"Jane Kelly?" he asked.

Great voice. Warm and mellow. He smelled good, too. Musky and citrusy at the same time. And his dark hair had the faintest, and I mean faintest, of an auburn tint, a shade women pay big, big, HUGE, bucks for.

I nodded, wondering if I should check for drool on my chin. You can never be too careful.

"I'm Jasper Purcell."

"Hello."

"Thanks for meeting me. I know I didn't give you a lot of time."

I cleared my throat. "No problem. Marta Cornell said you wanted to see me about your family. She wasn't specific."

"I wasn't specific with her." He hesitated, his eyes squinting a bit as if he were wrestling with confiding in me. After a moment, he said, "It's about my grandmother, Orchid Purcell."

I looked interested, waiting for him to continue.

"She named all her girls after flowers. But it's the only crazy thing she's done until now."

Mental illness runs in the Purcell family. . . . "What's happened?" I asked cautiously, but Jasper Purcell didn't answer me. He appeared to be lost to some inner world.

Eventually he surfaced, glancing around, seeming to notice his surroundings for the first time. "Nice place. I've never been here."

Since Foster's was a Lake Chinook institution I was kind of surprised. The Dunthorpe area—where the Purcell mansion had been for the last century—was just north of the lake. If Jasper Purcell grew up there, the restaurant seemed like a natural.

"How can I help you, Mr. Purcell?"

"Sorry." He leaned across the table and shook my hand. The heat of his fingers ran right up my arm. I was dazzled by that incredible face so close to mine. "Call me Jazz."

"Jazz?"

"Short for Jasper. My cousin Cammie could never pronounce it."

Nowhere in my research had anything been said about this man's extraordinary good looks. Was Cammie as beautiful as Jasper—Jazz—was handsome? I made a mental note to ask Dwayne.

Instinctively, I knew I should stay out of whatever he had in store for me. But I really wanted to help him. Really, *really* wanted to help him. Call it temporary insanity. But every cell in my body seemed to be magnetically attracted to him.

Jazz looked down at the table, then across the patio toward the lake. Light refracted off the water's green depths, glittering in soft squares of illumination across his cheek and jaw. I lifted my glass and nearly missed my mouth. My gaze was riveted on his face.

"Do you know anything about my grandmother?"

"I know she's a philanthropist, active on all kinds of boards."

"Was. Her health's been failing her. It could be anything from simple forgetfulness to Alzheimer's to another form of dementia, to—according to my aunt—a nasty trick she's playing on all of us." He gave me a look. "Between you and me, that's just not possible. My grandmother isn't made that way."

"So, what do you think?"

"She's definitely not as sharp as she once was. She doesn't drive anymore. We have someone taking care of her during the day who Nana likes, but it's tricky."

I thought carefully and said, "I'm not sure what you'd like me to do. I'm certainly no expert on that kind of thing."

Missy, Foster's most generously endowed waitress, hovered nearby. Jazz smiled, but shook his head at her. She cast a lingering look over her shoulder as she swayed off. "I'd just like someone else's opinion."

"How about a doctor's?"

He smiled, briefly and bitterly. "If you can figure out how to get Nana to see a doctor, that would be fantastic. She's afraid we're trying to railroad her. Wrest the family fortune out of her hands."

I could hear the beginnings of a very loud inheritance squabble revving up. "Is it what you're trying to do?"

"Not unless it comes to that," Jazz said grimly. He lightly drummed his fingers on the table, frowning. "I just want you to meet her. Someone outside the family who has no ax to grind. A woman. My mother doesn't really trust strange men."

"You mean your grandmother."

His head snapped up. "Yes, grandmother. What did I say?"

"Mother."

I swear his skin paled a bit. "How Freudian," he murmured. "My mother's dead. Died not long after I was born. Nana gave me Purcell as a last name, and she raised me." He sighed. "Guess I'm throwing all the skeletons out of the closet. Feels easier than holding back, although other members of my family wouldn't agree."

"What caused—your mother's death?" In my research, I'd learned that Lily Purcell had died in a sanitarium when she was still in her teens. She'd had Jazz at a very tender age indeed.

Jazz's eyes met mine again. I felt slightly breathless under their solemn regard. He said, "She died in a mental hospital of complications that arose when the staff tried to restrain her. The whole thing was hushed up."

Not sure how to respond, I took a sip from my Sparkling Cyanide. The color of my martini was very close to the shade of Jazz's eyes.

"There have been all kinds of rumors over the years. My grandmother even thinks my mother was deliberately murdered."

"Murdered?" Disbelief rang in my voice. "At the sanitarium?"

"So, Nana believes. She says my mother was one of the meekest women on earth. Not a resistant bone in her body. Having to restrain her doesn't fit."

"Drugs can make people act like maniacs, sometimes."

Jazz inclined his head. "Nana believes there's more to that story, though frankly, I'm not so sure. But that's all past history. What matters now is Nana. Will you meet her? Just get an overall impression? That's all I'm looking for," he said, his gaze turning toward the lake. A sleek, black-and-white Master Craft pulled up to the dock outside Foster's patio.

I didn't talk about the cost. I didn't mention that I was barely an apprentice. I didn't say anything to jeopardize the moment. Under Jasper Purcell's spell I could only give one answer: "Yes."

That brought a brilliant smile to his lips. He gave me his full attention again and clasped my hands between his own. My knuckles tingled. "Thank you," he said, his gaze so warm my internal temperature shot skyward. *Whew*. I was going to have to order another drink . . . and pour it over my head to cool off.

Marry in haste, repent in leisure. One of my mother's favorite axioms slipped across my mind. So, okay, I wasn't marrying the guy. It wasn't like he was even interested. But I sure ended up with a lot of time wishing I hadn't been so hasty.

Every time I say "yes" it gets me in a shitload of trouble.

Chapter Two

"So, how'd it go?" Dwayne drawled.

I'd stopped by his cabana to pick up my cell phone, which I'd left charging merrily away on one of his end tables. I'd really hoped to avoid a tête-à-tête with him because I wanted to absorb and process my meeting with Jazz. But Dwayne stood in his living room, an unbuttoned white shirt over his tanned chest, hands on his hips, in jeans and bare feet. He looked solid and interested. Fobbing him off wasn't going to be easy.

"Have you met Jazz Purcell?" I asked.

"Seen him. Haven't spoken to him."

I hesitated. "I know you're a guy and all, and this'll be hard for you, but did you think he was . . . really attractive?"

Dwayne heaved a sigh. "They're all crazy, Jane. No matter how good they look. You got it right the first time." He gestured toward the printer table where my Purcell history document lay in an untidy heap. I snatched it up along with my cell phone and charger. My laptop was already in the Volvo. "Mentally unstable, to a one."

"Can you change my cell phone to vibrate? It's got this whiny ring I can't stand."

"You won't hear it on vibrate."

"I plan to carry it in my pocket."

Dwayne took my phone and made some lightning adjustments. It was easier than reading the manual or trying to fight my way through the phone menus.

"Is Camellia as gorgeous as Jazz?" I persisted as he finished, handing the phone back to me.

Dwayne's smile was knowing, sliding across his face to a wide grin.

"What?"

"He got to you, didn't he?"

"I'm just asking," I said, slightly annoyed.

"You like him."

"Not that way."

"Yeah, you do."

I detest it when Dwayne—or any man, for that matter—attempts to tell me what I feel. "The man's physically attractive. You can't miss it."

"Woke you up?"

I gritted my teeth. He was loving this, I could tell. And Dwayne knows better than anyone that I'm emotionally rocky on the whole man/woman thing right now. I'd made the mistake of trying to rekindle a past relationship and it ended badly. I'm still feeling raw about it all and whenever my mind touches on memories—which it does a lot—a sense of sorrow fills me that I can't rationally shake myself out of. "What does Cammie look like?"

He had the sense to let it go. "Not as as good looking by half. But I'd say those looks come from the Purcell side. Some of 'em are knockouts; even the ones in their fifties. For what that's worth," he added with a snort. "They're scary-nutty, Jane."

"Jazz seemed okay."

"Watch him. They're smart." He shook himself all over as if he had the heebie-jeebies. "They give a new spin to weird."

"You're talking about Cammie, specifically? Clue me in. What did she do?"

"Darlin' . . . give me a week."

"Come on, Dwayne."

He ran a hand through his light brown, sun-streaked hair. "The woman's unstable as nitroglycerin. Flashpoint anger. Comes out of nowhere. When I showed her pictures of her cheatin' husband's other family, she goes all white. Her lips just turn gray. I thought she was going to faint for a minute, so I moved closer, in case I needed to catch her. Suddenly she grabs me. I mean *claws* my arm. Jesus. I had to peel her off."

"The picture of the flower kids—Jasmine and Blossom?"

"You got it. Cammie just went into this zone. Closed her eyes. I swear the woman did not breathe. And I mean a long time passed. Minutes. Then she opens her eyes, gazes at me with that really crazy look . . . you know the one. Something about it's just not right. And she says, 'Okay, thanks. That's all I need.'" His gaze flicked to the report I held. "Keep that. Good to know what that family history is. Especially since you're planning to get involved."

"Overall, it doesn't sound that crazy. All families have something." I'd met Dwayne's sister and niece and their relationship was dysfunctional enough to make me give them a wide berth. "The Purcells might have a little more strangeness than some. Money'll do that."

"I got a bad feeling about all of them."

"You want me to make decisions based on your feelings?"

"Damn straight. Trusting my own instincts is what's saved me a time or two. Pay attention to your own instincts, Jane. What are they telling you about this *Jazz* Purcell?"

"I just said I'd meet his grandmother."

"That ain't all, darlin'. Don't believe it."

"Dwayne Durbin, thy middle name is 'paranoia.'"

"This grandmother hold the purse strings?" I nodded and he grimaced. "Tricky stuff, family inheritances. All kinds of strange things emerge when there's big money involved."

"It's a question of sanity, apparently. Some of the family members think she's losing it. Others aren't so sure."

"They're the last group I'd ask for a recommendation on mental capacity."

"One meeting . . . what can it hurt?"

Dwayne's phone rang. As he turned to answer it, he said over his shoulder, "Read over your own report, Jane. And FYI: you counted up the current middle-agers wrong."

"What?"

"Orchid Purcell had four children, not five."

Fifteen minutes later I pulled into the driveway of my cottage at the west end of Lake Chinook. I parked in front of the shed-cum-garage as there's no room inside it for my car. My landlord, Mr. Ogilvy, keeps god-knows-what within its faintly leaning, shingled walls. When it rains, I curse him. Today was so beautiful, a warm, glowing Indian summer afternoon, that I almost opened my arms and embraced it.

As soon as I entered my front door my pug, The Binkster, trotted toward me, her body wriggling like a contortionist. Her black mashed faced and bulbous eyes looked up at me expectantly and we exchanged kissy-face "hellos." I'm getting really weird about my dog. She'd been thrust on me by the grace of my mother, who'd honored some shirt-tail relative's request to find the little beast a home. I'd resisted for all I'm worth, but I must not be worth much because here she is. The Binkster, sometimes called Binky—which is enough to start the gag reflex, in my opinion—is a sweet-tempered, constantly shedding, stubby overeater with a serious bug-eye problem. However, I've grown way, way too attached to her. Whereas before I was looking out for Number One and holding my own, barely, now I was looking out for her as well. At night, this extra responsibility creeps into my conscious and my subconscious, too. I've woken more than a few times yelling at the top of my lungs at some imagined threat to my dog. This gets Binks going as well. Growling low in her throat from her little bed in the corner, she then jumps to her feet. She seems to sense my weakness in those moments and she makes a bee-line for my bed, practically jumping into my arms and snuffling her way beneath the covers. I make faint objections which we both ignore.

Walking into the kitchen, I gave my refrigerator the obligatory check and was surprised and delighted to relearn that I'd purchased some groceries a few days back. Yes, yes. I'd been in a buying mood. I actually had sourdough bread and margarine and Romaine lettuce. Almost a meal. There was a small carton of milk which I'd purchased for reasons that escape me now. I'm slightly lactose intolerant so I generally restrict my dairy to cheese. I drink my coffee black.

I slathered the bread with margarine, added the Romaine, slapped another margarined slice of bread and bit in. I pretended I was eating roast beef. It's not that I'm so poor I can't afford it. I just can't make myself pay the highway-robbery prices very often. I coulda used some cheese, though.

Binks set her chin on my leg and gazed up at me. This is a ploy. An effective ploy, actually. I gave her a smidgeon of my crust because I was too lazy to get up and find one of her doggy treats. Besides, I like to ration them out, and not just because of the price. Binkster's supposed to be on a diet as she's about as wide as she is long. Okay, that's an exaggeration . . . but not by much.

While we both munched, my eye fell to my report on the Purcells. With Dwayne's admonitions still rolling through my mind, I decided to remind myself what I was getting into. Tucking a last bite of sandwich into my mouth, I read:

Jane Kelly, Durbin Investigations
Purcell Family History
  Mental illness runs in the Purcell family. Their history bears this out. When James "Percy" Purcell arrived in Oregon in the early-to-mid-1800s he came with dreams of building a giant city at the juncture of the Willamette and Columbia Rivers. Other men joined in his vision and Portland was born, though Percy still managed to put his individualistic stamp on a lot of the city's architecture. To this day more than a few buildings have scrolled "P's" embedded into their stones and bricks.
  Percy appears to have been sane enough (if you count marrying six times as sanity). Wives one and two died from unspecified diseases. Wife three ran off when she learned Percy was determined to

leave Boston for Oregon. Wife four signed on in St. Louis as Percy was making his way west, then fell overboard to her death when the Purcell's Conestoga half-slipped off its raft as it swiftly floated down the Columbia River. Percy himself, and apparently most of his belongings, made it safely to the new and frantically growing city of Portland, Oregon, in one piece. He spent the next several decades building up what has since become a huge fortune by buying up every scrap of real estate he could get his greedy hands on. During these years he remained determinedly single; some felt he was past marrying. But at the youthful age of seventy-two he took Wife #5 who promptly bore him two sons: Garrett and James Purcell Jr., his first and only children. As soon as Junior came squalling into the world, Wife #5 began hemorrhaging violently. She slipped into a coma and into the next world. Percy Junior was handed off to a wet-nurse whom Percy hurriedly married. Wife #6 tended to both Garrett and Junior.

I finished off the rest of my sandwich and set the plate on the floor for Binks. She inhaled the scattered, teensy pieces of leftover bread as I reflected on how much different life was now. A wet-nurse? No thank you.

By all accounts Wife #6 was thin, wiry, ill-tempered and nothing much to look at. Whether Percy loved his sons or not is unclear. He did not love Wife #6, however, and took to whoring around the riverfront bars. He died in the arms of a lusty Madam who went after his fortune tooth and nail. Percy, however, had the foresight to leave everything to his sons. Wife #6 jealously took control of the two boys and sought a share of the estate, but she could never quite get the money for herself. She was still immersed in a legal battle she couldn't win when she was thrown from a horse, cracked her head on a stone and died at the age of thirty-nine.

By this time Garrett and Junior were in their teens. Always quiet and artistic, Garrett made it to his twenty-first birthday as a near recluse. But on that noteworthy day of his birth he walked to the center of the Steel Bridge, stood for a moment with his arms in the air and his face toward the heavens, then stepped into the Willamette River—some hundred feet down. Upon his death twenty-year-old James Purcell Jr. inherited everything. James waited ten more years before finding the woman of his dreams, Willamina Kersey. Willamina bore James a son and a daughter: James "Percy" Purcell the Third and Lilac Grace.

I surmised this, then, was the beginning of the whole flower thing.

Lilac was slow to develop and saw visions. James Junior and Willamina died in their midsixties, about six months apart from each other. Heart trouble in James's case; a loss of interest in life in Willamina's now that her beloved James was gone. Lilac Grace Purcell, unmarried and odd, moved into the family home where she spent the remainder of her life resting on a chaise longue, writing stories in a language of her own. She was in her forties when she died, eyes wide open, still on her chaise. The last words that she wrote—at least anything anyone could read—were prophetic: The End.

Weird, weird and weirder, I thought. Not a lot of happiness floating through the years.

Percy III inherited the entire Purcell estate. He also inherited his grandfather's interest and savvy in real estate. Throughout his adult life, even while his parents were still living and Lilac was growing older and odder, he steadily increased the family fortunes. He married Orchid Candlestone who bore him five children: Garrett (again), James Purcell IV, Dahlia and Lily, who was sent to a sanitarium as a young woman and died there several years later.

Orchid, currently in her eighties, is the surviving matriarch of the Purcell family. Her husband, Percy III, suffered from heart trouble. He died in his late fifties when, after driving home one night from his downtown Portland office, he climbed from his car and collapsed onto the ground outside the Purcell mansion. Orchid discovered him the next morning while she was getting ready to drive her daughter to school. She never remarried.

Orchid has several grandchildren and two great-grandchildren. James IV, a painter, has never married and seems to be a bit of a recluse. (Like Lilac Grace and Garrett I? Let's hope not.)

Daughter Dahlia married Roderick and gave birth to two children, Benjamin and Rhoda (could this be short for rhododendron? The mind boggles) *who died from SIDS as a baby. Benjamin is alive and well, in his early thirties, unmarried and still lives with his parents. He has no discernible employment and/or income.*

Garrett and his wife Satin (as if all the flowers weren't bad enough) *have one daughter, Camellia—or Cammie Purcell Denton, Dwayne's client. Cammie has a daughter Rosalie with soon-to-be-ex-husband Chris, who, working on being a bigamist, also has Blossom and Jasmine from his "other" marriage.*

Lily Purcell gave birth to Jasper Purcell while she was institutionalized at the tender age of sixteen. Jasper and his wife Jennifer—who died this past December in an automobile accident—have Logan, who is currently about twelve years old.

I hadn't known Jasper called himself Jazz when I'd written the history. Now I tacked on that information as a footnote, intending to put it into my laptop later on. I also counted up the middle-agers and realized Dwayne was right: there were four, not five. I corrected my report and set it aside.

The rest of the day I debated on calling Jazz, but every time I picked up my cell phone I hesitated. I'd told him I would meet with his grandmother. All I needed to do was set a time. But talking to Dwayne had set me back a bit. He'd emphasized the fact that the Purcells weren't exactly the poster family for mental stability. Still, I couldn't see how meeting Jazz's grandmother could be such a problem. What were my exact duties, anyway? Check to see if she was crazy or not? By my own standards? Maybe try to talk her into seeing a doctor for a professional opinion?

It wasn't like this was a pass/fail assignment.

So thinking, I picked up my cell phone and dialed Jazz's cell number, chastising myself for my ambivalence. This was easy money.

He answered on the third ring. "This is Jazz."

"Hi, it's Jane Kelly."

"Oh, hi, Jane," he said warmly.

It was more than enough to bolster my confidence. "We never set an exact time for me to meet your grandmother."

"Well, when can you do it?"

"Pretty much any time," I admitted. My calendar wasn't exactly overextended.

"Tomorrow evening?"

"Sure."

"You have the directions I gave you? Why don't you meet me at the house around five? Might as well get this show on the road, right?"

"Right." If my voice lacked a certain amount of enthusiasm it was because I'd gotten used to having my evenings to myself and was in the habit of curling up on the couch to watch TV with the dog. Binkster had a tendency to lay her chin on my leg and pretend an interest in whatever comes on the television. She never fights me for the remote.

I realized I could be in a serious rut.

"Tomorrow night at five," I told him.

"I'm looking forward to it."

I jogged to the Coffee Nook the next morning. The air was cooler, as if autumn had suddenly lifted its head, looked around, and decided it was time to come to the party. The air felt heavier, not quite foggy, but full of moisture. I'd left Binkster at home, still curled in her bed. She's not the earliest riser.

Out of breath, I sank onto one of my usual stools. Julie, The Coffee Nook's owner, asked me if I wanted a latte but I went for

my usual black coffee. I looked around for Billy Leonard who
generally shows up about the same time, but I was alone this
morning. My only fellow coffee fiends were strangers. They sat
on the end of the bar, a man and a woman dressed for the office.
There was something going on with their hands beneath the bar
that had her laughing and playfully slapping at him. He just had
a grin on his face and wasn't giving up.

I can't say why, but it sort of pissed me off. *Get a room.*

Julie set their drinks in front of them and they headed out the
door. He slipped one hand in the back pocket of her jeans. I
could see him squeezing her butt all the way to their separate
convertible Mercedeses. Both had their tops down and neither
bothered to put them up as they shot out of the parking lot with
rather more speed than necessary.

"That's Spence and Janice," Julie said, aware that I was watching them. "They're always like that. Usually come in a little earlier."

"Are they married?"

"To other people."

"Ahhh. . . ."

"They work together in downtown Portland. They're both
hotshot lawyers at some law firm. Their spouses come in sometimes, but they're always alone."

"Think they know?"

Julie shrugged. "'Spence and Janice aren't exactly keeping it a
secret."

"Do you know the Purcells?"

Julie didn't find my change of subject odd. I have a sneaking
suspicion she expects strange behavior from me. "I know of
them."

"I'm meeting Orchid Purcell today. The family matriarch."

"Are you working for her?"

"For her grandson. Jasper Purcell."

Julie shook her head. Clearly she'd never had contact with the
family. As she turned to serve some newcomers I slid off my stool
and jogged back home.

Binks was awake and hungry. I gave her some kiblets, then stepped into the shower. She can let herself out my new dog door to the backyard for bathroom purposes.

Forty-five minutes later I was dressed in tan capris, flip-flops and a black T-shirt. I grabbed a bottle of water and walked onto the back deck. Binks was in the fenced yard, rooting through a few fallen leaves. With the help of a handyman friend, Dwayne had cut the doggy door into my back wall. Mr. Ogilvy, my landlord, had been duly informed of the renovation and had okayed the change, though he'd come by several times to suspiciously eye the work. I'd paid for the improvement myself, but Ogilvy's always looking for a way to charge more. I wouldn't be surprised if he called it "added value" to the property and upped the rent. The term "skinflint" doesn't even come close to describing him.

Once The Binkster was back inside and had begged a couple of extra kiblets from me, I was ready to go to work. There were still hours before my meeting at *Chez* Purcell, so I took the time to go over my finances. Fifteen minutes into the task I had a blinding headache. There was no way I could see how I was going to make it to the end of the month. I keep a certain amount in savings—enough to eke out a six-month stretch if work drops off—and I refuse to dip into it unless I absolutely-lutely have to. This had only happened once so far and I like to keep it that way. What it meant for today was that I needed extra cash.

I drank a glass of water for my headache, which subsided to a dull throb. I could take aspirin, but hey, you actually have to have some on hand. I decided to see how far I could go without drugs. Snagging the keys to the Volvo, I headed to Greg Hayden's office.

I was halfway there when it occurred to me that I should call in advance. Greg answered his cell on the fourth ring. He's even more electronically challenged than I am, so I half-expected to be cut off before we made contact.

"Hello," Greg greeted me.

"It's Jane. Got any notices to post?"

"Nah. Everyone's paying on time."

I stared out the windshield. Just my luck that the deadbeats weren't out in force. How was I supposed to make a living? "Nothing?"

"Are you anywhere near here? I've got a twenty. Get a couple of Standish's burgers and keep the change."

"It'll take a thirty."

"All right."

Well, okay, free food was worth it. Especially since I'd already eaten up the gas for this trip. I stopped in at Standish's, which is a Portland institution known for their plate-sized burgers, and placed the order. Greg's always concerned about calories and nutrition so I didn't order the mammoth-size burgers. We each got a normal-size one.

Twenty minutes later I was at Hayden's office, transferring his burger to him. He gave me thirty dollars and I congratulated myself that I'd cleared over ten. The food and cash took care of the headache and I was good to go.

I took a slow drive back to my cottage. Coming up my drive, I was surprised to see a familiar, slightly battered Honda parked in my usual spot. Cynthia, my arty friend who is the new owner of the Black Swan Gallery, was still seated inside the car. I parked to one side of her and came around to peer through her windshield at her. She had one hand in a death grip on the steering wheel, the other clenched around her cell phone. I signaled her that I was heading inside and she gave me a curt nod. I was pretty sure the curtness was for the caller.

Binks was thrilled to see me. She did her little happy dance and ran to her bowl. She seems to feel that any homecoming requires food. I hated to break her gluttonous little heart, but I have to be firm. Instead of food I opted for one of her stuffies, a pink elephant with drunken looking eyes. It was the only dog toy that called to me the last time I was at PetSmart. Or, Pets R Us. Or, Petco. I can't be required to remember the names of these stores, can I? Pet ownership should not be so taxing.

Binks and I were playing a game of tug-of-war when Cynthia

entered in a rush of air that seemed to vibrate with her own internal outrage. Binkster's ears lifted and she eyed Cynthia with interest but her jaw remained clamped on the elephant.

"Everyone who works for me is either a moron, a backstabber or a fucker."

"What constitutes a fucker?"

"They need to get the fuck out of my life." She threw herself onto the sofa. I didn't have time to warn her about the dog fur. She wore a black knit skirt and matching jacket with a silky chartreuse blouse underneath. "God, I hate being management. What was I thinking?"

"You wanted your own gallery."

She ran tense fingers through her spiky, dark brown hair and made a growling sound. Binkster dropped the elephant and stared at her. "I started sleeping with Ernst."

I ran the names of Cynthia's friends through my mind and drew a blank. "Ernst?"

"He works for me. A painter . . . sort of." She snorted. "He's like forty, going on six. He's a moron. And a fucker," she decided as an afterthought. "I'm an idiot."

"I take it you're not sleeping with Ernst anymore."

"Not for a good six hours."

"Oh."

"Do you know what that piece of shit said to me? He said I was too old for him."

Cynthia is around my age, thirtyish. "He's *forty?* Does he want to be killed where he stands?"

"He meant my soul, or so he says. I'm an old soul. Which I have to say, I thought was a good thing until I heard him say it. Then it just sounded wrong."

"He must believe he's a young soul."

"He's a larva. No . . . he's an egg. A louse egg."

"A nit," I supplied.

"Is that what a louse egg is?" She was momentarily diverted.

"Yep."

"That pretty well says it all. Now I don't know what to do. I've got to fire him but he'll probably sue me for sexual harassment or something. I can just smell it."

"Then you must put up with him."

"Oh, puh-leeze. Like that's gonna work. If I could only sleep with him but not have to work with him. This is like some terrible marriage. I can't explain how I feel. And what's worse, I think he feels the same way. He can't stand me, except in bed. What does that say about us?"

I shrugged. Nothing good. Cynthia isn't one to have tons of relationships. If she was involved with this guy it had to be for some reason that she wasn't revealing. She's a tough cookie, but once in a while I sense her vulnerability. I'm always at a loss at those times. Should I be this great huggy friend? It's not my style. And Cynthia's pretty prickly most times. Besides Dwayne, she's my closest friend, but it's a fine balance. Friendship can be so tricky.

She clammed up about further information on the mysterious new lover/employee and I let it go. She hung around the rest of the afternoon, making phone calls and generally wasting time. Fine with me. I had nothing to do but wait.

By the time she got up to leave it was after three. At the door, she said, "Thanks, Jane."

"For what?"

She just waved at me and left. I watched the Honda back down the drive. Because of an incident earlier in the summer the Honda bore a few more scratches. The incident was my fault and I suspected Cynthia might hold a bit of a grudge. Maybe not. It's all long over now, but I felt better thinking I may have helped her in some way this afternoon. She was enough of a loner for it to be a rare thing for me, or anyone, to be there for her.

My good feelings lasted until I had to fret over my wardrobe. I'm not that great at "outfits". But . . . I was meeting with the Purcells and this required some thought. I dug through my closet, even though I know I've only got a couple of dresses I save for funerals and weddings. Eventually I settled on a dark brown knit dress with a large silver belt. The belt was a gift from Cynthia, as were the slightly worn, brown boots which I pulled out from behind my cheapie flip-flops and strappy sandals. I examined the boots critically, then shrugged and pulled them on. Cynthia deplores my lack of fashion sense and has taken to dropping off items of clothing now and again that she swears she doesn't want or use any longer. I could take offense to her charity but that requires more energy than I care to exert. Besides, the boots looked damn good. They could easily turn into my new favorite thing.

I had no fears of being too warm this evening, even though the sun had been fierce all day. Fall nights cool down rapidly in the northwest, and as I walked to my car a brisk breeze was blowing leaves across my drive, planting them against my tires. More leaves and branches rustled overhead.

It was still hot in the Volvo, however—greenhouse effect—so I rolled down a window and started the engine. As I headed out of Lake Chinook I noticed pumpkins on people's porches. None carved yet. Halloween was still a few weeks ahead, but fall was fast taking over. You gotta look out for November 1st in Oregon. September and October can be really nice. Warm. Sometimes *really* warm. But come November it's like crossing a line. Wind, rain and generally gray nastiness hunch down on you. Darkness in the morning, darkness at noon, darkness at night. In my opinion, the reason hibernation was invented.

I drove up Macadam Avenue toward Military Road and one of the main turnoffs into Dunthorpe. I headed uphill for a mile or two, switchbacking and curving around to a headland. Perched on the eastern edge were the view houses.

Jazz had given me the address but I'm not all that familiar with the winding roads that sometimes are barely wide enough for one car, let alone two. I took a couple of wrong turns, passed by the same lady walking her Pomeranian twice, and finally found myself on a dead-end street named Chrysanthemum Drive. Well course. Flowers. It was the Purcell theme. I could see a small metal plaque with the P logo tucked into the shrubbery at tire height, so I turned in.

The Purcell mansion stood at the end of a narrow, winding, tree-lined drive, oak and maple limbs creating a canopy above my Volvo that very nearly scratched my roof. This place would be hell on SUVs, but then I guess James Purcell hadn't really planned for the automobile when the place was built at the turn of the century.

I drove into a clearing. The lane curved in front of the house, which had a slate floor portico that extended outward to cover space for two cars. There were several more uncovered parking spots beyond.

I realized that this was actually the back of the house; the front faced the Willamette River. I gazed up at the second-story windows. The house was built in what's locally termed "Old Portland" style with shingles and pane windows, rounded pillars and rock facing the entire first floor. A slate path curved off from the portico, presumably toward the front door. On the rear side were two doors, one entering into a funny apse on the left; one on the right that appeared to head into the kitchen. It amazes me that people ever build homes where visitors have to search for their correct entry, but there's more than a few of them in Dunthorpe and ortland's West Hills.

I pulled in front of the portico and slotted into a spot beside low-slung sports cars. Made sense, considering the tree/drive ion. There was also an ancient vanilla-colored Cadillac, pos-Nana" Purcell's mode of transportation. I'd neglected to hat Jazz drove. The idea of entering this family manor im daunted me.

g out of my car, I slowly locked the doors, taking my e gilding afternoon sun I could see the towering had dropped a carpet of needles atop the house's ooked as if the gutters hadn't been cleaned in this vo L-shaped wings jutted from each side. I tried to estimate the rambling mansion's square footage and failed. Big. Really big. But in a state of long-term neglect that had left its once awesome grace moldering into disrepair.

I swear there was a faint odor of something dying or dead.

Shadows formed where the lowering sun could not reach. I shivered though it wasn't cold.

After a few minutes I followed the path to the front of the house where sweeping grounds rolled toward the edge of the cliff. In the name of safety a wrought-iron fence had been erected along the perimeter, but spokes and curlicues were broken out in places and briers had climbed inside, tendrils reaching through like thorny fingers.

The lawn was freshly mowed, however, and the path I followed was swept clean. Dead ahead was the front door beneath another, smaller portico. The slate path swooped up into several stairs which were missing pieces of rock. I climbed the steps and stood for a moment looking at twin wrought-iron rings hanging on massive wooden doors. Not exactly in keeping with the architecture. Definitely monastic. I lifted one and let it fall. Its *boom* sounded like a wrecking ball.

Out of my peripheral view I noticed a side building. I turned to look at it and saw that it was a playhouse. Child's size. Its front door was bright red and freshly painted. The rest of it looked scary and decrepit. Worse than the house, even.

The door in front of me swung slowly inward revealing a gloomy interior. I had a mad desire to sing cheerily, "Avon calling!" but managed to hold myself back.

A figure moved into view. A slight, middle-aged man, his skin wrinkled in that used-up kind of way, blinked at me in the quickly fading light. "Yes?"

"Hi, I'm Jane Kelly. Jasper—Jazz—invited me to meet him here?" I couldn't help making it sound like a question. I was hoping somehow this skinny guy would help me out.

His expression grew faintly anxious. "Here?"

I wasn't sure whether to go into the whole thing about Orchid and her mental condition. I thought about trotting out a lie but sensed that might get in my way in the long run. I opted for a nod and a bright smile.

"Jazz doesn't live here." He glanced behind him, as if he were afraid of imparting a huge family secret.

"He said his grandmother lived here. Should I wait outside?"

This really threw him off. He clearly didn't know what to do with me. After a hesitation that lasted long enough to embarrass us both, he finally stepped from the gloom onto the porch. "I'm not sure if I should have you come in. The family's here." He tossed another glance to the still open door.

I got my first good look at him. He definitely carried the Purcell gene for attractiveness, even with his dried-up appearance and mannerisms. His eyes were gray-blue and his hair was thick and lustrous, only shot sparsely with gray. If he'd given any thought to physical fitness, which by his stooped posture and generally soft appearance didn't seem possible, he would be one good-looking man. I pegged him somewhere in his late fifties but it was hard to tell. He could have been much younger. He just *seemed* old.

His worry about "the family" was starting to amuse me. Or, maybe it was just relief that I didn't have to go inside without Jazz. I leaned forward and whispered, "Should I wait in my car, then?"

"Yes . . . yes . . . maybe . . ."

"James!" a female voice called from the gloomy bowels.

James started as if he'd been goosed. "That's Dahlia," he murmured.

So, I was looking at James Purcell the fourth and waiting for his sister Dahlia to appear. I did a quick recap in my head. James was a bachelor. Dahlia was married to . . . Roderick . . . that was it. She had given birth to two children. A son and a daughter. I couldn't recall the son's name but the daughter was christened Rhoda before she died in infancy from SIDS.

Dahlia clomped onto the porch. Where her brother was slight, Dahlia was large. Everything was—her body and her features.

She had huge eyes and lips and there was a wave to her ash blond hair that kept it about a half-inch off her skull, all over. Where James resembled a handsome professor gone to seed, Dahlia was a stevedore whose only real physical attribute was a set of even, white teeth.

She fixed her gaze on me through eyes that were a pale blue like a sky filled with white clouds. I almost felt sorry for her. She'd so clearly missed out on the family's good looks.

"Who the hell are you?" she asked in a melodious voice that surprised me enough to leave me momentarily speechless.

"Jane Kelly." I held out my hand.

She shook it firmly. "Yes? And what do you want?"

"She's here to meet Jazz," James put in. He'd taken several steps away and was gazing toward the edge of the property.

"What for?"

I suddenly didn't want to say. Dahlia narrowed her eyes at me, but before I had to confess my reasons, there was a commotion deep inside the house and the sound of voices greeting a new-comer. Dahlia whipped around and headed back the way she'd come without another word. James cast me a worried look and followed. I didn't wait for an invitation and just took up the rear, hoping to high heaven that Jazz had arrived.

He had. And he had a boy with him. His son, no doubt. Logan, I remembered.

"You have a guest," Dahlia said in a tight voice.

Jazz saw me and broke into another brilliant smile. It was enough to make me catch my breath.

"You went around to the front door," he said, coming toward me. "Hey, Logan wait . . ."

Logan, who'd been making a beeline for the stairs, reluctantly slowed, turning on one designer basketball shoe signed by an NBA player outside of my limited knowledge of the sport. "Yeah?"

"This is Jane Kelly. Jane, my son Logan. Jane's here to see Nana, so why don't you wait downstairs with Aunt Dahl—"

"She's here to see Mother?" Dahlia demanded. "Why?"

We were standing in the entry hall, which rose two stories. A gallery ran overhead between the two wings. Exclamations of surprise or disgust, or both, shot from the open doors to the main salon. Jazz glanced to his left, his expression carefully neutral. I stepped forward and looked inside the salon. A group of people were headed my way. The middle-agers. And, I guessed, Cammie.

They collected in the doorway to the entry hall and gazed at me with varying degrees of alarm. It wasn't what I would call a warm welcome.

I turned to Jazz expectantly. Instead of explaining my presence to them, he seemed flummoxed by the question. He shot me a "rescue me" look. My heart suddenly went into overdrive. What was this?

"Jazz asked me to meet Orchid," I said slowly.

"Who are you?" a male middle-ager demanded. I pegged him as Garrett Purcell. He, too, possessed the extraordinary good looks, but he'd let himself go and now was paunchy and soft. An overriding belligerence, which seemed to be a part of his makeup, also took away from his appearance. A few more years and his attractiveness wouldn't even be an issue. He would just be an older man with an attitude problem.

"I'm a private investigator."

The man actually reared back. He glared at Jazz. "What the hell are you doing, man?"

"Jane is here to see about Nana's sanity."

At least he'd come back to the point, but now all the Purcell gang regarded me with flat-out suspicion. "So, when do private investigators determine someone's sanity?" another man asked in a really snarky tone. I figured he must be Roderick, Dahlia's husband.

"I guess when Jazz asks them to," Dahlia answered, equally snarky.

"Why don't we all go in and sit down?" Jazz gestured toward the room they'd just exited, and we all trundled back inside.

The salon was furnished in fern green and gold. The Purcell

clan took their seats as if they'd been choreographed, apparently reclaiming the ones they'd just vacated. I stayed standing alongside Jazz. Logan flanked him on the left, but it was clear he didn't want to be anywhere near any of us. I sympathized.

"I know we've all been worried about Nana," Jazz said as an opening salvo.

"You've been worried," the bullish man corrected. He had a barrel chest, a pugnacious chin and salt-and-pepper hair. "The rest of us know what's wrong with her. Dementia." The woman seated beside him on the green and gold striped divan—his wife, I was sure—stiffened at the word. Her head was bent and she seemed intent on her fingernails. I watched her play with them. Her hair was coiffed in that flippy style so beloved by Ann Landers, if you could still believe the picture. It was dyed an unnatural black, the scary kind that seems to absorb all light.

"I'm Garrett," he added, rising again to extend his hand. Steely blue eyes searched my face. "That's my wife, Satin. Jazz said that you're . . . ?"

"Jane Kelly." We shook hands. His grip was one of those crushers. He squeezed my fingers and kept his gaze on my face, watching. I managed to keep my eyes level with his and luckily didn't tear up from the pain. Abruptly, he released his grip and turned away.

Geez, Louise.

"I'm Roderick," the other man said with a nod. He was lean with hair an even brown tone that spoke of coloring as well. I smiled at him in acknowledgment, all the time wondering when I could get the hell out of Dodge.

"And this is Benjamin," Roderick said, gazing at a young man who sat apart from the group, flipping through a magazine. Benjamin's head stayed bowed. There was something about his slouched posture and desire to be alone in a crowd that made me think he was a teenager, but when he deigned to look at me I was surprised to see he was closer to my age. He alone of the Purcells possessed brown eyes, a light shade, close to my hazel color, a gift from his father.

"Benjamin, say hello," Dahlia muttered automatically. She must have done it a million times before.

"Huh-low." Benjamin flicked a sideways glance my way. I got the feeling he wasn't trying to be rude, he just had no interest in me or anything else going on among us.

Cammie Purcell shifted position in a fawn wingback chair. I assumed it was Cammie because she was the only woman in her thirties in the room and her hair was an icy blond. Dwayne had described her as perennially unhappy. The downward bow of her lips spoke volumes. "So, what's this all about, Jazz?" she asked. Her gaze briefly touched mine. There was something going on in her eyes. Something manipulative and determined. Dwayne's admonitions reverberated through my brain.

Jazz seemed a little bemused by his family's suspicions. "I just wanted another opinion."

"She's not a doctor," Garrett pointed out. His attention appeared to be on Satin, whose gaze was fixed on the middle-distance. The smile on her lips looked permanently carved.

Cammie said flatly, "You work with Dwayne Durbin."

"Yes."

"We don't need a private investigator," Roderick said to Jazz. "What's got into you?"

"Nana won't see a doctor. We're all trying to figure out how to help. Nana relates better to women; we all know that. Let's just see what happens." A defensive note crept into his tone.

James Purcell IV entered the room, moving like a wraith. He didn't say anything, but hovered near the curtains, his attention outdoors to the darkening sky.

I wanted to back out. I wanted to leave. But there was the promise of payment and I'd said I would meet with Orchid.

And I couldn't bear the thought of returning to Dwayne, saying, "You were right. I should have listened to you. They're all crazy!"

"Come on," Jazz said to me as he turned to the door. His cheeks were flushed. Maybe he'd expected them to greet me with open arms.

"You can give us a report when you return," Garrett called as Jazz hurried me into the hallway. His tone was supercilious and edged with something mean. He was the oldest sibling and he wore his need to control like a cloak. Though he possessed the Purcell good looks, he pushed all my buttons. I was glad to get away from the lot of them.

Jazz walked ahead of me up the stairs. Logan had slipped from the room a few moments before us and was nowhere in sight. I followed behind Jazz, counting the steps. It was one of those stairways that turns at a landing, then turns again another half flight up. The rail was dark walnut, ornately carved but scarred and nicked by time. I could imagine what it had looked like once upon a time. The whole place was imposing, rich, deep. But now it smelled of neglect and the passage of time. I could feel them all waiting for Orchid to die. To collect the inheritance.

I shivered involuntarily.

"Are you cold?" Jazz asked. "Here . . ." He clasped my hand and held onto it all the way up the stairs in a way that made me feel slightly light-headed. *Phew.* I'm normally less affected by the male sex, especially overly attractive men, but I was aware of Jazz in a way that defied description.

Maybe I was still suffering the leftover malaise and loneliness of a love affair gone sour. It hadn't been that long since I'd suffered my loss. In any case, I was inordinately aware of Jazz's hand holding mine, the heat and good feelings their joining sent through me. Maybe I was ready to date again. Or, was it just the opposite? Was I still so raw and unhappy that I was reeling out of control emotionally?

Jazz stopped at the top of the stairs and turned toward the north wing. At the end of a hallway covered in nearly threadbare cabbage roses carpet stood a pair of massive, dark walnut doors that looked as if they might not shut properly, and probably stuck if they did. I had a mental picture of someone old and bent over with witchy long nails and rheumy eyes waiting behind them.

I put a hand on Jazz's forearm. "I gotta be honest. I'm here because you asked me, and because I'm trying to be a private investigator—working toward it—but really, this isn't a job for me. They're right." I inclined my head toward the open stairway. "You need a doctor. An estate lawyer. A professional."

"I want you," he insisted.

I tend to melt at that kind of cheerleading. Who wouldn't? But I was determined to get a few things straight. "I'm not the person for this job."

"Who is, then? She won't talk to professionals. She won't talk to anyone but Logan and me. She distrusts the whole family."

"I just think this might be a mistake."

"Jane, I need help. Please."

I gazed at him. I am such a sucker sometimes. This was a fool's errand but I was already in too deep. Drawing a breath, I acquiesced with a shrug, following Jazz down the hall to meet "Nana."

Chapter Three

I was prepared for anything, given the buildup I'd received. A woman anywhere between Medusa and Mother Teresa. Okay, maybe that was stretching it a bit, but I figured she could be a grim, hard-bitten monster with a whip hand, or a dotty old lamb in search of love and assurance.

In actuality Orchid Candlestone Purcell was, well, a disappointment. She was so middle-of-the-road that after my initial meeting, I was hard pressed to remember much about her appearance beyond the basics: hair, eye color, body size. Her behavior was more memorable, but that was only because she reminded me of my grandmother.

Her hair was iron gray turning to white. It still had a fullness to it; no cottony fluff. It was clear she went to a hairdresser steeped in the art of spray till it hurts. The concoction moved with her head in a way that reminded me of a jockey's cap. It stuck out in the front a little, too, as if it had a bill. Give her some silks and she'd be away to the races.

Her eyes were Jazz's electric blue. A little bit starey. Her skin was soft, powdery and wrinkled, like bread dough. Her mouth seemed to be in a perpetual half-smile. The Mona Lisa had nothing on Orchid.

She was sitting in a chair and I had the impression of a body folded in upon itself like an accordion. She was wearing some kind of blue suit with a short jacket and a gray, blue and black scarf artfully tossed around her neck and over a shoulder—the kind of thing that would drive me to distraction. Her feet were clad in black leather slip-ons that looked sturdier and far more sensible than the outfit.

Jazz stood aside to let me enter first, and I walked in and moved to the center of the room, feeling ill-at-ease, wondering once again what my role was.

Logan sat on a stool, deep into Game Boy. He'd turned the sound down low but I could hear little whistles and blurps and tinny voices. He didn't bother to look up at our arrival.

"Nana, how are you?" Jazz asked, heading toward her with enthusiasm, reaching for her hands.

She seemed to expect this because she held them out. "I'm fine. Help me up."

He pulled her to her feet, sliding a supportive arm around her back as she struggled with the effort. I saw that the accordion effect had been correct. Once she straightened out she was far leaner than I'd expected. The suit seemed to fit her better, too. The hem of the skirt hit her just below the knees.

"Who's this?" she asked, peering at me. One hand dug in the folds of her skirt and she pulled out a pair of blue-framed glasses. She put them on and turned her blue eyes into owlish orbs which looked me up and down.

"Jane Kelly," Jazz said. "She's the private investigator I told you about."

"Private investigator?" She sounded mildly alarmed.

"I'm actually more like an apprentice," I murmured.

"I wanted her to meet you, Nana. You know. Like we talked about? You said you would prefer a woman?"

She frowned, trying to recollect. "Is this about the money?" She gave me a studied examination then. "They all want my money. It was my husband's but now it's mine."

I couldn't really think of a comment for that one.

"A private eye," she repeated, sounding skeptical.

"Have a chair," Jazz said to me. He touched my elbow and gestured to a small sofa. A white crocheted antimacassar lay across its back, which was pretty strange since the sofa was that bright sky blue so popular in the 1950s—satellite blue—and its frame and design were contemporary to the extreme. It was the Victorian age meets mid-twentieth-century space age.

And the damned thing was hard as cement.

I shot another glance over at Logan, envying the fact he was in his own world. The tinny music kind of pissed me off. Its little beeps and whistles started sounding a lot like someone sing-songing *nanny, nanny, nanny . . .*

In the strained silence that followed, Jazz threw a glance toward Logan, before saying to me. "Maybe we should leave you two alone," he said.

"Um . . . no . . ." I smiled at him through clenched teeth.

"You afraid to be alone with me?" Orchid questioned.

I turned my attention to her. She was smirking. I could see it. "Mrs. Purcell, you'd be better advised—"

"Call me Nana."

"—to meet with an estate lawyer."

She folded her hands in front of her, then, with Jazz's help, settled herself back on her divan. "What's your name?"

"Jane Kelly."

"I'd rather talk to you."

"Well, okay . . ." She regarded me expectantly, waiting, so I added, "Nana," though it sounded false on my tongue.

It must have satisfied her, though, because she sent me a big smile—this one full of enjoyment. "Go on, then." She flapped a hand at Jazz.

"We'll see you downstairs," Jazz said. "Come on, Logan."

"Not yet. I'm almost to the end guy."

"Put it on pause and let's go."

"Uh-uh. I wanna stay here."

Jazz looked a little nonplussed. He rubbed a spot just abo his temple and closed his eyes, as if he were in pain. "Do argue . . . please?"

"Fine!" Logan switched off the device and threw it onto the chair next to me. It bounced on the cushion once and slid to the floor, hitting the hardwood with a crack.

Jazz looked pained. If Logan felt chagrined he hid it behind a sneer as he stomped from the room. Jazz followed him, closing the door softly behind them. I could hear Logan's angry clomping on the stairway until he reached the first floor and it faded away.

I was left with Nana.

She said, "I shouldn't feel this way, but Logan's my favorite." Her face shone with love.

Maybe she *was* crazy.

An hour and a half later I was back at my cottage and desperately in need of a drink. I didn't care whether it had alcohol in it or not. Water would be fine. I just wanted to pour something down my throat and close my eyes.

I called Dwayne and listened to his drawl on the answering machine. He might be home, he might not. He feels no compulsion to answer his phone while I can never hear a ringing phone without dashing to pick it up. Many times I've had to hold myself back. Sometimes you just know it's a telemarketer.

"Dwayne, come get me," I said after the beep. "By boat or car, can't care. I need to talk to you about the Purcells."

was in the process of hanging up when he clicked on. "I got at docked in front of the house."

ll, bring it on over."

compliance was a grunt.

ne's cabana does have a boathouse and a lift, the latter ted and scary, kind of like huge metal teeth floating just water's surface, so it's not really usable. Consequently, is boat at one of the easements around the lake. It's rom his place, so it doesn't delay him much, but having tly parked right out in front shaved off at least es.

you to believe as much. But he can turn it off so fast I sometimes wonder what's real and what isn't.

"What happened to your real mother?"

"Vamoosed."

I could tell he was shutting down on me. I didn't want the conversation to end, so I decided to sweeten the pot by throwing in my own dirty laundry. "My dad married his secretary. I have a passel of half brothers and sisters. I lost count at three. And I don't know their names."

"And you don't wanna."

"Damn straight."

"So why did you agree to call this woman 'Nana'?"

"I'm on a case. I'm playing a part."

"Bullshit. You just didn't have the *cajones* to tell her no."

"She's old and a bit confused."

"Crazy," Dwayne stressed.

"You're pissing me off."

"Like that's something new."

We lapsed into silence. Dwayne acts like he knows me so well, and yes . . . okay . . . he does . . . but there's something so annoying about it that sometimes I just want to launch myself at him in full fight mode.

I pondered these simmering feelings as we pulled up to his place. Across Lakewood Bay I could see the lights of Foster's On The Lake twinkling in strands around the trees. It was just starting to get dark. I didn't want to be mad at Dwayne, but I wanted . . . something.

He tied up the boat and sat back down. We swayed in the soft lavender evening light, neither of us climbing out to his dock. With a deep, uncomfortable awakening I realized I wanted to be kissed. By Dwayne? *No.* Proximity doesn't make things work. So he was right here. So what? I'm not an idiot . . . usually. Dwayne was off limits.

I had a raging internal argument with myself on the issue. Recognizing my feelings is not helpful. It makes me feel vulnerable and I just hate that. With an effort I pulled my eyes away from his chest. He was wearing some beat-up blue shirt that looked as if it had been laundered way too many times. The top button had given up the ghost and I could see the smooth, tan muscles of his chest. His jeans were even worse; typical Dwayne. He wore leather sandals that were a little out of character: Dwayne's strictly a sneakers or boot man. But he had nice feet.

For some reason it was all a seductive combination.

"Are we going to Foster's?" I asked.

"You hungry?"

"Aren't you?"

"Jump out and we'll fire up the truck. Forget Foster's. I feel like a chili dog."

I did as he suggested, more because I didn't care than because I was eager to leave the lake. I climbed into the passenger side of Dwayne's battered pickup. I hadn't been inside it in a while but it hadn't improved much over the last month. There'd been an incident where Dwayne had to pick me up at the hospital. He'd helped me inside but as a luxury ride it left a lot to be desired. I'd made it home and collapsed on my couch. Still, Dwayne had been there for me.

We drove to Lou's, across the river in Milwaukie. It's one of those institutions that's been around since the dawn of time—a prefab building shaped like a trailer. It's more about basic product than palate, more concerned with delivering up the same foot-long-chili-dog meal than worrying about an ultra-high rating from the health department. Not that they're slouches. Their focus is just different.

Dwayne really knows how to eat this sort of food. We settled onto one of their indoor painted picnic tables, seated across from each other on long narrow benches. I watched him bite into the foot-long dog, stuffing enough into his mouth to make me marvel. And he can do this without looking like a pig or a slob. I, myself, do not share this talent. I bit into mine and immediately had to wipe excess chili sauce from my mouth.

"So, okay," Dwayne said, chewing. "Tell me about 'em."

"Jazz left me alone with Orchid."

"Nana."

"Yes, Nana."

"And?"

"She was really nice. Kinda dotty. Some of the time, anyway. Other times she was really sharp."

"That's typical of dementia, isn't it?"

"Yeah, I guess. Although she was pretty clear on current issues. Well . . ." I made a face. "And then she'd kinda go off track. But she knows the family wants control of the money. She's bound and determined to keep their hands off it."

"Because she wants control, or because she doesn't trust them?"

"Maybe a little of both. I told her she needed an estate attorney."

"What did she say to that?"

"Oh, at first she acted like she didn't hear me. She kind of rambled about her husband, where they went on vacation, how they met. She wouldn't stay on the subject. She lives in this suite of rooms, no phone, no intercom that I could tell. But the door isn't locked, so it's not like they're keeping her prisoner." I lifted my shoulders. "I don't know what to tell Jazz about her. His son, Logan, is her favorite grandchild."

I thought I was keeping my recitation objective, but Dwayne must have heard something in my voice, because he asked, "What's wrong with him?"

"Logan? Nothing."

"You don't like him."

"He's twelve. What's to like?"

Dwayne swallowed his last bite, looking like he could eat five more. "Lots of twelve-year-olds are likable."

"Name one."

"My brother's son. Del."

"You have a brother? How come he didn't get mentioned when you listed your family?"

"I don't like him much. He's a stepbrother. Del's okay, though."

"Any other family members you haven't mentioned?" I said dryly.

"Scores. We talkin' about me, or the Purcells?"

"Both, maybe."

"So, what's wrong with Logan besides his being twelve?"

Dwayne clearly wasn't going to get sidetracked onto his family. I gave up and went back to the Purcells. "He's rude. Miserably rude. Jazz seems overwhelmed by him."

"Doesn't know how to be a daddy?" Dwayne guessed.

"Logan's a handful. Jazz seems worn down. Orchid did get kind of chatty about Logan. She talked about Jennifer—Logan's mom and Jazz's wife—who died last Christmas in an auto accident. It was a hit and run. Logan and Jazz were in the car. Jazz ended up in the hospital for a bit, but Logan was unhurt."

"You want to feel sorry for the kid but you don't like him, so it's hard."

That about summed it up, all right. "The kid probably has lots of issues." I was trying to be fair but Dwayne can read me like a book.

"Doesn't mean you have to like him."

"Nope."

"Okay, so back to Nana. Give me more about that meeting."

I took a bite and closed my eyes, partly because I wanted to put my interview with Orchid in order, partly because the chili was hot and spicy and better than it had any damn right to be. I wanted to hurry through one bite so I could get to the next. I envied the way Dwayne could eat a third of the foot-longer in a bite. I had ordered a regular size dog and now was wishing I hadn't been such a girl about it. Give me fat and nitrates and lots of 'em.

I started talking. Dwayne, for all his faults, can be a good listener. He waited while I told my story.

In Orchid's presence, I'd felt a bit like a parent or a jailer. She'd talked on and on about Logan, like a girl with her first crush. Any attempt I made to change the subject was met with resistance. I swear she invented ways to bring him back into the conversation. I couldn't shake her from talking about him, so in the end I just let her go on for the better part of an hour. I learned that Logan was genius smart, that he was handsome enough to be a model, or maybe an actor, and that he was patient as a saint as he'd taught Orchid how to operate Game Boy—and oh, goodness, she'd gotten so good at it! Those little buttons were so small, but dearest Logan had showed her the menu screen. She just loved that it was called a *menu*.

At this point she'd actually clapped her hands and chortled. Honestly, all the praise for dearest Logan was gaggy enough to make me want to puke. I kept an interested look on my face by sheer willpower.

Finally, as she ran down, I said to her, "Jazz is worried that no one's looking out for your best interests."

"Come on, girl. Tell the truth. They're all worried about the money."

"Jazz just wants to make sure you get what you want, not what they want."

"You make it sound like a war."

"I don't know what it is," I told her. "But I think everyone would agree that you should meet with an estate lawyer."

"Like Mr. Neusmeyer?" She smoothed her skirt.

I instantly felt my insides contract. Of all the lawyers in the state of Oregon—and believe me, they're thick on the ground— she had to contact Neusmeyer? I'd had a run-in with the man a few months prior. In a bid to gain information, I'd pretended to be someone else—someone other than an investigator—someone with even less scruples than I possessed myself. Jerome Neusmeyer was known for casting an eye toward younger women, so I'd assumed a fake name and approached him, making clear that I was interested in being an estate beneficiary and that I could be bought. Neusmeyer had jumped on the idea—and jumped on me. Extricating myself from the situation had been tricky. I could still feel the imprint where he'd squeezed my breast. The idea that he was involved with the Purcells left me searching for an exit *toute suite*.

I would have run from the room right then and there, but

Orchid had turned away to glance out the window and stare up at the sky. The gnarled oak that reached toward the house was losing its leaves. She said, as if in conversation with it, "I don't remember what happened to her."

I'd been lost in thought at that point, wondering if Dahlia might not be right and that this dementia-thing was an act. She knew who Neusmeyer was, all right. Now, I keyed into what she was saying. "What happened to who?" I asked.

"I think it was my Percy's fault. But he was a good man," she added instantly, as if afraid she might be overheard maligning her late husband. "He didn't mean to drive her away."

"Are you talking about your . . . daughter?" I moved closer to her, craning my neck to look up at the sky, too. What was this? Some kind of confession?

"Sometimes I think she'd still be here if we'd just listened a little more. That's the way it is with children, don't you know. You have to listen to what they're not saying more than what they're saying."

"Yes." I agreed with her. She seemed entirely sane. Thoughtful, even.

Then she suddenly glanced around furtively and whispered, "I just don't want anything bad to happen."

"Nobody does," I answered automatically. She looked unsure, so I added, "Nothing bad's going to happen."

"How do you know?"

"I don't, I guess."

"I want her back." Orchid's face tightened, and she suddenly looked as stubborn as a two-year-old. Then her expression cleared. "But I have Logan. And Jazz!" as if she'd just remembered.

"Yes," I agreed, and that was pretty much the end of our discussion. It definitely left me feeling undecided about her mental state, not exactly the news Jazz would want to hear. Now, I said to Dwayne, "She needs to be looked at by a professional."

Dwayne, who'd been listening intently to my story, asked, "You think she meant Jazz and Logan's mother?"

"Lily's the one that's gone."

"She died in the sanitarium?" I nodded and Dwayne added drily, "Doesn't speak well for how she feels about the rest of her family."

"No, it doesn't."

"What about them?" Dwayne asked. "You think they're tryin' to steal her money?"

I chewed thoughtfully and mentally ran through my impressions of the Purcells.

"Hard to say. I think they pretty much keep her isolated and confined to her room. There's no phone, and I didn't get the feeling she has lots of visitors. Maybe she likes it that way. Maybe it's a protection for her. She could be easy prey for anyone trying to get a chunk of Purcell money. Beyond that, Orchid's got some deep fear. Or, maybe that comes from starting to lose your mind. She needs a doctor *and* a lawyer."

"Your buddy. Neusmeyer." A smile played around Dwayne's lips. He knows all about my "relationship" with the estate lawyer. "So, what did you tell Jazz?"

"I haven't really told him anything yet. He wants to meet tomorrow. He asked me a couple of questions and then we just sort of left it."

Actually, I'd walked downstairs after the meeting with Orchid and breathed a sigh of relief to see that most of her children had dispersed. The main salon was empty except for Jazz, Logan and Benjamin. Logan was thumbing through a book and perfecting his bored look. Benjamin was standing at the window, looking up at the sky, much as Orchid had. Jazz was lost in thought, his brows drawn together, his expression sort of grim.

When I entered the room Jazz jumped to his feet. His smile nearly distracted me. "What do you think of her?" he asked eagerly. "Isn't she great?"

I wasn't sure what I thought of her, in point of fact. She'd seemed kind of spooky, and sometimes cagey, sometimes clear. She'd lamented her husband's treatment of Lily, but then seemed oddly scared to talk about it.

"I don't think she's ready to give up control."

"But should she? Is it dangerous, do you think?"

I shrugged. "Call an estate lawyer. Or, maybe the family doctor. Maybe they can figure out if she's *compos mentis*."

"What's that?" Logan asked, eyeing me darkly.

"If Grandmother's in her right mind," Benjamin said, his voice sounding dreamy and distracted.

We all looked at him. My thought was: Now, why doesn't *he* call her Nana?

"I hate doing that," Jazz said. "It feels like such a betrayal. I really think she just needs someone with her."

"She's got Eileen," Benjamin said.

Logan made a choking sound. "Her? She's a thief! She stole those jewels."

"We don't know that," Jazz reminded.

"Yes, we do. We just don't want to do anything about it, 'cause no one wants to take care of Nana."

Logan sounded fairly knowledgeable about the situation, especially for a twelve-year-old.

"I take it Eileen's the caretaker?" I put in.

Benjamin nodded.

"You ready to go?" Jazz asked me. I got the feeling he wanted out of there even worse than I did.

"Sure."

We headed through the back door to the portico and our vehicles. Jazz drove a silvery BMW convertible. The other two sports cars were gone. The vanilla caddy still sat parked, looking for all the world that it had been there an eternity and would be there for another one. Bits of moss had taken up residence around the wipers, and the cream body was streaked with dirt.

I glanced at the entrance drive, which curved into the portico and exited out again, angling down another long, leaf-canopied lane, then at Jazz. He was in profile, looking at the house. He could have been posing for a J. Crew print ad. He looked wonderfully clean and beautiful against the decaying property. Briefly, I wondered what he did for a living. Did he even have a job? Or, was he on the dole with Nana's money? He seemed so . . . untouched . . . that it was difficult to believe he'd ever toiled at any-thing.

A stiff breeze had kicked up and leaves swirled over his convertible BMW and my Volvo wagon. They settled onto his upholstery but Jazz didn't appear to notice.

"Sorry I couldn't be more help," I said. My job was done, and I was kind of wondering when Jazz planned to break out the checkbook.

I don't know what I expected to come next, but he suddenly shook my hand, then impulsively hugged me. I could smell his scent, that same citrus cologne, and I felt the first stirrings of sexual interest. The man was just so attractive. He released me before things could become uncomfortable, which was probably a good thing.

"Thanks," he said.

"No problemo," I said lightly, turning toward my car. My stomach growled, and I realized it was dinnertime. My thoughts ran ahead to food and a debriefing with Dwayne. I was about to ask Jazz where to send the bill when he reached into his pocket, pulled out a roll of cash, then ripped off six one-hundred-dollar bills and handed them to me.

I was dazzled by the money.

"I'll call you tomorrow and we can talk about Nana in depth," he said, climbing into his car. "Oh, and I didn't say it in front of Logan and Ben—but Eileen's been let go."

"The caretaker? You really think she stole?"

"I don't know. The family decided she had too much influence on Nana."

I got into my car slowly, carefully tucking the money into a safe little pocket of my wallet before starting the engine. I had no idea whether I was still employed or not. Meeting Jazz the next day held definite possibilities, but there was a niggling doubt associated with his family and their accusations concerning Eileen that followed me all the rest of the evening and through dinner with Dwayne.

Dwayne and I left Lou's in companionable silence. It wasn't

until we pulled into my drive that we brought up the Purcells again, and it was Dwayne who broached the subject. "So, they want you to be the caretaker."

"No. That's not what I said. Where do you get that?" But I knew. Somewhere in the back of my mind the same thought had been circling.

Dwayne's mouth uttered the thought perched on the tip of my tongue: "Why else were you there? Sounds like Jazz told you Eileen was out for a reason."

"I'm not a caretaker. I wouldn't know what to do. I don't want to do it, whatever it is. And besides, they'd have to pay me far more than what the job's worth."

"Good."

"I mean it."

"Even better."

"You don't believe me?"

"I want you to do something for me," Dwayne said, adroitly jumping to the next item on his mental to-do list. "And I don't want the Purcells to get in the way."

"What do you want?"

"You any good at shadowing?"

I gave him a look. He knew darn good and well that I suck at following people. I have no gift for subterfuge. "No."

"I need someone to follow someone for me. A woman. And this woman spends a lotta time at the spas: massage, mud packs, painting the toes and fingers, facials. I don't know what all. It's boggling. I need someone to follow her there and see who she's meeting."

"To a spa?" He nodded. There was a hint of amusement around his eyes. He knows that I'm not the spa type. But I could tell he was serious about the assignment. "Okay. What do you want me to do and when?"

"Tomorrow. Follow her into Complete Me. It's on Hawthorne. Fancy. Order up whatever's she's getting. Her next appointment's at one."

"How do you know?"

"Her husband's the client. Thinks his lovely spouse is cheating on him. Thinks Complete Me gives a whole new meaning to hot rock therapy."

"Who's paying for my spa experience?"

"The client." Dwayne smiled. "It's a freebie, Jane."

Free and be. When hooked together, two of my favorite words. "And after Complete Me, follow her to her next destination?"

"And wherever else," Dwayne agreed.

"I can do that."

"What if Jazz Purcell calls and wants you to take over as Nana's jailer?"

"Dwayne, it's not going to happen."

"Keep tellin' yourself that."

"I mean it."

His answer was a smile that said he knew better.

Chapter Four

I made my nearly three-mile run to the Coffee Nook the next morning. I was still out of shape from a couple of months of recuperation after surviving a nasty fall in August. Consequently, by the time I arrived at the Nook, I ended up hanging on one of the door handles, struggling to catch my breath, dripping sweat. I'd thought about bringing The Binkster with me, but she's really not in love with jogging. Even long walks cause her to try and sit down halfway through. A circle or two around the backyard makes her happy. Sometimes I force her to come with me, and afterward she acts like she needs to sleep for a week. So much for the myth that dogs have more energy than humans. Maybe terriers—or chihuahuas.

Billy Leonard was inside, seated on one of the stools. "Hey," I greeted him, glad to see a friend.

Billy's a CPA but you'd never know it. His appearance is not what I'd call buttoned-down. Today he looked like he'd just stepped out of the tumble dryer. "What are you working on, Jane?"

"A job."

"Process serving?"

"No . . . do you know the Purcells?"

"*The* Purcells? Don't know 'em personally. Know a few stories. Your job involve them?"

"Jazz Purcell . . . Jasper . . . asked me to meet his grandmother and see if I thought she was still mentally capable of controlling the finances. The family's worried she'll give away the farm, the jewels, whatever isn't nailed down in a trust."

"Orchid Purcell?"

"That's right."

Billy thought a moment, running his hand quickly through his hair several times. It had been pretty well combed before this ravaging. Now he looked wild. "What about the daughter? The one that went to the mental asylum?"

"Lily was Jazz's mother. She died at the asylum."

"Big investigation, right? Lawsuit . . . sanitarium responsible?"

"I don't really know."

"Something went on there. The old man die right afterward?"

"James 'Percy' Purcell the . . . third, I believe? Orchid's husband? I don't think so. I thought he lived quite a while."

Billy snapped his fingers. "He was never the same. Kinda took his mind, I think. Killed his will to live. He was always a big mover and shaker, then *bam*. No more. What's the son's name? The older one?"

"Garrett?"

"Yeah, yeah. He's the only one I've met. Saw him at Jake's Grill one night. Really not a friendly guy. He was pushing and talking and telling everybody what he knew." Billy laughed. "It wasn't much, if you know what I mean."

"I do." I could just picture Garrett thrusting his opinions on anyone within hearing range.

"He was with his wife, I think. I thought she was drunk. She looked kinda glassy-eyed."

"That's just how she looks. I just met her yesterday. Garrett might be worried Orchid isn't capable of handling the money, but he wasn't thrilled that Jazz brought me to meet her."

"Families . . . They don't wear gloves in battle. Look out you don't get your head knocked off."

Julie handed me a cup of black coffee. Usually I fill it up myself but sometimes Julie anticipates my wishes. I gave her a grateful smile. It makes me feel special when someone does something unasked for. Sometimes I worry that I expect too little. Maybe I need to raise the bar when it comes to acts of niceness.

Billy left and I sipped my coffee. I debated on running back to my cottage or heading downtown. Dwayne's cabana is just on the other side of Lakewood Bay. I could be there in twenty minutes to a half hour.

I started out in that direction, then switched back to my original plan to run straight home. I needed the exercise and time to think. By the time I walked through my front door my cell phone was vibrating. I'd left it on the kitchen counter and it damn near walked off the edge. I just managed to snatch it up before it thrummed itself into a death dive.

"Where ya been?" Dwayne demanded. "Miriam's going to be at the spa at one."

"I know. I'm running through the shower now."

"The husband tried to meet her for lunch but she told him she was getting a massage. I need you to follow her *today*."

"I'm on it, Dwayne." Sheesh. "I just ran six miles," I added for good measure.

"You walked a lot of it." I made a strangled sound and would have argued with him just for the sake of it—even though he was right—but Dwayne swept on, "You got a two-hundred-dollar allowance to get yourself buffed and puffed as well."

I was impressed and worried. I wasn't sure what kind of treatment that would buy me, but I knew it wouldn't be anything I wanted. "How am I going to know Miriam?"

"You can't miss her. She's a redhead, and the collagen lips will enter the door before she does."

"Okay . . ."

"Try to enjoy yourself." He hung up.

I gazed in consternation out my back kitchen window. I heard Binks, who'd been sleeping in her bed in the corner, stagger toward me. Her doggy toenails clicked on the hardwood floor, heralding her arrival. She touched the back of my leg with a paw. Normally I pet her, but I was only half-conscious that she was even there. I was thinking about massages and mud packs and hot stones and steam. Sorry. I know a lot of people think this is the end-all/be-all in pampering but I find it slightly worrisome. So help me, I imagine foot fungi in communal dipping pools. I could get a skin rash from some so-called lotion that's good for my body. And maybe I've seen too many horror movies, but there's something about a mud pack slathered over my cheeks and nose that makes me fear I could lose a breathing passage.

I wasn't even sure what to wear. Knowing I was overthinking the whole thing, I showered and washed my hair. Then I put on fresh sweats—the horrible baby blue ones my brother and his fiancée had given me after my fall and trip to the hospital. I'd thanked them and stuffed them in a drawer. Not that they weren't pretty. But sometimes "pretty" makes me look like I'm playing dress up. When I'd donned them the first time, I'd had an instant vision of Barbie getting ready for an exercise date with Ken. Now I steadfastly zipped up the stretchy-tight jacket and slipped into my Rite-Aid flip-flops. Would a little eyeliner be too much, or maybe a prerequisite? How about some chandelier earrings?

Binkster came over and sniffed my ankle suspiciously. "Don't even go there," I muttered.

By the time I was ready, I still had an hour to kill before one o'clock. In the interest of surviving another day I stopped at the grocery store and picked up wheat bread and Havarti cheese. The young male clerk gave me a bright smile. "Cute workout gear."

"I'm going to a funeral."

The smile didn't waver. "Wow. Cool."

This depressed me. I hate it when I mean to be screamingly funny and above-it-all and someone takes me at face value.

I drove into Portland down I-5 and took the Hawthorne Bridge to the east side of the river. Hawthorne's this cool street with fun little coffee shops, restaurants and music stores. It's become chic in a mostly affordable way. Not too gentrified as yet, which suited me just fine.

I had a small bit of difficulty parking. The side streets are narrow with cars choking the roadway on either side. A great many of the houses were built at the turn of the century with Victorian or Craftsman style influence. Try to turn around in one of those skinny drives and you could pop a tire. A garage is a rare event.

A guy in a black Mercedes scowled at me as he cruised by. He'd wanted the spot but I'd muscled in first and he'd been unable to play chicken with his newer car against my older one. He mouthed something at me as I climbed out of my car. Something fairly rude, I was sure.

I cupped my ear with my hand, pretending to struggle to catch his meaning, then dashed through the door to Complete Me.

The place was a far cry from the historic older homes and quaint shops. It was glass and chrome and the anteroom soared several stories. Young women with hair gelled and curled and makeup expertly smoothed on about a quarter-inch thick greeted me with blinding smiles. One asked me if I had an appointment. I said no, I was waiting for someone. More smiling. Could they get me herbal tea? A scented, warmed neck pillow?

I wavered on the tea, though I often struggle with something that smells like weeds and is a strangely yellow-green color I just know isn't from this world. Before I could even reply I was handed a small cup without a handle. The cup was dark gray so I couldn't quite tell the hue of the concoction. I sipped it carefully. It wasn't terrible. I waved off the neck pillow.

"Love your outfit," one of the girls told me with a smile. "Blue's your color."

Bullshit. I'm better in pink. But I'll be damned if I tell anyone that. "Thanks."

I'd brought my cell phone with me and had a sudden urge to call Cynthia. I should have asked her to join me. She's better at navigating this stuff. She likes massages and rubs and I've heard her actually purr at the thought of turning her body over to experts.

But this was a job. I needed all my concentration, because by God I wasn't going to go through this twice.

The reception girls saw me with my phone and lines of consternation etched between their shaped brows. One pointed to a sign that very nicely said that, as a courtesy to their other customers, cell calls were to be made outside. I reluctantly put my phone back in my pocket.

I was debating on whether to ask for another cup of herbal tea. I could see where this stuff might be addictive. It made me worry about just what kind of herbs might be used in the brewing. I was actually heading toward the counter when I saw a redheaded woman approach the glass doors. Her frosted pink lips entered the spa a half-second before the rest of her. Ducking my head away from her, I put my cup on the counter, pulled a sad face and said to Girl Number Two, "I got a text message from my friend. She's not going to be able to meet me after all. Maybe I could get a massage . . . or something . . . and this trip can be salvaged?"

Girl Number Two made clucking sounds, checking her appointment book. "I just hate it when my girlfriend plans get ruined."

"Amen."

"Miriam Westerly," my quarry introduced herself to Girl #1 in an abrupt, breathless voice. "I've got an appointment with Trevin."

"Ah, yes, Ms. Westerly." She flashed her pearly whites. "Someone will guide you to the relaxation room in just a moment. I'll let Trevin know you're here."

"Sure." Miriam glanced toward the door to the inner sanctum, strolling to the center of the room and back again, fueled by nervous energy. Her eyes kept returning to the door.

I felt she could use the relaxation room and wondered how I could get there myself.

Girl Number Two told me, "You can have hot stone therapy with Bryce."

That sounded scary. "Um . . . any chance for a plain old massage?"

"Deep muscle?"

"Okay."

"Trevin's our best . . . and Julia's not in today . . . hmmm . . ."

"How long will Trevin be?" I asked.

The girl glanced at Miriam, then back to me . . . I tried to read her expression. Was I imagining the slight irony when she said, "Oh, it'll be a while. Actually, I think Drago's free. Let me check."

Drago? I wondered if I might have been too hasty. Hot rocks with Bryce sounded better.

She put a call through to Drago as Girl Number One invited Miriam into the inner sanctum. Miriam bolted like a colt, scurrying inside as if she were about to wet her pants.

Drago, as it turned out, was free. It was my turn to pass through the door, but I was escorted by my own girl guide who directed me down a thickly carpeted hallway lit by polished-nickel wall sconces. There was also ankle height lighting that guided our way in evenly spaced pools of illumination. We passed a door where a woman was moaning as if she were being tortured.

My enthusiasm—already low—drooped ever downward.

We entered a "holding" room. My girl gestured in the direction of the showers, explaining that they had lockers for my belongings. I could change my clothes there and lock them inside. I was to put on the Complete Me robe, and I would receive a key attached to a plastic wrist band with which to secure the locker. Then I was to come back here where I could avail myself of the showers—some of which were behind bamboo walls that left my head and feet visible—kind of like something out of *South Pacific*. And, please avail myself of the relaxation pool as well. She swept another arm and half turned toward the gently bubbling dark blue, glass-tiled pool that swept around one corner of the room. It was lit by directional spotlights and I could just see the top

curved tile step that led into the water. The pool's surrounding
seat was adorned with clusters of ochre, white and red orchids. I
didn't hear much else of the tutelage, though my guide rambled
on effusively, because my eyes were searching for Miriam. Either
she was in the locker room or she'd charged right past relaxation
to muscle thumping with Trevin.

"... when you're finished here just pass into the Autumn Room."
She half-turned toward a door done in more bamboo poles. The
handles were wrought iron formed like small branches. "Take a
seat there. Read a magazine. We'll call your name when your
body therapist is ready for you."

"Drago," I said, gauging her reaction.

She smiled blankly, as if the name meant nothing to her. I didn't
take it as a good sign.

I gave the locker room a cursory search but no Miriam. An attendant handed me a plastic wrist band with a key attached, labeled with the letter G. She then gave me a white plush Complete
Me robe that smelled faintly of vanilla. I inhaled deeply, before
claiming locker G. Taking off my clothes, I stuffed them inside,
then wrapped myself in the robe. The plastic wrist band was pale
yellow, the key shiny chrome. I slipped the band over my hand
and kind of enjoyed the feeling of my spa "bling."

Passing through the bamboo door, I looked hard for Miriam,
who'd miraculously escaped into the bowels of the place without
my further detection. Chagrined, I glanced around for a seat, settling in to a comfy espresso-colored leather chair. The Autumn
Room was another, smaller holding room sporting more low-
lighting and cushy luxury. Spread artfully on a black occasional
table lay the kind of magazines that tout makeup, lite diets and
how to keep your man happy in bed. Makeup didn't interest me
today and since I didn't currently have a man, and didn't feel like
I'd had any complaints in that department anyway, I skipped
right over to salads made from kelp.

The magazine girls eating the salad sported impossibly white
smiles, the kind I suspect could send streams of laser illumination into the stratosphere bright enough to confuse small aircraft.

Their haircuts were dramatic, leftover strands of hair falling into one or both eyes. The salads looked pretty, but I wasn't convinced they'd pass a taste test. I'm cool enough to have moved from iceberg lettuce to Romaine. I wasn't cool enough for field greens, which I kind of think might be weeds that some chef somewhere is having a huge belly laugh over—sort of like the Emperor's new clothes. I knew I was not ready for seaweed of any kind. It's one of the many reasons I struggle with sushi.

There were two other women in the room. An attendant came through a sliding paper door, like in upscale Japanese restaurants, and intoned, "Diana."

The heavier set woman climbed to her bare feet and padded after the attendant. I was left with woman Number Two and a sense of time slipping away. I hadn't been that far behind Miriam. What had happened to her?

The Autumn Room door suddenly opened, answering my question. Miriam stepped inside, fresh from a shower. Her hair was wet and combed away from her face. She seemed snuggled into her robe, yet there was a sense of energy thrumming through her. Her blue eyes glowed as if lit from behind. Her mega-lips looked even plumper, if that were possible. I could smell the anticipation of a sexual encounter, as if the woman herself were emitting pheromones.

"We'll call your name when we're ready," the attendant informed us all as she disappeared behind the paper door.

I flipped through the pages of the magazine, surreptitiously studying Miriam. She was making me curious about Trevin. The other woman in the room, a lithe, stylish blonde in her mid-thirties, seemed to sense Miriam's excitement as well and view it as a call to arms. She straightened in her chair and ran a hand through her long mane with manicured pale pink fingernails. She said coolly, "Are you interested in that magazine?"

Miriam wasn't interested in anything but her upcoming appointment. "Oh, no. Help yourself." Her voice was breathless as she handed over a magazine with a woman wearing Kabuki makeup on the front cover.

Blondie gave Miriam a sidelong glance full of repressed venom and flipped through the pages without looking.

The attendant returned. "Miriam."

Miriam leapt up. Her robe uncinched briefly and I caught a glimpse of skin starting to ripple. Quickly she recinched and followed the attendant, nearly giving the woman a flat tire in her haste to reach the inner sanctum and Trevin. Blondie, having caught the same quick peek as myself, subsided into satisfied contemplation of her lovely nails, a faint smile on her lips.

I exhaled carefully and congratulated myself on missing out on these deadly female battles that pop up randomly and for no seeming reason.

The hostess returned. "Jane."

I followed after her, shooting Blondie a puzzled glance on my way inside. She caught the look and said, "I'm waiting for Christine. She's running a little behind but she's incredible."

"Ah."

I followed my attendant down an inner hallway. The carpet was thick and spongy beneath my bare feet. I heard laughter from one of the rooms. Miriam's laughter. "Oh, there's Miriam," I said softly. "I wonder . . . could I be next to her room?"

"You're already in the room adjoining. Would you prefer to be together? There are two beds in the room Trevin's using today."

"Oh, no. Thanks. This is fine." Yikes. Wouldn't Miriam just love that.

She opened the door. "Drago will be here shortly. Make yourself comfortable. You can hang your robe there.

"There" was a heated hanger next to a tray of various oils and masseuse/personal care products which stood against the wall near the head of the bed.

"Thanks."

As soon as I was alone I hurried to the south wall where Miriam and Trevin were getting into their massage. I pressed my ear to the wall, looking around for a tumbler glass or any other conduit. Nothing.

I could make out a few snatches of conversation. Miriam said something about hating to wait so long. Trevin asked her about Stan, or maybe Lance. She responded with a raise in her voice. Very clearly, she said, "I can't live my life like this. I won't!" Trevin suggested she lie down and relax. She said she was glad how things were, now that they were over. Or, maybe she was sad how things were for the lovers. Or maybe it was something else entirely.

I strained, but soft music began emanating from the speakers in my room. At the same moment, there was a knock on my door. My pulse skyrocketed. I glanced around the room like a caged animal.

"Helloooo," Drago said in a deep voice, cracking the door. "May I come in?"

"Um . . . not . . . yet?"

"Do you need help getting onto the table?" He had a faintly European accent that may or may not have been fake.

"Nope. Just need another minute."

As soon as the door closed I stripped out of my robe and slid bare-ass naked beneath the top sheet, lying on my stomach on the bottom one. There was a hole cut into the bed itself near one end, a place for my face, apparently. I settled myself down, heart thumping. Maybe I should have left my underwear on. I felt . . . well . . . naked, which I guess was the point. I glanced around once, noting the nearby table with the oils and little scrubby bead what's-its, Q-tips and neatly stacked cloth napkin things.

Drago knocked again. "Ready?"

"Yes."

I got my first look at him as he entered and gently closed the door behind himself. He wore a blue outfit similar to a surgeon's scrubs. His hair was dark brown; his skin lightly tanned. He was rubbing his hands together in an alarming fashion. "You want a deep massage."

I wanted to get the hell out. But I'd been granted two hundred dollars, and I knew it wasn't really my money. If I didn't use it up, I wasn't going to get it as a bonus. "Sure."

Self-consciously, I pushed my face into its special cradle.

Drago came up next to me. I heard him rubbing oil between his hands. I squeezed my eyes closed and reminded myself that this was something people paid for because they actually enjoyed it. My breasts pressed against the soft cotton sheet beneath me. The sheet came around my body and held me tightly to the faux-leather covered table.

Drago pushed back a section of top drape, exposing my left arm and shoulder. I jumped when his hands connected with my skin. "You are skittish," he observed.

No shit, Sherlock.

My cell phone lay on the side table with all the masseuse accouterments. I could almost reach it if I stretched out my left arm. I kept it with me when I'd undressed. Now, I wanted to clasp it in my palm; a true security blanket. Instead I closed my eyes and fought to succumb to the sensation. He was pushing my lats with hard palms, fingers and thumbs.

Deep muscle? It damn near brought tears to my eyes. I'm not sure massage can really be good for you.

"You work out. Firm muscles. You have a good body."

"You should see my teeth."

"Pardon?"

It was quiet in the room. I could hear his breathing and my own. I wondered how long we'd been at it, so I checked my watch. Four minutes. I used to periodically go to a tanning salon, and I could find a way to relax enough in those glass beds to actually zone out. It's a good thing they're on timers or they could fry a person. Now, I tried to figure out a way to achieve that level of relaxation by letting my mind wander aimlessly on a variety of thoughts. I had a jolt of surprise when Drago flipped up the bottom part of the robe and began working on my left leg. I was highly sensitive to his fingers on my upper, inner thighs. I couldn't help the tension. I tried, I really did. I fought to stay in the moment and surrender to the whole massage thing.

All I could think about was where his fingers were and what I would do if they strayed where I didn't want them. Logically, I know this is unlikely. I mean, would it be worth me screaming bloody murder? But it just felt like it could happen.

A few more minutes went by. I was faintly relaxing. Enough to let loose my death grip on the sides of the bed. Drago had moved to my right arm and I was feeling relief.

"Yes, relax," he said.

I was. I did. Okay, it was good. Kind of hurt in a healthy, you're doing something great for yourself way. Kind of felt good, too. I sighed deeply. Maybe this was all right. Maybe I'd missed the whole point. Maybe I would make this my new life mission and—

"Mind if I chant?"

My eyes popped open. *Chant?* "Uh . . . go ahead."

"Thank you. It will be good."

I tensed anew as his rubbing became more rhythmic.

"Ohmmmmmmmmm. Ohmmmmmmmmmm. Daaaaaroooooohh hhmmmmm. . . ."

I stared through the face-hole to the floor. His chanting reverberated through the room.

"Ohhhhmmmmmmmummmmm . . ."

My inner vision saw the little glass container of Q-tips. I desperately desired one. I wanted to stick it in my ear and dig away for all I'm worth.

"Ohhmmmmmmmmm. . . ."

I tried to squeeze my ears shut against the vibration. The tickle was excruciating.

"Daaaaaroooooohhhhhmmmm . . . daaaaroooohhhmmmmm . . ."

Was that a 747 taking off?

"Daaaarooooohhhhmmmmm . . ."

Every muscle clenched.

"Ohhhhmmmm . . . mah . . . mahhhhhhh . . ."

I needed to relax. I couldn't make myself.

"Bahhhrrrrkoooohmmmm . . ."

"Drago," I whispered.

"Yesss . . ." His voice sounded sleepy and sated.

From the next room I heard some thumping and moaning. There was the sound of flesh being slapped and cries of ecstasy. It brought Drago out of his trance, for he stalked to the opposite wall and dialed up the music. I caught the thunderous look on his face as he returned to me.

If I'd thought my massage was deep before, I soon learned we'd been in the kiddies' pool. My breath was lodged in my throat, and when he asked me to turn over I wasn't sure I was capable. Instantly he was contrite. "Too much? You should have said so."

"I'm okay."

"I will be careful with you."

Staring at the ceiling was even worse. I felt more exposed. But at least for the time being his chanting was over. I could tell he was bugged at what was going on in the next room.

"My friend Miriam likes a little more than massage," I said, injecting just the right rueful tone.

His dark eyes shot to me. "You do not feel the same."

"No. Heavens, no. Not me. I struggle with just a massage."

"Your friend should be more . . . careful."

"She thinks Trevin's the one," I said, feeling my pulse race once more. Lying, and the fear of being found out, release some chemical from my brain that gets me going. Adrenaline. Maybe endorphins. Whatever. I could feel myself growing high on my own chemistry.

Which is just about hell when you're completely naked.

Drago eyed me clearly. "Trevin is one."

Either he didn't get what I'd meant, or he did and was making a play on words.

"One what?"

"He is one . . . type of man." Disapproval filled his tone and the deep massage grew deeper.

"I think I'm done now," I squeezed out.

"Your hour is not up."

"I'm okay with that."

Drago gave me a long look. My smile was tremulous. I couldn't help it. I felt tired all over. He took pity on me and nodded curtly. "You should take a sauna. Ease those muscles. You know where the sauna room is?"

"Yes," I lied.

"Along this hall to the left." His mind clearly wasn't on my answer.

"Thanks."

"I'll be right outside if you need me."

He left rather stiffly, as if I'd insulted him somehow. Quickly I climbed off the bed and grabbed the robe, which was deliciously warm. My muscles felt liquid. I had to concentrate on them to keep them moving. Tiptoeing hurriedly to the wall, I listened hard. The damn music was in the way. Carefully, I dialed it back down.

There was faint murmuring and laughter coming from the other room. Love talk. I could picture them enjoying a postcoital herbal tea or lemon water cocktail.

I headed out the door where Drago stood with a bottle of water. In truth, I was dying of thirst. I thanked him, unscrewed the cap and glugged half of it down as I headed for the sauna. Looking back down the hallway, I saw Drago watching me and I gave him a quick, parting wave.

Once through the door, I dropped my phone in my locker, then headed to the showers to rinse off the leftover oil. Then I returned to the relaxation pool, hanging my robe on a hook above my head. I groaned as I melted into its depths. All my muscles were protesting and I felt faintly headachy. An attendant asked if I would like more herbal tea and I eagerly accepted. I hoped to hell it was loaded with some escapist narcotic the FDA hadn't figured out was harmful yet.

There were several other naked women already in the pool, their heads turbaned to keep their hair safe from moisture. I found my inhibitions had left me. I sipped my tea and tried to think good thoughts. The surrounding mist and ferns fed a seventies feel-good revival.

It took Miriam another half hour before she appeared. By that time I was seriously pruned and ready to get the hell out. But I waited. She looked flushed and blotchy. If she and Trevin hadn't massaged a few parts not recommended in the Complete Me handbook, I was a monkey's uncle.

My other pool buddies had left by the time Miriam headed straight toward me. As she dropped her robe I started thinking about her having sex with Trevin and sharing water with me, and I was instantly sure this was a bad, bad idea. Now, I know you could say the same thing about a community swimming pool. You don't know what the other pool-ees have been up to before joining in the water. And I'd just been with several other women who hadn't flipped me out at all.

But Miriam reeked of sex.

I moved to the far end of the tub and reminded myself that chlorine is a germ killer. This was no time to let my phobias overtake me. Not with a God-sent opportunity to interrogate the woman.

I smiled at her. She flicked me a look. I realized then that her suffused skin was from a different emotion entirely: anger. She was infuriated. Rage pulsed through her like an electrical charge.

Uh-oh.

I said, "How was your massage with Trevin?"

Chapter Five

Miriam Westerly's skin turned redder yet. I kind of shrank back, afraid her head might pop off. She said in short, bitten off words, "How—do—you—know—I—was—with—Trevin?"

I blinked, shifted into acting mode. In confused innocence, I said, "I was at the front desk when you arrived."

It didn't pacify her. She turned her head. I saw she was fighting back tears. It made me feel like a heel, but I wasn't getting paid to start commiserating with her.

"Are you okay?" I asked.

"Do I look okay?" she snapped.

"No . . . actually." She sniffed loudly and her jaw tightened. I could tell she was torn between breaking down completely and erupting into a shrieking rage. I wasn't sure which one I'd vote for.

"Goddamn it!" she hissed, making her choice. "The suck-up, brown-nosing bastard. I'd like to smash my fist in his mouth."

"You mean Trevin?" I tried to look concerned and understanding. If she managed to actually hit Trevin, I thought his lips might look like hers. There was something ducklike to her mouth that drew my gaze like a magnet. How many sessions did it take to achieve that effect? One? Two? Twenty?

"Yes, Trevin." Her lower lip pulled down in disgust. Beneath the pink lips, there wasn't quite the attention to dental hygiene there might be. I'm pretty sure I detected some plaque. As I hate to have my teeth cleaned, but do it religiously to keep the choppers working great and looking good, I feel everyone else should have to endure this gum-ripping experience on a regular basis as well. When someone cheats, like Miriam, I get all judgmental about them. There's just no substitute for good dental hygiene. Collagen lips ain't gonna cut it without the pearly whites shining brightly.

"How do you know Trevin?" she demanded. "Are you a . . . client?" Those pink wads twisted into a sneer.

"This is my first time to Complete Me. I guess that makes me still incomplete."

"You think you're funny?"

Well, now that really pissed me off. Here I was trying to be all friendly and understanding and she was using me as a substitute for her anger. "I'm a regular laugh riot."

"I don't know why I'm even talking to you. I don't know what I'm doing here. I've got things to do. Important things. This was supposed to be . . . to be . . . a time . . . when . . ." Her voice started to shake. More tears welled. We were moving from fury to self-pity pretty fast. ". . . When . . . I could have something for *me*."

This last part was a squeak. "What did Trevin do?"

"I've been going to him for over a year. And he said he's quitting! He's going to Australia. To be a scuba diving instructor. Can you imagine? A scuba diving instructor!" Her eyes were awash in tears. She looked stunned, like a thwarted child.

"How old is Trevin?"

"Twenty-four . . ." Her chin wobbled. I clocked her as being somewhere in her mid-forties. "He said this was our last appointment."

"There are other masseuses," I said.

She said bitterly, "Oh, sure."

That pretty much ended our conversation. I started wondering how much I had left on my spa allowance. Was Trevin already out the door? Or, could I possibly schedule something with him? Not that I was really eager to be on the bed beneath his hands, but I really wanted to know what he was all about. It was something I could put in a report.

I didn't really think I would need to follow Miriam from the spa. She and Trevin were done and she was heartbroken. Whatever had transpired between them was over. But Trevin might be able to provide some insight.

However, I didn't think I could handle any more massage today.

What then? How could I meet with the guy?

Miriam left the pool a few moments later, dejected and miserable as she slid her arms into her robe. "Jesus." Her head snapped up as if pulled on a string. "He's got my money!"

What money? I wanted to ask, but she was suddenly frothing at the bit, padding quickly to the locker room. I grabbed my robe and followed, throwing on my blue jogging suit over skin still wet. I slid my feet into my flip-flops and nearly beat Miriam out the door. Unlike me, she actually took some time with her appearance, but then she had to save face as she left the spa.

I followed her to the initial waiting room and watched her saunter through the glass doors to the street as if she didn't have a care in the world. She did glance back once, longingly, and I bent my head over a brochure. But her eyes were searching for Trevin and she didn't even notice me. She grabbed her cell phone and placed a call. I hoped it was to her bank. If she'd given Trevin a check she could put a stop payment on it. Or, if she'd given him a credit card, she could cancel it. But if she'd given the guy cash it was all over. I kind of felt sorry for her.

As I debated on whether to ask for hot stone therapy with Trevin, a young man strolled in from the inner sanctum, his damp, dark, shoulder-length hair brushed away from his face. He was smiling, in that smirky self-satisfied way that bugs me for no reason I can name. I knew it was Trevin without being told, but Girl Number One suddenly brightened as if someone had toggled her switch. "Hey, Trev," she said.

"Hey, Gloria," he said in singsong voice.

"You're not leaving today, are you?" She pretended to pout.

"Not till Friday. I'll come see ya before I head Down Under."

"You'd better."

He gave her a wink and sketched a wave.

I quickly explained to the girls that I was Jane Kelly and I had a credit to use for payment. They took their time finding the paperwork and I wanted to scream. Lucky for me, after Trevin stepped outside he stopped to dig into a pocket for a pack of cigarettes. I watched Mr. Masseuse/Scuba Instructor light up a menthol—like, oh, sure, that's going to save your breath—and finally Girl Number Two pronounced me "Good to go."

By this time Trevin was striding across Hawthorne, trying to dodge the traffic. This was not something I planned on doing. Unlike Trev I have great respect for cars and what they can do to the human body. I kept my eye on him and walked along the opposite side of the street. I caught a crosslight and hurried quickly over to his side of the street. He was nearly two blocks ahead of me and I had to beat feet to catch sight of him as he turned into a doorway. I hurried to where he'd disappeared and saw he'd entered a small bistro that served coffee and luscious looking non-fat/non-sugar pastries. What *are* those things made out of?

My stomach growled and I realized I hadn't really eaten anything since yesterday's evening's chili dog. I should've got the foot-long dog. I knew it.

I hoped following Trevin had been the right choice. My quarry had been Miriam but, seeing her defeat, I'd jumped ship. Now I fretted my decision. Clearly our client wanted the goods on his cheating wife, and though it made me feel kind of sleazy to follow the would-be lovebirds, I'd signed on for this tour of duty.

Entering the bistro, I pretended not to notice Trevin. Not that he was paying me the slightest bit of attention. He and some guy pal were standing near a table, loudly discussing the merits of scuba diving in various parts of the world. It was a pissing contest with guy pal seating himself at the table, hands wrapped around an iced mocha thing that brought saliva to my mouth. Trevin stood over him, intent on making his point, something about the Great Barrier Reef. He was waiting for his order as I walked up to the counter.

"May I help you?" a young woman with serious piercings asked me.

I pointed to guy pal's iced coffee. She rang it up and asked for nearly four dollars. I paid reluctantly. Normally I'm better at price checking. Now, as I eyed the pastries, I wondered if it was really worth making this stuff my late lunch and even later breakfast. Oh, hell. This is where Trevin had led me, so this is where I would eat. I pointed to a rolled thing oozing marionberry filling. I gave her my name—Veronica—my favorite alias, then forked over some more dollars. Carrying my bounty carefully, I chose a small table with a straight-on view of Trevin and his friend.

"T," the girl called, holding out a whipped milky concoction in a glass mug.

Trevin picked up the mug. I cut off a piece of my pastry with the side of my fork and shoved it into my mouth. Either I was really hungry or it was really good. For a moment my attention was taken by my pastry. Wow. Non-fat/non-sugar? Who knew?

In that second Trevin leaned toward guy pal and said something too low to hear. Guy pal whistled and said, "You dog." They both chuckled. I strained closer, but just then my cell phone, which I was in the act of pulling from my purse, started vibrating in my hand. I nearly jumped from my skin. It felt like a huge, flying insect had landed on my palm and was thrumming its wings. I had to stifle a surprised gasp. Unfortunately, it caught Trevin—T's—attention and he gave me a look. I smiled and checked my caller. Jazz.

Trevin's gaze slid down me, hesitating somewhere around my chest. He was one of those.

"Hey, there," I greeted Jazz.

"Hey, yourself," he said warmly. "I was wondering when we could get together?"

Ah, yes. The debriefing. "Later this afternoon . . . evening?"

"Let me take you to dinner."

He was talking my language. "That'd be great. Should I meet you?"

"Sure. You pick. Where would you like to go?"

"What price range?" I asked cautiously.

"I don't care." He sounded amused. "Sky's the limit."

"Dangerous words. I can pack the food away, given half a chance."

"How about Hill Villa? I'll make reservations for six. That work for you?"

"I'll be there."

I hung up, pleased. Hill Villa was one of Portland's premier restaurants. It was perched on a hillside with a spectacular view of the Willamette River and Mt. Hood. I'd eaten there exactly once, a long time ago, but I still remembered the prime rib fondly.

Trevin had gone back to an animated conversation with his buddy. His cell rang and he slid a look at Caller ID. "I think this is her. Looks like it might be international. I'd better go."

"Tell her G'day. And to hang onto her wallet 'cause T's coming south!" He guffawed.

Trevin sent him a dark look, called him a dick and left.

I followed a couple of seconds later, pretending to place a call on my phone as I sauntered out. The damn thing buzzed in my hand again, and I nearly dropped it, then juggled like mad to keep it from hitting the painted concrete floor. I just managed to save it. "Hello?"

"You still at the spa?" Dwayne asked.

"Nope. On the job."

"Following Miriam?"

Trevin seemed to be heading back to Complete Me. I kept him in my sights while I threaded through the looky-loos strolling along Hawthorne. I'd felt hot when I'd left the spa but now a stiff breeze was blowing my hair and sending a chill down the back of my neck. "I'm actually walking behind the other party."

"She met someone at the spa?"

"Works there. Worked, actually. Just quit."

"He the boyfriend?"

"Pretty sure. He's moving to Australia to teach scuba diving. There's a girl waiting for him there. And I think he might have got a chunk of money out of our client's wife. He seems to be known for this behavior. A friend of his teased him about it."

"Does Miriam know he's leaving?"

"Uh huh. Didn't take it well."

"I'll bet."

"She was—distraught."

Dwayne grunted. "I'll call Spence and give him the update. If the wife's upset, maybe she's ready to come clean with him."

"Spence?" My antennae lifted.

"Yeah. Knew his wife was cheating on him. He's pretty torn up about it."

"Does he go to the Coffee Nook?"

"Not sure," Dwayne said, losing interest. "Yeah, maybe. I've seen him with those dark red paper coffee cups. I think they're from the Nook. Your friend Julie probably'll know. I can ask him."

"No," I answered quickly. "No big deal."

Dwayne hung up and I crossed back across the street, still following Trevin. But in my inner eye I saw Spence and Janice playing footsie underneath the counter.

Yeah. He was really torn up about his cheating wife.

I met Jazz at Hill Villa around six PM. I'd had to really spend some time thinking about my appearance because he'd already seen me in my two favorite outfits. I'd had to take it up a notch, donning a silvery blue dress that I seldom wore—mainly because it was the kind of thing that would serve me well if I ever became a lounge singer. The neckline was demure, but it plunged down the back, which created problems for wearing a bra, so I didn't bother. Still, I'd been complimented on it more than once, so I kept it around against my better judgment. It was my "wedding" dress, the one I wore to all formal occasions. I'd nearly made myself crazy the whole way over to the restaurant, wondering if I'd overdressed. Though Hill Villa is fairly swank, casual seems to go everywhere these days, and I just plain struggle with being dressed up.

So, when I entered wearing my dress and the pair of silver sandals that I'd recently bought to team with it—I'd walked into the store to take them back, walked back out again, then clutched them to me like they were the answer to the world's salvation—I was feeling a trifle insecure. I know lots of women who wouldn't think twice about being the chic-est peacock in the room, but it ain't me, folks.

I'd brushed my hair down straight and added some faint, curling-iron curls at the ends, burning the side of my neck in the process. (Had to cover the redness with serious cover-up, then fretted about that, too.) I refused to ask myself what all the fuss was about. I knew anyway. Jazz Purcell was handsome and I didn't want to completely shrink into the wallpaper. There was no competing with him, but hey, I wanted to at least look worthy. I didn't want to read the looks on the other patrons' faces that said, What the hell is he doing with *her?* Maybe they would anyway, but at least I could try and mitigate it.

The maître d' took one look at me and said, "Ms. Kelly?"

This was a good sign. "Yes."

He smiled warmly and nodded to a girl holding a pile of maroon leather menus in her arms. "Mr. Purcell's waiting for you."

She led me to a table for two by the window. Jazz half rose as I walked toward him. Silly me, my heart skipped a beat or two. Good God. He was all in black. Black collarless shirt, again something silky and primal, black slacks. His hair was brushed back artfully. I kinda liked that it was longish. Not too much. Not scary, ex-hippy ponytail stuff. Just brushing his collar . . . if he'd had one.

"You look great," he said, trying to hide his surprise.

This was more gratifying than annoying. "I clean up good."

Outside the window was a dizzying view down to the Willamette River and east toward Mt. Hood. It was spectacular, so crisp and clear it was as if someone had taped a picture of the mountain to the window in lieu of the real thing.

As I sat down Jazz reached across the table and covered one of my hands with his own. Surprised, I nearly jerked back, just managed to keep my hand in place.

"Do you believe in fate?" he asked.

I hesitated. I didn't want to spoil the moment, but I always feel the compulsion to lay down ground rules even when there appears to be no need. "Not really," I hedged. I worried he was going to go all mystical on me.

"I've had a life-changing year. It really started last Christmas when my wife died in the car accident. I've been trying to get past it, and move on, but . . ." He gave me a look out of those killer blue eyes. "You know about the memory loss?"

"Memory loss . . . ?"

"They didn't tell you?"

I wasn't sure who "they" were. "I guess not. You mean your family?"

"They all liked you. I just thought maybe one of them took you aside and explained."

I was still struggling with "they all liked you." Clearly Jazz was overstating the situation. "I really didn't talk to any of them other than Orchid."

"Nana loved you," he gushed. "Just loved you."

I heard distant warning bells. "What memory loss are you talking about?"

"After the accident, I couldn't remember anything for a little while. I guess it's common after a head injury. No memory of the accident. But I haven't had much of a memory even past that," he admitted. "I knew who I was. And I knew Logan and Jennifer. But it just seemed like kind of a mess. Like I had pieces of somebody else's life . . . a movie . . . that wasn't mine, in my head. It all came back pretty fast. Well, in a couple of weeks, but I lost a lot of my short-term memory. Now, it's hard to learn new things."

"How did the accident happen? Do you know?"

We paused while the waiter brought a bottle of red wine that Jazz had asked for before I'd arrived. I'd been thinking of having a cocktail, but when Jazz questioned if I liked the name of the particular zinfandel he'd already ordered, I said, "I'm sure I do," and left it at that.

The waiter began the uncorking ritual and poured us each a glass of a deep red wine that looked luscious, reflecting bloodlike from the light of the table's votive candle. "I don't recall, but I've heard them say it enough times. It was just before Christmas. Logan and Jennifer and I were shopping. We'd been in downtown Lake Chinook and were driving home. We were on the hills when a car came around the corner too fast and pushed us off the road. We actually went over the side of the cliff but got hung up in the trees."

. . . *Over the side of the cliff* . . . I had a mental image of Jazz's car careening off one of the steep Dunthorpe slopes. A finger of fear coldly touched the base of my neck. I'd had a similar experience not too long ago. I hadn't had the benefit of an automobile, if it was a benefit. I'd lost my grip on a tree limb and fallen to the ground, which had been a long, long way.

Giving myself a mental shake, I asked, "Who was the other driver?"

"Don't know. They never came forward."

"A hit and run?"

"Maybe they never knew. Or, maybe that's something I tell myself because I don't want to believe anyone would be that callous. The police asked me to describe the car but I couldn't. Logan thought it was yellow or tan. They tried to find a vehicle with a crumpled right fender, but it never turned up."

"How have you been coping?" I sipped the wine and thought it tasted better than my usual stuff from 7 Eleven.

"Not so hot. I had to quit work. I've just been . . . waiting, I guess, for time to pass and things to get better. But then Nana started deteriorating. Well, it's been going on for a while, but it's just so much worse now."

"How were you employed? Before the accident."

"Oh. I worked for the family. We have some real estate investments. And some stocks . . ." He made a face. "I don't really know. There were some apartments downtown. Dahlia said I managed them, but I don't really remember. It's one of those things that's missing. Dahlia took over, or, maybe Cammie. I think Garrett handles the other financial stuff."

"Is everyone in the family employed by the family?" I asked the question lightly, trying not to make a judgment call. These things are tricky.

"We're all trust fund recipients," he admitted. "I think that's why Garrett's so worried. It's not all locked up. You'd have to ask him about it, but I guess Nana could rewrite everything if she wanted and cut us out."

I nodded while the waiter took our order. I ordered prime rib with a loaded baked potato and a Caesar salad. Jazz had invited me, so it was a good assumption he was paying. If not, I had enough cash left over from his earlier payment to take care of myself. Either way I was going to have a fabulous meal. If I saved some of the meat for Binkster, I could maybe squeeze in room for crème brûlée.

Jazz refilled my glass and I felt a little glimmer of that first wine buzz. The outside light was fading. Mt. Hood glowed faintly orange, lit by the setting sun, and grayish-purple shadows slanted across the landscape. It was a feast for the eyes and I kept my gaze trained out the window until the last solar illumination faded away.

Melancholia sneaked in and took hold of me. Maybe it was the Spence/Janice/Miriam/Trevin thing. Maybe it was a recognition of my own "singleness." I drank more wine and distantly worried that I wanted Jazz to fall in love with me. I needed to feel desired. I tried to talk myself out of these dangerous thoughts but for the moment I couldn't.

"I want to hire you, Jane. To come and be with Nana."

Oh, Dwayne, I hate it when you're right.

In a faraway corner of my mind I knew I was in trouble. "I'm not a caretaker, companion, babysitter . . . I would be terrible at it. I'm too impatient. I like my freedom."

"I'll pay you triple your usual rate. Really. It's not a matter of money. I can get money. I just need someone reliable and trustworthy to take care of my grandmother."

"How do you know I'm reliable and trustworthy?"

He smiled. "I might have trouble with my memory, but I've got pretty good instincts."

I squinted at him. He was looking even better, by this time. I sensed other patrons gazing at us with a kind of curiosity and wistfulness. Did we look like a couple? Well, of course we did. Jazz had reached for my hand. "Instincts, huh?" I asked. To my own ears I sounded sober.

"Yeah . . ." There was meaning in there somewhere.

The food arrived. Knowing I needed to be clear, I dug in with gusto. Okay, I was really hungry, too, and the prime rib felt as if it melted on my tongue. After a good ten minutes of pure eating, I said, "I think you're wrong about your relatives. They did not love me."

"They told me they thought you'd be good," he insisted. "Nana's been a worry. She needs someone there. I promise I'll find someone else. We'll keep interviewing, but this would be a great opportunity for you to get to know her, to talk to her. A lot."

I was hovering. I closed my ears to Dwayne's devilish laughter, which I could hear before it even began. But I'm weak. And . . . well . . . I can be bought sometimes.

"I'm not staying nights. I have a dog."

"Nana's in bed by nine. We can take it from there."

"You live at the house, too."

"No." He sounded regretful. "I live in the West Hills."

I realized belatedly that I'd completely forgotten about his son. "How's Logan doing?"

"He's okay."

"Good."

"Jane . . . ?" His blue eyes gazed at me in a way that made me want to reach over and touch his face, run my hand down his smoothly shaven jaw.

I also, however, wanted to face-plant into my bed and not wake till noon. I said, "When do I start?"

He grinned. "Tomorrow. Thank you. Thank you."

Chapter
Six

I showed up at the Purcell mansion at eight o'clock sharp the next morning, as instructed by Jazz. He'd told me he wouldn't be able to meet me and to just make myself at home. In his giddy joy over having coerced me into the job he hadn't specified the particulars of my employment. Maybe that's why I grabbed Binkster at the last moment and settled her in her fuzzy, little car seat. Or, maybe perversely I simply wanted to let them know what I was all about. Hire Jane Kelly, hire her dog.

Binks has a tendency to sit up in her seat like a person, her butt down, her front legs dangling. Her tail, being curled, doesn't get in her way. There's something so humanoid about her that I find myself confiding in her about all kinds of things. On the way to the Purcells, I suggested that she ingratiate herself with Orchid so that I could keep bringing her. This was motivated by fear on my part that I might be in this new job a *loooonnnggg* time. I also wondered what my rates should be. Since Jazz was tripling them, this could be quite a windfall.

Clipping Binkster's leash to her collar, I climbed out of the Volvo and she scrambled to the ground beside me. I nearly choked her as I dragged her from sniffing every leaf, fir needle and clod of dirt on our short trek from the car to the Purcells' back door. What is it about dogs, especially their first time out each day? I swear it's like they're reading the morning paper. I've heard they get something like fifty different bits of information about the animal whose urine or feces they're smelling. Maybe it's more. Whatever it is, it's like ambrosia to Binks. Since she has no nose to speak of, she gets her whole face so close to the loathsome poop or pee that I suspect one of these days she'll get some on her. And then I think about how she licks me in delight, washing my face with that pink tongue whenever she gets the chance. Germanophobe that I am, those chances are few. It's enough to send me to the shower just thinking about it.

Once in a while though, she takes one quick whiff and backs up as if she's been stung. Makes me wonder about the dog that left that information.

A young Hispanic woman met me at the back door and instantly looked worried about the dog. A rapid-fire stream of Spanish brought another Hispanic woman—this one a bit older—who said, "Mrs. Dahlia does not allow pets."

Mrs. Dahlia herself appeared at that moment. A look of distaste crossed her broad face. "You brought a dog?" she said incredulously.

Although I had no reason to be, I was instantly irked. A few months earlier and I'm sure I would have had the exact same reaction. But now I'm a dog person. And being a nouveau dog person, I ignore the fact that others don't feel the same way I do.

"The Binkster is well behaved."

"Just because Mother loves animals doesn't mean we let them in the house."

"I told Jazz I was bringing Binks." I'm an opportunistic liar, if there ever was one. Dahlia had unwittingly given me information I could use, and by God I was going to use it. If Mother loved animals, then *voilà*, I had the animal for her.

Her lips compressed. "He should have checked with me."

I waited. Dahlia gazed at me hard. She didn't have the male Purcell beauty but she had those eyes. I found it a little unnerving. Some people just look kind of crazy.

In my own thoughts I heard a remnant of Dwayne's recital about Cammie: ". . . She opens her eyes, gazes at me with that really crazy look . . . you know the one. Something about it's just not right."

"Make sure his feet are clean," she grudgingly said, holding the door.

"Her."

"What?"

"Binkster's a girl."

We followed Dahlia inside and upstairs. Binkster tugged on the leash like she was at a race, but I held her in check. Dahlia hesitated outside Orchid's rooms, her hand on the knob.

"You should know, it wasn't our idea to have you take care of Mother. Jazz was insistent, and well . . ." She looked me up and down as if to say, "This is what it's come to."

"I understand." I wanted to tell her that it wasn't my idea, either.

"This is just an interim thing, until we replace Eileen."

"Absolutely."

I expected her to move out of the way, but she bent her head and added in a confidential tone, "We're trying really hard to get Mother to see what needs to be done, for her benefit as well as the benefit of the family. It's not easy. She rambles on about things that didn't happen. She confuses her dreams with reality."

"Jazz simply wanted me to do a personal evaluation of your mother—just as an outside party—and since I was on site . . . that's why I'm here. This isn't my usual job."

"You're a private detective."

"Information specialist."

She sighed. "I really don't know what Jazz was thinking."

She was starting to thoroughly bug me. It's okay for me to ask these questions of myself; it's not okay for someone else. I was saved from a response when she finally pushed open the double doors. Binkster shot inside. Wriggling and twisting her tan and black little body, she greeted Orchid affectionately. Orchid exclaimed in delight and leaned down toward her. Binks snorted right in her face, giving Orchid's sprayed hair a puff of doggy wheeze that didn't alter its shape one iota.

"Oh, he's so cute. Come here, sweetheart. Oh, aren't you lovely!"

Although her hair was done, and makeup was applied—a little clownlike, I might add—definitely too much fuchsia going on there—she was still in her bathrobe. That made me think that breakfast might still be forthcoming, which was immensely cheering.

Dahlia did not follow us inside, which was a win as far as I was concerned.

Orchid cooed over Binkster, who moved on and sniffed the thick, cream carpet in a way that made me worry we should have made a potty trip first.

"Binks," I said sternly.

The dog looked at me. I motioned her to come to me, but she prowled around the room, performing her usual perimeter check, her pushed-in muzzle picking up all the hidden Purcell scents.

"Is the dog for me?" Orchid asked expectantly.

"She's just here for a visit," I said quickly, slightly alarmed. "The Binkster is my dog, and I just thought I'd have her come along." I was suddenly wishing I hadn't been so bold and pushy. This whole thing looked like it could backfire without much provocation.

"Oh, she's a girl!" Orchid was even more delighted.

The door opened and Dahlia stepped inside. She'd allowed us a whole three minutes together before checking in. Big whoop. Binks looked up, but quickly went back to her exploring.

"Did you see the doggy?" Orchid asked. Her eyes joyfully followed the pug around the room.

"Mother, Jane's here to help you look over those papers."

My ears sharpened. Papers? I skewered Dahlia with a look.

"Oh . . ." Orchid gazed around the room in a lost way, then climbed to her feet with an effort and toddled over to her desk. She picked up a sheaf of about four pages. "These papers."

Dahlia nodded, folding her arms under her breasts. I got a pro-file shot of the woman. Her weak chin slipped into her neck.

"You really want me to sign these, don't you?" Orchid said to her daughter. "So afraid . . . so afraid . . ." She slid me a cagey look. "You agree with them?"

Dahlia said impatiently, "Mother, it's a power of attorney. You know what it is. How do you expect us to take care of you, and everything Daddy left you, if you won't even sign?"

"I didn't say I wouldn't."

"Everybody agrees it's for the best."

"Do you think Eileen was stealing?" Orchid asked me.

Dahlia made a strangled sound and lifted her gaze to the ceiling.

"I never met Eileen," I answered truthfully.

"Eileen's the nicest girl and they ran her off and gave me you."

"Mother . . ." Dahlia sighed.

"All right, fine. I'll sign it."

I blurted, "Don't do it unless you want to," which earned me a lightning blue glare from Dahlia.

Orchid gloated at Dahlia. "Then I'll leave it here till later. Come here, doggy. What's his name again?"

"Binkster. Her name." I watched Orchid set the papers back down on the desktop, my thoughts uncomfortable. We'd just gone over Binkster's gender. Was it "old age" or serious memory problems that made her forget so quickly?

Dahlia stared at the sheaf, her jaw clenched. Then she slid a look my way. I realized very clearly that I'd been wrong: my time on this job was going to be very short. Muttering something about checking on breakfast, Dahlia strode stiffly from the room.

Orchid stretched her arms toward me and said, "I'm ready for my bath now."

"Be right back." I practically ran straight downstairs. When I found the younger Hispanic woman, I pantomimed what was required. The girl nodded and headed upstairs to take care of the situation. Bath time was definitely outside of my job description.

Relieved, I hung around downstairs. The smell of eggs and bacon made Binkster start to whine. I wondered if I was on the list for breakfast. The caretaker protocol was still a little vague. I was making up rules as I went.

I wandered around the hall and main salon for about fifteen minutes when the older, English-speaking woman brought out a tray with a plate that held one egg, a piece of toast and two strips of bacon. I could see the string from the tea bag hanging over the china cup's rim. She headed for the stairs, but saw me look at the food. "Would you like some breakfast?"

"Thank you. That'd be great," I said with feeling.

"I will be back soon."

She was good as her word. As soon as she was finished taking the food up to Orchid, she waved me into the kitchen. I parked Binkster at the newel post, wrapping her leash around several times. She tried to follow me, but I shook my head and she sat on her haunches and eyed me patiently. She seems to get it that I will return with goodies.

Inside the kitchen I perched on a stool, my mouth watering as I watched Reyna—my keen detecting skills took over when the other girl, momentarily back from her bath-preparation, called her by name—expertly fry up two eggs and a couple more slices of bacon. There was miserable whining heard from the other room. Reyna cocked her head and put part of an egg on a plate without my asking. Throwing her a look of gratitude I picked up the plate and carried it to the dog. Binkster received this bounty with a happy dance, then got to eating with a concentration I can relate to.

I returned to my own plate and a cup of black coffee, shaking my head to her offer of cream. I ate with appreciation, though I tried to be polite and not wolf it in like I'm wont to do. I also tried to manage some conversation but Reyna was very reluctant to say more than was required. Whether this was from difficulty with the language or reticence over appearing too friendly with me, the new, half-baked caretaker, I couldn't be sure. I figured if anyone knew what was really up in the household it would be Reyna. She might even have a pretty good idea what the truth was about the much-maligned Eileen. As I was a member of the help, I could see how this might work to my advantage.

I spent the rest of the morning doing basically nothing. After Orchid's bath and breakfast she went down for a little nap and I was off babysitting duty. I used the time to acquaint myself with the first floor of the house, which, besides the entry hall, main salon/living room and kitchen, yielded a wing devoted to maids' quarters, which were obviously unused as the rooms were cold, musty and bare; a laundry room; a little room called the ingle-nook filled with glass shelves which in turn were filled with an array of knickknacks; and a library done in rich mahogany-stained wood complete with one of those cool ladders that slides around on a rail. Two oxblood chairs with high backs and brass studs were collected around a table near the floor to ceiling pane windows. I looked outside to a view of trees, the Willamette River far below, and a distant view of white-capped Mt. Hood.

I skipped lunch because I honestly don't eat three meals a day, and for once in my life I wasn't hungry. I talked to Orchid while she again ate in her room—this time a brothy soup and toasted cheese sandwich—but she seemed distracted and in her own world. It occurred to me that I hadn't seen any of the other members of the Purcell family since Dahlia's morning greeting, though I knew most of them lived in the house. They'd moved back in recently, a result of taking care of Orchid. But nobody wanted the actual chore of babysitting her. Hence Eileen, and now me.

Deciding to walk the grounds, I was on my way out when Orchid stopped me with, "I really don't want things to be like this."

"Like what?"

"The way they are." She regarded me beseechingly.

"I'm not sure what you mean."

"She had to leave." Her eyes filled with sudden tears and she started to gently weep.

I froze by the door, uncomfortable at her sadness. Binkster stared at Orchid, then went over to her and licked her leg. Orchid broke into sobs and hugged Binkster who, having offered up her sympathy, grew a bit alarmed at the sudden tight squeezing. She wriggled free and trotted a few steps away. Orchid swiped at her eyes to no avail. "I didn't . . ." She hiccupped, still crying. "I didn't . . . want it to happen . . . and she knew it would . . ."

For lack of any idea how to comfort her, I said soothingly. "I'm sure it's okay now."

"That place . . . that mental place . . ."

"The sanitarium?" I suddenly tuned in. I had a few questions of my own about Jazz's mother's incarceration.

"Yes."

"You're talking about Lily?" I wasn't sure how knowledgeable to appear. I didn't want to scare her into clamming up.

"Lily," she breathed. "Nobody wants to talk about her. Nobody wants to talk about either of them. After what happened, being her older sister . . . it was just a matter of time . . ." She shook her head, unable to go on.

"Both of your daughters?" I glanced at the door, where Dahlia had left in such a huff earlier.

"Yes . . ." She bent her head.

I let the moment spin out. I didn't know what this was all about, but it was terribly sad for her. Whatever it was, it had deep tentacles inside Orchid, pulling at her emotions.

She drew a shaky breath. "And the boys were . . . they were . . . hard to control. Percy tried . . . but . . ." She started weeping softly.

I sensed something ugly. Some family secret that included all of them. I suddenly didn't want to know.

Orchid's blue eyes were swimming with tears. She looked at me as if for salvation. "I want her back."

Silently, I sat down on the couch beside her and held her hand. She clasped mine with both of hers and cried and cried. She cried herself to sleep, actually, slipping sideways against me.

I was squished into the cushions. Almost instantly, she fell asleep, breathing deeply, like a small child.

I stayed until my right leg fell asleep, then gently moved her aside and tiptoed out of the room, Binkster in tow. I found Reyna sweeping in the kitchen. "Orchid's sleeping on the couch. She's very sad. I think she's missing Lily . . . ?"

Reyna nodded. "She is sad often."

"I'm going to head outside for a few minutes."

"I will look in on her."

"Thank you."

Binks and I practically race-walked to the back door. She was in need of a potty trip, and I was in need of fresh air. I unclipped her leash, then leaned against the back porch, drinking in the warm afternoon air and view over the Willamette. I was pretty sure this was my only day as Orchid's caretaker and I can't say I was sorry. No amount of money would convince me to switch careers. You simply couldn't pay me enough to take care of someone else.

Watching Binks nose around the backyard, I pulled a plastic baggy from my jeans pocket. Normalcy. Thank you, God. I'm pretty sure this was the first time I was glad my dog was about to poop. It kind of put the world in perspective. I followed after her. I've become adept at scooping up dog shit with a small plastic bag and finding a waiting receptacle. Binks zigzagged across the back lawn, looking for the "perfect place" to offload her usual diet of dog chow. Low-fat dog chow and egg, in her case.

Binks did her business and I scooped it up with a plastic wrapped hand. Then I left the baggy on the ground for the time being. I would pick it up on the way back inside and either toss it in an outside trash bin or flush the contents down the toilet.

The afternoon sun was surprisingly hot; no chilly little autumn breeze stirring things up. Binkster started panting and I felt like doing the same. In the waving heat devils, the playhouse beckoned, looking mirage-like. I squinted at it. There was something so determinedly cheery in its design and demeanor, even with

the encroaching decay, that it creeped me out a little. I sometimes experience this same sensation at theme parks with loud,
bubbly music and sculpted, painted creatures wearing nightmarish
grins. It's just too *fun*. These are places any self-respecting adult
should just avoid. That said, I was kind of drawn to the Purcells'
playhouse in spite of myself. With Orchid's melancholia fresh in
my mind, the playhouse seemed a likely place to offer insight
into the Purcell youngsters. What had they been like? What had
happened that Orchid wished hadn't? To both daughters. I wondered if I could come out and ask Dahlia without appearing
overly nosy. I didn't bet so, but maybe it was worth a try.

I walked toward the playhouse. Binkster trotted at my heels
through the unmown grass.

The flower boxes under the playhouse's two front windows
had not received the same fresh paint as the door. What had once
been bright orange was now a faintly pinky color, like that old
medicine my grandmother used to put on our cuts before
Neosporin came into play. I stood outside the red door and found
myself hesitating to cross the threshold. Maybe it was Orchid's
crying. Maybe it was something else. I had to give myself a good
talking to in order to make my hand reach for the doorknob.

Binkster brushed my legs and whimpered. I flicked her a look.
Her gaze was fixed on the playhouse door, the fur at her neck
standing straight up, her skin rippling beneath her pelt.

Gooseflesh broke out on my arms.

Irritated, I said, "Stop that." The dog had pulled back a safe
distance and stood stiffly, one front paw in the air, as if she were
about to gingerly step backward, as if she were afraid of disturbing the playhouse occupants. "There's nobody here," I told her.

She set her foot down but her skin kept rippling. My uneasi-
ness mounted. Dogs know stuff. Lots of stuff that we don't. If
The Binkster didn't like the playhouse, neither did I. I could feel
something odd and unnerving in the air surrounding it.

I almost turned around. A chicken side of myself, one I listen
to whenever it starts clucking, nearly took over. But then the ra-

tional side of my brain started asking questions and belittling me. *What do you think you're going to find there? It's just a little house. It's empty. It's been empty for years. What do you care? You're letting Orchid's sadness infect your judgment. You're thirty years old and you're afraid to set foot inside a child's playhouse? Is this for real? And you call yourself an information specialist?*

I pushed open the door and held my breath. Nothing jumped out at me. No cobweb-covered skeleton grabbed me around the neck. No bat swooped over my head. Calling myself all kinds of names, I looked inside.

The interior was covered with dust. The furniture was child-size. Perfect little replicas of the chairs I'd seen in the Purcell dining room. Perfect little velvet gray couch. Perfect table, set for three, with little china tea cups and teapot, all painted with lovely little violets in a magenta color. The place had the dry scent of disuse. The air was still and dead.

Binkster started growling low in her throat in that odd, hesitating way that sounds a bit like a slow Geiger counter. She would not step a foot across the threshold, though I tried to persuade her. I even lied to her about possible "treats" inside, but she steadfastly kept about two feet back. I knew how she felt. I wanted to run away like a scared girl. But now it had become something of a dare. I mean, come on . . . all this drama was just dumb.

Ducking down, I entered the door. The front room ceiling was low enough that I had to stoop. Looking around, I slowly sank into a squat. My flip-flop-encased feet looked huge in the space. On the child-size maple buffet there was more of the violet dishware. Some of the plates held plastic fake food. I recognized a wedge of cheese, once orangy-yellow, now kind of a dirty butter color. Various plastic vegetables were scattered around, as if any self-respecting kid would really eat asparagus, broccoli and spinach leaves. Plastic cupcakes, chocolate-colored with little white flower icing, sat to one side. My mouth watered at the sight, which gave me pause. Maybe I should have opted for lunch after all. Would it be gauche to return to the house and ask if afternoon tea was being served? I had an overwhelming desire to return to the kitchen, Reyna and safety.

There was a buzzing sound. A large honey bee was banging itself into one of the pane windows over and over again. The death dance of a drone, kicked out of the nest by the female worker bees. It sank to the sill, stunned, suddenly silent. My skin felt as if insects were walking all over it.

Oh . . . for . . . God's . . . sake, Jane.

Girding my loins, I squat-walked sideways, giving the bee a wide berth, to the west side of the playhouse, which elled back to form a second room. Around the corner stood a perfect twin bed. A real bed. Adult-size. The coverlet had once been red but now was kind of dusty rose with brownish water spots. A few dead bugs nestled in its folds. It was quilted, the white stitching in the shape of lilies.

In the quiet that seemed to descend I thought I heard childish whispering and the hair on my neck lifted. Outside, Binkster gave a sharp little worried bark.

I ran out of there like my pants were on fire, banging my elbow on the door jamb, catching a thread of my pocket on a nail. Instantly I dragged air deep into my lungs. I was annoyed to feel my limbs tremble.

Binkster's eyes, always huge, looked like they took over her whole face.

"You trying to scare me?" I demanded.

When I made a move to head back to the main house she bolted ahead of me. I'm ashamed to say I beat her there.

I almost screamed to find someone hovering in the shadows of the back porch. It was James IV, his own eyes widening a bit in fright at my reaction. "What happened? Are you all right?"

"Oh . . . no . . . I'm fine." I was breathing hard.

Binkster squeezed in-between us and stared through my legs in the direction we'd come.

James's gaze followed hers. "What's the matter with your

dog?" He started a bit to realize Binks was fixated on the play-house.

"We were just fooling around. Kind of chasing each other."

"Where were you?"

"Over there." I waved vaguely in the direction of the cliff. I didn't want him to know the playhouse had spooked me.

He seemed to want to say something else but kept his silence. Finally, he said, "Well, we're all home now. I was sent to tell you we're having a meeting in the main salon in half an hour. We want to talk to you."

A powwow. Great. "Who's 'we'?"

"All of us."

"Jazz?"

"Um . . . yeah . . . he's coming in a while. But if he isn't here in time, we want you to join us anyway. Garrett and Satin are here. Dahlia's just getting back. Roderick's coming down. Oh, and Cammie's on her way."

"Okay." Like, oh, sure, I really wanted to go to this function. I had a feeling they would be serving up my head on a platter.

He led the way inside, saying, "Can you leave the dog out here?"

"Why don't I put her in my car." I was already heading around the side of the house.

The Volvo was parked in the lengthening shadows thrown by the house itself. The sun was sinking, the heat rapidly dissipating. If I cracked the windows, Binks would be perfectly comfortable. Personally I would have liked to have her with me. Someone on my side, so to speak, but I could tell that wasn't going to fly.

Reyna caught me as I was coming back inside. "Mrs. Orchid wants to see you."

"I'm supposed to meet the family in half an hour . . ." Something about her look made me trail off. "I'll check on Orchid first," I told her, and she nodded and offered the ghost of a smile.

I braced myself for more crying, but Orchid was pacing around the room when I entered, if pacing is what it could be called. She kind of rocked on her feet, holding on to pieces of furniture for support as she passed by. "There you are," she said in relief. "I'm worried about these papers. But you don't want me to sign them."

"I'm not really the one to ask about this, Mrs. Purcell."

"Nana."

"Nana."

"You think I should call that Neusmeyer fellow?"

I nodded.

"They're trying to take my money away. They don't trust me. And they keep blaming me for what happened. I couldn't help it, could I? I didn't even know! And Percy wouldn't want me to be blamed." Her voice caught a bit.

I really didn't want her heading into that distraught world again. But I was also in the untenable position of defending the motives of people I didn't entirely trust myself. I picked my words carefully. "They just want to make sure the money—your money—is being taken care of by the best person."

"And that's not me?" She sounded belligerent.

"Do you think it's you?"

She blinked, surprised that I'd asked. "Well, I don't know. They want me to sign." She waved a hand toward the papers. "Should I?" When I didn't answer, she skewered me with a look that could have cut through steel. "You're not fooling me with this act. You're with them on this. I can tell."

I straightened in my chair. "I'm not with them. They want you to sign that power of attorney, but I'm not—"

"What power of attorney?" she demanded, cutting me off.

"The papers Dahlia brought earlier." This circular conversation was worrying me. Orchid did appear to have some serious cognitive flaws. She faded in and out, and there was no telling what you were going to get. "If Jerome Neusmeyer's your lawyer, give him a call."

"I have to go downstairs to call, and I don't have the number." She looked fretful.

"I'll get it for you. I'm meeting with the family in a few minutes?"

"Garrett."

I nodded. "And some of your other family members. Jazz, too, I think."

"And Logan?" She brightened.

I sure hoped not. I lifted my shoulders rather than answering.

"Should I be going with you?" She pressed a hand to one cheek. "Oh, I don't want to."

I didn't figure they wanted her, either, so I said, "Why don't I ask them?"

"Tell them I'll be in my room. Will you come right back? As soon as you're done?"

"Sure."

She visibly relaxed and sank back into her couch. She was wearing a similar outfit to yesterday's, this one a cranberry color, and it folded in on itself the same way, making her seem small and squashed.

I headed toward the door.

"Thank you, Eileen," she said on a contented sigh. "Come right back when you're done."

They were all assembled by the time I entered the main salon. Luckily Logan wasn't there, but then neither was Jazz yet. Garrett and Satin sat on the green and gold divan again; James was in a ladder-backed chair that was straight enough to be a form of torture; Roderick lounged in the fawn wingback, his ankle propped on his opposite knee; Dahlia was in another chair across from him, frowning, looking like she might scoot her chair next to his; Benjamin had arranged himself in the window seat, his limbs loose and tucked like a cat; and Cammie burst in right behind me with a fair-haired girl in tow. This must be Rosalie, I recalled, as I moved to one side. Her face was pulled into a pout and Cammie had to push her forward a few times to get her in far enough to close the door behind them both.

"Damn traffic," Cammie said darkly, settling on the love seat. Rosalie wriggled from her arms.

Garrett didn't actually check his watch but I could tell he was annoyed at our tardiness. He said to me, "I thought James said to come right in. That we were having a meeting."

"He said half an hour. I checked on Orchid first." I propped my back against a wall, wanting them all in my sights, nobody behind me.

Dahlia waved an impatient hand. "Let's just get on with it. She hasn't signed the papers yet. Maybe she won't. Jane told her not to."

Their accusatory gazes swept my way. Defensively, I said, "I told her to call her lawyer. Aren't you supposed to have witnesses for those things? Don't you want it legal? I don't know what the proper procedure is here, but Jerome Neusmeyer will."

"You know Neusmeyer?" Garrett snapped.

And how . . . I'd damn near ralphed up lunch after his breast squeezing. "I understand he's the family estate lawyer."

"Do we need him?" Dahlia demanded, gazing at Garrett.

"We need mother to comply. And we *don't* need interference."

Cammie said, "Nana doesn't know what she's doing."

"And my dear wife thinks her mother's faking it," Roderick put in lazily. He seemed to be enjoying this proceeding as if it were comic art.

"Well, she seems to, half the time," Dahlia defended.

Cammie looked exasperated. Her eyes followed Rosalie's progress as she headed toward the window and Benjamin. The little girl wanted to crawl up there with him, but he froze her out with a cold shoulder. Cammie said, "I'm just glad Eileen's gone. I'm tired of feeling like everybody's stealing our money."

"It's not *ours* yet, darling," Roderick pointed out, amused.

"And it won't ever be, unless we stop Nana from giving it all away! Rosalie, come over here." Cammie patted the love seat cushion beside her.

"No!" Rosalie's pout increased.

"Stop bothering Benjamin." She got to her feet and headed for Rosalie, who started screeching and running away. Cammie caught her on the fly. Rosalie's limbs flailed and she bucked for all she was worth, but Cammie held her tightly, her mouth grim. Rosalie collapsed into a limp, wailing rag and Cammie settled her on her lap. She made cooing noises and petted Rosalie's head until the little girl stuck her thumb in her mouth and subsided into hiccups, tiny teardrops standing on her cheeks as if they were glued there. Cammie's hard gaze softened and she looked down at her daughter with love. A kind of scary love, actually. Something possessive in it that fractured my attention for a moment.

"Can't we be witnesses?" James asked. "Dahlia, you're the person we've chosen. What's it called?"

"The agent or attorney in fact."

"Then, can't we witness Mom's signature? Does it have to be someone outside the family?"

"We can witness it," Garrett said positively. "She just has to *sign* it. What part of that aren't you getting?"

James flushed and subsided into silence. Benjamin, who was already giving us his back, stiffened and stared fixedly out the window.

I wasn't sure what the truth was. I didn't much care. All I knew was that I was beginning to feel protective of Orchid, and I didn't like the way the rest of the family seemed to think so little about her as a person.

There was a soft rap on the door. Everyone looked at the panels expectantly. Since I was closest, I answered the knock. Reyna's assistant came in with a tray of tiny, powdery cakes and a teapot. My mouth watered at the sight of it. So, they did do afternoon tea. I couldn't believe my wish had come true.

Garrett flapped a hand at her. "Put it on the table, Carlotta. Thank you."

She hurriedly did as she was bidden and disappeared, softly closing the doors behind her.

Nobody jumped on the food. I wondered if I could just step forward and help myself. I had a feeling that no, that would not be okay. I was the help, after all.

To underscore this Garrett turned to me and said, "I know Jazz hired you as Mother's caretaker in some capacity. Frankly, I'm surprised you took the job. I thought you were a private investigator. In any case, we won't tolerate interference. And I think we're perfectly capable of taking care of her ourselves. My wife would be happy to keep Mother company."

Satin's eyes widened in surprise. I got the feeling this was not okay. She instantly bent her head and began playing with her fingernails again as if it were an Olympic sport.

Dahlia regarded her brother with disgust. "Oh, Garrett. We need somebody outside the family."

I'd been a bit surprised that Dahlia was the one chosen for power of attorney. I'd expected it to be Garrett. Now, I saw why. Garrett's ham-fisted way of handling all things Orchid had put her off—and probably everyone else in the family as well. Dahlia was the next choice, and she was a better one.

And Jazz had said his grandmother didn't trust men.

"I don't see why," he huffed.

"She doesn't really listen to me," Satin said softly.

Garrett's nostrils flared. "If you'd just try a little harder, it would be fine. If everyone would just *step up* this would be resolved."

I reached in my pocket for my cell phone, more to finger it like a talisman than any urgency to call anyone. It wasn't there. I lost my focus on the conversation for a moment as I was sure I'd taken it out of my purse. Nobody seemed to notice my attention lapse, nobody but Rosalie anyway. She stared blankly at me through huge blue eyes. Kinda creeped me out anew.

There was a lively discussion about whether to bring in Neusmeyer now, or try to coerce Orchid into signing first. I kind of blanked out. I thought about Binkster in the car. She would probably need another potty trip soon. I thought of Orchid upstairs waiting and decided my cell phone had dropped out when

I'd comforted her on the couch. I wondered if I could make a quick stop at her room to check, or if I would get wrangled into staying on, an idea that seemed distinctly unpleasant. I was tired of the family after just one day.

I also wondered if Dwayne had called me while I was phoneless. Or maybe Jazz? This momentarily lifted my spirits. Momentarily, because this job was bound to be short. No more money and maybe no more Jazz.

I shifted my weight from one foot to the other as shadows lengthened outside the windows. Soon there was out and out darkness. But the Purcells just kept talking. I finally decided I'd had enough. I mean, was I even getting paid for this? I was about to simply up and leave when the family meeting finally broke up though there was no resolution in sight. I murmured a good-bye and raced outside before they could buttonhole me. Binks was curled into a ball, asleep, but when I opened the door she popped up. I clipped on her leash and took her for a stroll in the opposite direction from the playhouse. When we were finished and I was on my way back to my car, Reyna appeared at the back door, her dark brows an anxious line.

"Something wrong?" I asked.

"Mrs. Orchid is missing."

"What? Missing? What does that mean?"

"She is not in her room."

"Well, she has to be," I insisted, though there was really no good reason to feel that way. "Does she ever leave? I got the impression she was pretty much confined to her room. By choice, mostly."

"She never wants to leave. The only time was when Eileen was not coming back. Then she said she would go, but she stayed."

"Well, when *was* the last time she left the house?"

"A month . . . maybe . . . leetle more? Doctor's appointment."

"Then, I suspect she's around here somewhere. We were all here all afternoon. She could be on the grounds." My inner eye saw the drop-off at the front of the house and my heart clutched a little.

"Carlotta and I were in the kitchen except when we go downstairs." She looked even more worried.

"What's downstairs?"

"Linens. Food supplies . . ." She cupped her chin in her hand. I could practically hear her thinking. I sensed that Reyna and Carlotta might have been gone for a while. Reyna was clearly afraid she would be blamed for Orchid's disappearance.

"She's got to be here," I assured her. "I was just going to check on her."

I put Binks back in the car and went up to Orchid's rooms myself. True to Reyna's fears, Orchid was nowhere to be found though I walked through all four rooms of her suite, checked the closets and even under the beds. A long shot, but stranger things have happened. I half-expected her to be playing hide and seek.

In the main room—the living room of her domain—I stood by the satellite blue couch and called, "Orchid? Nana? It's Jane Kelly." When that didn't work, I said, "It's Eileen, Nana. Where are you?"

No answer.

I could feel the lines form between my brows. I didn't like it one bit. It had only been a couple of hours since I'd seen her— though the Purcell meeting felt like an eternity—but the plain truth was: Orchid was gone.

Before I left, I dug through the couch cushions. My cell phone was tucked behind one, right where I'd expected to find it. For that I sent up a small prayer.

Slipping the phone in my pocket, I headed out of Orchid's suite. There was another bedroom at this end of the gallery and I twisted the knob and peeked inside. I was met by the faint scent of cloves. Further exploration revealed a series of candles, unlit, emitting the scent. There was a lived-in feel to the room though it now looked abandoned. I surmised it had been Eileen's room. I searched it quickly and thoroughly, but there was no one hiding inside, and there was nothing of a personal nature within it other than the candles.

Crossing the gallery, I sent a glance down to the entry hall

where Purcell members were saying good-bye to those leaving—
which basically was Cammie and Rosalie. James looked upward
and I waved. They clearly didn't know Orchid was missing, yet.

There were three doors on the south end of the gallery.
James's rooms faced east, toward the river. I know because I'd
gotten a quick look when the door had been ajar earlier in the
day. James had been standing in the aperture, and I'd smiled and
said I was acquainting myself with the house. He'd simply
blocked any further view, and I hadn't deemed it important to
snoop. Now, I tested the knob and found it locked.

Dahlia and Roderick's rooms were at the end of the hall, done
in the same green and gold as the salon. They'd moved in hastily,
clothes strewn about. There was an adjoining door to a smaller
room which must be Benjamin's, though I thought he was kind
of old to be moving around with Mom and Dad.

"Temporary," I reminded myself. They'd all come home to
roost for Nana.

Both Dahlia and Roderick and Benjamin's bedrooms had a
bathroom attached, a modernization that also extended to the
suite of rooms behind the third and last hallway door. I pushed it
open and entered an alcove with sloping ceilings that looked like
they could take out unsuspecting visitors. I could imagine
smacking my forehead into one and going out cold.

These rooms were occupied by Garrett and Satin, and one
door led to another room and to another, and then the bathroom.
Dormers allowed just enough headroom to make them livable. I
walked through the rooms, opening each door and closing it behind me as I went. The first room was a bedroom done in white
and blue, the second room was a sitting room with an ancient
chaise longue. I hesitated a moment, imagining Lilac Grace lying
on its dusty gold brocade surface, writing stories in a language
only she understood, then I hurriedly opened the door to the
next room, which was full of dolls in varying outfits: red, blue,
purple, black, ecru, chartreuse . . . you name it. I stood in frozen
horror in the doorway. I'm sure I must have played with dolls at
least once, as a kid, but faced with all their little painted faces, I

felt my heartbeat thunk hard against my chest and my palms
sweat.

There was a little pillow in the center of the daybed with
crewel embroidery stitched onto its lacy cover. The dolls surrounded it like a shrine.

I looked closely and read: Rhoda.

These dolls were for the baby who'd died of SIDS? Or, had
the dolls come first?

Either way, I backed out of the room and into the hallway—directly into a human body. I emitted a little shriek before I caught
myself.

"What are you doing?" Cammie demanded.

I whipped around. She was frowning at me, Rosalie propped
on her hip. "I'm—"

"Snooping?"

"Searching." I sounded slightly breathless. No wonder. My
pulse was still rocketing along.

"Searching for what? Something to steal? Something to have
my grandmother give you as a *gift?*"

"I was searching for your grandmother," I answered, pulling
myself together with an effort.

She gave me a pissy look. "Nana's rooms are at the other end
of the hall."

James reached the top step and headed for us, looking a bit
wild. "What's going on? What are you doing here?"

I wished I'd had time to unlock his door. It was secured with a
privacy lock, the kind on any residential bathroom, the easiest
type to breach. All you need is a thin piece of metal to poke in
the little hole beside the knob. I'd managed this trick more than
a few times when Booth and I had chased each other around the
house. He was great at locking himself away from me; I was great
at finding my way in.

"I brought Rosalie up to play with the dolls and I found her
here," Cammie told him.

"Nana's missing," I said.

Cammie started. "What do you mean?"

"Missing?" James repeated.

"Reyna went to her rooms and she was gone. I was looking for her."

My phone buzzed. I whipped it out and examined the LCD, hoping for some kind of rescue. But it wasn't Jazz or Dwayne or even Cynthia. It was my mother. I pushed it back in my pocket. This was definitely not the time for one of my convoluted conversations with Mom.

James and Cammie looked at each other, absorbing what I'd said. Cammie said slowly, "Well, you were the last one to see her."

"How do you know?" I asked.

"Well, weren't you? You were with her this afternoon. Was there someone else there?"

"They could have visited after me. A lot of people live here."

"Is this a riddle? I'm trying to get information and you're just making it so hard!"

"I'm just saying you can't assume I was the last person to see her," I answered, holding on to my temper with an effort.

"Call it an educated guess."

James cleared his throat. "Maybe she went for a walk."

"Nana?" Cammie turned her glare on him. "Since when?" She flipped back to me. "Wasn't this your job, to take care of her?"

"Glad you brought it up," I said. "I'm not exactly sure what my job is."

"Well, was she upset? The last time you saw her? Did she say anything? You're supposed to be the one who examines this stuff, aren't you? Dwayne seems to think you know what you're doing. Where is she? Why don't you know?"

Her voice grew in volume throughout this speech as did my temper. I wanted to take her on, but instead, remembering how Dwayne said she'd grown crazy with rage, I kept my tongue in my head and my mouth shut.

James looked scared. "What are we going to do?"

"We're going to find her." Cammie stalked toward the stairs. Within ten minutes she'd alerted the whole family that Orchid wasn't on the premises. I thought this was premature as there was a lot of ground to cover on the Purcell property. She could be anywhere and I didn't really believe Orchid would just take off.

Everyone searched the house. Nothing. Garrett, Benjamin and Roderick started pacing off the grounds, covering every square inch. James went into his rooms and returned, declaring his mother hadn't found her way to his space. I made a mental note to check his rooms myself, if I were given the chance. There was just something fishy about him that begged to be explored.

Night descended and the breeze kicked up to a cold wind. The Purcells began returning from their respective searches, huddling in the main salon. It had been several hours, and it was growing clear that Orchid was definitely missing.

As this realization took root, they all started looking my way. I wanted to be angry with them, and I was, but I was also really worried. Alzheimer's sufferers who wander off sometimes come to horrifying ends. I didn't want this to happen to Orchid. And I sure as hell didn't want it to happen on my watch.

I called Dwayne for help and got his answering machine. He wasn't picking up his cell, either. I gritted my teeth. He was probably on a job.

By seven-thirty, after the house and grounds had been scoured, we knew she was not on the premises. Garrett and Satin drove around the area, hoping to find her, but she was gone.

Roderick looked at me and asked, "What did you say to her that caused her to leave?"

Oh, sure. Blame the outsider. I stated flatly, "Nothing."

"You must have said something," Dahlia insisted.

My phone buzzed again. I yanked it from my pocket. Seeing the caller was Jazz, I answered, "Hey, there. You haven't seen your grandmother, have you?"

"Nana?" Jazz asked. "You mean, today? No. I've been at a school function with Logan, tonight. One I didn't remember. Kind of a Meet the Teachers meeting. The school counselor wants to make sure Logan stays on track, especially since the accident. I'm still learning the ropes about this being a single parent. Jennifer took care of everything. Now it's me." He seemed to recognize something in my continued silence, because he added, "So, how did it go with Nana today?"

"Not great."

"Why? What happened?"

"Well, it looks like Nana's missing." I glanced around at the sea of angry, set Purcell faces. "You might want to get over here before your family decides to skin me alive."

Chapter Seven

When Jazz arrived, everybody in the family started playing Cover Your Ass. Accusatory glances came my way in a steady stream. I might have felt really bad except Jazz wasn't giving his family's attitude serious consideration, at least for the moment. I hoped his allegiance would last once they started working on him, but you just never know.

"Someone must have seen her," Jazz said. "She couldn't just walk off and disappear."

"Nana's not that fast," Cammie agreed. "She's got to be around here." She hiked Rosalie up on her hip. Both of them looked cranky and tired. "She couldn't have gone far."

But the truth was, Nana was nowhere to be found. Which made me wonder if she could have had help. Maybe she'd plotted her escape all along. "Did she receive any calls?" I asked.

"No," Garrett said immediately. "We would have heard the phone."

"Does she visit anyone?"

"Oh, God. Eileen." Dahlia looked horror-stricken.

There was a mad dash to the phone. Garrett demanded Eileen's number and Dahlia pulled it off her cell phone. She reeled off the digits and as Garrett dialed, I committed them to memory. Eileen seemed a key player in the Purcell drama, whether they wanted her to be or not, so while they were entrenched in locating the ex-caretaker, I plugged her number into my cell phone.

It turned out that no, Eileen had not seen or heard from Orchid. Eileen made this clear to Garrett herself, adding that she was terminated most unfairly by all of the Purcell children and though she hoped Orchid was all right, she suspected the lot of them had been thinking only of themselves and Orchid's well-being was overlooked yet again. I picked up this sentiment by Garrett's ever-more succinct and furious responses just before crashing the receiver down in a fit of temper. Satin bent her head and tried to disappear. Dahlia seemed stumped. Jazz's handsome face was full of worry, which gave him more character somehow. I let myself concentrate on him as a means to weather the Purcell storm.

"Good riddance," Garrett muttered. The dark red color beneath his skin had not subsided. I didn't like him much, but if I were examining him objectively I would have to admit that he had been given the gift of the Purcell good looks. In his mid-fifties, he was still a handsome man, even with the extra forty pounds he carried and his pain-in-the-ass, thumb's-down personality. I glanced around at the others. James IV was too slight and anxious to rise to his own attractiveness. Dahlia had missed out; part of the unfair delineation between the men and women in the family. Benjamin was exotic, catlike and androgynous. He had his father's dark hair and eyes but there was something Purcell in the shape of his face and his mouth. If he ever actually smiled he might be devastating. As it was, he didn't do anything for me, speaking strictly from a female point of view.

Rosalie seemed like she might escape the "Purcell girls are plainer" thing and be a looker. But she had that *Children of the Corn* kind of blue-eyed look I couldn't quite get past.

Recriminations, anger and growing fear fueled the heated discussion, but nothing was decided. I couldn't stand it and went outside and patrolled the grounds myself, checking the playhouse as well, though I still felt averse to the place, but it was to no avail. When I returned to the salon, everyone looked at me hopefully but I shook my head. Jazz came and stood by me, which was heartening, but when I suggested alerting the authorities, nobody seemed to want to place the call.

Time crawled by. They were literally and figuratively wringing their hands. At a stalemate, I finally announced I was going home. I was tired and hungry, and it was past dinner time, fully dark by now. But I wouldn't leave until they phoned the police, so more as a means to get rid of me than deciding on a positive plan of action, Garrett placed the call.

There was nothing further to be gained by hanging around, so I headed toward the back doors. When I got outside, Reyna was waiting for me, her dark eyes full of worry and questions. She had her coat on as the day's heat was completely gone but she was still shivering. I said, "I'm sure Orchid's fine. Maybe a friend picked her up?"

"She is not on the grounds?"

"Doesn't seem to be."

She glanced back at the door. We could faintly hear the voices of the family. "I hope she is okay."

There was something about her unconvinced tone and her stolid, careful expression that said she didn't trust the other Purcells. Did she think they had something to do with Orchid's disappearance? I seriously doubted that, not because I would put it past any of them, but the last I knew Orchid hadn't signed the POA, and until that was accomplished I didn't see how anyone would mess with her.

Well . . . unless they wanted to coerce her . . . somewhere away from the rest of the family?

Jazz stepped outside as I entertained these unsettling thoughts. How did Orchid's will read? I wondered if the estate was evenly divided. What would happen if she up and kicked off right now? Who would win out?

Jazz caught up with me at my car. I smiled wanly at him, then glanced inside my passenger window. Binkster was curled up into a little ball, her chin on the edge of the bed. She looked up at me and wagged her tail.

"This isn't like Nana at all," Jazz said. "This has never happened before."

My whole chest was heavy with dread. It felt like it was my fault, even though I knew it wasn't.

"The police are coming over," Jazz said. "I hope it's not too early for them. What's that rule about how many hours a person has to be missing?"

"With Alzheimer's or dementia patients, I'm betting that rule doesn't apply."

"I hope they find her." He looked at me. The outdoor lights sent ribbons of light across his face. He was like a luscious candy. Something rich and beautiful where you wonder if you should really bite in and destroy its beauty, but yet you can't help yourself. My thoughts were bouncing all over the place—a means to try keeping ahead of my own fear.

"What if she spends the night outdoors?" Jazz asked.

"It's not too cold." But it wasn't exactly red-hot, either. A night outside without protection would be really uncomfortable. For someone Orchid's age, it would definitely be ill-advised, maybe dangerous

"What if something bad's happened to her?"

"Keep good thoughts. She can be very lucid, very aware. In fact, most of the time she seems fine. Better than fine, actually."

"You think so?"

Right up until the time she called me Eileen. "Do you want me to stay?"

"Yes. For me." He almost smiled. "But no . . . go home. Get some rest." He didn't say it but I saw he thought we might be in for a long siege.

It felt like some kind of action was called for, but for the life of me I didn't know what it would be. The police were on their way.

I opened my car door. Binks stretched and blinked. Then Jazz placed a hand on my forearm. I could feel the heat of his palm against my skin and my heart fluttered a bit as I turned toward him. Even though it was late, his jaw looked freshly shaved, and his clothes were crisp and clean. He wore a tan cotton sweater pushed up his forearms and khakis. Casual chic. The guy knew how to dress, that's for sure. I was in my usual work uniform: jeans, Nikes and a black V-necked T-shirt.

"You want to come to my place?" he invited.

"You mean . . . now?"

"I've got a house in the West Hills—Portland Heights, actually. It's got a great view. Jennifer picked it out but now it's just Logan and me. We could wait for news together. It would be great to show it to you . . . and . . ."

My phone vibrated again, cutting off that tantalizing "and." I wasn't quite sure what Jazz was asking. I wasn't sure I wanted to know, but adrenaline kicked in as my mind buzzed with thoughts.

"I could order dinner in," he said. "I'm worried about Nana. And I don't want to be alone."

"What about Logan?" I asked.

"Well, yeah, he's around, of course, but I'd like to be with another adult. I'd like to be with you, Jane." He sounded hopeful.

The thought of Logan really put a damper on things as far as I was concerned. But I understood wanting to wait out the hours of Orchid's disappearance in the company of friends; the same feeling tugged at me. And it would be nice to be with Jazz and learn more about him.

Still, I sensed something inside myself . . . an unsettled loneliness . . . maybe even a need to prove my own attractiveness . . . and I knew I would be in dangerous territory. Jazz was wonderful to look at, and he'd been nothing but nice to me, but was I ready to get to know him better? Was now the time? I felt so bad about Orchid that I could picture myself jumping into bed with Jazz, searching for the kind of transitory comfort that could come back to bite me in the ass.

Sometimes my own self-awareness pisses me off.

"I think I'll have to take a rain check," I said regretfully.

He seemed crestfallen, but he nodded.

"Call me if you hear anything."

"I will." He moved away from me.

All the way back to Lake Chinook I silently railed at myself for chickening out. I would have liked to be with him. I would have liked to hold his hand and allay my fears. I would have liked to be there when—if—the call came through about Orchid. I'd even had The Binkster with me, so we could have all settled in for an evening together.

What do you want, Jane?

The question circled my brain. I felt frustrated, tentative. On the verge of turning around and heading back toward Portland Heights. I could call Jazz on his cell. I could be with him in twenty minutes and let whatever might happen between us, happen. We could commiserate, worry and talk. And though Logan wasn't exactly part of my ideal "date package," he would probably be off playing video games or talking to friends via the Internet or whatever kids his age did.

I actually nosed into a side street, intending to circle around. Then I hesitated, tapping my fingers on the steering wheel. Damn it all. I yanked the wheel back toward Lake Chinook, a sound of frustration rumbling in my throat. Binks lifted her ears and looked at me.

"What?" I asked her belligerently.

At my cottage, I poured her a small bowl of delicious, lo-cal kiblets, then listened distractedly to my message from Mom. Actually, she'd left three messages. I wasn't sure how I'd missed the rest of them, but I don't really understand cell phone intricacies and I don't care to learn. Each Mom message was progressively longer, as if she'd decided I would never answer my phone or call her back so she might as well have a one-way conversation that took care of everything.

The gist of it was, she was coming to Lake Chinook. She'd made her flight reservations for next week. There was no more putting her off. There was no more talking about it. She was on her way and that was that.

I scrambled to call her back. It's not that I don't want to see her. I love my mother, but family can be so tricky—the Purcell family a case in point. And the warmth of my relationship with my brother Booth ebbs and flows; with my mother it's just a certain amount of stress and responsibility. And now with Orchid missing . . .

"Mom!" I said when she answered her phone. She is not a cell phone user but she hangs by her land line pretty closely.

"Jane? Is that you?"

Since I'm her only daughter I'm pretty sure that's the kind of thing that doesn't require an answer, but I always feel compelled to make a joke. "No. It's the Dalai Lama."

"The Dalai Lama's a man, so I guess it's you, Jane."

I grimaced. Okay, I wasn't really in a joking mood and it showed. "I listened to your messages. You've got a flight for next week?"

"Yes." And she proceeded to give me all kinds of information about how she'd chosen the airline, and where the seat was, and how much luggage it would require, and she wasn't sure if she needed those Sky-Cap people to help her or not. I wrote down her flight information and told her I'd pick her up.

"I can't believe Booth's getting married," she said at the end of her report.

"I know."

"And she's black." She said the word tentatively, as if afraid the politically correct police would haul her in for not using African American. Personally, I don't care whether someone calls me white, Caucasian, or sickly pale. It's all fairly accurate about my flesh tone. Which reminds me, I'm still not over the fact that Crayola got rid of the crayon "flesh" apparently because it only portrayed white flesh. They changed to peach back in the sixties, but I had an ancient box of crayons that my mother had possessed from when she was a girl. For years I didn't recognize the switch. Now, I wondered why it couldn't be called white flesh. Or Caucasian flesh. I colored with that crayon a lot when I was a kid, depicting friends and family, and it just didn't seem like peach.

I closed my eyes. It was easier to mourn for something dumb than think about Orchid, maybe lost, scared, crying. I felt so damn helpless.

With an effort, I struggled hard to stay on track with Mom. In the beginning my brother had been cagey about his engagement to Sharona. I think he'd hoped that I would spill the beans to Mom and save him that little drama. But I'd been really careful about steering clear of the whole thing. There were pitfalls I was simply not going to trip into if I could help it. My mother had been insistent about making the trip to Oregon, however, and eventually Booth had broken down and had a long, long talk with her. Sharona is tall, black, beautiful and possessed of a steely determination that awes me. I just don't think I'll ever have that power of conviction. But apparently Booth gave Mom a fairly accurate depiction of his soon-to-be wife, because my mother sounded like she was still processing.

"She's a lawyer," Mom said, as if trying the word out on her tongue. "She practices criminal law."

"I know, Mom."

"She deals with criminals, I guess."

"Or innocent victims. Booth's with the police," I pointed out.

"I guess that's how they got to know each other?"

She'd learned all of this information weeks ago. I wasn't sure why I was called upon to ensure its veracity. Maybe she thought that upon first meeting her, Sharona would give her a test.

"Do you like her?"

I heard the hope in my mother's voice, and though my immediate response was to answer "yes," I honestly wasn't sure if I liked Sharona or not. I don't know Sharona that well yet, and she's kind of prickly. I'm sure it was her idea to get me the baby blue jogging suit.

I was afraid she would question me further, but apparently there was more on my mother's mind. She moved on to other topics without waiting for my response. There appears to be a ritual only she understands, so we chatted away about nothing while I kept one eye on the clock. I was hungry. The little fairy cakes and tea hadn't come my way after all. No one had the decency to grab for one. A damn shame and a terrible waste. Now, I was in desperate need of food. I wanted to call Dwayne back. I wanted to see Dwayne and have a debriefing.

Finally, she came around to what she wanted. "Booth and Sharona are planning to get married in Oregon. Not in a church. At some hall or something."

"Yeah, but not for six months or so."

"Next summer, but these things take so much planning."

I had no idea how involved Booth's wedding plans were. My brother wasn't the type to make it a big deal, but maybe Sharona wanted the whole enchilada. I had a sudden gaggy thought about bridesmaids and bridal gowns and where I fit into the scheme of things. "Seems to me that sounds like enough time."

"I was just thinking about the guest list." Another pause. "Do you think Booth will invite your father?"

Her words stopped me cold. Of all the things I'd expected, this wasn't one. My mother and father had divorced when Booth and I were two, and he'd stayed away from us like we were a bad smell, so it wasn't like we had any real connection to him. He'd been a deadbeat dad; barely managing child support, though by all accounts he was a successful lawyer. He'd married his secretary at some point and pumped out a trio of kids. Maybe more by now. I had no idea. I'd never had anything to do with any of them. Neither had Booth, as far as I knew. "I doubt it. Geez, Mom. I'm surprised you even thought so. We don't talk to him."

"Oh, good." She was relieved. "I didn't want to impose my wishes, but it would be awkward."

No shit. I couldn't picture what I would say to the man who'd run away from his first marriage and children as if they had leprosy. The idea that he'd fathered a new family and found his way to love and cherish them bugged me in a way that would probably send a smarter person than I to the psychiatrist's couch. As it was, I was in complete denial and glad to be there.

"I'll see you soon," Mom said as she hung up.

I called Dwayne, again, and left a blistering message on his voice mail about people who never answer their cell. Frustrated, I dug through my refrigerator. Failing there, I opened the freezer door and grabbed a small frozen meal of pasta, chicken and Alfredo sauce, refusing to look at the pull date. I microwaved it. As soon as it was cool enough for me to test my tongue on it, I gave it a taste. Not much to recommend it except that it was right in front of me. In that it met the only criteria I cared about. I dug in with gusto.

I put in a couple more calls to Dwayne, just to bug him. It felt good to transfer my worry over Orchid to annoyance with Dwayne. I sang the first few bars of a camp song on the second call, a dirty ditty that I'd learned from an older boy who'd tried hard to get into my pants when I was about thirteen. He'd pretty much struck out with everyone of the female sex; I'd been way down the list. He didn't score with me, either, as I had ideas about love, marriage, and happily ever after that didn't jibe with stolen moments of fumbled and hurried sexual encounters in the great outdoors. Also, he didn't brush his teeth well.

I wondered if I should call Jazz. Or go to his house. I'm a terrible, terrible waiter. To distract myself I called Cynthia. She answered but said in hushed tones that she was on a date with Ernst.

"A date?" I questioned.

"Stop by the gallery and meet him later this week," she urged.

"Okay."

A date . . . The very idea made me feel blue. I picked up my keys. I *would* go to Jazz's. Why not?

"Damn," I muttered through my teeth, placing a call instead. He answered on the second ring.

"Oh, I'm glad you called," he said, and my spirits lifted a bit. We talked about Orchid's disappearance at length, well, Jazz did the talking/worrying and I just hung onto the phone for human contact. Hearing Logan in the background, complaining about something, made me relieved I'd stayed home after all. Jazz was just warming up on the fretting, and I listened quietly, inwardly stewing and worrying myself. Instead of making me feel better, it made me feel worse, and pretty soon I pretended exhaustion and hung up. I grabbed my living room/TV watching green quilt, cocooned myself inside and curled up on the couch. Binks came up to me and scratched at me with one paw. I scooted back to give her room and she jumped up and nosed her way under the blanket. We adjusted into sleep mode with me trying to shut my brain down and Binks snorting and snuffling as she settled down by my feet.

I thought it would never happen, but we were both asleep inside of ten minutes.

Bang. Bang. Bang.

I shot to my feet, disoriented. It sounded like the roof was caving in. Stumbling around, I tried to get my brain to catch up. Where was I? What time was it? Two A.M.? Three? I squinted at the clock above the fireplace. Nine-thirty? Impossible. I looked again. Nine twenty-five, actually.

Binkster woofed a couple of times, and dug herself from beneath the blanket. She must have been convinced I was in no mortal danger; otherwise she would have trotted after me. She's a notorious chicken, but in the face of a real threat she can rise to the occasion. She looked toward the kitchen with dark, liquid eyes as I realized someone was pounding on my back door.

It felt like all the hair on my body had lifted. My skin tingled. Unlike Binks, I wasn't sure who or what had come to visit. Was this related to Orchid's disappearance? I tiptoed forward, my mind casting about for a weapon, just in case. I'd dragged my feet to get licensed to own a gun. I can't quite make myself carry one. Now, I sternly reprimanded myself. It would just make me *feel* better to think I had protection from anything that came my way.

I peeked around the corner to the kitchen. A man was framed in the glass of my back door. My heart clenched and I made an involuntary squeak of fear. Binkster jumped from the couch and came to my aid, a growl beginning in the back of her throat.

The growl turned to a yip of joy as Dwayne rattled the lock and peered inside at me. He was holding two bottles of wine. "Are you going to open the damn thing?" he demanded.

Muttering under my breath, I flipped the lock. Damn Dwayne. "You could give me a heart attack. It's late," I groused, as I switched on the light. I blinked in the blast of illumination that followed.

"Late? You gotta be kidding." He stepped inside, set the wine on the counter, then squatted down, playing with Binkster, who wriggled and twisted and wagged her tail in sheer joy. She jumped up and licked him on the face a couple of times, too. He petted and nuzzled her right back.

Dwayne glanced up and read whatever showed on my face. "Tough day at the geriatric ward, darlin'?"

"You don't know the half of it."

"Have you got anything to eat around here? I missed lunch."

"Look who you're talking to."

He took a gander inside my refrigerator anyway, snorting in disgust at what he found. Or, more accurately, what he didn't find. Flipping open his cell phone, he pushed speed dial, connecting with a local pizza joint. I listened while he ordered a large pepperoni with double cheese and though it sounded like trouble for one with on-again/off-again lactose intolerance, saliva formed in my mouth.

"What are you doing here?" I asked.

"I wanted to debrief you."

"Yeah? You coulda called."

"Your phone's dead. But I enjoyed the song. Maybe later you could sing me the rest of it."

I yanked the phone from my pocket and looked down at its blank face. "I'll put it on my list of things to do before I die. I don't get this. It's dead. I swear to God, this battery sucks."

"Who gave you the hickey? Jazz?"

I clapped a hand to the side of my neck as I headed to my bedroom to plug the phone into its charger. "An accident with my curling iron."

"Good thing you don't like guns."

I set up the cell phone, glad to see it beep and whir to life now that it was being fed with electricity. Before heading back to the kitchen I examined my "hickey." Grimacing, I wondered if Jazz may have thought the same thing.

When I returned to the kitchen Dwayne had put one bottle of white in the refrigerator and had uncorked the second. He was pouring us each a glass. Handing me mine, he arranged himself on one of my barstools. He wore a light blue shirt with snap-on mother-of-pearl buttons and his ubiquitous pair of disreputable denim jeans. His blondish-brown hair had grown longer than usual; it actually came over his ears a bit. Dwayne is nowhere near as classically handsome as Jazz, but there's something distinctly male about him that I try hard to ignore. If I've had too many drinks he starts to look good to me in dangerous ways. His blue eyes aren't as brilliant as Jazz's but they're sharp and astute and ironic.

"Orchid—Nana—is missing. I was the last one with her, and I seem to be the one everyone blames." The weariness settled over me again.

Dwayne nodded as I sat down on the barstool next to him.

"You knew?" I asked incredulously.

"Cammie called me and said the Purcells wouldn't be needing your services any longer."

I could feel the back of my neck grow hot. "Well, thanks for telling me."

"Darlin', things are just getting interesting. Sounds like Grandma decided to get the hell out before they made her start signing things she didn't wanna."

"Maybe she just wandered off," I said, but I'd begun to think that wasn't likely. My gut feeling said there was something else going on.

"You didn't find her anywhere on the grounds or nearby. And you looked pretty hard."

"Cammie can't fire me. Jazz hired me. And since when are you still talking to her?"

"I told you. The woman just keeps calling."

"They're the weirdest bunch," I said with feeling. "All of them. And it doesn't help that the men are a lot more attractive than the women. It's like some lesson off the Discovery Channel: see how the males' plumage makes them bright and colorful, while the pea hens hide in dull camouflage in the reeds."

"So, what are you gonna do next?"

"I don't know. I'm going to think about it."

Dwayne nodded. "Tell me more about your day at the spa, then."

The pizza delivery boy rang the bell at that moment, sending Binkster shooting toward the door, her tail wagging furiously. Her nose told her what blessed gift had arrived.

Dwayne paid for the pizza and brought it into the kitchen. Binks sat down beside him, face turned attentively upward. I am a sucker for this, but Dwayne ignores her completely until he's done. Then, he might break off a small piece of crust, but he never totally indulges her. It may be that he would be a better dog owner than I, but I'd rather rip out my tongue than admit as much to him.

While we ate I gave him all the details about my travails at Complete Me. Dwayne listened, nodding occasionally, grunting in agreement once in a while. This is one of his best attributes, the ability to really listen without cutting me off before I'm done. I don't know if it's me, or if other women have the same problem, but I rarely seem to be able to tell a whole story without having some man interrupt me. Is it that the male gender is disinterested in what I'm interested in? Or, is it that my telling of said story is such a snore that they can't bear it?

"You haven't talked to our client about Trevin, yet?" I finished.

"Nope."

"I gave you this information when I was at the spa."

"You just gave me the highlights. Didn't want my head handed to me until I had all the facts."

"Well, it's too bad if he doesn't like what he hears." My voice was laced with judgment and Dwayne gave me a "what gives?" look. "He hired you to follow his wife while he's meeting with Janice every chance he gets."

"Who told you that?"

"I saw them at the Coffee Nook the other morning. Playing footsie under the counter. And I understand Miriam goes in there sometimes. Always alone. So, maybe she was just looking for love in all the wrong places."

"It's Spence who's paying us," Dwayne pointed out.

"Paying you."

"You're really pissed about this."

"I'm pissed about a lot of things."

Dwayne shrugged, clearly disaffected. "Well, maybe Mr. Australia dumped her, but Miriam hasn't broken down and fessed up to Spence, as far as I know. It's still a secret."

"She's probably licking her wounds. Trevin is a shit."

"She chose poorly."

"Well, maybe if your buddy Spence wasn't with Janice, Miriam wouldn't feel compelled to choose."

"Spence is not a buddy of mine, and we're not investigating him."

"Well, maybe we should."

"And who's going to pay us for that?" he asked, maddeningly logical.

"It isn't always about money."

"Since when, Jane Kelly?"

"Since I had to listen to those damn Purcells worry that Orchid wouldn't sign the power of attorney."

He slid me a look out of the corner of his eyes. "Is Jasper one of those 'damn Purcells'?"

"I'm worried about her. Dementia patients wander off and bad things happen to them. Injury. Death. I don't want to be responsible."

"You're not responsible."

"That's not what I mean."

"What do you mean?"

"Dwayne, damn it . . . don't go there with me right now. I'm just . . ."

"Irrational?" he guessed.

We stared at each other a moment. My mind cataloged nearby objects I could use for weaponry: pots, pans, lamps, the pile of books I'd left on a corner of the counter. I really, really wanted to throw something at him.

He watched my expression intently. "You know what I think?"

"What?"

"I think you should find Orchid Purcell on your own. You're not going to feel right until you do. It's not your fault. You know it's not your fault. But the lot of them are going to act like it is, and you need action."

My anger slowly dissolved. "The police have been called and there's no money in it."

"All right. This time you need something better: validation."

It's the rare day Dwayne can admit there's something more important than collecting clients' greenbacks. It's even rarer that he thinks I should spend my energy in such pursuits.

But it made me feel lighter to hear him give me the go ahead. Rolling around in the back of my head had been the desire to take on finding Orchid myself. I said, "If Orchid's still missing to-morrow, I'll join the search for her. She can't be far, but I wouldn't put it past one of them to hide her. Maybe coerce her into signing the power of attorney. I don't know."

"Who would that be?"

"I don't know."

"How would they do it? You said they were all at the meeting when she turned up missing."

"I don't know, Dwayne. I'm just guessing. Someone could be hiding her at the house, for all I know. I didn't get to search James' suite." I looked away, not wanting to meet his gaze. Jazz hadn't been at the meeting. He hadn't made it to the Purcells until after Orchid was missing, but I couldn't believe this was anything to do with him, and I certainly didn't feel like explaining that to Dwayne. "Whoever did it could have had help from outside," I theorized. "It just feels like there's something else going on."

"You going to tell Jazz you're doing your own search?"

"Maybe. I'll see."

He nodded, draining his glass of wine and pouring another.

I thought about telling him my feelings when I was inside the playhouse, but changed my mind. Dwayne works in facts. An attack of the willies isn't something he would relate to. Instead, I said, "There's something . . . off . . . with the Purcells. Something happened with Lily, Jazz's mother, and it's eaten away at all of them. Orchid was crying about Lily and how her husband treated her. I know dementia patients can get sad and upset and there's no consoling them, but this seemed like something festering inside her. Something secret and dark. So, I'm going to look into that, too."

I half-expected him to accuse me of being fanciful, but all he said was, "Put it down in a report. Then give me a copy."

"What for? Posterity? You think someone's going to pay you for it?"

"You just never know, darlin'."

He finished a third piece of pizza and the rest of his wine, then tossed Binkster a teensy piece of crust. At the back door, he stooped to give Binks a couple of hearty pats on the head before he disappeared. I latched the door behind him, listening as I heard the engine of his boat rev to life.

I felt better. I had a plan. Corking the still half-full bottle, I glanced down at the pug who was staring through the glass at the inky night, hoping for sight of Dwayne. She looked up at me in silent recrimination, clearly blaming me for ruining her evening.

"Oh, get over it," I said, and we both headed to the bedroom.

Chapter Eight

In the middle of the night I clawed myself awake from a dream about annoying insects that were buzzing and buzzing and tangling in my hair. I thrashed an arm out to ward off a cloud of some kind of wicked, stinging black hornets, effectively waking myself, and that's when I heard the little buzzing sound. It came from my desk. Vaguely I recognized it was happening every few minutes. As I came to full wakefulness, I realized it was my cell phone. On vibrate mode, it was telling me I had a message.

I brought the phone back to bed with me and punched in the numbers to access my voice mail. After the female computer voice instructed me to please enter my password, I pressed in the four-digit code—1, 1, 1, 1. (I never claimed to be a security expert.) I had two unheard messages.

The first was from Lorraine Bluebell, a real estate agent in Lake Chinook whom I'd befriended last summer. "Hi, Jane. Believe it or not, I have a gift certificate to The Pisces Pub. Are you free for lunch tomorrow? I'm buying . . ." She left her cell phone number and I saved the message, so I could input it to the phone later. I probably had one of her business cards floating around, but I didn't want to chance it and miss out. There's something about The Pisces Pub that doesn't lend itself to the "gift certificate" criteria. It's a beat-up, shit kicker kind of place whose theme was once something to do with the sea and now is mostly ranch or cowboy.

The second message was a sales call for a reduced interest rate on a credit card. They wanted me to call the number back immediately. I squinted at the phone. Telemarketing on my cell phone? That was low.

I snuggled deeper into bed and Binkster took it as a means to lobby for entry under the covers. I allowed it and she curled her furry little body up next to me. I put my arm around her and felt incredibly protective and possessive. I don't get what's come over me. All my affections seemed to be targeted at her. I fell back asleep wondering if this was the result of a nonexistent love life—or a symptom of something worse.

I was up at the crack of dawn the next morning, determinedly shaking off my blues of the night before. Any thoughts I had for a run to the Nook were dropped when I saw the streaming rain pouring down from the heavens. I drove myself instead, my thoughts on Orchid. I hoped she was inside somewhere, safe and sound.

Things were hopping at the Nook. No Billy Leonard, but the crowd was intense. Julie was working like she had six arms, and her right-hand woman, Jenny, was also delivering orders at top speed. Julie and Jenny are the Coffee Nook's sugar and spice: Julie's sugar; Jenny's spice. Kind of jalapeno spice, actually, since you never know when you're going to get zinged. Jenny can zap you good but her sharp repartee is a major draw for the Coffee Nook customers.

I poured myself a cup of black coffee and blew across the top, searching for a place to sit. One stool was empty but someone had her purse on it, so I stood in the center of the room and watched Julie and Jenny serve the customers. There was no sign of Spence or Janice this morning; too early, perhaps. Since I didn't want to run into Miriam, either, I was going to have to keep my eyes peeled.

Seeing Jenny reminded me of Jennifer, Jazz's deceased wife. I wondered if Jazz was still mourning her more than he let on. I also wondered what effect his short-term memory loss had created. Had the accident changed him? What had he been like before?

I called Lorraine at eight o'clock. Early, yes, but she struck me as the kind of person who got going in the morning. She answered promptly and was thrilled that I could join her. We settled on twelve-thirty.

I next called Jazz but I got his cell phone voice mail. I thought about leaving him a message but changed my mind. I didn't feel like telling him Cammie had "fired" me through Dwayne, and I knew if there were any news on Orchid he would let me know first thing.

Blessedly, the rain turned to a fine mist on its way to stopping completely. Back at the cottage I wrote up the hard copy report about my trip to Complete Me for Dwayne to give to Spence, then I read it over and fixed a few typos. I afterwards examined my online banking report and was pleased at the five hundred dollar deposit I'd made. I'd kept out a hundred dollars to use as mad money from Jazz's first payment. I wondered vaguely if he would pay me for yesterday. Does it count if you lose the woman you're supposed to be looking after?

Around ten I had a *mazda:* I decided to call Eileen. Punching in her saved number, I eagerly waited for her to answer with no clear idea of what I planned to say. But she didn't pick up her phone, so I left a message saying who I was and what my connection to Orchid had been before her disappearance.

At ten-thirty Jazz got back to me with the information that Nana was still missing, and the police were taking down a detailed record of Orchid's daily life and schedule. I mentioned to him that I was thinking about conducting my own investigation. He didn't jump on the idea of "hiring me" for that as well, but clearly his mind was full of other things—worry, chief among them. We ended the conversation with "let's get together later" words of good-bye.

Around noon I headed to The Pisces Pub. The front door has a carved mermaid who looks as if she's been abused by every patron who's walked through the doors. She lost her breasts years ago and her fins aren't in the best of shape. Her face has been hacked at or eroded, too, so she looks perpetually pissed off.

I could relate.

Lorraine wasn't about when I entered so I sat myself at the bar right in front of the wooden fish statue that is bolted to the front counter. Said statue wears tiny spurs, a western vest, chaps and a hat. Since the last time I'd been here someone had added a string tie around the fish's neck adorned with a turquoise clasp. Our little fishy cowboy friend also had a new sheriff's star on its right breast. "Jewels Verne" was imprinted into the star's dull copper finish.

"We had a contest," the bartender said, catching me examining Jewels. "That's the winning name. Want anything?"

I chose a light beer. Having tended bar in California, I always examine the style of the bartenders with a critical eye. I liked this guy's easy manner. And I liked The Pisces Pub for its lack of pretension and its kitsch. I hadn't been here for a few weeks but apart from the fish's name and get-up, nothing had changed: same scarred wooden floor, same wagon wheel overhead lights, same random mix of the seven seas meets the wild west.

I was halfway through my glass when Lorraine burst through the doors. Her brown hair is cut short and feathered, and a white streak slashes across her bangs. She has to be in her mid-fifties but she seems to be fighting the middle-age middle fairly well. Her deep purple pantsuit fit well, the kind of cut that spoke of designer tailoring. She looked thinner than when I'd last seen her, and I complimented her as she sat down on a stool beside me, loading her current big-ass purse onto the counter beside Jewels. The purse matched her outfit: dark purple and gold. She even wore gold flats.

"I've been at class all morning," she said, turning her attention to the bartender. "Do you have a decent Chardonnay? I don't care if it's good. But decent I have to have."

"It's decent. Barely," he said.

"Bring it on."

Lorraine gave me her full attention. "Luckily I don't have to go back this afternoon."

Real estate agents are always taking classes. Part of the ongoing requirements to keep licensed in the state. "I'm glad you called."

"I have an ulterior motive," she admitted. "I may need some help. I sold a property to a friend and now one of her neighbor's flipped out and seems to be sabotaging her home."

"How?"

Lorraine shook her head. "She lives in First Addition. It's one of those tricky neighborhood association things. They've got a rogue player causing havoc. He doesn't like all the construction going on around him, and those that agree with him are turning a blind eye to the vandalism. I was wondering if you could do a stakeout at my friend's, catch the guy in the act? He's been pretty actively targeting her since she added an addition and second story."

"Did the renovation affect someone's view, or something?"

"No. It's all about stopping progress using any means possible." Lorraine sniffed. "Some of the longtime residents feel the homes are getting too big . . . that they're moving away from the original concept of the neighborhood. A lot of First Addition was built in the forties, and the homes were two-bedroom cottages with one bathroom. New people moving in are paying high prices and they want more. And yes, they're making them bigger." She gave me a look. "The guy's stolen items from the job site. He's broken tile. When she went out to her mailbox, it was filled with dog poop."

Yuck. "I'll see what I can do." Since I was working for myself on the Purcell case unless Jazz decided to butt heads with Cammie and hang onto me, I could use another job.

"Thanks." And as if reading my mind, Lorraine added, "Bill me your usual rates."

I nodded. Note to self: *I'm going to have to get some of those.*

I took down the particulars on her friend's house. First Addition is close to Lake Chinook's downtown business area, and it's always been a desirable neighborhood but in the past few years the prices have gone from hot to blistering. I knew someone who owned apartments in that area, so I jotted down a note to call him and catch up.

We settled into the business of ordering food. I chose the coconut shrimp, knowing they'd be probably frozen, heavily battered and rubbery. But when in The Pisces . . . Lorraine chose a small bowl of chili. "You can't trust the salads here," she said in an aside.

"I've got some questions for you, too," I said as they brought our orders. My shrimp were exactly as I'd expected, and I soaked them in a gingery salad dressing that they served in a small, clear plastic cup. Honestly, they were dang good.

"What do you need?" Lorraine asked.

"Do you know much about the Purcells?"

"Hmm . . . yes and no. Don't know them personally, but they've got amazing real estate. Not just in Dunthorpe but the West Hills and Portland Heights. Central Oregon—Bend and Black Butte. And you can't miss that "P" on a lot of commercial buildings in downtown Portland."

"Know anything about the family history?"

"The usual, I guess. One of them ended up in a sanitarium."

"Lily," I agreed encouragingly as the bartender brought her drink.

Lorraine took a swallow and made a face. "Should have ordered a martini," she said. She was a woman after my own heart. "Mostly what I know is rumor. What are you searching for? Are you doing work for them?"

I suppose it was slightly unethical of me, but I brought her up to speed on my adventures in senior-sitting. I figured it wasn't exactly client-investigator privilege, and the police were involved now, too. Lorraine's eyebrows lifted upon hearing Orchid was missing. "That's too bad," she said.

"I kind of expected her to turn up today. Maybe they all did. I'm going there next and making finding her a priority. It's not what they hired me for, but I can't just walk away and forget about her."

"Don't you go feeling responsible," Lorraine cautioned me.

"Well, I do. I can't help it." I didn't add that I felt the Purcells were responsible at some level, too, but it was what I was thinking.

Lorraine's brow furrowed in thought. "Maybe I can help you with Lily. . . . As I recall, there was some rumored scandal surrounding her. All of the Purcells went to private school, not public, which isn't a surprise but it means I didn't ever meet them personally, and I don't know any of their classmates. I went to Lake Chinook High. They were at some school on the east side of the river, I think. Lily was around sixteen when she was sent to that place on the Willamette somewhere around Salem? Or, maybe Eugene? Oh, what's the name of it . . ."

I didn't comment. Didn't want to disrupt her thought process.

"It's River, something. River . . . river . . . River Shores! And I think it's closer to Salem. She wasn't there long. She died of something."

"She was there almost a year, I think. She had a baby. A boy. Jasper Purcell."

"Oh, that's right. And he's the one who hired you. What did you call him? Jazz?"

I nodded. "Do you remember anything about his father?" This was a question I hadn't wanted to ask Jazz, figuring if he wanted me to know he would bring it up himself. But I wasn't above a little rumor-mongering if it helped my cause.

"Was he from the sanitarium?"

"I don't know. I guess it depends if she was pregnant before she arrived or after she got there. Jazz says Lily was known for her meekness, but she died from being held down and restrained. The whole thing was hushed up. Orchid even believes she may have been murdered, but Orchid can be—fanciful."

"Is she losing it?" Lorraine asked.

"Seems like it," I admitted. "There are some signs. I never really had a chance to talk to her about Lily's death. It didn't come up, and honestly I didn't know how to mention it without sounding like a ghoul."

Lorraine nodded. "Well, I wish you luck. Are you going to go to River Shores?"

"Maybe. It'll just be for my own edification, though." I checked my watch. "Right now I'm going to the Purcells. Finding Orchid is a priority."

An hour later I turned into the Purcell "in" driveway and headed toward the house. I wasn't sure about the reception I would receive. I wasn't really looking to be "rehired," but I refused to be pushed aside, and as long as I had my connection to Jazz, I intended to use it.

I'd barely moved into the drive when I stopped the car, my mind catching on a thread of possibility. Backing out again, I kept on Chrysanthemum Lane for a bit, then edged the Volvo's nose into the Purcell's "out" drive. Shoving the wagon into neutral, I kept the engine idling. Through the windshield I stared down the tree-canopied drive toward the house, which, from this vantage point, was invisible as it was hidden by shrubbery. Twisting around, I looked behind me, across the road. There were several houses on the opposite side of the street, all of them also down lengthy drives. I could see their slate-and-tile roofs and stone or brick chimneys peeking through walls of thick foliage, protective hedges and trees.

Once again I backed onto the road and just stayed there, wondering about the driveways. Orchid could have left by either one of them. Maybe someone drove her. Maybe she just toddled onto the street. No one was likely to see unless they happened to be going by at that exact moment.

As I sat in my idling car, a kid of about fourteen shot out of one of the neighboring drives on a skateboard, skidding to a stop when he saw my car sitting in the street. He wore an iPod, the ear buds inserted in his ears. A dark blue Mariner's cap covered his head but I could see unruly, red curls sticking out from under it.

I rolled down my window. "You live there?" I yelled, inclining my head to the drive from where he'd just come.

He unhooked an ear plug. "What's it to ya?"

He sounded more curious than angry. I said, "I know the Purcells. Actually, I was taking care of Orchid Purcell until just recently." Okay, I made it sound like it was a long-term job, but it wasn't exactly a lie.

"The old lady? The one they're looking for?"

"You haven't seen her, have you?"

"I told them already. *No.* That grouchy dude practically accused me of lying." The memory brought a scowl to his face.

"Would that be Garrett Purcell?" I guessed. He and Satin had canvassed the neighborhood.

"I guess. He said he was her son. He's a fat-ass."

"He's probably just worried. She's been missing overnight."

"Why'd you go in the out?" he asked, gesturing toward the exit drive.

"I don't know. Just looking around, I guess."

He snorted. "The only people go in the out are gettin' it on in the backseat."

I thought that over. So, the Purcell exit drive was a lover's lane of sorts. "Cars park there?"

"All the time. Same ones, mostly. Nobody leaves that place after eight o'clock, so it's not like you're gonna block 'em in. Cars come around midnight. I see the lights from my bedroom." He grinned. "Sometimes I sneak over and scare the crap out of 'em."

"Sounds like a worthwhile endeavor," I said. "You remember any cars here yesterday?"

He shrugged. I got the feeling that, even if he did, he wasn't ready to talk about it. Since I was just fishing in the dark, I let it go.

"What's your name?"

"What's it to ya?"

This appeared to be his favorite response. "I'm Jane Kelly. I'm trying to find Orchid Purcell, and I'm doing some investigating for the family." Okay, this *was* a lie. "If you think of anything, I'd like you to contact me."

"You're a private investigator?" he said, his grin widening. "Gimme your number and I'll program it." He whipped a razor-thin cell phone from a jeans pocket and flipped it open. I told him my number and was awed by the swiftness with which he added me to his phone. Feeling inadequate somehow, I asked for his number in return and though I managed to program it, I wasn't half as fast and I could tell by his smirk that he'd noticed.

"I'm Nate," he said when I asked. "If I think of anything, I'll call you."

"Cool."

Nate took off and I put the Volvo in reverse and backed up to the entrance lane. I was lost in thought as I pulled up to the house. Something about that exchange with Nate had triggered a memory, one I couldn't quite latch onto.

Jazz was already at the house. In fact, he and Reyna were standing beneath the portico. Reyna's face was strained and pale, and Jazz looked puzzled and upset. He gave me a wan smile of greeting, but if I'd hoped for more since last night, I was disappointed.

"No word on Orchid?" I asked, as I climbed out of my car, slamming the door behind me.

"No," he said.

Reyna looked miserable. "They are blaming me."

"What? Oh, come on. They can't blame you. Last I heard, they blamed me."

"They're just worried," Jazz muttered.

Yeah, they're worried their meal ticket is M.I.A. I wondered, if Orchid remained missing, what that meant for how—and if—the Purcell money would continue to be distributed. What provisions had been made?

Reyna clasped my arm. "Would you help me? If they fire me, I will not get another job."

"They're not going to fire you." My voice lacked conviction, however. They'd already kind of fired me.

The rest of the family members were all squabbling in the

main salon as Jazz and I walked into the entry hall. I really didn't see what good it would do for me to face them again. I was through with recriminations and interested in action. Besides, I wanted to check James's rooms, so I told Jazz I needed to head to the bathroom, then I scurried upstairs, keeping my steps light and fast. I hadn't really been thinking of a plan, but I headed straight to James's door. My purse was tucked under my arm, but now I pulled it off and dug through it, my fingers closing on a paper clip. I'm fairly tidy about my things, but inside a pocket of my purse I keep small items such as the paper clip, string, nail clippers, even a tiny measuring tape, just in case. There's a suitcase thrown in the back of the Volvo with extra clothes and shoes, too, and a flashlight and compass are tucked into the side pocket on the driver's side. Very Nancy Drew of me. Actually, Dwayne's been instrumental in setting me up for surveillance work—although I still haven't figured out the bathroom break thing for stakeouts and the like. It would be just my luck that when I ran to the loo, that's when my quarry would act. Dwayne has a contraption only a male can use. I've cursed my female anatomy more than once, but then I don't have to shave my face or buy oversized wheels for my car, so I guess it evens out in the end.

I quickly unwound the paper clip and inserted it into the keyhole. A couple of jabs and the lock sprang open. James was going to have to do more than basic interior privacy door handles to keep his secrets safe.

I twisted the knob and let myself inside.

Three steps in, I stopped short. My breath caught in my throat, and I felt my eyes widen.

The room was filled with painted canvases. They were on the walls, leaning against the furniture, propped up against entry to the private bath directly in my line of vision.

And nearly every one depicted knives.

I had to blink several times to take it all in. I counted twenty paintings. Blue knives, black knives, red knives. Even a sinister dark, mustard yellow that had something brown dripping from its tip that made my lips pull back in distaste. They were painted in many ways: upside down, held tightly in a wound fist, lined up in dozens as if ready to be thrust at an unsuspecting victim, stuck into mounds of flesh that could, or could not, have been human. I was repelled in a way I couldn't define.

Footsteps on the stairs. Quick as a cat, I pushed the lock, backed into the hall and closed the door softly. Facing its panels, I knocked softly, pretending to have just arrived. "James? James, are you in there?"

"James is downstairs." I turned around and faced Roderick, his amused smile in place. "But I'm sure you know that. What are you trying to do?"

"I was looking for him."

"Really. Jazz said you were looking for the bathroom."

"That, too."

"Why do you want James?"

I sensed I wasn't going to be able to fob him off with some lame story, but then all I had were lame stories. "I wanted to know about the playhouse," I said, the idea bursting onto my lips before it had fully assimilated in my brain. "It's kind of creepy, don't you think?"

Roderick seemed taken aback. "Why do you want to ask James?"

"He's the first one of you I met. I looked at the playhouse and when I came back, he was waiting at the house. He seemed to think I'd been there. Is there someone better I could talk to?"

"Better? I don't know what you're looking for."

"Orchid." I can carry on a circular conversation with the best of them. Double talk is better than half-baked explanations any day. "Isn't that why we're here?"

He sized me up. There was something leering and lustful in his eyes. "You sure like to tap dance, don't ya?"

"Figuratively or literally?" I started to edge past him, but he shifted to block my way. I could smell his aftershave, something spicy and strong from another era. If he touched me I was going to kick him in the balls.

"Well, now, come on. This isn't getting us anywhere."

"I'm going downstairs, now."

"Might as well take your time. They're rehashing and rehashing." He put his hands in his pockets and rocked back on his heels, watching me closely. I could see his hands move inside the pockets. Was he doing a quick search for Mr. Perky?

The doorbell suddenly rang through the house. It gave me an opportunity to brush past him. Roderick was momentarily diverted. But then he was quick on my heels, as I headed across the gallery, his breath hot on my neck. In one of those moments of pure synergy that sometimes happen my mind suddenly touched on Jerome Neusmeyer and the last time I'd fended off unwanted advances of this nature.

And then Jerome Neusmeyer himself walked into the entry hall below. He looked up and saw me crossing the catwalk, Roderick practically climbing up my back.

Shit. I had no disguise and he thought my name was Veronica . . . Ronnie. I had visions of racing out the back door—well, actually, the front door—anything to delay another round with Neusmeyer. Instead I peeled off to the upstairs hall bath. I practically slammed the door in Roderick's face, then leaned against the counter, my heart pounding.

Damn it all to hell.

I could see Roderick's shoes shading the light that came through the crack under the door. The bastard was waiting for me.

What is it about me that invites the lecherous to misbehave?

My decision to outwait him took ten minutes. A *looonnnnggg* ten minutes where I nearly bolted from the room several times. It felt like I'd been trapped for hours. But then Dahlia came upstairs and demanded to know what Roderick was doing. It was time he came downstairs. The meeting was in progress and she needed him right now! He left his post reluctantly.

I'd used some of those ten minutes to wash off the little bit of makeup that I'd applied this morning and snap my hair into a ponytail with a leftover hair band I'd discovered in one of the bathroom drawers. Yes, it had given me a moment's pause about whose hair band it might be, but I was desperate. If I ended up lice-infested, creepy and disgusting as that was, I could always delouse myself with chemical products available at my local pharmacy. But if there was any way to disguise who I was from Jerome Neusmeyer, I was going to take it. I'd dressed up to meet him last time. I'd been flirtatious and played like a gold digger. I'd showed legs, a little cleavage and unveiled interest. This time it was pure, boiled down Jane Kelly: jeans, boots, dark T-shirt, scraped back hair, no cosmetics.

I gave myself a hard assessment: thirty, going on nineteen. It would have to do.

Letting myself into the hallway, I peered over the gallery to the entry hall with trepidation. They were closeted in the main salon with Neusmeyer. Chicken-heart that I am, I really considered just vamoosing. But I'm also nosy. And I was bound and determined to help find Orchid. She wasn't in James's rooms, so I believed she was not in the house. And several groups—myself included—had already searched the grounds.

I was going to have to look for her off-site.

Creeping downstairs, I listened at the salon keyhole. Reyna appeared from the kitchen and looked at me. I waved and she simply turned away.

". . . Didn't hear about this yesterday," Jazz was saying, his voice a bit higher than normal. "I really want Jane to hear this. I'll go find her."

"She's locked herself in the bathroom," Roderick said lazily.

"And she's not working for us," Cammie added. "Pay her any amount you want, Jazz. You want to buy women, go right ahead. But don't expect cooperation from the rest of us. Personally, I think she should be held liable for Nana's disappearance. If anything's happened to Nana because of that woman . . ." She left the thought unfinished but my heart clutched.

"You think Reyna should be held liable, too," Jazz stated.

"What are you talking about?"

"She just said you blamed her."

"Oh, she's a . . ." I couldn't hear the rest but Cammie sounded fit to be tied.

James had a Rodney King moment, saying something about everyone needing to get along.

"Let's get back to the matter at hand." Neusmeyer's voice came through the door, cool and smooth. Sweat broke out on my skin. "I'll keep a copy of the POA. With everything in order, things will continue to run smoothly. But, of course, finding Orchid is of utmost importance."

POA? Orchid had signed the Power of Attorney? My mind flew to possibilities. Had someone coerced her to sign it?

"That goes without saying," Garrett told Neusmeyer. "We're all terribly concerned for her."

"And we've alerted the news media, too," Dahlia said.

"When did you do that?" Jazz was surprised. He wasn't the only one. I wondered who'd initiated that part of the bargain.

Dahlia tried to fob him off with, "You act like we've forgotten about her. She's my mother."

"I'm getting Jane," Jazz responded and this time his footsteps strode my way. I hurriedly scuttled to the kitchen and jumped on a stool. Reyna was making dinner. She glanced at me but kept her own counsel. Jazz appeared a few moments later, his cheeks suffused with color. He said with relief, "There you are. They all act like I've heard things before, but I don't think so. Maybe it's because I can't remember. I don't know. It's so frustrating."

I wanted to ask him about the Power of Attorney. When had Orchid signed it? Yesterday they were all about it. Today, it was suddenly just *there?*

"She signed a POA," he said, as if reading my thoughts. "Can you believe that?"

"When was this supposed to have happened?"

"I don't know. They're saying they already told me. Did they? I don't know." He shook his head. "Come with me," he said, urging me to follow him. I stood where I was, and he stopped at the kitchen door. "You know this isn't right. Nana didn't sign anything."

"No . . . but . . . I wasn't with her the entire day yesterday. I saw her in the afternoon. The papers were there for her to sign."

"You think she signed them?"

My gut instinct was to say no, but I really had no idea. It seemed too opportune. "I'm just saying it's possible, time-wise, I guess."

"They never told me," Jazz stated emphatically. "I would have remembered something this important. They're using my memory loss against me." I thought he might be right, but there was no way of knowing. "Dahlia just dropped the bomb this morning," he went on. "She's the attorney in fact. James witnessed it."

Reyna shared a look with me as I followed Jazz into the entry hall. We entered at the same time Neusmeyer and the rest of the Purcell gang spilled out of the salon. Before I could prevent him, Jazz clasped my hand and dragged me forward. He introduced me as Jane Kelly to Neusmeyer with puppy-like eagerness, as if he really wanted to impress the man with how he'd handled this whole Nana problem.

The attorney shook my hand and stared at me. My insides felt like ice. I'd forgotten how short he was until I realized if we were to stare straight at each other I would be gazing at his forehead. But I didn't meet his inquiring look. Instead, I kept my focus off to one side, as if I were kind of lost in thought, not completely in the moment. I didn't want anything to cue him that we'd met before, and I've found sometimes being purposely vague helps make people remember your behavior over your appearance.

I could see his brow furrow but he didn't put it together. It probably helped that my V-neck was discreet and there was no hint of cleavage. Last time he'd been more interested in my boobs than about anything. This time I just smiled a little when he introduced himself. Jazz said my name was Jane Kelly.

Nobody else in the family showed me much interest, which

was fine by me. I practically bolted out of there. Since I'd convinced myself Orchid was not in James's rooms, there wasn't any reason to hang around. Maybe he could have had her hidden somewhere, but there wasn't a lot of space for much besides his "art." And it felt more like he would want to hide his curious obsession with knives from his mother than subject her to it day and night. And what point would it be to confine her anyway?

No, I sensed Orchid was off the premises. Where, I didn't know, but I intended to find out. I just hoped she was still alive.

Chapter
Nine

Jazz gave me a good-bye hug and said he'd call later. I strode quickly to my car, feeling like I was poised on the brink of a relationship. I asked myself if that's what I really wanted as I drove out the Purcells' exit to Chrysanthemum Lane. I didn't have an answer.

Glancing over to the roof of the house just visible above the maple trees, I recalled the elusive thought I'd been unable to grasp earlier. It was the vision of Nate inserting my phone number into his cell phone with such alacrity, as if he were a born computer programmer. I don't have the love of electronics that seems to voraciously infect young men. Some young women, too. I've never actually reviewed the CD about "You and Your Cell Phone" that the salesman had heralded as an absolute must, but I've fumbled my way through learning all the menus, tweaks, bells and buzzers. I've always felt I could be good at it, if I just cared a little more.

Now I pulled over, parking the Volvo cockeyed at the end of another long, tree-lined drive to a home I couldn't see. Dragging my cell phone from my pocket, I turned it over in my hands. Orchid, the prisoner, hadn't had a phone in her room, but she loved, loved, loved Logan, who'd spent every moment that I'd been around him glued to his Game Boy. I suspected he possessed a cell phone as well. If not his own, then he probably had Jazz's from time to time.

And Orchid liked to spend time with Logan. He was her favorite.

So, how do you keep a kid like Logan interested? What do you talk about when you're in your eighties and he's barely a teenager? You engage him in a discussion—or possibly even a demonstration—of something he loves. Or, maybe you just sit there and he, lost for something to say to you, decides to show you all about the wonders of the cell phone.

And Orchid loved menus.

I cursed myself for not viewing the How To CD and learning to be more cell phone savvy. But I wasn't completely at a loss, either. I pushed the button with its green phone icon and got a list of recent incoming and outgoing calls. I didn't recognize all of them. I didn't have them cataloged on my contact list like real cell phone whizzes do. I picked out an outgoing number from yesterday afternoon with a Lake Chinook prefix but no identifying name and pushed the call button.

"Lake Chinook Adult Community Center."

Bingo! I was almost surprised that I was right. After a moment's hesitation, I responded, "I'm looking for Orchid Purcell."

The voice, momentarily welcoming, took on a careful tone. "May I ask who's calling?"

Since I'd learned the Purcells had alerted the police and apparently the media, I didn't see any reason not to be forthright myself. "My name's Jane Kelly. I'm a . . . private investigator hired by the family to help find Orchid. I'm sure the police have already contacted you about her disappearance . . . ?"

"Oh, yes, yes. But we told them we haven't seen Orchid for months. Ever since the family decided it wasn't a good idea."

"She hasn't contacted you?"

"No, ma'am."

My cell phone said differently. It had been stuck inside the cushions of Orchid's couch, and since I knew I hadn't made the call, someone who'd been in Orchid's rooms had. It made sense that it was Orchid herself.

"Were you working yesterday afternoon?"

"Yes."

"And you're the person who most often answers this number?"

"Well . . . yes, I suppose."

"And Orchid did not call anytime yesterday?"

"No. Of course not. I would have told the police that."

"Could she have called when you were away from the desk?"

"No one left any messages, if that's what you mean." Her tone grew tart. "I don't leave the desk unattended. There's always someone here."

"Who would be there, if it wasn't you?"

There was a moment of silence. I could tell she was trying to outguess me. I didn't want to alienate her, but I needed the information. "I told the police that none of us had heard from Mrs. Purcell in months."

"What about friends? The police must have asked who she would contact."

"I gave them a list of her friends." Now, her tone was out and out frosty. I was apparently questioning her ability and she didn't like it one bit. I sensed that if I asked for the same list she'd tell me where to stick it.

"Oh, good," I said enthusiastically. "Hopefully the police plan to give that list to Garrett. He's so upset. He's really on the warpath. I told him I'd tried to jog things along, you know, so that we could keep the family involved. The police are great, but it's kind of a long grind, y'know? So much protocol. It's just so difficult. We're all so worried."

"I can imagine . . ." Her tone warmed a fraction.

I pushed a little harder. "If you could do anything to help speed up the process . . . ?"

"There aren't that many people who come to the center who know Orchid. And she hasn't been well for a while now, bless her heart, and when she did come she sometimes said things that were hurtful, not that she meant to."

"She hasn't been herself lately," I said, adding, "but she was always a gracious woman."

"Exactly. Tell Garrett I gave them William's name and address, and Bonnie's."

"Could you give them to me, too? So, Garrett doesn't have to bother?"

"Let me see . . ." She put down the phone and returned a few minutes later, rattling off both addresses and phone numbers.

I was about to hang up, but then asked, "Were either William or Bonnie at the center yesterday afternoon?"

"Both of them were here for lunch."

I thanked her profusely, then did a happy dance in the Volvo bucket seat. I was feeling pretty damn smug about my investigative skills. I possessed the same information that the police had with the added knowledge that someone had called the center yesterday from my phone, presumably while it was inside Orchid's suite.

There was, of course, the off chance that someone had used it somewhere else, but that someone would have had to be able to stuff it back inside the cushions where I discovered it. That someone would have had to do it deliberately, and that would mean there was an out and out plot to hide Orchid. Now, I was betting the answer was far simpler. My money was on Orchid.

Both Bonnie Chisholm and William DeForest resided in Lake Chinook, and both of them also lived in First Addition, not far from the Adult Community Center. I drove out of Dunthorpe and back to Lake Chinook proper, cruising through First Addition, admiring the Craftsman-style cottages, counting up the new developments of condos and larger homes that were muscling out some of the older, smaller houses. I wondered which place was home to the vandal who was giving Lorraine's friend such fits.

I drove past an apartment building undergoing major reconstruction, possibly in the throes of a condo conversion. The builder's name was on a sign with a telephone number. Someone had tossed eggs at it, and the yellow, runny yolk had slid over the letters and numbers in a nasty obscuring slime. I realized the apartments were owned by the guy I knew. If I needed more information, I would contact him and see who he thought was behind the vandalism.

Bonnie Chisholm's house was a dilapidated cottage about four blocks from the Adult Community Center. A fortyish man was mowing the front yard using a push mower. He was making small headway against a thriving field of daisies and buttercups, but he seemed determined. Laurel bushes looked like they were about to swallow the house from all sides. He was going to need serious clippers to get those monsters under control.

I pulled in the drive. When the man turned his mower in my direction he looked up at me and frowned.

I got out of the car. He mowed to the edge of the driveway and stopped. "I'm looking for Bonnie Chisholm."

He was in pretty good shape, a tad paunchy maybe. Wiping his brow with the back of his wrist, he said, "My mom's at a doctor's appointment. Something I can help you with?"

"I'm working for the Purcell family. We're trying to locate Orchid Purcell, who's a friend of your mother's. She's missing. Have you seen it on the news?"

"No. What happened?"

"We don't really know. She seems to have walked away from the family home."

"She the one who's batty?"

"She's suffering from some dementia," I agreed.

He leaned against the mower's handle. "I don't think my mom likes her much. She's always complaining about her. The Purcell woman thinks she's too good for everybody, or something. They're all just old and kinda, you know . . ." He twirled a finger beside his ear.

"Think I could talk to your mom later on?"

"Sure." He shrugged. "She'll be back later this afternoon."

"I'll try to stop back by."

Clearly the police hadn't checked with Bonnie, yet. Or, if
they'd tried, they hadn't connected. I climbed back in the Volvo
and headed to William's house, which was on a corner lot and
built of red brick faded to a rose color. It was a two-story, commanding residence with high, mullioned windows and a mansard
roof. It looked out of place among the cottages and I felt it must
be far newer than its appearance would lead you to believe. The
yard was manicured and edged. Little mushroom-shaped lights
lined the walkway to the front door, which was surrounded by
narrow, beveled windows—lights, as they're called in building
parlance. The doorbell was a brass lion's head with a lighted circle in its mouth. I pressed it and listened to a long, tolling peal fit
for announcing His Royal Highness.

It took awhile to get any response. I rang again and was about
to push the bell for a third time when I saw movement through
the sidelights. I half-expected some somber butler, or a maid in a
black dress with a frilly white cap and apron to open the door.
Instead I got a stooped, older gentleman in a dove gray sweater
and matching slacks. His hair, too, was gray—what was left of
it—and it lay in greased-down, comb-over strands across his
head. He wore wire-rim glasses, rather natty and hip, and he
looked straight at me through suspicious, intelligent blue eyes.

He opened the door a crack and asked, "May I help you?"

"Are you William DeForest?"

"Yes. Who might you be?"

I introduced myself to him as I had to Bonnie's son. William's
eyes assessed me with unwavering criticism as I gave my spiel. I
was therefore surprised when he suddenly swung the door wide
and bade me to follow him down a hall to the TV room.

He swept some books and papers from a leather La-Z-Boy for
me, then settled himself onto a couch covered with a red and
green knitted afghan. The La-Z-Boy's leather felt warm, as if
a body had recently been sitting in it. The Daily Crossword was
folded, half done, and left on a nearby table next to a pair of
glasses.

"I haven't had the TV on today," William said. "I didn't know about Orchid. Wha'd she do? Walk off again?"

"Again?"

His brows were gray and bushy. When he drew them together he looked like a Schnauzer in glasses. "Didn't they tell you? She's wandered off a time or two. Damn near fell over the cliff once. That caretaker girl caught her, but one of the family was supposed to be watching her." He smiled smugly. "I called the police myself, that time, when Orchid told me. Warned them about her kids."

"She's actually wandered off the grounds before?" I was picking my way carefully, trying to discern what was real and what wasn't. I hadn't heard that from the Purcells. And William struck me as the kind of guy who liked to embellish and place himself in the hero role at every opportunity.

"Now, I didn't say that. You're putting words in my mouth, girl. But Orchid's not the lady she once was, more's the pity. Still a beautiful woman, but she's confused a lot now."

"You've known her a while."

"I've known her a hundred years." He chuckled. "Knew Percy—James—too. What a rascal. You know about him, don't ya? Him and his little ladies?"

"I . . . don't think so."

He flapped a hand at me. "Well, it's all old news now. Orchid's a fine woman, but she deserved better. And after what he did to his own flesh and blood. Sending her to that place. I felt sorry that Violet left, too."

"You mean . . . Lily?"

William gave me a sharp look. "Percy didn't want to admit that Lily was just like him. That's why she went to the Haven of Rest."

I was a bit confused, wondering if this was his euphemism for death. "He thought she was just like him how?"

"Didn't I just say? Couldn't keep her pants on."

"I'm sorry. I was under the impression that Lily was meek and mild."

"Who told you that?"

"Her son. Jasper."

He snorted. "Well, he never met her, did he? 'Course Orchid didn't want to believe it. She argued with Percy. She didn't want him to send her there, and she was right, as it turned out. Look what happened. The girl barely gets there and she's knocked up and then killed. They could've named it better, couldn't they? Haven of Rest. Stupid."

It felt like we were having two conversations. "Lily went to River Shores Sanitarium."

"Well, sure. They fancied up the name after the scandal, but it's the same place. Lily died at the Haven of Rest. Not exactly good for business, you know?" He gave a short bark of laughter. "Some bright boy musta pointed out that it would be a good idea to change completely, sweep all the bad stuff under the rug. Poor Lily got forgotten."

"Jazz said it was Orchid who made sure he was part of the family, that he had the Purcell name."

"Well, it wasn't Percy," William allowed. "But he never got over it anyway. I guess he thought he was doing the right thing, but it killed him in the end. A lot of things happened. And I don't think Orchid ever forgave him. When he died, there wasn't a lot of mourning."

"You seem to be pretty well informed."

He skewered me with a look. "Can I trust you with a secret?"

"Sure," I lied. I always say the same thing when someone asks me that question. I mean, come on, if it's a secret about something illegal, I'll be the first to spill. If it's not, I sort of choose whether to tell or not. This is why I believe there are no real secrets. People just can't keep them, and they don't want to anyway.

He leaned in toward me, and I leaned in toward him. "Orchid and I have been in love for years."

"Really."

"Oh, it isn't the kind of cheap, tawdry thing that Percy indulged in. And it's not the kinda sick thing that"—he stumbled a moment, then glanced at the dark, blank eye of the television screen—"you see on TV all the time now. It's just something we both know. But Orchid didn't want her family to know about us, so it's been something we kept to ourselves."

"I see."

"You don't believe me?"

"I'm just wondering why you don't seem really worried that Orchid's missing, since you're so in love."

"Of course I'm worried! I'm terribly worried." Color swept up his neck. "Damn, girl. Orchid's everything to me. They took away her phone and kept her from seeing me. It's been months. I don't know how you can accuse me of not caring."

"I stand mistaken," I said.

"Well, I should say."

We both sat in silence for a few moments. I was pretty sure William wanted to throw me out on my ear, but he seemed to be fighting his own impulse. After a long few minutes, he said stiffly, "You should go on down to that place and see for yourself."

"River Shores?"

"Fancy schmancy," he muttered. "Yeah, that place."

"I might just do that," I said, watching him. I couldn't tell exactly what was going on, if he was giving me a clue or just trying to dismiss me.

I left a few moments later. It was getting long after lunch and my stomach was growling. I went home to Binks and leftover pizza, and gave Lorraine a call to get the particulars on her friend's house. It wasn't that far from William's, so I decided to do a bit of surveillance after the sun went down.

I was planning my stakeout wardrobe—pretty much my usual everyday wear—when my cell phone buzzed. Again I didn't immediately recognize the number on Caller ID, though it was a 503 prefix which meant it was somewhere in the Greater Portland area. "Hello?" I answered.

"Is this Jane Kelly?" a female voice asked.

"Uh huh."

"This is Eileen Knopf. You called me?"

I'd been critically examining my jeans, determining if they needed a trip to the wash. Now, I zeroed in on the conversation. "Oh, yes. Hi," I said enthusiastically. "I'm working for the Purcells, and I'm—"

"You're an employee of theirs?" she cut me off.

"Well . . . of sorts . . ."

She snorted. "Be careful they don't accuse you of theft or worse. Orchid's a lovely woman but the rest of them aren't worth two cents. Except maybe Jazz," she added grudgingly. "He's at least nice. They don't care about Orchid at all. They're just waiting for her to die. And since you've probably already heard, the jewelry she gave me was a gift. And it was costume jewelry. Just *stuff*. But they act as if I stole the family's heirlooms. I say good riddance to all of them, and I hope Orchid's all right. Have you checked the playhouse? She seems to have an obsession with it. She's wandered before and I've found her there."

"The playhouse was checked. It was empty."

"Yeah? Well . . . that would be my guess."

The playhouse had been scoured by me and numerous Purcells, but her words brought up an interesting point. "Do you know why Orchid is drawn to the playhouse?"

"God, no. But she's haunted by it. I've found her crying there, more than once."

I tried to quiz Eileen more about the Purcells but apparently I'd tapped her out. She was far more interested in defending her own innocence. Just before we hung up I asked her about both Bonnie Chisholm and William DeForest.

"Orchid has a love/hate relationship with Bonnie. Two little old ladies trying to up one another, but Orchid had the money and prestige. Bonnie's kind of . . . sour. William thinks he's God's gift to women, and they fawn over him. The only able-bodied male who hangs out at the Community Center, I guess, and I think he has some money. Bonnie always tries to catch his eye, but he's all about Orchid."

"He intimated they've been friends, maybe even lovers."

She laughed. "In his own fantasy world. Orchid's too prim.

She did confuse him once for Percy, and that time she hauled off and hit him right across the face. Crack! I mean, I thought he might lose some teeth. Then she screamed, 'It's your fault she left.' She's never forgiven Percy for sending Lily away."

I thought of something else. "Does she ever call Lily Violet?"

"Yes." Eileen sounded surprised. "How did you know?"

"William said the same thing."

"He's a sweetie but such a putz. He parrots anything Orchid says. He's just like that."

"Thanks."

I hung up lost in thought. I'd been getting a lot of information about the Purcells although I wasn't certain any of it was truly helping me. Hearing Dwayne's voice in my head yammering about hard copy, I spent the rest of the afternoon and early evening writing down my new information, adding in William and Bonnie and the discovery of James's knife paintings. It was really an exercise in futility as I had no client to bill, but it made me feel productive. As soon as we both had some time, I was going to talk the case over with Dwayne.

About seven that night I grabbed my soft-sided, blue, insulated cooler and stuffed in a water bottle and the last of the now foil-wrapped pizza. What I wouldn't give for a salad. Sometimes my diet worries me. I wondered if I could talk Jazz into taking me out to some really healthy restaurant with lots of veggies, especially sprouts. I am not a sprout eater by nature, but having grown up in SoCal I feel it's an homage to my roots. Actually, that's a lie. I never want to eat sprouts. I made a mental note to drop them from my list of edible food, right alongside field greens.

I parked the Volvo about a half a block from Lorraine's friend's residence, just around a corner. First Addition is laid out in blocks with no sidewalks. The yards just sort of peter out into the roads with maybe a scattered edging of gravel. You'd think somebody would scream at the city to put in curbs and walkways, but it seems to be a source of pride to the inhabitants to keep it as it is and was.

There were other cars parked around, some of them in drive-ways, some of them jutted onto the grassy edges of their lawn. Many of the homes do not have garages. Others can be accessed by rutted, gravel alleys that bisect the blocks, so that the homes' garages face each other, and the houses face each other as well across the streets.

Lorraine's friend lived on a corner lot and it looked to me like she'd made the colossal mistake of adding a second story with high gables, higher than William's house by a number of feet. She'd edged her yard with a low, stone fence, and the driveway was new concrete that fanned toward the street, crowned by an asphalt apron. She'd also hacked away at a couple of once drap-ing cedars, probably to save her roof and gutters. I bet that really got the other residents' panties in a twist. Trees were more valu-able than children around here sometimes.

The overall impression of the home was of a well-tended, beautifully appointed house whose owner cared for it. It was hard to see what the ruckus was all about, but then what do I know when it comes to neighborhood politics. My landlord, Mr. Ogilvy, seems to be at war with the City of Lake Chinook on principle. He's "parked" his trees over the years, turning them into tele-phone poles with frilly green tops. It's saved him a lot of ground maintenance and given me a better view out my back window to the bay. I'm sure I have the wrong attitude, but I just keep my mouth shut whenever a group of Lake Chinookers start com-plaining about how people aren't saving the trees, the lake, the atmosphere and/or Mother Nature in general.

I have become a dog person, however. That also seems to count for a lot around here.

I settled into my seat. My view through the windshield cap-tured two sides of the house, and I could see partway down the alley. If anyone sneaked around the back side I would see them. If they were bold enough to show up at the front of the house, I would miss them, but I was pretty sure the vandals were cowards who would choose darkness and stealth.

I wasn't sure how many hours I wanted to devote to this endeavor. Stakeouts are notoriously boring. Without the proper zen attitude a person could snap. I used the time to half-nap, my thoughts zigging and zagging alone different lines.

About an hour and a half into my vigil I saw a circle of light bobbing along the back alley. A flashlight. My attention sharpened. Was I lucky enough to catch the perp on my first try?

Slouching in my seat, I peered through the darkness. I'd wrapped my hair in a black stocking cap and I hoped the lightness of my face didn't show much through the window.

The newcomer shined the light on the back of the house. I was poised, every muscle ready for action. I wasn't sure exactly what I was going to do, but one thing I knew, I was going to find out who this guy was.

And then the flashlight circle returned to the ground and jerkily headed my way. I sank my head into my shoulders. A moment later I saw the perp was a neighbor who'd chosen the alley as the route home. Was he my guy? He was singing to himself and stumbling a bit. In fact, as I watched I realized he was dead drunk. He tripped over a loose stone at the edge of his lawn, swore good-naturedly, righted himself and dug in his pockets for his keys. He suddenly threw back his head and screamed the refrain from Bon Jovi's "Livin' on a Prayer." At least I think it was. Several dogs started barking and howling.

Not him.

Disappointed, I settled back down, but the adrenaline spike in my bloodstream had made me itchy and anxious. After a couple of minutes I got out, locking the car behind me. I just couldn't stand it; I had to move. I left my post to take a brisk stroll around the neighborhood, sensing that my surveillance was an exercise in futility anyway, at least for tonight. Exercise seemed like a much better alternative, so I made a large circle around the blocks. The streets are letters one way, numbers the other. I started out on F and 9th and made my way to A and 3rd before heading back again, and I made a point of turning by William's house.

The warmth of the La-Z-Boy seat came back to me. Someone, or something, had been sitting in it moments before I came in. It hadn't been William because there were papers and books placed on the seat. Why would he put them there, if he was just getting up to answer the door? What was the point, unless he was trying to hide something, say, the fact that a guest had been sitting there? And the guy was pretty spry, too. What had taken him so long to answer the door? There was definitely some subterfuge going on. Who'd been with him? I wondered. Someone who called the Adult Community Center looking for him, perhaps?

And what about those eyeglasses . . . hadn't they had blue frames? Didn't they look a lot like Orchid's?

I glanced at my watch. Its glowing LCD said it was about ten P.M. I punched out Nate's number and waited for him to answer. I didn't think it was too late to call, and I decided I didn't care if it was. He picked up on the fourth ring.

"Yo," he said sleepily.

"Sorry, did I wake you? It's Jane Kelly. I'm the private investigator searching for Orchid Purcell?"

"Oh, yeah, sure. I just fell asleep playing Fissure. Ever played it? It's like Los Angeles falls into the San Andreas fault, and then it just keeps cracking. You're trying to stay alive but the world's coming to an end. Ya gotta stay ahead of the game. Cool."

"Sounds exciting," I said, wondering how you snooze through the end of the world. "I was thinking about Lover's Lane . . . the Purcells' driveway?"

"You want me to go check it?" He sounded suddenly wide awake.

"Actually, I just wanted to know if you could describe the last few cars you saw there."

"What's it to ya?" he asked.

"Part of my investigation."

"Well . . ." I waited while he seemed to tick through his thoughts. I could picture him sprawled on some couch, a Mariner's cap smashed atop his red curls, video game controllers surrounding him, chasms on the TV screen opening into a nightmarish hell of molten fire and smoke as people were falling and screaming as the ground broke up beneath their feet. "I mighta seen some yesterday," he admitted.

"Can you tell me about them?"

"Do you want to know about the nighttime ones, or the one I saw in the daytime?"

My attention sharpened. "Let's start with the daytime one."

"A parent car. Sedan. Buick, I think. Maybe ten years old. Light green or tan. Really bad. My parents drove that, I'd walk."

"You didn't tell me this earlier."

"Hey, I didn't know you then."

Yeah, like we were longtime buddies now. "Tell me about the nighttime ones," I said, but I only listened with half an ear because they were all newer vehicles with way more pizzazz that just screamed young people.

I had a feeling William DeForest might drive an older-model Buick.

I got off the phone from Nate as soon as I could. Since I'd awakened him, he seemed to be in a chatty mood. Maybe Fissure wasn't as all consuming as he made it sound, or maybe he just enjoyed the idea of talking to a real, live P.I., even if I was female.

The lights were off in William's house except for the TV room around the back. He had a high enough wooden fence surrounding that part of the yard that I couldn't see inside. I glanced around for an object to climb atop, but there was nothing. I could have maybe tried a neighbor's tree, but none of the lower limbs looked all that accessible.

I jogged back to my car. I was about to slip my key in the lock when I saw movement behind Lorraine's friend's house. I stared in disbelief. Damn it all to hell. *Now*, he shows?

Cursing my luck, I stealthily crept forward. I had a feeling William was hiding Orchid. I would bet my bottom dollar she was his guest for reasons I could guess at. Most likely he wanted to get back at the family for keeping her from him. Maybe it had even been Orchid's idea. I could just see her toddling down the exit lane, in cahoots with her good friend William. Maybe they got a big laugh about it. Whatever the case, I was going to have to wait until I took care of my vandal buddy before I could find out.

As I approached I heard the metallic rattle of the mixing ball inside a paint can as he warmed to his task. Indeed it was my neighborhood eco-terrorist. Graffiti tonight, apparently. I heard the *pfffttt* as the spray started. Tiptoeing close, I rued the fact that once again I was weaponless. Mace would have been nice. The cool kind that comes in those classy neon-colored containers. Or, maybe stainless steel. Gotta get me one of those.

He was around the corner, alley-side, just out of my sight. My Nikes moved noiselessly across the grass. I wouldn't be able to disguise my arrival as soon as I hit the alley gravel. After a moment of hesitation I made an executive decision: I ran at his black-clad figure, yelling at the top of my lungs.

"Fuck!" he cried in shock. I hadn't intended to hurl myself on him. I'm just not that into physical contact. But my momentum drove me forward and when I tried to stop, one foot jammed and sent me at him in a flying tackle. I hit him with an *ooof* and we went down in a heap.

He started punching and swearing. That pissed me off. And *hurt*. I clawed and twisted and threw elbows. The impotence I'd felt over the whole Orchid ordeal turned to rage. I wanted to jam my knee into this guy's groin. I went after him like my life depended on it. He seemed to sense my fury and it must have convinced him I meant business because he scrambled along the ground belly-down, protecting the family jewels. I was on his back, grunting and pounding like an animal. "I'll kill you," I gritted out in a voice I didn't recognize as my own.

He stilled instantly. All you could hear was our twin breathing.

Half a block away I heard faintly, "Ohhh-ohhhh, livin' on a prayer . . . livin' on a *prayer!*"

"Who are you?" my captive muttered against the ground.

The voice was familiar.

It was the lawn mower man, Bonnie Chisholm's son.

Chapter Ten

I climbed off his back, staggering to my feet. Now that I had his identity, the rest would be easy. My heart was still beating hard from exhilaration and a certain amount of fear. His flashlight was sending illumination toward the back of the fence where he'd written *McMansions are for frying* in orange Day-Glo.

"You were gonna torch this place," I accused.

He tried to get up but I placed my Nike firmly on the back of his neck. "No, no!" he denied. "It was just a threat. Just to stop all this building madness. Everyone's sick of it. Nothing was going to happen. Really. It was just to let them know."

"Let them know?"

"That making things bigger doesn't make it better!" He was breathing hard, scared maybe, or incensed. My anger was cooling a bit now that I had him under control. I was starting to think it might be a good idea to make tracks before he figured out who I was. Once he was released he could start thinking how unfair it was, how embarrassing. Anybody who'd sneak around and create havoc like he did wasn't likely to suddenly have an epiphany and be grateful that he'd been shown the error of his ways. More than likely, he'd stew and stew until he came up with some method of retaliation. And I didn't want him retaliating against me.

"Don't move for five minutes, or I'll call the cops," I threatened. Then I took my shoe from his neck. He was trembling, but he stayed on the ground.

"Who are you?" he asked again.

"What's it to ya?" I responded, then I ran lightly away, opposite of my car and Bonnie Chisholm's house and in the direction of William DeForest's.

If a stakeout is bad in the comfort of one's car, it's murder on a crisp to chilly night, standing on one's feet. I tucked myself into a dark corner nearby William's house, next to a hedge of arborvitae and the blasted fence I couldn't scale. Soon my limbs grew numb. I wished I could get a look inside William's garage but the doors were windowless. The whole place was shut up tight.

If I'd been able to I would have given up and driven home, hoping I would be hit by inspiration in the course of the night. But I wanted to stay away from my car as long as possible, in case Chisholm decided he remembered me and my vehicle. Luckily, he hadn't seemed to recognize my voice, and my older, slightly dirty, blue Volvo wagon fits into the First Addition landscape without causing a second look.

A part of me felt like simply laying on the doorbell, waiting for William to admit me, then brushing past him to search every nook and cranny of his house. Would he call the cops on me? Not if he was harboring Orchid. But if I was wrong I didn't relish the idea of going over my crime with the LCPD. I imagine that would constitute a trip to the county jail. No, thank you.

Another part of me debated on calling Dwayne and asking for backup, or at the very least, advice. But honestly, I wanted to figure this out myself. I had William's phone number. I could give the sly weasel a ring-a-ling.

And then what . . . ?

I thought about it for another ten minutes, then placed the call. It took him a while to answer and he sounded pretty groggy. "Your car was seen . . ." I hissed into the phone, then I clicked off. Maybe he had Caller ID, but even if he did I was betting my cell phone didn't cough up my name. I half-expected him to call me back, but joy of joys, a few minutes later lights came on in the upper floor. I could see the progression of illumination as he moved down the hall toward, I suspected, the stairway. Was he heading to the garage? I waited on pins and needles. Sure enough, suddenly there was a thin band of light showing beneath the garage door.

Gotcha.

I could hear voices. And then the garage door started to swing upward as William fired up his car. I squeezed back into my hiding place, eyes peeled. Moments later a pale green Buick backed slowly out of the drive, damn near taking out one of the arborvitae. I pulled back. The guy wasn't exactly a driving ace.

And then I saw Orchid sitting beside him in the passenger seat, big as life.

They put-putted away. I counted to five . . . well, it was more like ten 'cause they weren't exactly burning rubber . . . then I dashed to my car, on the lookout for Chisholm just in case. But I was fast and it was easy to pick up Orchid and William's trail. It was much harder to stay a discreet distance behind so they wouldn't realize they were being followed.

I was annoyed with William. The old coot had given us all a terrible couple of days! But I was gratified Orchid was all right. And I was thrilled beyond thrilled that I would be able to take the guilt off myself. It wasn't my fault she'd gone missing. Hell, they were probably in it together, giggling like schoolkids about their caper.

It didn't take a rocket scientist to see they were headed to Dunthorpe and the Purcell home. I tootled along behind them. La, la, la, la, la. I was far enough back that I didn't see them actually turn into the entrance drive, but I cut my engine and rolled down my window and then I could hear William's engine as his Buick moved farther down the lane. So, he was taking her home.

I yanked my wheel to follow them. I was sure as hell going to be there when the family realized she was back. This I had to see.

William was still helping Orchid out of the car when I screeched

up beside them, jamming on my brakes with a jolt just to let
them know I'd arrived. They both turned my way, eyes wide.

"Now, now," William said as I slammed out of my car. He put
a protective arm around Orchid, who lifted a hand to touch his.

"Nice of you to tell me," I said to him.

"I was going to bring her back. She just needed some time,
didn't you, dear?"

Orchid's gaze was on the house. I couldn't tell if she was happy
to be back or not. "It's always good to take time . . ." she said
vaguely.

The back porch light flashed on. The door opened and
Cammie looked out. I hadn't paid attention to the other cars
parked outside the portico, but Cammie's black Range Rover
was still jockeyed next to one of the Purcell sports cars. "Nana!"
she exclaimed in shock, one hand to her chest. Then, arms out-
stretched, she flew to her grandmother's side.

If she wasn't truly glad to see her it was masterful acting.
Whatever else Cammie was, she certainly seemed to care about
Nana.

From there Orchid was bundled inside to the bosom of the
family. William and I brought up the rear. Cammie's cries of delight were heard by the rest of the family, who rushed around
throwing on bathrobes and slippers, or in Satin's case, strolled in
from the den fully dressed but more than a little sloshed. So,
Billy Leonard was right: she was a drinker. She hiccupped a couple of times, earned a sharp glare from her husband, and took
herself upstairs, hanging tightly to the rail as she ascended.

Questions rained from all sides. Where had Orchid been? Who
found her? Did she wander off? Was she all right? Had she had
enough to eat? My God, she scared them to death! Who was to
blame for all of this?

William wasn't ready to cop to anything. I wanted to blab that
I'd found her, that it was because of me that the old joker had decided to bring her back, that if I hadn't pressured him, he could
have squirreled her away forever, which I fully believe he in-

tended to do. I feel I showed admirable restraint in merely clenching my teeth in a grimacing smile and pinning my hard glare on William, daring him to take any credit at all.

He tried, the wily snake. "Orchid was *sooooo* unhappy. I didn't know you thought she was missing, otherwise I would have called you all right away."

Utter bullshit. I glanced around to see how the Purcells were taking this. They seemed baffled on how to proceed. A thoughtful frown on her face, Cammie ushered us into the salon while Dahlia headed to the kitchen to put a pot of coffee on.

Orchid settled into a chair, blinking and murmuring about being back home. She seemed happy enough, but there was a wild look around her eyes as her family pressed in closer. I didn't blame her. I asked if anyone had called Jazz, but none of them were listening to me, so I placed the call myself, disappointed to get his voice mail. I left him the news, glad I hadn't seriously believed he could be involved in Orchid's disappearance.

Meanwhile, William was insisting that Orchid had called him and begged to be liberated. What was he to do but come to her rescue? This explanation was greeted with shock and shared looks of consternation among the Purcells. How? On what phone? There was no phone in her suite of rooms; they'd made certain of that. Had she used the hall phone? When had she gone downstairs? As she was leaving the house? How come nobody happened upon her?

I didn't enlighten them about my cell phone. I figured I didn't owe them any explanations, and I don't think William really knew. I would have liked to talk to Orchid alone and see if I could glean anything further, but that wasn't going to happen. She was besieged by her family. Someone, James, I think, finally suggested that she be taken upstairs, and then there was a mad dash to be the "bestest" family member, the one who showed Nana the most care. Garrett won. "Come on, Mother," he said, surprisingly tender as he reached for Orchid's hands, which she held out dutifully. He helped her to her feet and guided her toward the door at the same moment Jazz buzzed me back. I gave him the news about Nana. He was thrilled beyond thrilled and was ready to head right over. I told him Nana was being tucked into bed, but it didn't deter him. He promised to be there in twenty minutes, maybe fifteen.

"Thank you, Jane," he said effusively. It was gratifying to know he, at least, assumed I'd been the one to find Orchid.

While Nana was being helped to bed, Dahlia passed around cups of coffee. I dutifully drank mine, wondering if the caffeine would keep me awake all night. Sometimes it does, sometimes I'm immune. I suspected this might be one of those immune times because I was starting to feel really, really tired. Every bump and bruise I'd sustained in my skirmish with Chisholm suddenly seemed to come alive. My right shoulder, still tender from its injuries a few months earlier, felt weak; my arm leaden. My face and jaw were sore. My right elbow throbbed. I'd been running on pure energy for a while. These adrenaline highs are killers; there's always the piper to pay afterward, a downward spiral that sinks into a hangover worth four martinis or more. I had a feeling tomorrow morning might be a tough one, but at least Orchid was no longer missing. That was worth every scrape and bruise.

I'd sort of drifted into my own world so I was surprised when Cammie suddenly said, albeit a bit grudgingly, "It sounds like we have you to thank, Jane."

I gazed at her and hoped I didn't look too amazed. Jazz, okay, but Cammie? She'd never shown the least bit of compassion or graciousness before.

William objected, "What do you mean? I brought her back! *I* kept her safe."

"You met her at the end of the lane and hid her from us," Roderick pointed out. "It's pretty clear Jane flushed you out."

William's mouth dropped open. "Orchid wanted to be with me!"

Garrett caught the tail end as he returned to the salon. "We don't appreciate any of this." He threw a look my way, just to let me know *he* didn't think I deserved any credit, but he was pissed at William. "We're glad she's home, Mr. DeForest, but your choices were ill-advised."

William's skin turned a mottled red. In his world, I suspect he'd fancied himself the hero. "Well, you were ill-advised in keeping her locked up in her room!"

"Let's move on," Cammie said wearily.

"And cut out the melodrama," agreed Garrett. He said to me, curtly, "Though I'm glad you found my mother, this has all been a huge embarrassment and waste of energy and time. I'm sure Jazz would agree it's time for our family to be involved in its own problems."

"She just needed a break," William insisted. "Some sunshine and friendship." He was totally torqued.

"You're lucky we're not pressing charges against you," Garrett told him through tight lips.

"Charges?"

"She was missing for two days. As far as we knew, she was kidnapped."

I thought William might have a stroke. He glared balefully around the room, his expression landing on James. "What about you?" he demanded. "You're going to still let your brother speak for you? Make all your decisions?"

James frowned. "Garrett's right, Mr. DeForest. We were worried sick about Nana."

"Sure."

"I'm tired," Dahlia said, and truthfully, she looked done in. "Let's all go to bed."

William seemed disinclined to leave, but the family inexorably moved him to the entry hall and the back door. Garrett went to phone the authorities and let them know Orchid was home. I followed the tide, glad to have the evening come to a close.

I was dead on my feet.

Benjamin, who'd hovered in the background throughout the proceedings, caught up with me. "Did you get in a fight?" he asked.

I hesitated, halfway through the door to the porch. Touching my face, I wondered what I looked like. "Something the matter?"

He shrugged, catlike, his brown eyes dark beneath the entry hall chandelier's uncertain light. "I guess not."

I drove home with exhaustion weighing on me. I half-expected the Lake Chinook police to pull me over on general principles. It was after midnight and once you hit the witching hour, all you have to do is drive through the center of town to risk being pulled over on some minor infraction. A favorite of theirs is "you were weaving" or "you crossed the center line." This is a ploy to check to see if you've been drinking. But tonight the streets were devoid of any kind of activity. No cars, no pedestrians, no cops. The traffic lights glowed in lines of green, and it felt like I was the last person on the planet.

When I got home Binkster didn't even have the courtesy to get up and greet me. She was tucked into her little bed in my bedroom. She did switch her tail back and forth a couple of times, and when I crooked my finger she staggered toward me for a chance to climb into my bed. I picked her up and lifted the covers, which she nuzzled underneath, and she headed for the foot of the bed.

When I looked at my reflection in the bathroom mirror I saw what Benjamin had been talking about. A streak of dirt ran across my right cheekbone, and my skin was hot pink in patches, as if it had been scraped hard.

I took off my shirt and saw I had a bleeding strawberry on my elbow. I was bound to feel the effects of rolling around on the ground. Bruises would surface. Still, there was satisfaction in catching Chisholm in the act.

I cleaned myself up and joined Binks in bed.

* * *

In the morning I pulled one eye open. Groaning, I rolled out of bed, crying out from pain at the trophies I'd received from tackling and wrestling with Chisholm. Gritting my teeth, I forced a stretch, then threw on my running gear and jogged my usual route to the Coffee Nook. It hurt like hell, pain in every jarring movement. Once again I wondered about Dwayne's belief in me as an information specialist/private investigator. I'm not really great at the whole pain and torture thing, and unfortunately catching bad guys had a certain amount of that built right into the equation.

It was Saturday, so teenagers were manning the store instead of Julie and Jenny. Several girls' soccer teams seemed to have taken over the chairs and the order of the day was hot chocolate with plenty of whipped cream. I got my usual black coffee, belted it down, then walked the nearly three miles back to my cottage. While I chomped down cold pizza, Binkster ate her kiblets, then went outside to relieve herself.

I called Dwayne and gave him the news about Orchid. He was relieved for me and also in a mood to talk, so I didn't have a chance immediately to tell him of the rest of my night's exploits. He was working on some new case that involved robbery, but I wanted to know how it went with Spence.

"We had a small argument over money," Dwayne replied to my query. "He wanted some of his retainer back, and I said no. Sometimes it happens that way. He started to become unreasonable, so we had to have an attitude adjustment talk."

"How'd that go?"

"About what you'd expect from a lawyer who's cheating on his wife. There were veiled threats on his side. Out and out ones on mine. I should've charged him more for the aggravation." Dwayne sounded as if it were all in a day's work.

"Which reminds me: what are our rates?" I asked. "The question came up, and I didn't have an answer."

"Darlin', I don't have rates. You can, if you want," he added magnanimously.

"Well, how does it work, then? I mean, if we're going to be in business together, I need to know these things."

"Here's how I look at it. Each job is its own entity. Each client has his or her own problems. Now, you can give 'em an hourly rate if you want, but they start bitching and moaning almost instantly, watching every minute that goes by. When I meet with a potential client, I assess them and tell them straight up what the job'll cost. If they don't like it, they leave. Otherwise, they pay me up front. If the job turns out to be easier than I thought, I may renegotiate and refund some money. If it's harder, I just take it in the shorts."

"How often does that happen?"

"Never." I could hear the smile in his voice. "Make it worth your while at the outset. And be clear that you get paid whether there are results or not, and whatever those results are. Some people get pissed if things don't turn out the way they wanted them to. Spence is a case in point."

"What happened?"

"He didn't really believe honey-bunch would look for some other guy when he wasn't coming home at night. Some guys just don't get it. What was good for the gander, apparently wasn't good for the goose, in his opinion. Spence never dreamed she'd start sniffing around."

"But he was the one who had the affair first," I said.

"Yep. But you forget the male ego. It's easily bruised."

"He was so blatant about it!"

"Doesn't matter. Spence is burned now. He broke it off with his lover. Now, everybody's mad."

"I wonder how Miriam's doing," I said, remembering how heartbroken she was upon learning what a schmuck Trev was. "I hope she got some of her money back."

Dwayne said, "Their problems are just beginning. Spence cut his losses with Janice but now, if he had a lick of sense, he should beg for forgiveness from his wife. But hell, I don't get paid to offer advice. It's all about reality. That's what he paid me for."

"He doesn't sound like the type to forget she had an affair."

"He isn't," Dwayne assured me.

I started considering the actual dollars and cents of the job. "I get a percentage of that, right?"

"Of course you do, darlin'."

Sometimes I love Dwayne.

It was my turn to talk, so I told him about my run-in with the First Addition vandal. "You actually attacked this guy?" Dwayne sounded both impressed and a bit horrified.

"More like I ran at him and tripped, but once I was in the fight there wasn't much else I could do but kick and punch."

"Feeling the effects today?" His voice sounded casual but I suspected he really wanted to know.

"I'm okay." This was essentially the truth, although even the scrape of a comb against my tender scalp had had me squinching up my face in pain. "I'm going to call Lorraine and give her his name. She can decide what action to take."

"Charge her four hundred."

"Really?" I find it difficult to bill friends for anything, even if they beg me for the figure. I'm cheap, yes. I love to wangle a free drink out of Jeff Foster at Foster's On The Lake, but when it comes to financial negotiation for my services, I feel strangely sheepish and embarrassed. Maybe it's an inferiority complex, like I believe I'm underqualified in everything I do. But then again, I wouldn't have any trouble demanding cash from Spence.

"You gotta make it worth your while," Dwayne said. "Sounds like you deserve hazard pay. You didn't get any payment up front?"

"I'm still learning."

He grunted. "Glad you're okay. You're tough, Jane. You were made for this stuff."

"Hah. You know I'm a chicken through and through."

"You can rise to the occasion."

"Do you want something from me?" I asked. "I get the feeling I'm being set up here. I mean, I'm not that good."

He laughed. "I trust you to troubleshoot your way through anything."

We were about to hang up, when I said, "Oh, one more thing—I put this in my report, the one I'm working on, haven't given you yet—when I was in James' room, I found some paintings that were—unsettling."

"What were they?"

"Knives. All of them."

I described a few of them to Dwayne, who thought that over for a while. "Sounds like the guy needs a serious head-shrinking."

"Yeah, it struck me that way, too. And . . ." I hadn't put this into words—I hadn't really had time to let the thought coalesce—but visualizing those images again, I added, "The paintings were phallic, sexual."

"A lot of art is," Dwayne said.

"They creeped me out."

"You think they have some special meaning?" he asked.

"All I know is, James doesn't leave the house much. The rest of them have other lives. Other homes. They have families outside of Orchid. But James is like this recluse." I shook off another attack of the willies. "Well, anyway, Orchid's back now, so I guess it doesn't matter how weird James is."

Dwayne snorted. "Goes with the Purcell territory."

After we hung up I called Lorraine and told her what I knew about Bonnie Chisholm's son. She decided to talk to her friend about how to proceed. When she asked me how much she owed me, I took a deep breath and said, "Four hundred dollars." She didn't even hesitate, just said she would drop a check in the mail. I gave her Dwayne Durbin Investigations' post office box address, and she told me it would be taken care of that afternoon. Afterward, I felt surprisingly energized. I mouthed to myself, "You're a private investigator, Jane Kelly," and decided things were pretty good.

It was going on eleven by that time, and I debated on whether to make today the day to go to River Shores. Should I even bother, now? So there were secrets floating through the Purcell family. Did I really care? Orchid was home, safe and sound. Jazz had initially hired me to evaluate her mental condition, to find out if she was capable of handling the family fortune, and that issue was resolved with Orchid's signature on the Power of Attorney.

And what would Jazz think of me if and when he learned I'd gone fishing for information on his family outside of what he'd requested? How would I explain myself? Still . . . I wanted to go. I was going to go. It defied reasoning, but I didn't care. In the end I thought "to hell with it" and changed into my loosely flowing tan skirt, brown sleeveless top and Cynthia's boots.

Before I left I attempted to cover my bruised cheek with makeup, but it wasn't much use. Binkster cocked her head in concern at my, "Ouch, ouch, goddamn it, *ouch!*" as I combed my hair, pulling it into a ponytail, with a little more finesse than my usual snap-it-up-and-forget-it job. As I headed out, the dog toddled after me and looked forlorn. "Next time," I told her. Even though I planned to be gone awhile, I didn't want to take her with me. I'd seen on the news where a woman in Milwaukie had lost her two black pugs when they were stolen out of her car. I've been slightly paranoid about leaving Binkster in the car ever since, especially if I'm not at someone's home.

Remembering I'd promised Cynthia I'd stop by her gallery, I drove into Portland first. The Black Swan is located in the Pearl District, which is in the northwest section of the city. What was once an area of warehouses and industrial buildings has become one of the chi-chi-est areas of town to live. Sort of like SoHo-Portland. Cynthia's gallery, a recent purchase for her, was located on a corner. I'd been there before, but not since she'd taken possession. Pulling into her tiny parking lot around the back, I muttered about the Chevrolet Tahoe crowding my space. Since when are those things a "compact"?

Cynthia's an artist herself, a watercolor painter whose favorite subjects seem to be wild animals of the fierce variety: jungle cats, fanged snakes, rhinos, unnamed creatures of the deep, etc. She puts a spot of humor in their poses as they peek out from behind some arty camouflage. I find them all mildly disturbing, and as I stepped through the front door and a little overhead bell *dinged* my arrival, my eyes searched the varying pieces of displayed art. Straight ahead was some kind of bear peering at me from behind bamboo. It was black and white, but it didn't look anything like a big, cuddly panda. There was something smug and treacherous in its gaze.

I thought about James's knives again and wondered about the artistic mind. Maybe it's just as well I'm so right-brained. Half the time I just don't get it.

I didn't immediately see Cynthia, so I strolled through the gallery. The Black Swan represents artists who use a variety of mediums. Someone named Kayla fashions glass into stemmed flowers and also paints glass pictures. A couple of months earlier Cynthia had given me a dozen red glass roses and they currently sit in a blue vase in a place of honor on my mantle. Now, I admired a glass picture of birds in a tree, keeping one eye on the bear. Looking at him from the corner of my eye, I swear he started grinning. I had to shake myself out of the heebie-jeebies.

There was a row of dark paintings lining the back wall depicting faintly human shapes engaged in varying positions of copulation. Tiny spotlights shone on these renditions, making them seem almost animated. I examined one closely, wondering if there were four bodies or five torqued around each other, their mouths either sucked onto another body's anatomical protrusion or open in an "O" of ecstasy. Oh, yeah. This would be just what I wanted in my living room with Mom on her way. Nothing says welcome to my home like ravening mouths, stiff penises and rock-hard nipples.

"I see you are engaged with *Eventide*. Does it speak to you?" a deep male voice inquired.

I turned around to see the newcomer. I would bet my money this was Ernst, the employee and artist who'd found his way into Cynthia's bed, much to her dismay. He was thin and dark and sneery with long fingers and even longer hair, greased or sprayed enough to be held back from his face like a mane. His nose was a beak; his eyes, dark brown, almost black. Was this what they call ugly-sexy? Because surprisingly, there was something compelling and male and predatory about him. Not that he appealed to me, but I did feel a faint pull at some baser female level.

"Ernst?" I asked.

"You could read my signature?" He was surprised.

"Actually, I'm a friend of Cynthia's. Jane Kelly." I stuck out my hand, which he stared at for a moment of heavy thought, then shook weakly. If I had a stereotypical "serious painter" mold inside my head, he would fit.

"Cynthia will be back soon." He waved vaguely toward the windows and the greater outdoors.

I now understood her great reluctance to admit that they were involved. Ernst wasn't exactly regular boyfriend material. His being an employee was only part of the problem. I would bet nothing good could come out of this, certainly nothing long term. But then, I suppose it's whatever you're looking for at any given time that matters. Honestly, I would find going to bed with him repellent, like cuddling up with a reptile.

My gaze slid toward the nasty bear painting. But then Cynthia's tastes ran a different path than my own.

We made some small talk. Very small, as we had absolutely nothing in common. I told him I liked to drink cheap wine and deliver eviction notices to deadbeat lessees; he said he liked sex.

When I heard the door open and saw Cynthia enter, I turned to her in relief. She took one look at Ernst and something flickered across her face. I swear to God it looked like anxiety. Cynthia? Who's always in such control?

"So, you got a chance to meet," she said.

"Sure did." I sounded bright and fake, as if I were hiding some big secret, but I couldn't help myself. Ernst made me feel dirty and sneaky.

Cynthia's gaze slid from me to Ernst. She was wearing a dark chestnut colored pantsuit that showed off her slim body. Her hair is short, dark and spiky and she always looks feminine-tough. I sometimes yearn to be more like her, but today Ernst was putting the kibosh on that big time.

"You have a lovely face," Ernst suddenly said to me. "So nat-

ural. And your body is athletic. Very firm and supple." His dark
gaze rippled over me. "You would make a good subject, but you
should really be more careful with your skin."

He reached a hand toward me and I pulled back automatically.
"Oh. My cheek. Yeah, I bruised it."

"No, this." He touched the side of my neck. "What have you
been doing?"

Damn curling iron. At least my burn apparently didn't look
like a hickey any longer. "It's the beautification ritual I engage in
each morning. Sometimes it's hazardous."

"Don't you think she would make a good subject, Cyn?" he
asked.

We both looked to her for her opinion. Now, I was the one
feeling anxious. Ernst was wormy and icky. I could sense that he
could ruin my friendship with "Cyn" without even trying.

"Oh, leave her alone." Cynthia went behind the massive,
baroque, carved oak desk and picked up some receipts. My anxiety level diminished a bit. She was on to his ways. "I'm glad
you're here, Jane. I'm dying for lunch. Let's grab something
around the corner. Have you got time?"

"Absolutely."

"Ernst, Mrs. Clooner's picking up the Suji painting. She said
she'd be here at one."

"The Suji's amateurish," he sneered.

"Don't piss her off. We'll be at Zen and Now," she added.
Cynthia grabbed my arm and steered me out the door and down
the street to a pan-Asian restaurant known for its sushi. I was so
relieved Cynthia seemed to realize I had no interest in Ernst that
I let myself be dragged to the restaurant without protest. Sushi
and I aren't on the best of terms. It's something I'm learning to
like, but apart from California rolls, I'm highly suspect of the in-
gredients.

"What's the deal with Ernst?" I asked as Cynthia and I were
guided to a wooden booth at the end of a row of such booths.
Above our heads red sailcloth partitions divided us from the customers dining on either side of us.

"I'm losing my mind. Why do I like him? Why do I do it? I don't know. I really don't."

"So, things aren't going any better than before?" A waitress passed by carrying a fish with head and tail still attached. The fish gazed balefully at me though dull, puckered eyes.

"I don't have an explanation," Cynthia went on, snapping open her menu.

"Maybe you like him."

"No, that's not it."

"Maybe he's fine for now."

"Jane, he's never fine."

I shrugged. "All right, I'm out of options." I was also a little horrified by the prices. If I'm going to pay that much for food it better be damn good.

"I'm going to have to let him go. I can't work with him. It's not fair, I know, but it can't go on this way. He makes me crazy." The waitress came by and looked at us expectantly. I chose the California rolls and Cynthia ordered eel and a rainbow roll, which was beautiful when it arrived—red, watermelon, green, white— but I could tell it was layers of raw fish and avocado. "Here, have some," she said, dropping a pale white section of fish wrapped around rice on my plate. She was distracted, lost in her own personal dating hell, so she didn't notice my lack of enthusiasm. I smothered the thing in as much wasabi as I dared, soaked it in soy sauce, then chewed carefully. I gotta say, it was okay.

Cynthia nibbled on dark red raw tuna. I retreated to my California rolls—rice, crab, a little avocado. Safe. "I'm going to break it off soon," she decided at the end of the meal. "This week." I was digging in my purse for some change, but she threw down her credit card, and said, "On me. Thanks for listening."

"You don't have to."

"I'm just glad you're here, offering support."

I didn't see that I'd said anything that could qualify as supportive. "This was pretty good," I admitted, pointing to the empty plates.

"Better than good. Great." She gazed at me seriously. "What

do you think of him? Honestly. I know he's not the usual, but I could never go for a Barbeque Dad. It's not my style." It was uncomfortable to see how much my answer mattered to her. Momentarily, I seesawed, wishing I could duck the question. Though at times I'm an accomplished liar, I just can't do it with my friends.

Still, there's no reason to be harsh, so I said with a light shrug, "He doesn't do it for me, but what do I know?"

"Has it just been too long for me? I've always been sure of what I was getting into, but now this. I'm really struggling to give him up. I know I have to. It's really not good for either of us."

"Maybe you're pushing too hard. Let it run its course."

"I wish I could. Boy, do I wish I could. But sometimes things get toxic." She shook her head. "When we first started I was reluctant. Careful. I told myself I'd be sorry right from the get-go." She gazed off into the middle distance. "There was this other guy a couple of years ago. I didn't give him enough of what he needed. I should have, but I didn't. I really wasn't sure what I wanted. I was so focused on my career, I just quit paying attention to him, us, everything. He slowly stopped calling, and I never picked up the phone and tried to resurrect anything. I've always been sorry."

"What about now? Is he still reachable?"

"He's married." She signed her name to the bill. "Lives in suburbia. Probably owns a riding lawn mower. I'm sure she's either pregnant or will be soon. A Barbeque Dad."

We got up to leave. There wasn't much else to say, as I knew better than to try and tell her what kind of man to choose. Her dilemma made me consider my own dating situation. I felt if I pushed Jazz a little that he would eagerly turn us into a "couple." Sometimes you just know.

"You do look great, by the way," Cynthia said, gesturing to my outfit. "What's all this for? I'm glad to see you out of those jeans and black shirt for once. And the boots are working for you."

"I've got a mission this afternoon."

"Work related?"

"Yep. Can I ask you something, as an artist?"

"Sure."

"What do you think of knives as a subject?"

"Knives?" She gave it some serious thought.

"Sexual, right? Phallic . . . plunging . . . whatever . . ."

"It's also a symbol of power," she said. "Dominance." She must have seen something on my face, because she asked, "What?"

"It's just that the guy who painted all the knife paintings isn't domineering in the least."

"Maybe someone dominated him."

As I thought that over, she asked, "Can I come by the cottage later tonight? I'm going to break it off with Ernst this afternoon, and I may need support."

"Sure."

"Do you have wine?"

"Not anything you'd drink."

A smile broke across her face. "If I get through this afternoon, I'll be happy to drink axle grease, if that's what you've got. I just don't want to *dread* my life anymore.

"See you tonight."

"Thanks, Jane."

"*De nada.*"

Chapter
Eleven

An hour later I was on I-5, heading south to River Shores
Sanitarium, feeling slightly nauseous. Probably psychoso-
matic, but I couldn't get that fish's eye out of my mind.

The day was chillier, no rain but not much sun, either. Gray
clouds filled the sky reminding everyone that October was autumn, folks. No more fooling ourselves it was late summer. The
fields alongside the freeway were full of tan stalks, dried grasses,
stiff and hollow. There was a damp, smokey smell hovering in
the air, the remnants of field burning somewhere out of my range
of vision.

I probably should have asked Dwayne if he needed help on
his robbery job. All he'd said was that the client didn't want to report it to the police for reasons that were unclear. But if Dwayne
had really wanted me, I reasoned, he would have said so. The
fact that he hadn't meant I was faced with free time, and in the
interests of putting some questions of my own to bed, I was on
my way.

So, I was driving down the freeway, attempting to shrug off a
sense of dissatisfaction, of a job left half-finished. Maybe I would
learn something from River Shores, maybe not. Either way I was
doing something, and it felt good. I could never work in an office
all day. And I could really never be able to do those jobs like

casino work where you're stuck inside in an artificially bright room, and there's no telling whether it's day or night, or winter or summer, or if we're even still on planet earth. Though driving can often be a pain in the ass, if the traffic's okay it can be therapeutic, too. I drove down to Salem in forty-five minutes, and I was at the gates of the sanitarium in another ten.

And gates they were. I looked through my windshield at ten-foot-high wrought spikes, the kind with fancy little arrowheads across the top. Gazing down the fence line, I could see it turn into an equally high chain link. And yes, a strand of razor wire could not be discreetly hidden behind the laurel hedges, though River Shores sure gave it a hell of a try. Once you were admitted there might be no any easy way getting out.

What fun.

There was a kiosk at the gate with an attendant wearing a sage green uniform. I hadn't expected to encounter this first line of defense and it must have showed on my face because he said, "You're here for the birthday party." He was already pushing a button as I offered him a grateful smile.

"I was worried I wasn't going to be admitted."

"No problem, ma'am."

It occurred to me that if I were in my jeans and T-shirt, I might have been questioned more thoroughly.

Note to self: *proper camouflage is important in the animal kingdom.*

The hospital drive was a ribbon of asphalt. It swept around in a large horseshoe, like the Purcells' entrance and exit lanes, but here you could see both ends across an expanse of lush, carefully tended grass. Zinnias and chrysanthemums bobbed heavy heads at me in oranges, yellows and purple. They looked about to fall over from their own weight, but they were cheery. The building itself was a massive brick monster. It looked nearly a century old, though I learned later that this was not the truth. Most of the sanitarium was newer, spoking back from this imposing facade, long halls of concrete that connected mazelike around several inner courtyards.

I parked in a visitor lot on the side painted with fresh white lines. There were half a dozen cars taking up space, and two spots over stood a van with its cargo doors open. It was filled with a variety of party supplies: helium balloons, pink tablecloths and napkins, gaily wrapped presents, noisemakers—the kind that every parent wants to rip from the lips of their kids—several sprays of flowers studded with pink carnations, and a banner that I couldn't make out beyond "–ppy birthd–." A family had already tumbled from the van: dad, mom, three children of varying ages, maybe an aunt and uncle or two. As I watched the little boy blew a noisemaker at his older sisters, who turned toward their parents with that long-suffering "Could you make him stop, please?" look. Junior took this as an invitation to blow the damn thing harder, over and over again. I was glad when dad jerked it from his mouth because I might have stepped in myself and screamed STOP IT in the kid's ear. Dad's actions caused Junior to squawk about how unfair it all was and he didn't want to see great-grandma anyway because she *smelled*. This earned Junior a whack on the butt as mom swooped in with a rolled-up magazine of some kind. I passed by close enough to see it was a brochure extolling the wonderful amenities offered here at River Shores Sanitarium.

Junior held one of the Mylar helium balloons aloft. Both sides depicted a big pink cake groaning beneath candles stacked upon candles. The caption read: MORE CANDLES MEANS MORE FUN!

Junior bitched and whined and dragged his feet as mom pulled him by his arm to the front doors. Oldest sister used the time to gaily trip along beside dad, slipping her hand within his, a little goody-two-shoes I would have liked to whack as well. Middle sister stolidly walked behind them. She cast a look back at aunt and uncle who seemed to lag behind on purpose.

I didn't get the feeling this birthday was going to be loads of fun, but as they were my ticket inside, I kept just a couple of steps behind the reluctant couple. The middle girl eyed me with a grave, unabashed stare. I stared right back. If it was a silent game of who's gonna flinch first, I was taking her down.

I don't think I have the right attitude for motherhood myself. Children annoy me and I worry I might not feel any differently about my own.

Except I do have a serious soft spot for my dog.

We all entered the reception area together. I'd passed the lagging couple by this time, and I held the door for them. They smiled at me and I smiled back. One big happy family.

It was 2:30 PM by the clock behind the crabby-looking receptionist. She had a permanent frown line dug between her brows. I didn't want to gaze at her too directly, inviting questions, so I pretended to wait while Mom and Dad checked in with her, my attention on the reception area. The place was done in tones of yellow and chocolate with a highly polished dark wooden floor expanding from one end to the other. An ecru lisle carpet delineated a square in the center around which were grouped boxy chairs and a dull, brick-red leather couch. All very welcoming. But my nose detected a faint antiseptic scent. I'm not a huge fan of hospitals of any kind. Putting lipstick on this pig didn't make it anything but what it was.

The fifty-something receptionist behind the counter now turned her smile, if you could call it that, my way. There was something about her attitude that sent warning signals along my nerves. I leaned down to the middle girl as if we were the best of friends. Her serious gray eyes widened slightly.

"Think Great-Grandma will remember me?" I asked. "I haven't seen her in so long. I'll bet she'll remember you, though."

"Which courtyard is it?" Mom asked. She already seemed frazzled.

The receptionist was diverted. "Just past the orange wing. Go straight back, past the double doors. Take the first left. That'll take you to Blue, and you'll see the double glass doors. You know the code to get out?"

"1 2 3 4," Dad said. "I think I can remember." He and oldest daughter shared a smile and a laugh.

And I thought my code was bad.

"1 2 3 4, opens up the door!" Junior sang. "1 2 3 4, opens up the door!"

We all trundled through to the orange wing. Aunt and uncle were falling farther and farther behind. I swear one of them, or both, smelled of gin. Junior kept right on singing and by the time we made it to the double glass doors, I was close to asking them if they'd brought the bottle with them.

The family seemed to accept me without question. They were wrapped up in their own dynamics, too busy and distracted to care who the hell I was. We pushed through the glass doors to five concrete steps and a wheelchair accessible ramp that led to a back patio area. Great-Grandma had been wheeled to a spot of honor at the edge of the patio. She'd been turned to face the group, of which there were maybe thirty to forty people. Another helium balloon said, "Ninety-nine years young!"

Junior and company were lining up to wish her well and I tagged along. What I really wanted to do was dig through administrative files and learn about past patients, but I was at a loss on how to accomplish this task. It would be just lovely if I could ask somebody for Lily Purcell's records and have them hand them over to me, but people in the health care profession are notoriously loath to impart personal information about patients to complete strangers, more's the pity. Several days earlier I'd refilled a prescription for some allergy medicine that keeps me from serious pollen attacks and I'd had to stand ten spaces back at the pharmacy, behind a line of blue tape stuck to the floor, so I supposedly couldn't hear or see what was happening to the man at the counter. Of course he was deaf as a post and shouting everything anyway. Also, he dropped his vial of pills and couldn't reach them, so I'd leaned down to pick them up for him. He'd taken the opportunity to give me the once-over. "For the old ticker," he said, leering. "Don't need no Viagra, though. You wanna find out?"

"Sure thing," I answered. "Let me pick up my genital wart medicine, and I'll meet you outside."

He blinked a couple of times. "You're a funny lady." But he didn't stick around to see if I was putting him on.

Now, a table on wheels was rolled over in front of Great-Grandma. It held a huge sheet cake smothered in white frosting and red and pink confectionary roses with green leaves and stems. HAPPY BIRTHDAY, GERALDINE was laid out in lovely gold script. Little clusters of candles were tucked all over its face. There actually could have been ninety-nine. About six dozen cupcakes, all with candles, were nestled in groupings around the cake.

The courtyard opened to a large expanse of grass that ran from the back of the main complex and disappeared over a slight hillock. Apart from the razor-wired fence, out of sight from where we were, it was a decidedly pastoral view. Shafts of sunlight drove like beams from heaven through a gray cloud cover, glittering the placid surface of the Willamette River about a quarter mile away. Serenity abounded. But I tried to imagine a sixteen-year-old managing in this setting, no matter what her problems were, and failed.

Everyone was in party attire, though jackets and sweaters had been broken out against the cold bursts of wind that would suddenly whistle around the corners of the buildings. The women were hugging themselves tightly and the men had their hands in their pockets. The kids ran around chasing each other.

Geraldine was swathed in layers of sweaters and blankets. She had the shrunken, creased look of old age, and her skin was a mottled design in differing tones of brown and beige. Her hands and neck were wrinkled into knots of flesh. People were leaning close to her and wishing her well. A man in front of me, not of my little "family," said, "Hi, I'm Jim Paine. Are you with the Kirkendahls?"

"Mmmmmm," I said. "Doesn't she look great?"

"Fantastic," he agreed enthusiastically. "Who knew she'd last this long? With that asthma? I thought she'd die long before Uncle Ralph."

"We all had bets on it," I improvised.

"No kidding. What's your name? I'm sorry I can't remember."

"I'm Jane. It's hard to remember everybody, isn't it?"

"Oh, yeah." He was relieved I felt the same.

We moved up to Geraldine and Jim had to break off from me to greet her. He leaned down and said a few words, then moved to one side, waiting. I could see he was going to be a problem. I had plans to break away and do some exploring of my own and I didn't want company. Maybe this wasn't the fortress the razor-wire would lead one to believe. It's not like this was a home for the *criminally* insane. It was merely a place to improve mental health.

I leaned down to Geraldine. "Congratulations. Ninety-nine. Wow."

"How old are you?" she asked in a thin, raspy voice. It was the first time I'd seen her speak to anyone, and it kinda took me aback.

"Thirty."

"You're not getting any younger, are you?"

I squinted at her. Well, now that was kind of calling the kettle black. "I guess not."

"Better find yourself a husband before it's late."

"Before what's too late?"

"The end of your looks, honey. And don't give the milk away before he buys the cow."

I moved away from Geraldine to make room for the next well-wisher. Okay, she was an inmate at River Shores. Was I really supposed to listen to her?

Jim hovered by me. "That's her favorite line. She says it to all the women, even the married ones."

"Hmmm . . ." I hadn't seen her dispensing it to anyone else. I glanced around for escape. Someone had propped open the door to the main building.

One of the party guests was cutting thick slices of cake with a wicked looking knife. Junior was jostling older sister for position in front of the food line. Older sister stomped on his foot and he screwed up his face, turned it toward the heavens and screeched like a banshee.

I made a bathroom excuse and headed back inside, walking up the handicapped ramp as birthday party guests had taken over the stairs. I wondered vaguely if I should shut the facility's doors, but nobody seemed to care. Glancing back, I saw Jim watching me and I sketched him a wave before disappearing inside.

The hallways were covered in commercial carpet, and as I was in the Blue Wing, everything was blue. There were signs on the doors with the patients' names. Some of the doors were ajar, and I glanced in to see elderly men and women watching television from chairs and beds. They didn't notice me.

The employees all wore sage green short-sleeve shirts and pants with name tags. They smiled at me as I cruised the halls, clearly unconcerned to have me around.

In my wanderings I found a set of locked doors. I punched in the code and was admitted to the Alzheimer's wing. The color here was yellow. A number of patients sat in chairs in the hallway. Others wandered restlessly, talking to themselves, sometimes almost marching. Hands reached out and touched the fabric of my skirt as I passed. "Nice," one woman said. A male patient continually rattled the handles to the door at the end of the hall that led outside. Staring out the window, he said, "She went there. She went there. She went there . . ."

I left quickly, returning to the main facility through the same door I'd entered after punching in 1,2,3,4 again. I looked around, making sure nobody walked out with me, then I headed toward the main part of the building, following a sign on the wall that pointed to reception and administration. Administration, okay, but I sure as hell didn't want to leave the inner sanctum and face the pinch-faced receptionist again. As I headed toward the front of the building, I found the jog in the hallway that led to the administrative offices.

I hesitated a moment, wondering what story I could cook up. As I stood there, a man came around the corner, nearly running into me. "Whoa," he said, holding out a hand to keep from barreling into me.

"Hi." I kind of laughed.

"Sorry," he apologized. "Are you lost? Reception's back that way." He hooked a thumb toward the front of the building. He was sandy-haired, a tad pudgy, sporting a nice smile. His tag read Dr. Cal Bergin, and his eyes lingered on me as he added, "Unless . . . I can help you?"

A godsend. I gave him my best smile. "I was just wanting to talk about River Shores. Do you mind? Are you busy?"

He glanced at his watch, but it was all for show. "Come on in."

He led me into a rabbit warren of offices, walking briskly as if he didn't want any of the administrative staff, mostly young women, asking him any questions. I took note of the partitioned areas. Computer monitors sat on almost every desk, whether they were manned or not. I wish I were better with electronics in general, computers in particular. I'd love to be an ace hacker. The information available at the press of a few buttons is mind-boggling. What I did know was human nature, and I would bet money that, if given fifteen minutes alone at one of those cubicles, I would be able to find the passwords and/or User IDs needed to access the system. I'd learned from someone I knew in the medical field that many hospitals, clinics and institutions make their personnel change their passwords every six months for security reasons. And you aren't allowed to use any password you've used before. This being the case, those passwords cannot be committed to memory. They're scratched down on a piece of paper somewhere, or hidden in a book, or taped to the inside of a drawer, but they're just waiting for someone to discover them.

"What can I help you with Ms . . . ?"

"Kellogg," I said, reaching a hand across his desk. We shook hands and I smoothed my skirt and sat down. "Call me Veronica. Actually, call me Ronnie."

"I'm Cal," he said.

"I know the Purcell family," I said, trying out the name on him. It didn't immediately click, which was a plus in my mind.

Around Portland you can practically assume everyone's heard of the Purcells, but start heading toward the suburbs and beyond, and they're not as well known. "They've spoken highly of River Shores. I believe it was called Haven of Rest once?"

"Oh, way back. It was changed over thirty years ago."

"That's about right, then. One of the Purcell daughters was a patient here for a few years when she was in her teens."

"Our facility's known for its young adult treatment. We also handle alcohol- and drug-related problems, which, unfortunately, are a major part of the teen culture."

"But also, more serious ailments . . . ?" I was groping, struggling to find a way to ask for the information I sought. "Schizophrenia?"

"Yes." He looked properly sober. "Schizophrenia often manifests itself at the young adult stage."

"Actually, I believe Lily's problems were depression related." More utter bullshit. I was running blind. "My own sister suffers from depression as well. I was wondering, do you still have the records for Lily Purcell? I'm not asking to see them," I said hurriedly. "I'm just feeling my way here, trying to determine if River Shores is the best facility for her."

"Oh, I'm certain you'll find River Shores one of the best institutions in the state. I've been here for five years."

"Is it possible for you to check the files on Lily?" I gestured toward the computer.

"That long ago, her records wouldn't be on computer. They'd be stored in our records room."

"Records room," I repeated.

"All the old files are in the basement. Some newer ones, as well. I could go down and check your friend's file, but I wouldn't be able to give any information to you. It would have to be a member of the family." He gazed at me a little uncertainly.

"Oh, don't worry about it," I gushed. "My friends just didn't seem to have saved any of the records, and since I was in the area I thought I'd drop in and check out things for myself. If I need more information, I'll ask them to contact River Shores. Should I have them ask for you?"

"Sure."

I got up hurriedly and extended my hand. I hoped I hadn't overplayed my part.

Cal shook my hand, looking like he wanted to linger, but I headed out of the administration offices and back toward the party, my eyes peeled for stairways leading downward. I was nearly to the open doors to the backyard and Geraldine's big event when I found the stairs. There was no second story on the building, so these had to head to the basement.

I actually stepped outside for a moment, letting everyone think I was just another party member. The birthday party itself was winding down. Junior had frosting smeared across his sweater-vest. He was chasing another little boy and shooting at him with his thumb and forefinger. The other little boy was shrieking with laughter and "firing" back at him. A sugar high. With weapons.

Heading back inside, I was just starting for the stairs when a woman jumped in front of me, surprising me. I stopped short. She wore a pair of brown polyester pants that covered a round belly, and a loose top smeared with pink frosting and white cake. Her gray hair was crumpled on one side, as if she'd just gotten up from a nap. Her mouth was open and her tongue lay on her bottom lip. Her eyes were rolling around in her head like marbles. In one hand she clasped the NINETY-NINE YEARS YOUNG! Mylar balloon; in the other the serving knife.

With growing dread, I reheard my discussion with Cal Bergin about schizophrenia. Maybe that wasn't what it was, but something was definitely not okay with her.

I saw again the Alzheimer's patient at the door. *She went out there . . . she went out there . . . she went out there . . .*

And Junior shouting at the top of his lungs: *1, 2, 3, 4. That's the code for the door!*

Despite the smeared icing, this was no party guest. And the

way she held the knife, her fist wrapped around it tightly, did not convince me her intentions were benign.

"Excuse me," I said, my eyes on the knife.

For an answer she jabbed it at me. I backed away quickly. My brain sizzled. What? *What?* I sensed she was simply reacting. She had no particular animosity toward me. That made it even scarier. No logic. No way to convince her to stop.

She lunged again. I danced to one side, my shoulder hitting the wall. She came charging again and I jumped the other way. There was no finesse. No art. She came at me, bullish and direct. Noises were issuing from my throat. Feral noises, full of fear. She hauled back and lifted the blade high. *Whoosh!* I twisted, but she caught a bit of my ponytail. My breath came out in gasps. I jumped away, but she charged. I stepped to one side and she slammed into me with her shoulder, sending me reeling. Pushing off the wall, I faced her, desperately dancing out of her murderous path. I wanted back outside but she caught my intention and leaped at me again. I slammed myself toward the opposite wall and she was on me. I kicked and she sliced, this time catching the side of my ear.

That *hurt!*

I was suddenly furious at the fates. Furious at myself. Furious at Dwayne! *Damn you, Dwayne,* I thought. Damn you for talking me into this! I knew better than to ever think I could be an information specialist!

"You—get—out—of—*here!*" she shrieked.

In the distance I heard running footsteps. "Gina!" someone yelled. "Gina, where are you?"

"Say a word and I'll kill you!" she whispered harshly. Her eyes wouldn't stay focused.

For an answer I screamed as loud as I could, a shrieking siren of a wail. Green-suited employees ran our way, pounding down the corridors. Gina glanced around and I shoved her for all I was worth. She stumbled forward, hand clutching the knife, slicing wildly at the arriving employees. Everybody backed off.

Outside, there was pandemonium at the party. My scream had

sent them into panic mode. One quick glance out of the side of my eye and I saw the guests were scattering across the lawn.

In a moment all hell would break loose. Questions, recriminations, God knew what else. I didn't want any part of it. Without consciously planning it, I simply slipped down the stairs and left Gina, now growling like a beast, in the somewhat capable hands of the frightened River Shores staff.

Sometimes I surprise myself. I really do. I wouldn't call myself a cool head in times of trouble. I'm certainly not overly emotional and reactive, but I don't think of myself as someone who can make calm choices in times of extreme upset.

However, it was as if I'd choreographed the whole thing. Swallowing back my anger at Dwayne, I hurried down the steps to the basement and simply strode toward the doors at the end of the hall. My heartbeat was light and fast; more adrenaline. A brief search led me to the records room. I fully expected the door to be locked and it was, but it was one of those winky, rattly door locks that says nobody gives a rat's ass whether it stays shut or not. I opened it with one hard kick.

No one was about. The whole basement smelled forgotten. If there'd been anyone on this level, the commotion upstairs had undoubtedly brought them to the surface. I strolled in, switched on the fluorescent lights, and took a look around.

The room was a large rectangle with several thick concrete posts holding it up in the center. Metal shelving ran from ceiling to floor around the perimeter, and there were more shelves lined up in the center of the room as well. It was like a poor man's library, cold, vacant and bare. Manila files, some in protective plastic sleeves, some not, took up every bit of available space. Nearby were stacks of computer disks. Everything was dated, so it was easy to pluck whatever information was needed without a lot of searching.

I had a pretty good idea when Lily Purcell had been a patient here, so I scanned the dates covering that five-year period around her incarceration. Within each year the files were listed alphabet-

ically. The gods of fortune must have been smiling upon me because I came across Lily's file within five minutes.

In the back of my mind was the idea of simply lifting it. I'd
given Dr. Bergin a hell of a lot of information about whom I was
looking for, and he might be able to finger me should something
backfire, but he didn't know my name, and honestly, I was in a
strange state of exhilaration where I didn't much care anyway.

I scanned the file. It was filled with copious writings about
Lily's day-to-day pharmaceutical and nutritional intake. I considered that she might have been heavily drugged, but that didn't
appear to be the case.

The doctors' notes were strange. I could swear they seemed
stilted, careful, as if they were overly concerned about who
would view them. Maybe families just don't want to know how
unhinged one of their members might be. Maybe that's what all
the euphemisms were about, such as "low-spirited"—read depression for that—or "not engaged"—sounds like antisocial to
me—or—"passive and quiet"—could be catatonia.

But then I read a passage that made me silently say, "*What?*"
to the empty room. I read it again, then heard approaching footsteps. Quickly I slipped the file behind my back and pressed myself to the wall, heart thumping.

Someone entered the room. I closed my eyes and prayed it
wasn't Dr. Bergin. I was pretty much tapped out of explanations,
and I was just too tired to come up with something new.

When my hiding place wasn't immediately discovered, I carefully peeked through the racks. It was a young, green-suited
woman, and she was gazing down at the pile of CDs. After a moment, she hauled up quite a stack of them, staggering under the
weight. She tried to slam the door shut behind her but it was impossible with what she was carrying. If she noticed the splintered
wood beside the lock, she didn't react.

Quick as a flash, I shoved the file into my purse, then scurried
out of the room, choosing a different exit to the first floor from
the one I'd used coming down. As I ascended, tiptoeing, I heard
footsteps descending on the route I'd taken down. *Hurry, hurry*, I

urged myself, all the while moving quietly forward. At the top of the stairs I peeked through the door. I was just inside the door that led from the waiting area to the inner sanctum. Through a panel of glass, the crotchety receptionist eyed me narrowly.

"What were you doing downstairs?"

"I damn near got myself killed by one of your crazy inmates!" I declared furiously, slamming the stairway door behind me. I stomped through the inner sanctum door to outside reception and glared at her through the front glass. "See this?" I pointed to my clipped ear.

Her lips parted in dismay. I hoped to hell there was a lot of blood showing. I hadn't had the time nor inclination to look, but head injuries are so gushy. I wondered if I should feign like I was about to faint.

Hurried footsteps sounded in the corridor. The inner door opened again and both the receptionist and I turned. It was Jim Paine. "There you are," he said. "Oh, my God. You're—you're *bleeding*."

The door flew open behind him. A crowd was pouring through to the front of the building, like lemmings to the sea. Dr. Cal Bergin was one of them. When he saw me, his eyes widened. He started to push past the crowd of birthday well-wishers currently clogging up the hallway.

"Jane, maybe you should sit down," Jim said, reaching for my arm to guide me to one of the boxy chairs.

All I wanted was to escape. "No, I'm fine. Really." Dr. Cal squeezed through some of the crowd. The group was loudly worrying about that "crazy woman who tried to kill someone."

Shit.

"I've gotta go," I said, but Jim hung onto me like a burr.

"Jane, I really think you should have that looked at. That woman attacked you? What happened?"

My teeth clenched. If he called me by my name one more time I was going to smack him. At that moment Dr. Cal made it through the door. "Ms. Kellogg, I am so sorry. We've got Mrs. Rowalski sedated. She's never done anything like this before."

I heard an echo of dog owners everywhere: *But, he's never bitten anyone before!* Like it was the victim's—*my*—fault, somehow.

"No problem. Really."

"This is so unfortunate. Please be assured your sister would be well looked after. Gina . . . Mrs. Rowalski . . . has episodes, but she's really quite docile."

Jim Paine, my new defender, looked down his nose at Dr. Cal. "That's not saying much for your institution, Dr. Bergin. I came here for my great-grandmother's birthday, but I'm going to rec-ommend moving her. You can't have paranoid schizophrenics wandering the halls."

"Mrs. Rowalski is not a paranoid schizophrenic, I assure you."

I was edging away. Nothing good could come of this. Jim looked around for me, but Dr. Cal was doing his best to convince him that this was just an unfortunate incident. I figured I'd over-stayed my welcome at the place, and was making tracks fast.

"Jane! Wait!" Jim called.

I sailed through the front door. I'd just known he was going to be a problem.

I took my time going home, stopping for a much-needed jolt of caffeine at a fast-food restaurant before heading back to Lake Chinook. I cruised over to Dwayne's cabana but he wasn't there. I have a key, but I really didn't want to hang around by myself and wait for him. Glancing at my watch, I swore softly. It was after seven, and I'd promised Cynthia I would be home. However I really wanted to talk to someone about the Purcells. Phoning Dwayne's cell netted me nothing but his voice mail. He was probably on the job and therefore under the radar.

But I didn't feel like leaving yet either.

I thought about Jazz. I felt the tug of wanting to be with him, but he was a Purcell, and I kinda suspected he wouldn't be all that crazy about my sudden desire to investigate his family's background. That wasn't why he'd hired me. It was bound to be perceived as snoopy and suspect. And what would he say if I brought up James IV and his knife obsession? Or, the fact that Orchid was haunted by the playhouse?

They're all crazy.

I'd gotten tired of Dwayne's assessment, but there was no denying it held more than an element of truth.

"Damn it, Dwayne." I punched out his number again and when his voice mail answered, I ordered, "Call me. I need to talk to you."

Using my key, I unlocked Dwayne's side gate and walked around to his dock. There was still some faint daylight, but it was growing darker by the minute. I sank into one of his deck chairs and sighed deeply. What—a—day.

Feeling tired all over, I called Jazz's cell. "Hey, there," he answered right away, sounding happy to hear from me. "Have I thanked you enough for finding Nana? I don't think so. Thank you. *Thank you!*"

"You're welcome." It was such a relief to hear uncomplicated gratitude. I lay my head back and threw an arm over my eyes. I closed my mind to the mess of Cynthia and Ernst, refusing to think about the ramifications of starting a relationship. Because that's where I was headed. If I saw Jazz, spent time with him, made plans with him, eventually we would end up kissing. And kissing led to more kissing. More kissing led to other things, explorative things, and well, once sex was in the picture, you were through the looking glass. Nothing was ever the same.

But was that so bad? Isn't it what I wanted, needed, *craved?*

"Jazz?" I heard the worry in my voice even when I just mentioned his name.

"Yeah?"

"I'm glad your grandmother's home. I hope that you can all work it out now, keeping the finances in order, keeping Orchid safe. I'm just . . . glad," I said again. Taking a breath, I plunged in further. "I just want you to know that I've been doing some background checking, kind of as a means to get a clearer picture." This sounded lame, even to my own ears. I hurried on, "So, I went to River Shores and asked them about your mother."

"You did?"

"Orchid—Nana—just seemed bothered by everything so much. I found out some things."

"What?" He sounded more curious than upset, so I doggedly drove on.

"You told me that Lily died from being restrained."

"That's true."

"Yes, it is," I agreed quickly. "But you also told me she was known for her meekness, and that's not what it looks like. She was restrained quite a few times before that final time. She was considered a problem to the other patients."

"A danger?"

"In a way." I plunged ahead with the information I'd found in her file. "There are references to her extreme sexuality. Apparently she was locked in her room to keep her away from the male patients. She even tried to seduce the staff."

Silence. I held my breath, aware that I may have seriously blown it.

"Well, that's just not true."

"Jazz, it was in her records. Do you think Orchid knows?"

"No . . . that doesn't make any sense." At least he wasn't slamming down the phone on me.

"I'm going to ask you this. If you think it's too personal, or you just don't want to speculate, just tell me and I'll shut up." I hesitated, then asked, "Do you know who your father is? Or, have any idea?"

"Not a clue," he admitted. "I've often wondered, but nobody really knows. Or, if they do, they're not telling."

I'd read Lily's file. Quickly, to be sure, but I'd seen enough to recognize several names and dates of people who worked for Haven of Rest. Someone named Zach Montrose had signed and initialed many pages of data. An employee of Haven of Rest, although what his job was wasn't clear. I'd gleaned information about her pregnancy, but I hoped a closer perusal would offer more insights.

Then Jazz asked, "Why are you doing this?"

I heard a forlorn, little boy quality to his voice, as if I'd really let him down. For reasons I couldn't explain it put a lump in my throat. I felt terrible. "I just want to help," I said, but it sounded feeble to my own ears.

"Helping who? Me?"

That sense of nausea—or was it revulsion?—that I'd felt after lunch returned. "I'm sorry. I wanted some answers. Orchid seems distressed and I thought if I had more information about Lily it might make her feel better."

He didn't immediately respond. "Did you learn anything else?" he finally asked. I heard a certain amount of trepidation in his voice.

"Not really. I'm not a member of the family. You may not want to, but if you'd like more information, you could ask them yourself."

"I think I'm okay."

I nodded, though no one saw me but an osprey gliding above Lakewood Bay, searching for a meal in the last glimmers of twilight. We didn't have much more to say to each other, and after we hung up I kicked myself for ever starting this. I felt bad. I'd let him down and perversely, now that it felt like it might be over, I wished I'd tried harder to kick start something with him.

Glancing at my watch, I made a sound of distress, then took a quick trip to the local Safeway. Cynthia was bound to be on her way. Grabbing more wine, both white and red, I raced through the deli, tossing cheese, crackers, olives and, my big splurge, a small, shrink-wrapped package of smoked salmon. Personally, I wasn't in the mood to eat; the food was for Cynthia. All I wanted to do was drink wine and lots of it.

I ended up juggling a couple of large grocery sacks, paper not plastic. The leftover sacks make good luggage—a multipurpose unit that can be a briefcase or an overnight bag or whatever you want.

By the time I got home it was completely dark. My headlights flashed across my driveway as I pulled the Volvo into its spot in front of Ogilvy's garage and to the east side of the house. Throwing the strap of my purse over one shoulder, I gathered up the bags, balancing them as I attempted to lock my car doors with my key. I don't have a remote lock. That's a luxury that didn't come standard with the '94 wagons, apparently. One of these days I might have to step up.

I could hear the traffic on West Bay Road as I headed to my front door. Not a ton; the street's narrow. But enough to make walking on it hazardous. There are no sidewalks and no shoulder. It's pretty much asphalt and private property. Lots of my neighbors have those little low fences that can put a crease in your door in seconds flat if you get too close to them. Sometimes I simply drive down the center of the road.

With the bags in my arms, I was fingering my keys to find the one for the front door. It had a little key hat on it. "Eureka," I muttered as I finally felt it, but threading it into the lock was a trick. I finally managed, but as soon as I was inside I tripped over something. "Shit!" I cursed, struggling to hang onto the bags. I bobbed and weaved, practically dropping them onto the coffee table with only minimal damage. The salmon flew out of the top and hit the floor. Binkster came over and sniffed it, but it was sealed, so then she wiggled around my legs, tapping me with her paw.

It was then I saw what she'd done to my strappy sandals. My one good pair. They were in pieces.

I think I screeched first. Then I yelled, *"Binkster!* Look at that! Look what you did!"

She stared at me in confusion. I was furious and hurt. *How could she?* I grabbed up one of the sandals and shook it at her. "You see?" I yelled. "You see?" She'd chewed through one of the straps. "They're *ruined!"*

Her tail went down and she cowered. I was too angry to make nice just yet. I tossed the shoe in the corner and it slammed against the wall with a crack.

That's when Binkster ran out the front door.

"Binks!" I yelled again, this time in fear. She doesn't go out front. She doesn't understand about the street.

And that's when I heard the car turn into the drive.

I yelled in pure fear. I ran out after my dog. Cynthia's headlights picked her up the split second before Binkster ran in front of her tire.

I heard a doggy shriek. I screamed.

Cynthia slammed on her brakes and my terror-stricken gaze fixed on the crumpled body of my little pug.

Chapter
Twelve

I ran to Binkster. She was lying still in the headlights. I was soul sick. Frightened and cold to my core. Cynthia cut her engine and stepped out.

Teeth chattering, I bent over my dog. Her shriek still reverberated in my ears.

My mind bloomed in a picture of bloody gore. I'd stop screaming but I was still screaming inside. So overtaken by fear that my eyes rained tears. I was totally at fault. I called myself names: *Stupid, stupid, stupid!* I'd even been warned by the gal who dropped Binks into my care that dogs just don't get it about cars. Especially little dogs, for some reason.

We were caught in the headlights' glare. Cynthia muttered over and over again, "Oh, God, oh, God, oh, God . . ." Her face was a mask of shock. "Oh, my God. Oh, my God. Is he all right?"

"I don't know. I don't know . . . she . . . I don't know . . ."

I was kneeling down beside her. Binks tried to sit in her little sidesaddle position but it must have hurt too much so she lay on the ground, panting, staring up at me with trusting eyes. I was useless. A hateful person. I shouldn't be allowed to have a dog. Any pet. I'd been thinking of myself. Only of myself.

"I—I—I need a blanket," I said dully.

"I'll get it."

Cynthia strode into my house. My tears fell onto Binkster's head. She blinked a bit and kept panting.

Cynthia returned with my TV watching quilt. Gently we lifted the dog onto the blanket. I carried her to Cynthia's car, and Cynthia got behind the wheel. I realized my front door was wide open so I called Dwayne, told him what happened, asked him in an ultra-calm voice to please come over and shut the door.

I knew where the veterinary hospital was. Not that I was responsible enough to have been looking for it. I'd just happened on it one day and thought, "Oh, look. There's a pet hospital. Good to know."

I directed Cynthia to Tualatin, which is the city just southwest of Lake Chinook. The dog hospital is inside one of the buildings of a quasi-industrial/quasi-commercial center on the edge of city center. We drove in silence except for Binks's panting. I couldn't stop crying. It was soundless. The torment was inside me. I have never hated myself so much, been so utterly helpless or so frightened.

We entered the front doors to a small waiting area. We weren't the only ones there. Someone actually had a black crow. "It flew into the window," the man holding the box with the crow told us.

I started feeling competitive about who should see the vet first. It was a good sign, as it brought me out of my stupor.

I held the dog and stood at the desk. Immediately a girl came to help and said, "Ohhh," in a soft, mothering voice to Binks. That started the waterworks again. I'd gotten myself under control but now I was just . . . gone.

Cynthia stepped up and gave the particulars. There was a tremor in her voice. Neither of us had ever had any experience in this mothering, care-taking, loving someone more than yourself thing.

It was *awful*.

They carefully took Binkster away. We sat back down as the guy with the crow was admitted to a back room. That left us with a woman with an obese orange tabby, and a family fighting over who got to hold the whining puppy with the piddling problem.

Mom and Dad had opted out, but the kids kept pulling it back and forth. Little droplets of pee were all over them and the floor. One of the staff came out and took the dog, which sent the kids into a whining match that neither could win. Both of them wanted to go through the door to be with the dog. Mom and Dad ignored them.

I, too, wanted to be with my dog. I had a little bit of blood on my suede skirt. It wasn't till the next day I realized it was my own. Then I was sort of pissed that my skirt was ruined by the knife wielder. But that night, while I thought it was Binky's, it drew my gaze like a magnet. I'd stopped crying but I felt drained and horrible, my eyes dry and scratchy.

"The dog's going to be all right," Cynthia said.

"I know."

Eventually we were called back to the desk. The Binkster was being anesthetized and then they would stitch her back up. She got nailed by the front bumper, but somehow managed to avoid the tire. She got a nasty slice up her thigh—which they would shave and stitch. The cut was deep and had sliced through muscle, but nothing else. She would be very sore, but in time she would be good as new. I was told not to worry; she was a brave little soldier.

That did me in again. My eyes teared and I hated myself some more.

They suggested we leave her overnight and pick her up in the A.M. They would call when she was ready to go home.

I shivered, as if stricken with malaria all the way home. Dwayne's truck was parked beside my Volvo, which brightened my spirits a little. I begged Cynthia to come inside and have a glass of wine. She dutifully walked through the door but said she couldn't force down a drink. She said she'd ended things with Ernst and would tell me about it later. Once she saw me inside, she left.

When I walked in Dwayne was seated on my couch, his expression grim. He stood up as soon as I entered. "How's Binks?" he asked.

"Back leg injury. She's going to be fine." And the tears just burst from my eyes. The sobs I'd held in check until that moment racked my body. "I'm an idiot," I said. "And I can't stop crying."

I went into the kitchen and found a chilled bottle of Sauvignon blanc. Uncorking it, I poured two glasses, one for me, one for Dwayne.

He said, "You sure you want a depressant?" as I sat down beside him on the couch. When he put a hand on my shoulder, though I appreciated the contact, I wanted to fall into his arms.

For an answer I gulped down half my glass. "I was feeling sorry for myself. And Binks ripped up my shoe . . . and I threw it against the wall . . ."

"She's going to be fine."

"I yelled at her . . . and . . . she ran out . . ."

"Shhh."

"It was horrible to watch," I choked.

"I can imagine." He was sober.

"It's scary to care so much about something." I shook my head, fighting for control. Giving up, I tossed back the rest of my glass, climbed off the couch, headed to the kitchen, poured myself another. "I think I'm going to get drunk," I said.

"I might join you," he said. "All right if I stay over?"

"Please do."

And we proceeded to work our way through two bottles. We might have uncorked a third. Things got pretty fuzzy in there somewhere but I was glad the world was dull. I found myself longing for Jazz. I was suffering from some serious self-loathing and I needed a cheerleader. I think Dwayne tried to help. I don't really recall. I vaguely remember trying to explain something to Dwayne—something about love, truth and the secrets to world peace, but I don't think he took me seriously.

Somewhere in there I found my way to bed. I'd never felt so low, so miserable, so weary. I'd drunk way too much wine and don't remember quitting. In the morning I woke with a low level sense of dread. I peeked through one eye and groaned. Sunlight was trying to creep between the slats of my bedroom blinds. I was on my side, so I reached behind me for Binkster before I remembered she was at the hospital. My heart sank just as my hand encountered a human leg.

My eyes flew open. And my head screamed with pain. And my throat cried, "Water!"

My guest heard me and got out of the bed, apparently heeding my request. The movement and the faint squeak of the springs caused my head to pound. Damn, but I hurt all over. I would have whimpered and stayed in bed all day, but I'd begged for this punishment, so I was going to take it like a man.

That lasted about two minutes as Dwayne came back into the bedroom carrying a glass of water. He'd been naked, I'm pretty sure, while in bed with me, but he'd had the decency to throw on his jeans in the meantime. I looked at his expanse of bare, broad chest, threw my arm over my eyes and groaned again.

"Did we have sex?" I asked. I feared if I dug through my memory too hard that's what I would discover.

"No."

"No?" I lifted my arm and looked at him. There was something way too satisfied about his appearance. "Oh, God, are you trying to spare my feelings? Don't bother. I can take it."

"You sure, darlin'?"

His drawl was in full force. It sounded like "Ya, shore, dahlin?" with a few extra syllables thrown in for good measure.

"Don't keep me in suspense," I said tiredly.

"We did not have sex."

I heard the ring of truth this time, and I tested my feelings. I was glad we hadn't done something foolish, glad I didn't have to deal with a new aspect to our relationship, glad I could focus on Jazz as a possible date/boyfriend/something in the romance department.

"Thank God," I said fervently.

Dwayne continued to stare down at me and I started to get a funny feeling. Something wasn't right. "We did not have sex," I repeated. "That's what you said."

He nodded.

"Did *not*."

"That's right. We did not . . . have sex."

I heard an unspoken "but" in there and I grimaced, afraid to ask. I waited until the suspense stretched to intolerable lengths. Staring back at Dwayne with dread, I said, "We did not have sex, but . . . ?

". . . we had soul-searing lovemaking," he said with a straight face. "The kind that makes the planets realign, the kind that explodes the myth that men don't feel as much emotion as women. I was transported to another world. I have never felt these *feelings* before." He looked toward the ceiling, placed a hand on his chest, and quoted earnestly, "'I've known love, but never have I known ecstasy and beauty in—"

I threw a pillow. He deflected it easily.

"—the light of true honor and worthiness and—"

"You're making that up."

"—and . . . damn. You've broken my concentration."

"Drop dead."

I realized belatedly that I was stark naked. I'd been too wrapped up in my pain and angst to sense that there was nothing covering my lower parts. A stab of panic. Maybe we had made love. Maybe he was trying to spare my feelings. I asked, hating the little note of anxiety in my voice, "Are you going to tell me the truth?"

"Now, that hurts, Jane. You can't even remember."

"I say nothing happened."

"Maybe it'll come back to you."

I lifted my head and guzzled the water. Pain shot from the top of my head and settled behind my eyes. Yep. I'd really done it to myself. "Is it time to get Binkster yet?"

"Not for a couple of hours. Want me to make breakfast?"

"Yes," I said in surprise. Something loaded with grease and carbs. True hangover food.

"Got anything to make?"

"You'll have to go to the store."

"Hmm."

He left the room and presumably put on his shirt, socks and shoes. I heard him leave my house, locking the door behind him. Dwayne has a key to my place as I have one to his. We'd exchanged them in the spirit of becoming new business partners. Now I wondered about the repercussions. Had I slept with him? No. He would never be so cavalier . . . would he?

Growling under my breath, I stepped from the bed. My stomach rolled over. I saw the baleful fish eye again. With a hand clapped over my mouth I sprinted to the bathroom. I threw up lustily until I was spent.

Thank God, I'm alone, I thought, curled up naked around the bottom of the toilet. I stayed that way long after Dwayne returned and began frying bacon and making toast. My mouth watered, more from leftover misery than hunger. I really wanted to make it back to bed but I couldn't.

Dwayne strode by the open bathroom door on his way to the bedroom, caught sight of me and stopped short. I'd curled myself in a ball so I didn't feel so exposed. I decided I was going to live because I started worrying about how big this position made my thighs and butt look.

Dwayne looked excruciatingly put together in his totally Dwayne way. I said, "I must have had more to drink than you did."

"Y'think?"

"Shut up. I'm paying the price."

Dwayne asked, "You want breakfast in there, or do you think you'll make it to the kitchen?"

I gave him the finger and he grinned.

My heart fluttered in a strange way, and I knew I was in big, big trouble.

Picking up Binkster was beyond stressful. I had Dwayne drive me. I'd ignored him throughout breakfast, what I could eat of it, and ignored him some more afterward. I had a new awareness of him that I did not want to acknowledge. Lucky for me, Dwayne didn't seem to notice. In fact, everything was so damn normal it was enough to make me want to scream. Not that I would, given my raging headache. I'd carefully taken some aspirin and water before we bumped in his truck back to the hospital. Dwayne was humming some country western song. He was really pissing me off. Cynthia had called and offered to be part of the pickup team, but I told her I wanted to go on my own. But then with Dwayne cleaning up the dishes and me feeling a bit lost, I didn't argue when he offered to take me.

They brought Binks out. She was glassy-eyed and her back leg was shaved, stitched and smeared with some kind of yellow/orange iodine thing. She looked like something out of a horror flick. There was this neck cone thing around her neck which I was told she should wear until I was told otherwise; they wanted to prevent her from trying to lick the wound. I pointed out that I thought "licking a wound" was supposed to be a good thing. They merely smiled politely.

Note to self: Steer clear of vet hospital; they know I'm an unworthy dog owner.

Binks desultorily wagged her curly tail, but she licked my hand over and over again as I held her in my lap on the way home. Normally, she's stingy with her kisses, but now she was so loving that I felt doubly awful. It was my fault she'd run outside. It was my fault for not being more careful.

Dwayne, too, seemed reluctant to leave Binkster, but he finally headed for the door. I admit I was kind of grouchy with him. Okay, I was really grouchy with him. I was irked that he wouldn't tell me the truth about what did, or did not, happen between us, and as time wore on and I began to feel marginally better, and my fear for The Binkster was lessening since I saw she was starting to act like nothing had happened, even with the sore leg and neck apparatus, I started to over-think the events of the night before. I did not believe *anything* had happened. If I'd slept with Dwayne I would know it. I would *feel* it. Physically and psychically. Okay, I pretty much felt muscles I rarely did, starting with my overtaxed stomach muscles from heaving my guts out earlier. It was possible I wouldn't know physically. But, I should know in my sense of self. In my world, Jane Kelly does not sleep with Dwayne Austin Durbin.

My mind touched on Ernst and Cynthia. Nope. Didn't want to think about them and whatever their lovemaking entailed. I thought next of my brother Booth and his fiancée Sharona. Last summer I'd sat with them at a restaurant and felt the sex vibes charging the air, that energy thrown off by couples who you just know are dying to get in bed together. I'd been envious. Actually, I was still envious. But I did not feel that way about Dwayne.

I'd taken a shower before picking up Binks, now I took a second one. I came out of this one feeling almost human. I'd barely done justice to Dwayne's breakfast, even though it was just what the doctor ordered, so now I nibbled on some leftover bacon and toast.

Binks toddled into the kitchen and looked up at me expectantly.

So, sue me, I gave her two whole strips.

Jazz called me up and invited me to a party. "It's a celebration for having Nana back safe and sound. It's just the family, really, and a few of her close friends. And we wanted you, of course. Without you, she'd probably still be missing."

"Is William invited?" I asked curiously.

"Still under discussion. The family doesn't want him, but Nana is asking for him, so . . ."

I didn't want to go. I didn't even think I belonged. And let's face it, I still didn't *feel* that great. Also, I didn't want to leave Binkster, and I'd be damned if I took her and had to explain what had happened. But I was also glad to be elevated from noxious interloper to sometime savior. I could take Binkster over to Dwayne's, and I could spend time with Jazz.

And maybe this would be the button on the whole episode.

After I accepted Jazz's invitation, he told me he would pick me up in a little over an hour. I next called Dwayne who said he would be happy to watch Binks at my place. I didn't know what to say. Though I much preferred keeping Binkster in her own home, right now having Dwayne in my space seemed like a bad idea. But to do the right thing by my dog I reluctantly accepted Dwayne's offer. He said he'd be at my house in an hour.

Sixty minutes . . .

I took a hard look at myself in the mirror. Good . . . God. The bruise on my cheek had ripened into an underlying violet with an alienish green tinge. My ear had a red cut nicked out of it. The hot curling iron burn on my neck was starting to scab but it looked like it might hang around a lifetime. My hair needed to see a brush, and my eyes were dull as dirt.

I had a thought of myself standing next to Jazz and I tore into a frenzy of personal beautification. Dragging out the bottle of liquid cover-up, I smeared it over my face. It pretty much took care of the bruising and turned the neck burn into a faintly bumpy discoloration. I went for the heavy, sparkling tannish eye shadow and dark brown liner. My lashes got a healthy layering of mascara. Examining my teeth, I brushed them for about the fifth time that day. Something about throwing up that makes the mouth crave peppermint or wintergreen or cinnamon for days after. I dug through the drawer and found a bottle of pinkish blush loaded with little sparklies. Dabbing some on my cheeks, I then pulled out my favorite lipstick. Actually, it was the closest tube I had at hand. I put it on, thought the color was pretty good, smacked my lips and examined my results.

Huge improvement. I brushed my hair hard and covered my nicked ear.

Finding clothes was another matter. I looked at my wedding and funeral dresses and blew a big raspberry. Binkster sat in her little bed in the corner of my bedroom. Her head was damn near swallowed up by the contraption keeping her from doing her canine best to heal herself.

I said to her, "I wore my good outfit yesterday and we both know how that turned out."

In the end I pulled out a pair of black pants—the dressy ones only used for special occasions. This was it. The last item of good clothing I possessed. If I saw Jazz after this, it was recycle time. Since Binkster had taken care of my strappy sandals I tugged on Cynthia's boots one more time. Okay, they're brown, not black. To combat this fashion faux pas I teamed the pants with a dark tan blouse made out of stretchy material that makes my breasts look bigger than they are. I rarely wear it because . . . well, I don't know why, really. Am I afraid of false advertising? Like, who's gonna care but me?

I stuck out my chest and looked at the dog. "See anything you like, sailor?"

My eyes took in Binkster's shaved, swabbed and stitched hind leg. It hurt to see her injury. She wagged her tail at me, and I felt terrible again.

I spent ten minutes rubbing her head and ears, petting her, and doing the coochy-coochy-cutie-doggy-goo-goo stuff that used to make me groan and roll my eyes upon witnessing it in others. Binks flopped over on her side and sighed contentedly. Okay, I can still make my dog happy. What's that line about aspiring to be the kind of person your dog already thinks you are? I was going to do my darnedest to make sure I never let her down again.

Dwayne knocked on the door and I yelled at him to come in. I was all about pretending nothing had happened between us. Just good old Dwayne. No need to answer the door. Let him come on in, make himself at home.

Binkster scrambled to her feet and tottered out to see him. Her affection for Dwayne is a source of concern to me; one I'm not sure what to do about. But for today I was going to be magnanimous and let them be all smoochy with each other and not care. Binkster deserved all the attention and Dwayne, well, I just wanted him to be distracted. I was pretty sure nothing sexual had transpired between us, but there had been a subtle shift in our relationship nonetheless, and I didn't know how to handle it. Answer: act like it doesn't exist.

"Hey," I said, coming out of the bedroom, affixing an earring. I hadn't planned to wear any, but it seemed like a good idea to be in the process of doing something when I saw him. Another form of distraction. It hurt my ear some, but I didn't care. I was all about appearances.

Dwayne was squatted down, petting Binks with one hand, holding a box of some kind of frozen food in the other. I realized it was mochis, a Japanese dessert, ice cream with a rice-gum and powder skin. It was something he kept on hand, and something Binkster had discovered to her ever-loving delight.

Unlike me Dwayne hadn't bothered with the dressing up thing. He was in his jeans, cowboy boots and a white shirt, sleeves rolled up, exposing tanned forearms. Binkster was licking him and wiggling ecstatically. Dwayne glanced over. Sometimes he wears a cowboy hat but he's got great hair. Light brownish and sun-streaked. He gave me a sideways look out of his blue eyes that made it hard for me to breathe. Those eyes swept up the length of me, then he turned back to Binkster.

"So, this little Purcell wingding is a 'welcome home' party?" he asked as he walked into the kitchen and shoved the mochis into my freezer.

"I guess so."

"You never said what you learned at the sanitarium."

"It seems kind of unimportant now."

"Does it? Why?" He came back into the living room and gazed at me directly. I found it kind of unnerving.

"Well, Orchid's back. The family has her signature on a power of attorney. Whatever their problems are, they're their problems. Every family has them. You said yourself that you've got a lot of family issues."

"Yeah, but I don't have to see my relatives much. No wonder the Purcells are nut cases. They have to live in each other's pockets."

The sound of wheels crunching on gravel announced Jazz's arrival. Both Dwayne and I turned toward the door. I felt absurdly shy all of a sudden. This was so dumb. Neither of them was my boyfriend, or lover—please, God, let it be so—so I was overreacting and feeling weird for no reason.

Jazz knocked at the same moment I turned the knob. He smiled at me and the light hit his eyes as if it were set for a photograph. His hair was combed from his face in a smooth, casual style. He wore a cream shirt and taupe chinos with Italian leather shoes. His scent was now familiar to me. He looked and smelled like money.

"These are for you," he said, and he held out a bouquet of a dozen yellow roses.

"Thank you." I could feel Dwayne behind me and heat crept up my neck. Oh, Lord, I was blushing. "Let me put these in water," I said, ducking from Dwayne's scrutiny as I race-walked to the kitchen.

I heard Jazz introducing himself to Dwayne and vice versa. I yanked down a vase from the cupboard above my refrigerator. It's the only one I have and I thought it might be a tad too small for the roses. I shoved them in anyway, avoiding the thorns, and ran water about halfway up the vase's neck. They were stunning, really, so I brought them out to the coffee table.

"What happened to your dog?" Jazz asked.

"Car accident." I found myself unable to explain more. It just made me feel so terrible.

"I'm the dog sitter," Dwayne said, his drawl more pronounced than ever.

I didn't look at him as Jazz and I left. Jazz tried to quiz me a bit on Dwayne, but apart from saying that he was basically my boss, I avoided the topic altogether. Dwayne was a worry, one I didn't want to look at too closely just yet. I was afraid, at a gut level, that I may have blown it with him and the delicate balance of our relationship. I didn't know what to think about that.

My anxieties over Dwayne made me overly attentive to Jazz. I wasn't trying to play some kind of game, but my fear was driving me in a way that defied rationality. I was scared and, unfortunately, kind of excited; every nerve ending felt raw and alive.

Jazz seemed to eat it up. "I'm so glad you came," he said enthusiastically. He dropped a hand over mine and I smiled at him. Part of me wanted to clasp that hand, another part didn't want to start something I wasn't prepared to finish. Apparently he was over being upset about my trip to River Shores.

"So, that guy's your boss?" Jazz asked.

"Yes. Sort of. I work independently, but he's the one who connected me with you, actually. He was working for your cousin. Cammie."

Jazz thought hard for a moment, then shook his head. "It's not there. One of those missing pieces, I guess."

I explained about Cammie hiring Dwayne to check up on Chris, wondering if I should go into the particulars of Chris's second family. It wasn't a secret, but it was apparently all new to Jazz. I expected him to have some follow-up questions, but instead he reached an arm around the back of my seat and turned to me as we pulled up to the Purcell mansion.

"Before we go in, tell me the truth, Jane. Why were you checking up on my mother?"

Okay, he wasn't over it. "The truth?" I asked.

"Why did you go to the sanitarium?"

"Ummm . . ."

"You said it was for Nana, but I was wondering . . . was it for me, too?" He was engagingly expectant. I just kind of stared at him. The man was damned attractive, and I didn't want to burst his bubble so I just shrugged, letting him think what he would. "I'm glad you haven't given up on us," he said, almost shyly. "I was afraid, now that the money issue is settled, that you would walk out of my life."

I smiled for an answer and thought about last night in bed with Dwayne. Naked. Drunk. It felt like this massive betrayal, and it bugged me no end that I'd gotten myself into this situation. "The money issue's settled, then?"

"Dahlia has the POA. Nana doesn't even seem aware of it, right now. We're all kind of relieved that that's been taken care of. So, anyway, the sanitarium? Who did you talk to? Did they tell you anything about my mother?"

"Like I said, they're going to need you, or a member of your family, to be the one to ask for information."

"But you learned something. You said she wasn't meek."

"The records imply that Lily suffered from hypersexuality," I said reluctantly.

"That's right. That's what it was. Sorry. I can't hold onto anything sometimes." He shook his head. "But it's not true. Nana—everyone—talks about my mom's meekness."

"I'm just saying what was in the file."

"Do you have that file?" Jazz asked.

"That would be stealing," I pointed out. Those papers were still stuffed in my purse. I suddenly had worries of the authorities chasing me down, yanking them from me and booting me into jail. I know this is fanciful, but I do fear incarceration. It keeps me semiresponsible in my job and life.

"I'd like to talk to someone there," Jazz said, taking me by surprise. "Will you go with me?"

"Back to River Shores?" He nodded. I'd opened the floodgates, apparently. Now he wanted to know everything there was to know about his mother and the secrets surrounding her. "Sure." Jazz didn't hear my lack of enthusiasm or chose to ignore it.

As we were getting ready to enter the house, Logan came out. He saw me with his father and his face darkened. "I'm not sure I'm going to let you into *my* house," he said, reaching for humor but coming off sounding bratty and spoiled.

"Logan." Jazz gazed at him as if he'd never seen him before.

Logan was too young to have the good sense to quit before he made things worse. "Well, it's mine, isn't it? Nana said so."

Jazz said to me, "Nana told him last Christmas that he was her heir. It's not really true."

"Yes, it is. I'm her favorite," Logan insisted. "She's leaving everything to me. She said so."

"You bothered her with this?" For the first time I could tell Jazz was growing angry with him. Personally, I thought it was high time the kid was taken down a peg or two.

"Nah. I haven't had a chance to talk to her. They're all going in and out of her room. 'Nana, would you like some tea? Can I get you anything? Let me get you a blanket. Can I kiss your butt?'" Logan snorted in disgust.

"Stop being rude and give Nana some space."

"Oh, yeah, sure. You sound like all the rest of them." He flounced off, heading around the side of the building, toward the front of the house.

Thinking about Orchid, I asked, "Does Nana ever talk about the playhouse?"

Jazz gazed at me oddly. "Why?"

"Someone said she seemed haunted by it." I wasn't going to invoke Eileen's name as anything about her seemed to be dismissed.

"Haunted by it," he repeated. "That's one way to put it, I guess. Sometimes she says things about it."

"What kind of things?"

"I don't know. I can't quite remember. Maybe you should ask James."

"Why James?"

He lifted his hands in a kind of surrender. "It just seems like you should."

We entered the house. Music was emanating from the main salon, a Frank Sinatra song. It was just ending as we joined the others and another one was beginning: "High Hopes." We were apparently listening to a CD compilation of Sinatra favorites. I guessed he was a favorite of Nana's.

The family was there in force, except for Orchid herself. Garrett explained that his mother was napping, that they were planning to wake her soon but that they were all so relieved that she was fine that they'd started the party early. There was a crystal decanter of port or sherry on the coffee table. Upon seeing me, Dahlia hurried to pour me a demi-glass. Her eyes were bright, and I wondered if she'd been imbibing heavily. I shuddered at the thought of even putting my lips to the rim. There was no way I was ready for any alcohol, after praying to the porcelain god early this morning, but I accepted the glass just to hold.

Behind Dahlia, Satin moved over and poured herself a refill. There was something secretive in her movements and I realized she was hoping the family's attention would stay on Jazz and me and no one would notice.

Cammie was sans Rosalie, who was also napping. "She's sleeping too late, and she'll be a bear when she wakes up, but what are you going to do?" She shrugged, took a sip of her drink and made a face. "Port. Yuck." She set the glass on the coffee table.

"Reyna's making Mother's favorite," Garrett said. "Southern fried chicken with biscuits and gravy. Personally, I'd rather have a steak, but I guess I'll survive." This was his little joke. I was kind of surprised he had any sense of humor at all.

James said, "Maybe we should wake her."

Satin floated by and Cammie said, "Yeah, before Mom gets to the bottom of the bottle." Satin flushed and sank into a chair. "Did you think I didn't see you pick up my glass?" Cammie asked.

"Leave your mother alone," Garrett ordered.

Benjamin viewed them with a jaundiced eye. He refilled his own glass as did Roderick. Father and son clinked rims. Dahlia gazed at Benjamin with a mixture of motherly love and possessiveness.

Jazz said, "I'll go get Nana."

"I'll come with you," I said, setting down my untouched drink. I glanced toward Satin, whose eyes were focused on my glass.

I was following Jazz upstairs when he suddenly stopped at the landing, turned around and looked down at me. "Let's not stay for dinner," he suggested. "After we take Nana downstairs and hang around for a little bit, I want us to go out somewhere. Just you and I. We can celebrate together. How does that sound?"

"Great."

We smiled at each other and then Jazz pulled me close and pressed his lips to mine. He took me completely by surprise, and therefore I was a little slow to get into the moment. I had to force myself to relax, but I managed. As kisses go, it wasn't bad: soft and searching, full of the promise of something deeper, more dangerous. I responded carefully. Jazz took his time but in my head I kept worrying what would happen if any of his family suddenly appeared. By the time he released me I needed to suck in a deep breath.

"Whew." I smiled. "That was interesting timing."

He laughed. "I've been thinking about it for a while, but somehow it never seemed like it was going to work." At that moment, the back door opened and Logan entered. He glanced up at us. Whatever he saw caused a stunned look to cross his face. Jazz moved away from me. "I'd better go check with him. He can be so sensitive."

I nodded. Yeah. About as sensitive as a Poloma bull.

"Go on ahead," Jazz said. "I'll be right there. Nana will be glad it's you."

I wasn't even sure Nana knew my name wasn't Eileen. But I sure as hell didn't want to be with Jazz when he had a powwow with Logan about what he may, or may not, have seen us doing on the landing.

I started thinking about Binkster as I walked toward Nana's double doors. I couldn't get my mind off my dog for long. I wouldn't mind getting something going with Jazz, but I was currently more interested in Binks's welfare than about anything else. This could be looked at as a flaw on my part, but I didn't care. Jazz was an iffy proposition; The Binkster was a member of my family.

I knocked, but Orchid didn't immediately invite me inside. I waited a couple of seconds, knocked again, and called, "Nana?" in a tentative voice I despised. I was going to have to give up and just call her Orchid, no matter what she wanted. I just couldn't do it. Nana was just too uncomfortable and rang false.

When there was still no response I tested the knob. I half-expected them to have locked her in now, after her grand escape, but I guess they felt they were all on alert now, all in the house, all aware of the exits.

The door opened and I stepped inside.

For a nanosecond I didn't notice anything off. Then my eye jumped to the mantel. A smear of blood. Then to the hearth. Orchid lay on her side in a heap, blood pooling beneath her left temple.

I stumbled forward and saw that her eyes were open and staring. I sucked in a startled breath.

Those electric blue eyes were sightless now. In disbelief I realized Orchid Candlestone Purcell was dead.

Chapter Thirteen

For the longest of moments I stood motionless, in a strange state of calm. I thought about checking Orchid's pulse. I'd never been faced with a dead body outside the trappings of a funeral home or church and it was the oddest feeling. Birth seems so right and natural; death feels like a cheat.

But I didn't check her pulse. I knew she was dead. Even if she'd risen up and starting talking to me I would have told myself I was dreaming and known it was true. That's how sure I was, and as it turned out, I was right.

Taking a deep breath, I turned on my heel and left the room. I walked right down the stairs and across the entry hall to the salon. Jazz was still with Logan somewhere, I presumed, because he wasn't with the rest of the family.

Garrett frowned and said, "I thought you were getting Mother? Where is she? Is she still napping?"

A whole lot of sick answers whirled around in my head on that one. In fact a little burble of hysteria had formed in my throat. I'd often heard stress makes people laugh inappropriately. That's exactly what I wanted to do, laugh and laugh and laugh. I just managed to hold myself back.

"What's the matter?" Benjamin asked, searching my face. The guy was intuitive in a way the rest of his family wasn't.

"It's Orchid. She's . . . dead."

They collectively stared at me. "Dead . . . ?" Roderick repeated. He looked at James, as if for confirmation.

I gathered my wits with an effort. "It looks like she fell against the mantel. She's lying on the floor."

"Is this a joke?" Garrett demanded.

"No."

Their faces reacted with shock. James declared fiercely, "She's not dead. If she's fallen, she could be injured!"

As if there were some off-camera signal, they suddenly surged as one toward the door. I was the rock in the current as they swarmed past me. As soon as I was alone I went straight for the inch of port in the bottle, looked around for a cup, realized I was out of luck, then simply tipped the bottle back and gulped it down. I didn't care if my stomach reacted now. I needed something.

Tears formed in the corners of my eyes and my nose stung, but the stuff did the trick. As soon as I was finished I felt stronger. Hair of the dog . . . time immemorial hangover cure and antidote for shock.

I heard voices in the hall: Logan and Jazz. They entered the salon and stopped short. "Where is everybody?" Logan asked.

"Where's Nana?" Jazz followed up instantly. Then, "Is something wrong?"

"It's Orchid . . ." We heard noises from upstairs. Raised voices. Logan turned and headed toward the commotion.

"Don't," I said, reaching a hand toward him. He hesitated, looking at me askance. Jazz grabbed my forearms and searched my face.

"Jane, what's wrong?" he asked.

"Jazz, she's dead. Orchid's dead. It looks like she fell against the mantel. Hit her head. Maybe it was an accident."

"*Maybe* it was an accident?" He looked shell-shocked. "Nana?"

"I don't know how it happened."

"Stay here," he ordered, and he hurried out of the room at a half-run to join his family upstairs, Logan on his heels.

I sat down hard in one of the chairs. I understood that I was in a mild state of shock, but it didn't help me pull myself together. I could feel a sense of guilt creeping in, as if Orchid's death were somehow my fault. Irrational, yes, but I couldn't shake it. What I wanted most in the world at that moment was to crawl beneath the covers of my bed, with my dog, and sleep for a week.

I wondered if they had any more port.

It could have been ten minutes, it could have been two hours, but in that weird interim while the Purcells dealt with the immediacy of Orchid's death, William DeForest opened the back door and announced his arrival. I turned toward the sound, waiting for him to appear in the open doorway of the salon. My first thought was: So they did invite him. My second: The old bastard kept her from spending some last precious few hours with her family.

This less than charitable conclusion couldn't be dislodged. I was angry with him. When William hesitated in the doorway, my lip curled. His natty gray slacks, white shirt, red bow tie and suspenders irked me. He was clearly puzzled at finding only me. "What's going on?" he asked, looking behind him as if the Purcells were hiding just out of sight.

Injustice fueled me. Later, I would wonder if I'd taken temporary leave of my sanity, but in that moment I zeroed in on William like a tracking missile. I said, in a conversational tone, "What the hell were you thinking, keeping Orchid from her family? You knew she was having cognitive problems. You call yourself her friend. But it's your fault she was missing these past few days. You did that. Nobody else."

His look of surprise was almost comical. "Where is everyone? Am I late?"

"All your little secrets . . . all your machinations . . . what did it get you? Nobody trusts you. And what were all those little comments about the Purcells, implying that you knew all the secrets. Blah, blah, blah." I scowled at him. "You're not a friend of theirs. You never were."

William did not know what to make of me. I was operating

outside the limits of good taste and acceptable social behavior. He eyed me critically. "Are you drunk?"

"Orchid's gone," I said, my fury dissipating as fast as it had risen. "She's dead."

He blinked several times. I was spent. Even more bushed than before. I didn't need port; I needed a bed.

He gulped. "What are you saying? What are you saying?"

Footsteps descended the stairs. I was glad. Let the Purcells deal with him. Let them explain it.

Dahlia entered first, her face blotchy, her eyes red. One look at her and William turned ashen. Stunned, he stared, nearly collapsing, then he headed for the stairs on wobbly legs. I should have felt sorry for him, but I didn't. I knew it was a classic case of transference, but I didn't care. I wanted to wring his lying, bow-tied neck. He wept as he climbed the steps and even that didn't melt my ice cold heart.

Long hours passed before Jazz could take me home, hours while the Purcells digested the news and decided what action to take. A call was put through to 911, the police showed up, the EMTs arrived and Orchid's body was taken away. Preliminary examination revealed what I'd already suspected: she hit her head on the mantel and fell to the floor. The head injury had probably caused internal bleeding in the brain, then death.

Once the body was removed and the authorities gone, Garrett had the bad taste to propose the idea of foul play. Cammie and Dahlia were horrified anyone could even think that was the case, but Garrett began trumpeting this idea as if it were fact. Satin kept her head bent and tried to become invisible. James stood by in silent, starey shock. Benjamin hung with Roderick, and they did find another bottle of port, which they kept out of Satin's reach, by accident or design I couldn't quite tell. For once Logan showed restraint. The shock of his great-grandmother's death had deeply rattled him. He stood by Jazz, who kept his arm around his son's shoulders.

I waited this out, staying in the background. My brain was too tired to think through the ramifications. The bottom line was

Orchid was dead. The worry and fret about her health, mental acuity, and overall handling of the finances was now a moot point.

Eventually Jazz and I climbed into his BMW convertible and headed out. We were quiet on the drive to my place, neither of us having anything to say. When Jazz pulled up next to Dwayne's truck and yanked on the emergency brake, he finally spoke. "God, I can't believe she's gone. She was my rock."

I nodded.

"She was always championing me, and you know how much she loves—loved—Logan." He swallowed hard. "I miss her already."

"I'm sorry," I said, and meant it.

Opening the passenger door, I stepped into a starless evening, leaning a moment on the car door to catch my bearings. I looked up at the night sky, then at my cottage. The air was distinctly chilly. I could see a bluish flickering light emanating through the slit that ran beneath the bottom of the living room blinds and the sill. Dwayne was probably lying on my couch, watching television.

"Jane?" I leaned down and peered in the window at Jazz. "That guy . . . your boss?"

"Dwayne Durbin."

"Is he something more to you?"

"No." I was positive. "He's not so much my boss as my business partner."

"Nothing more?"

"Nothing more."

He half-smiled. "That's the one good thing about today, then. You and me. I'll see you tomorrow?"

"Sure."

I waved good-bye to Jazz then walked into my front room and greeted Dwayne with a bitten off, "Hi." I wasn't trying to be rude; I just didn't want to go another round with him. I wanted whatever had happened between us to die a quick death.

Dwayne flicked me a look. "Hi." He was lying on the sofa, one arm tucked under his head. Binkster was sitting with her back to the cushions, her front legs and head splayed on Dwayne's flat stomach. The cone looked damn uncomfortable, and she held her stitched hind leg to one side as if it hurt, too.

"Binky," I murmured, coming over to scratch behind her ears. I'd had a hard time calling her this at first. Too cutie-patootie. But now it sufficed perfectly as she twisted her head around to lick my fingers.

"She's hungry," Dwayne said on a yawn.

"I know. She's always hungry." My voice was full of love. Hearing it, I thought about the Purcells and how they looked at their various offspring. I had so much to tell Dwayne and I just didn't know where to begin. Finally, I baldly came out with, "Orchid's dead."

"What?" Dwayne sat up in surprise and Binks shifted quickly.

The events of the night started to tumble out without any rhyme or reason. I needed Dwayne's clear thinking and investigator's mind. I didn't want to worry about what last night had meant, if anything. I just wanted everything to be the way it had been between us. Dwayne listened in silence as I told him about finding Orchid and the Purcells' varying reactions, then I backtracked and related my experiences at River Shores, trying not to leave out a single detail. Finally I ran down, finishing with the way I'd verbally attacked William when he'd walked through the salon door.

"I just wanted to kill him," I admitted. "I was so mad."

Dwayne snorted. "The seven stages of grief. Sounds like you skipped a few."

"Grief? Shock, maybe. I barely knew the woman."

"Yeah, well, you can't get over thinking she was your responsibility."

"Why does it always sound like you have all the answers? Why do you do that, Dwayne?"

My pique amused him. "I hear serious hostility, darlin'. You already attacked the poor old guy with the bow tie. Now you want to take a shot at me."

"Poor old guy, my ass. And you don't have all the answers. I'm beginning to realize that. You had me fooled for a while, but I know more now."

"I don't know what you're talkin' about," he marveled.

"You, Dwayne. You! I'm talking about the way you act. This kind of know-it-all male crap that's covered up with the 'aw, shucks, ma'am' bullshit always coming out of your mouth. I'm not listening to it anymore. That's what I'm saying. I'm not listening to it."

"You're just mad because I teased you this morning."

"Y'see? I hate that, Dwayne. I hate it when you provide all the answers. You don't even know what I'm talking about."

"Yes, I do."

"No, you don't." I was firm, my jaw tight.

"I know you're all worked up because you wanted to know if we slept together and I wouldn't give you a straight answer. I know that you can't decide whether you want it to be true or not. I know you've been thinking about it all day."

"I have not!"

"Oh, yes, you have." He climbed to his feet, settling Binkster onto the couch. She propped herself up on her front legs, her head turning from one to the other of us, as if she were watching a Ping-Pong match. "You've been wondering if we did the down and dirty together, and you've been pissed 'cause if we did, you can't remember. And you want to remember."

"You're unbelievable," I said uneasily. He was getting way too close to me. This was a new side of Dwayne I wasn't sure I liked. Yes, I'd poked and prodded at him, but now I was wishing I'd left well enough alone.

"Well, let me tell you something to ease your mind: No. We didn't do a damn thing together."

"I was naked when I woke up." I looked into his face, wondering why he seemed so different to me. It was scary and a little thrilling. *Don't do this, Jane. Don't find him attractive.*

"'Cause I stripped you down. Not because I had designs on you, because there was blood all over your clothes."

"What did you sleep in?" I asked, mouth dry, though I knew. I'd felt that bare leg.

"Not a damn thing."

"And we didn't have sex."

"No."

"Okay." I didn't mean to sound chastised, but I did. And a little disappointed, too.

"You wanna know why?"

"Because you knew I didn't want to?"

He almost laughed. "Didn't want to? Darlin', you were all over me! Begged me to make love to you."

"You are *so* lying!"

"Not a bit. I'm tellin' you the God's honest truth. I had to take a cold shower to keep from taking you up on the offer."

"That's not even true. Oh, sure. Make yourself the hero." I backed up a few paces. He was too damn close.

"Y'know what I told ya? I said if you still felt the same way today, I'd take you up on it."

"Well, I don't. I never did. I do not intend to be fuck-buddies with you, Dwayne. Ever."

"Fuck-buddies . . ." he repeated in disbelief, shaking his head. "Making it crass doesn't make it untrue. You tried to seduce me, Jane Kelly. It wasn't the other way around."

Had I? Maybe . . . Things were pretty darn hazy. But his words were dredging up memories from the depths of my brain, little forgotten pieces that suddenly burst into technicolor focus: my lips searching for Dwayne's, missing, me then laughing hysterically, trying again, managing a sloppy kiss, using my tongue . . .

I cringed inside. Oh, God. I *had* made a pass at Dwayne. "I don't believe any of this," I lied, mortified. "You're making it up."

"Nope."

"You have to be."

"C'mere," he said. His face was grim and set.

I could see I'd made things worse. And there was nowhere to

hide. Binkster gave a little yip and I glanced over at her. She wagged her tail and panted. I swear to God it was like clapping. She was enjoying the show.

"Okay, time out," I said, breathing a little sanity into the moment. "I don't know what we're doing here. I'm willing to concede that I could possibly be a little bit at fault. I've had a hell of a couple of days. You've gotta admit that. I'm not thinking straight, and if I seemed friendlier than I should have last night, well, I'm sorry. I was drunk and upset and I don't think I can be held completely responsible for my actions."

"So, you admit you came on to me?"

I narrowed my eyes. "No . . . I'm saying I wasn't myself."

To my shock Dwayne put his hands on my shoulders and pushed me against the wall. His face was close to mine. So close that I could see the darker, indigo striations in his blue eyes. I've always been a sucker for blue eyes. And Dwayne has some damn nice ones.

However, I hadn't planned on getting this close to them. "What are you doing?" I asked tautly.

For an answer he pressed his mouth to mine. My heart rate zinged and I let out a funny little squeak. Dwayne was *kissing* me. And he was kissing me, but good. Hard and demanding. My breath caught in my throat. I was so stunned that I stayed frozen, except my lips parted in dismay, or maybe invitation . . . it wasn't clear.

I could smell him. Sort of a musky scent that seemed to reach right inside me. Dwayne's eyes had closed and so did mine. There was just a brief instant, one of those sterling moments, when my mind chose between capitulation and outrage.

I sagged against the wall and Dwayne pressed himself against me. His tongue thrust between my teeth. I'm no great fan of French kisses. Half the time the guy nearly suffocates me with this wildly searching tongue. But Dwayne had it down right. His tongue slipped across the roof of my mouth. I wanted to damn near suck it down my throat. He tasted my teeth and my lips and simply kept going in a way that did me in. My mind was full of visions of grabbing him, rolling on the floor, wrapping my legs around him, stripping off our clothes.

I thought, succinctly: *I want you.*

It was about this time that I dimly noticed Dwayne wasn't as involved as I was. His body had pushed mine to the wall, yet there was something calculated about this seduction, something distant on his part.

I strong-armed him away from me and came up for air. Dwayne took a step back. We stared at each other.

"You're not into it," I accused. Now the outrage was there. And hurt. This really took a shot at my desirability.

"I'm gettin' there," he said, his accent thick. "Tryin' to hold back."

"Why?" My chest rose and fell like I'd run a marathon.

"Didn't want to rush the ending."

"Yeah?"

"Yeah."

His gaze dropped to my mouth. I realized he was struggling to hang onto his self-control. This was gratifying. But sanity was returning in a flood. I saw how much I wanted to sleep with him. I really, *really* wanted to sleep with him. But I didn't like what would happen next. Our relationship would digress. We would fight like lovers instead of friends. It would be hurtful and awful.

But as I looked into his eyes I thought it might be worth it.

"Goddamn it," I muttered, my own gaze fastening on his lips. He read me right. A moment later we were kissing for all it was worth. This time, when he pressed his body to mine I felt his urgency.

My fingers scrabbled for the tail of his shirt. I yanked it away from his pants, my hands running up the smooth muscles of his back.

In the midst of this insanity Binkster found her way between our feet. Her little body pushed and wiggled. I tried to ignore her. Dwayne did, too. We both sought to nudge her away with our feet. She made little growly noises. In the midst of a kiss I started laughing, silently, unable to help myself. Dwayne swore without heat against my mouth, his lips curving. We broke for a moment, both of us looking at each other, then at the dog. Binkster gazed up at us, her little black face inquisitive, her ears lifted, her head cocked. With the cone as a ruffle, she really looked like a clown. Dwayne and I both started laughing and Binks began digging at my leg for all she's worth—a ploy for attention.

"Want a mochi?" Dwayne asked her.

She instantly dropped to her four feet and stared at him, totally tuned in.

Dwayne took her into the kitchen. I heard him open the freezer and pull out the ice cream treat. I could hear Binkster smacking her lips as Dwayne gave her pieces.

I leaned against the wall. I felt exhausted and wired at the same time.

Dwayne returned, Binkster dancing around his feet, her face turned up to the half mochi left in his fingers. She gave him one sharp bark, just to remind him in case he forgot. He did forget, as it turned out. His gaze on mine, he popped the rest of the dessert in his mouth. Binks, on her hind legs, propped herself on Dwayne's leg with one paw, gazing up at him forlornly.

Dwayne said, "You look . . . well kissed."

"Yeah . . . well . . ." I gestured to his clothes. His shirt hung out, wrinkled and askew.

My cell phone, which I'd turned back to "ring" began singing away inside my purse. I grabbed at the diversion like a lifeline, picked up the phone and saw it was Jazz. While I debated on answering, Dwayne dusted his hands, showing Binks the food was gone. Then he strode to the bathroom, where I suspected he was putting himself back together. I straightened my shirt, rubbed my flushed cheeks and answered.

"Hi, there," Jazz greeted me warmly. "I just wanted to say good night, so, good night."

My gaze was pinned on the closed bathroom door. "Good night," I said woodenly.

"See you tomorrow."

I muttered a good-bye and closed my flip phone.

Oh . . . holy . . . shit.

Chapter Fourteen

The next morning I ran to the Nook in record time, chased by inner demons. I know better than to get involved with Dwayne romantically, I told myself like a litany as I ran. I know better . . . I know better . . . I *know* better.

It had been awkward when he'd walked back out of the bathroom. Well, that's an understatement, really. I'd kept my attention on The Binkster, using my dog as an avoidance technique. It worked better than I could have hoped for as Dwayne just said good night and left. I spent the rest of the night in a state of anxiety and mild sexual frustration. At one point I pressed my face into my pillow and screamed. Binkster growled low in her throat. I looked up at her, noticed the cone. Oh, yeah, she's fierce.

At the Nook I lingered around longer than normal, hoping someone would come in who would occupy my thoughts. My head felt full of problems, and I didn't feel like solving any of them. I didn't want to prioritize. I didn't want to think. I wanted all the problems to just go away so I could stop feeling so rotten.

I hadn't had a chance to really process Orchid's death.

I'd barely accepted the fact that my negligence had injured my dog.

I wasn't sure I wanted to get involved with Jazz Purcell, no matter how damn good looking he was, and my ambivalent feel-ings were all because of *Dwayne.*

I made a sound of annoyance under my breath that was drowned out by the espresso machine's noisy *fsssttt.*

Though I waited around hopefully, I couldn't cadge a ride from anyone, so in the end I was forced to drag my tired body back to my cottage on foot. As I walked, I crumpled the paper coffee cup in one hand to make it easier to carry. I took my time, dawdling, because I really didn't have anything pressing. The exercise made me feel better, but one look at The Binkster and my problems returned like a lead mantle on my shoulders.

After such an intense week I decided it was time to check out for a while, and I spent the next few days doing nothing but watching television, running to fast-food restaurants when I got hungry, tending to my dog and thinking. I also swore a lot. Every word I could think of, usually tied together in a string of profan-ity. I was surprised how quickly I ran out of them. There had to be more but my overwhelmed brain couldn't seem to come up with them. Luckily, they're the kind of coping tool that can be used over and over again.

Jazz called and we talked, but we didn't get together. This was my doing because although he was interested, I needed time to sort some things out. He didn't bring up our pending trip to River Shores again and neither did I. At first I thought it was be-cause, in the wake of Orchid's death, he suddenly had a lot more pressing issues. And maybe that was the case, but after a couple of days I began to suspect he'd also forgotten we'd ever dis-cussed the idea. His short-term memory loss was proving to have its advantages as I was so not interested in another trip to the san-itarium with Jazz in tow. Orchid was gone and whatever secrets she'd harbored had gone with her literally to the grave. If Jazz wanted to learn who his father was, that was one thing, but the mystery surrounding Lily had ceased to be a factor, at least in my opinion.

I didn't talk to Dwayne. Okay, I did, but it was just a sentence or two on a couple of phone calls. He was working and busy. I was not, but acted like I was. I pretended to be process serving day and night and unable to devote time to anything else. He didn't press me on the point. I think we were both relieved to take a break from each other. (At least this is what I told myself, though he occupied my thoughts far more than he should have and in new and disturbing ways.)

Thursday I was so into my non-work routine that I banged around in sweatpants and my IN-N-OUT T-shirt until nearly noon. It was while I was leaning one arm on my refrigerator door, wishing the shelves didn't look so bare, that I remembered something important.

"Shit!" I slammed the door shut and my gaze jumped to the kitchen clock. Eleven-forty-five.

I hurtled over Binks and slid around the corner to the bathroom, stripping off my running gear and leaving it in a trail behind me. Jumping in the shower, I didn't wait for it to turn warm as I swore pungently, running through my litany of words three more times.

Mom's plane was arriving in ten minutes.

"Shit!" I said again, rinsing the soap from my hair and leaping, skidding onto the tile floor before wet-footing it to the bedroom. I tried to yank on my clothes but the remaining water on my skin mocked my efforts. I swore some more.

By the time I was in the car I was ready to break every speed record known to man. Midday traffic isn't too bad. With luck, she'd just be collecting her bag when I pulled up to the curb.

Timing is everything with the Portland Airport, with any airport these days, actually. The pickup lanes are patrolled by security employees wearing Day-Glo orange vests. They have zero sense of humor—both a product of 9/11 and their own sense of importance—and I've been chastised for lingering too long when there was no pickup passenger in sight, and also for simply not maneuvering my vehicle into a good enough parking position. That one really torqued me. People drive crazy at airports; they can scarcely help it as they jockey into position around other crazy drivers. It's practically a free-for-all. I'd done the best I could given the constraints of a moron driving a Suburban in front of me and a kid in a red sports car with ski racks edging in behind me. The security agent, a woman with a snarl built onto her lips, told me I was taking up two lanes. Well, duh. I would have *liked* to have been in one, but I could hardly wedge myself over to the curb with the Suburban's back doors flung open. I would have also liked to point this out. I actually opened my mouth to give it the old college try but she ran right over me with a lecture that would not stop. Other drivers regarded me gratefully as I was taking the heat for them, their vehicles being able to hog two lanes with impunity.

It had really pissed me off.

With these thoughts in mind, I kept my eyes on the road, my brain moving ahead, planning my mother's pickup with the preparation I might give a bank heist. First: check the overall amount of airport traffic. Second: Get ready to abort pickup from the baggage level if need be, choosing the upper departure level instead. This would necessitate an instant decision that would probably infuriate the drivers behind me, but it was a viable option. Third: stay in the moving left lane as long as possible and then dart for the curb. Fourth: find God and pray for no fender benders.

Mom was coming in on Alaska Airlines, one of the carriers with the best schedules from Los Angeles to Portland. Alaska is at the end of the arriving passengers' section, so there would be ample time to make a change in plans if need be. When the security agent had yelled at me I was trying to drop off someone for Delta. Delta's too close to the start of carrier-row. I'd been easy pickings.

My fingers tightened around the steering wheel as I cruised up to the arriving flight deck, but today was fairly quiet and benign. I only felt like making one rude gesture at another driver. The security people didn't appear to be in attack mode. They were grouped along the divider between the pickup lanes and the roadway for hotel vans that ran in front of the parking garage.

Mom wasn't standing outside. I felt my first tickle of worry. If I pulled over, I would undoubtedly be swooped upon with all due haste, although there was a chance they wouldn't immediately notice. If I slowed down and just crept along, hoping Mom would suddenly appear, I was inviting unwanted attention and the chance for another lecture.

I tried to do a little of both. Moving into a slow, slow stop, I pulled up to the curb just before Alaska's sign and tried to be inconspicuous.

My efforts were wasted. My nemesis strode toward me, waving a flashlight like a billy club, her mouth twisted into its snarl. It was the same damn woman who'd yelled at me before. Why wasn't she down at the Delta area, that's what I wanted to know.

I chose deception as my means of defense by pretending I didn't see her charging toward me. Then I started waving furiously to a young woman standing at the curb as if we were long lost friends. The woman lifted a tentative hand. I climbed from the car and said, all smiles, "I thought you were coming in on Frontier! Get on in!"

She looked a bit confused. "Did George send you?"

"You better believe it."

From the corner of my eye I saw my nemesis slow down. She stopped about twenty feet away. "I'm Jane," I said, holding out a hand to the girl.

"Cheryl. You sure you're here for me?"

I shot the security guard nemesis a sideways glance out of the corner of my eyes. Her attention had been diverted by a young Asian woman who'd climbed from the driver's seat and was yakking on her cell phone. She was stomping toward the offender, her snarl in place. I smiled gleefully, thrilled to have foiled her, but Cheryl was gazing at me quizzically. "Actually, I'm not," I apologized. "I'm waiting for my mother. But hey, you saved me from security sending me out on a another loop around the airport. If you need a ride, I might be able to help."

"Ahhh . . ." She smiled, then swept a glance at her cell phone,

making a sound of disgust. "Battery's dead. Just when I need it."
Making a face, she added, "You don't look like a serial killer. I
might take you up on that ride."

"Take your time putting your suitcase in the back," I said
cheerily. I love thwarting authority. It's definitely some quirk in
my makeup, but I'll go out of my way to be a pain in the ass. It's
just so . . . gratifying.

Cheryl, it turns out, was totally up for being my partner in
crime. In fact, I was a little worried she was overplaying her part
when she acted like the suitcase was too heavy to lift. However,
when I tried to help her I realized the thing weighed a ton and a
half.

"What's in there?" I asked.

"Shoes, mostly. I love shoes. Went on a spending spree in L.A.
I hate paying sales tax, though."

Oregon's one of the few states that does not have a sales tax,
but we try to make up for it with property and income taxes.
"You were on the flight from LAX?" She nodded and at that moment Mom came through the glass revolving door, wheeling a
small red suitcase behind her. I was heartened by the idea that
Mom apparently wasn't planning to stay a millennium if that's all
the clothes she brought with her. With all the balls I was juggling
in my life, I didn't think I could take the distraction for long.

Introductions were made all around. Cheryl and Mom recognized each other from the flight and began a lively discussion
about some passenger who'd gotten so drunk and obnoxious that
the flight crew had almost returned to LAX to eject him from the
plane. I kept an eye on my nemesis who was now patrolling
around us, her gaze fierce. She suddenly blew her whistle and
motioned at me. "Move on!"

I took my time getting to my car door, then I asked Mom
earnestly, "Do you need help with your door?"

She looked at me as if I'd lost my mind. "How old do you
think I am?"

"It's kind of sticky. Let me help." I trotted around to the other
side of the car and opened the door for her. The Volvo obligingly

made a wrenching sound but it's done this for years. Mom settled in and the security woman looked like she wanted to thrust my car in gear herself to get it moving.

I lifted a hand in greeting and smiled as I slowly herded the car back onto the road. Mom watched this exchange. "Making friends?" she asked drily.

"Yup."

Cheryl lived in Beaverton and that took us out of our way about thirty minutes but it was worth it. Mom veered the conversation to my job, surprising me by telling Cheryl I was an "information specialist, which is a blanket term for private investigator"; I really never can tell what goes into her brain and what doesn't.

Cheryl brightened. "My brother, Josh, is a Lake Chinook police officer. Josh Newell. You should look him up."

I smiled and made agreeable sounds. I didn't tell her I avoid the Lake Chinook police on principle. I worry about their "no call too small" motto. And with my penchant for bending, or blatantly ignoring, the rules, the less they know about me the better. It's bad enough having an overbearing brother on the Portland PD.

But I committed his name to memory anyway. One never knows . . .

We dropped Cheryl off, then headed for Lake Chinook. As I pulled up to the cottage, I asked Mom, "Does Booth know what time you were getting in?"

She nodded. "We're all going to dinner tonight. This is the first time I get to meet Sharona, so it's kind of a celebration. I'm buying. Booth said you have a favorite place on the lake. Foster's, I think?"

I pictured myself at Foster's On The Lake with my whole family. "I don't have a boat."

"Can't you drive there?"

"Yes, but it's hellish parking."

"You don't want to go?"

I really didn't want to see Booth and Sharona at all. I'd kind of hoped they would take Mom out and I could be by myself, which was a pipe dream from the outset, but hey, it had kept my momentum up all afternoon. Now I pulled Mom's suitcase from the back of the car and sighed. "I might be coming down with something," I said as we walked to the front door.

Mom harrumphed her disbelief.

As soon as the door was open Binkster trotted up to us, wriggling in delight at meeting my mother. Mom gazed down into the dog's little black face. "Who's this?" she asked. "And what's with the lampshade?"

"Mom." My voice took that tone I despise in others, that one where you're holding onto yourself with everything you've got because you just might *snap*. "This is the dog you foisted on me. The one from 'Aunt Eugenie'? The friend of yours you promised to take care of her dog when she died."

"Oh, yes, yes. I remember."

Did she? I wasn't sure.

"He's cute, isn't he?"

"She. She's cute. She was in an accident earlier this week and the neck cone is to keep her from licking the wound."

"Poor little thing," Mom said.

Was there condemnation in that phrase? It sounded like a Mom thing to say, but I was so tender on the subject I was looking for blame in every syllable.

"I don't really want to leave her alone tonight," I said. "Maybe you all should go to Foster's without me."

"Nonsense. We won't be gone long. The dog'll be fine." She peered at me. "Honestly, Jane, I didn't know you had it in you."

"What?"

"You're pretty attached to him."

I said, succinctly, "Her."

My mother smiled, her point made. At fifty-five she's a shorter, plumper and more scattered version of myself: same straight light brown hair, same hazel eyes, same belief that everyone else is slightly off and we're the only sane people left in the world. I would never tell her that I think she might have gone over to the other side. Conversations with Mom can be tricky.

I took her bag into the bedroom over her protests, making it clear that I'm perfectly happy sleeping on my couch. I brought Binkster's bed into the living room, so she could sleep by me. She snuffled the cushions hard, making sure it was still hers, I guess, then promptly sat upon it like a throne.

"She's so cute," Mom said.

"You think she's too fat?"

"Well . . ." Mom trailed off, so I guess I had my answer.

I was itching to do something, but I couldn't rightly just take off. I'd called Greg Hayden and there were a couple of seventy-two hour notices to deliver, but he'd planned on giving them to someone else as he knew I was into the private investigation thing. I complained loudly. No, I wasn't through with process serving. I couldn't be. After all, I very well could have blown the whole gig with Dwayne.

Cynthia text-messaged me, asking how The Binkster was. I've tried text-messaging back but it's not the same as typing on a keyboard and I suck at it. I called her back, got her voice mail, gave her a thumb's up response, adding that Mom had arrived for her visit.

I tried calling Jazz. We hadn't talked today, as was becoming our habit, more his than mine, but there it was. I was beginning to get used to having him in my life. But I got Jazz's voice mail, too. I swear it's a plot. You either make calls and get everyone you want, or you make calls and no one's around. I next phoned Dwayne and this time I was glad for that robotic woman telling me to leave a message. I gave him the news about Mom's arrival, too, trying to sound normal and unaffected, but I think I might have been a bit stilted.

In the end I couldn't get out of dinner, but the good news was Jazz called back and accepted my invitation to join on. This was a bold move on my part, having my whole family meet him, but I thought maybe they could all talk to each other and leave me out of it.

As it turned out Jazz brought Logan along, too. Oh, happy day.

"Logan wanted to see The Binkster," Jazz said. "I hope you don't mind."

"Not at all," I lied. I was originally faintly suspicious of him wanting to be around my dog, but Logan seemed really concerned about Binkster's injury, showing more humanity than I'd seen so far. So, maybe he really was Jazz's son and not the devil's spawn. Time would tell.

Logan also opted out of dinner, which relieved everyone, I'm sure. It certainly didn't break Booth's heart as he settled Mom in the front seat of his Jeep and Sharona graciously took the back. Jazz and I followed in his convertible, the top up, as the weather hadn't known what it wanted to do for days. Sometimes sunny, sometimes rainy, other times blustery, and once in a while a shooting cold wind that made me wish for a down jacket.

Jeff Foster had opened a couple of tables on the patio, but the wind was flapping the umbrellas, sneaking beneath their canopies and threatening to emancipate them. One had actually rocketed its way from its restraints and into the lake. We chose to eat by the inside gas fireplace.

I was right about not having to talk; my family squeezed Jazz like he was auditioning for a game show. I ordered a hamburger—Foster's does them up right—and let the conversation float around me. Mom clearly thought Jazz was a keeper, and she asked lots of questions about his family. She was horrified to learn about his grandmother's recent death, and when Jazz attempted to explain how I fit into the equation—how he'd hired me to both check her mental acuity and be her temporary caretaker, and then she'd died—my mother gazed at me in that blank way that makes me think she wonders if I was switched at birth.

Booth regarded Jazz with suspicion, but then he's that way with everyone. Sharona was simply taken with his good looks, as were most of Foster's other female patrons. I thought back to my first meeting with Jazz, how bowled over I'd been, and assessed my feelings now. I'd really gotten over that initial hit, hadn't I? Even when he'd kissed me, I hadn't really sparked to life.

It was Dwayne's fault, I thought sourly. He'd ruined me for anything I could have had with Jazz.

Foster came by and was more than nice to my family. I took the opportunity to excuse myself and head to the ladies' room. Foster followed me. "So, the guy that looks like you is your brother, and you both look like your mother, so that explains that, but the black chick and Mr. GQ?"

"The black chick's a criminal defense attorney and my brother's fiancée. Mr. GQ is my date."

"Really." He turned to take another look at Jazz.

"He's Jasper Purcell."

Foster whipped around and stared at me as if I'd suddenly morphed into something beyond this world. "Jasper *Purcell?*"

"You got it."

I left him thinking that over. I was kind of pissed off later when we were finishing dinner and Foster sent over a crème brûlée and five forks, on the house. You have to be important to get any freebies. Sheesh. What a rotten world. I'd like to think bringing Jazz had lifted Foster's opinion of me, but that was bound to be a pipe dream. He knows me too well.

Anyway, the evening was fairly uneventful and maybe I've become an adrenaline junkie or something because I was definitely let down by the time we left for home.

At the house, Jazz looked like he wanted to kiss me, but it was all just too awkward. I walked him out to his car, Logan lagging behind. He regarded us in that freaked out "my parents can't have a love/sex life" way, so I just said we'd talk the next day.

"We're going to the lawyer's office tomorrow. Going over the will," Jazz said.

"Oh."

"Garrett's got the police involved. The medical examiner's checking Nana's body." He sounded repelled.

"Garrett really believes it was foul play?"

"I think he was just blustering, but . . ." He shrugged.

"There's no motive to kill her. Everyone in your family

seemed to love her, and you already had the POA, so the money was safe."

"I just feel awful," Jazz said on a sigh.

"Dad?" Logan called from inside the car. He didn't like us talking together.

Jazz gave me a quick, hard hug. "Next time we're together, let's get that alone time we haven't found yet."

They backed out of the drive and I returned to my cottage. Binks had taken up residence on the couch next to Sharona who was giving her all kinds of attention. "When does the cone come off?" she asked.

"Next week. Stitches out. Cone off."

Booth said, "Are you going to tell us about that guy, or what?"

"He's just a friend," I said firmly.

"He really seems to like Jane," Mom said proudly.

I'd only had one glass of wine with dinner, as it hadn't seemed like the drink to team with my hamburger. Now, I found my opened Sauvignon blanc, poured myself a glass and offered it all around. Booth chose to uncork a bottle of red and he and Mom indulged. After a while I walked out on my back deck, then down the stairs and across the flagstones to my empty boat slip. I stood looking over the black water of the bay. Across the way, my neighbor to the north's lights left wiggling lines of illumination across its restless surface.

I heard the back door open and close. I could tell by the approaching footsteps on the wooden steps—sharp, feminine footfalls—that Sharona was joining me. She stood to my right. I gave her a look and noticed she'd chosen some of my leftover white wine.

"There might be a bottle around that hasn't been sitting in the door of the refrigerator."

"This is fine," she said.

Sharona and I are still feeling our way as soon-to-be in-laws. We don't really talk to each other unless Booth is around. The fact that she'd sought me out, alone, made me wonder what was up.

"Jasper Purcell is awfully good looking."

"Yes, he is."

"He's not doing it for you, though, is he?"

"I guess not," I admitted.

"You want to talk about Murphy?" she asked.

I made a face. My second try with my ex-boyfriend hadn't been that long ago, but it felt like eons had passed. "Murphy isn't the reason I'm not into Jazz," I said.

"It's just not there?"

I shrugged. I didn't tell her I was having visions of Dwayne's muscular back. My fingers had felt that flesh and they wanted another chance at him. Not that I was going to let it happen.

"Well, I'm glad," she said. "I came down here to talk you out of him, if I had to, but it looks like I don't."

I looked at her in surprise. "Talk me out of Jazz?"

"He's beautiful, but there's not much going on there, is there? I noticed he rubbed his head a few times, as if he's constantly fighting a headache."

"He does that. He was in an accident. And he has some short-term memory loss."

"Oh."

We fell silent. I hated to admit it, but I kind of understood what she meant, all the same. There was something slightly unformed about Jazz. It was a minor thing, though. Jazz was nice, and he liked me, a lot, and he was gorgeous and wealthy.

My mind swept back to our first meeting again. I'd enjoyed the other women's eyes on him. I'd enjoyed being the one with the handsome man.

Hardly enough to base a whole relationship on.

We walked back toward the steps to the deck. I said, "I'll be right up. I've got to make a phone call."

I watched her join the others, then I whipped my cell from my pocket. I felt slightly furtive, like I wasn't being completely honest with Sharona as I placed a call to Dwayne. I was preparing my message when he suddenly answered.

"Hey, there," he said.

I didn't bother with preliminaries. I told him the M.E. was

closely examining Orchid's body, checking for signs of foul play, and I finished with, "Jazz thinks Garrett was just making noise and didn't really want an investigation. He's probably right. I can't think of any reason someone would want to kill Orchid. They had the POA."

"And the POA was legit?"

"I never heard differently."

"What are the terms of her will?"

"I don't know."

"Then the family should have wanted to keep her alive, otherwise they're at the mercy of the will. Grandma might have some favorites."

"Funny you should say that. Logan said Orchid promised that he would get everything."

"She told him that?"

"Apparently."

"Hmmm . . . nasty business, family inheritances. So, what are you thinking?"

"I don't know. I just wanted to talk it over."

There was a pause, and then Dwayne's drawl came over the line, raising the little hairs along my arms, "I think you miss me a little."

"Dwayne, don't go there."

"C'mon, Jane. Be honest."

"Are you trying to be a pain in the ass? 'Cause I gotta say, you're doing a hell of a job."

"You want to have sex with me."

I could scarcely find my voice. I was sputtering so much I sounded like Donald Duck. "First of all, this conversation is unreal. You and I are business partners and that's it, and that's all it'll ever be. And second . . . just so you know? I could never have sex with someone named Dwayne."

"You can hardly wait."

"Nope. It's in my rule book: No Dwaynes."

"I'm going to have to see that rule book sometime."

"Never," I said and hung up on his laughter.

Chapter Fifteen

The next day I put a call into directory assistance for a Zach Montrose in the city of Salem or the surrounding vicinity of Brooks/Keizer. There was one Z. Montrose. It was ten o'clock in the morning and Mom was in the backyard with Binks, and I was sitting around with time on my hands. My decision to follow up on River Shores and Lily was more an act of desperation than a real need for information: Mom was driving me crazy.

After my conversation with Dwayne I'd gone back inside the cottage to say my good-byes to everyone. As soon as Booth and Sharona were out the door, Mom took her turn grilling me about Jazz. I'd been forced to parry and thrust: every time Mom asked me about Jazz, I brought up Sharona. Yes, Mom thought Sharona was great. She was black, beautiful, successful and totally into Booth. And Booth was just as enamored of her. No, Mom had no problems with their relationship, but she had a ton of advice about mine.

I ignored her, begged exhaustion and flopped myself on the couch. This morning I pretended I had business to attend to, ergo the search for Zach Montrose. This, at least, got her attention diverted from me and back to the upcoming wedding, where it should be. I was just thrilled to be out of her cross hairs.

I dialed Montrose's number, expecting an answering machine

or voice mail in the middle of the day, but a woman answered. Her "Hello?" sounded distinctly cranky.

"I'm looking for Zach Montrose," I said, using my sunny, "not a darn thing to worry about" voice.

She made a disparaging sound. "Aren't we all? Why don't you try the gym? You got an appointment with him, talk to them. I'm not his secretary." She slammed down the receiver.

Hmmm. . . . I went online and found the name of six fitness centers around the area. On the fourth one I was informed that Zach didn't have anyone till noon. Would I like to be scheduled before or after? After, I told them, but I would call back. It sounded like Zach was some kind of personal trainer.

Debating on whether I really wanted to shoot down to Salem on what might be a fool's errand, I put another call into Greg Hayden. Wonder of wonders, he finally had a seventy-two hour for me to post. He'd saved it for me, he said. Gleefully I drove to his office, gleefully I picked up the notice, and gleefully I drove to the address. He needed to evict a group of apartment-dwelling druggies who played their music too loud, took over more than their share of parking spots and intimidated everyone over the age of thirty with their tattoos, sneers and body odor.

Greg was almost glad they were late on the rent. "Reason to move them out," he said.

So, I went to the apartment complex with my notice in hand. Mostly these kind of people really intimidate me, too. The more tattoos, the more cautious I become. Sure, they're cool now, but I sense something more than just "body art" going on there. An attitude seems to come with the territory. I've only met one guy with major tats who seemed like a sweetie. I learned later he was on some major tranquilizer to help him with his aggression problem.

But . . . it's a job, as they say. I pulled into the parking lot, my senses on high alert as I've had issues delivering seventy-two-hour notices. Dogs are a continual problem. But today I was feeling ornery. I had this sort of "bring it on" attitude that I sensed could backfire on me, but I couldn't talk myself out of it.

The complex was two stories, an L-shape wrapped around a parking lot in need of new asphalt. I knocked on the door to 215 and waited about half a minute. No answer. Fine. I taped the notice to the door. I normally like to put the paper in the hands of the occupant because then I know they've got it. No lying about it later. But if they weren't home, it was their problem.

The door opened just after I'd taped the notice up. I stared at a guy about my same height who appeared tattoo-less and wearing a sport coat and tie. "Well," I said in some surprise.

He took a look at the notice, snatched it off and crumpled it, then turned to me in that cold way that warns of serious psychological problems. "Fucking bitch," he sneered, smiling coldly at me.

Now, 999,999 times out of a million I would just turn and run. The notice was posted. I'd seen him grab it. The issue was resolved. Game over. But I was dealing with some psychological issues of my own: Dwayne, Binkster's injuries, the screwed-up Purcell family and my mother's visit. And I was dying to kick some butt.

I said in a steely voice, "Say that again, fucker."

"What?" His mouth dropped open in surprise.

"Say that again and I will mace you and tell everyone you attacked me." I slipped my hand inside my purse, keeping the lie alive. "And believe me, you'll be arrested for assault."

"You can't do that!" he sputtered.

"Watch me. Go ahead. Say it again."

"Are you crazy? I can't screw around with you. I've got a fucking job interview!"

"Then you'd better start learning how to address a lady, if you want that job."

I turned on my heel and marched down the stairs to my car. He slammed the door closed. I silently went through my litany of swear words, just to make myself feel better. A soccer mom with a couple of kids eyed me as I headed to my car. "What are you looking at?" I snarled. She emitted a scared squeak and herded the kids quickly inside her apartment.

I looked in the rearview mirror and admired the greenish bruises and scrapes on my face. No makeup today had been an inspired choice.

I felt a whole lot better about life.

Mom and I had lunch together. I took her to The Pisces Pub, where she admired the scarred wooden furniture and curly fries. I asked about the four-plex unit in Venice that we own together. Mom manages the four-plex, and she also owns a small house about two blocks closer to the beach. All the while Booth and I were growing up in southern California, Mom worked as an office manager for various companies. She bought the house she was renting from an older couple who wanted to move back home to Nebraska. Go figure. Then Mom got to know the owner of the apartment complex (I sometimes suspect she and he might have been lovers, but Mom won't cop to that) and he sold her the four-unit for a song. At the time of the apartment sale I was working as a bartender at a local bar, Sting Ray's. I lived with Mom—yes, this living arrangement lasted way past its pull date—and had saved a fair amount of money. Not that I was paid tons at my bar job, but I can live on next to nothing if need be; it's become kind of a habit. So, Mom let me buy in and now whenever I worry about my finances I just think about that piece of property, sitting in Venice, escalating in value at ridiculous rates. Better than therapy.

"I've got a problem with one of the tenants," Mom admitted now. "I might have to evict him."

Okay, nope. This was not what I wanted to hear. I get anxious about evictions when it concerns my own property. I've seen what angry tenants can do to a place. I almost asked, "What's wrong?" but stopped myself. I didn't want to know. I said instead, "What do you think Sharona's parents are like?" which sent my mother back down the wedding track like a fast-moving train.

I hustled her out of The Pisces as soon as I could, deposited her back at the cottage with Binkster, pled an afternoon's work ahead of me, then turned the Volvo south toward Salem. As long as I was pretending I was on a job, I might as well act like I was on a job. I might even learn something.

Zach Montrose worked at a place called The Body Shop. By virtue of its name alone, I might have expected to take my car in for a buff and puff if the woman on the phone hadn't said he was at the gym.

I drove into its front lot and up to a brick building with floor to ceiling windows along one wall. Inside, people were sweating on a variety of killer-looking machines. I figured this was one of those membership types of places and I was going to have to do a song and dance to see Zach. I sighed to myself. Sometimes the series of hoops it takes to get through a day makes me bone weary.

Wishing I could dig up some of the earlier aggression I'd felt when I'd delivered the seventy-two-hour notice, I walked up to the reception desk, searching for some kind of story to get me what I wanted. There were two young, buff males behind the counter wearing Crest Ultra smiles. I took it as a good sign; at least I wasn't facing another battle-ax receptionist.

"Hi, I'm Veronica. Ronnie," I said with a smile. "I'm looking for Zach Montrose." To my right was a glass wall. I could see a full gym to the left and the body-torquing machines to the right. The gym was half a floor down and a three-foot-high wall topped by a rail looked into it from the torture chamber.

"Zach's busy with someone right now." He glanced through the glass. I followed his gaze and saw a gray-haired man with an incredibly hard body helping some gal as she sat on one of the machines, lifting leg weights. I could see her strain from here.

I put Zach somewhere in his mid-forties. He could be older, but he was in great shape. At any rate, he was within the right age range to be the Zach Montrose who'd worked at Haven of Rest.

"Do you have a membership with us?" one of the buff boys asked. "I haven't seen you before."

"I'm just trying it out. Zach's been telling me what a great facility you have here."

"He has?" They exchanged looks. "Weird. I don't mean to be a jerk, but Zach hates everything and everybody. I don't think I've ever heard him say anything nice about anything." They both kind of laughed.

"I guess there's always a first time."

"I guess," he said dubiously.

Note to self: *Be more careful on this lying thing.*

I settled myself in a chair and waited for Zach's session to end. There appeared to be some flirty stuff going on between Zach and his client. I saw the two guys exchange another look, and I suspected Zach might be an older version of Complete Me's Trevin. I swear to God, how do these women fall for these guys? What is it about them that I simply miss?

Twenty minutes later Zach's sweating client headed for the showers. "You can catch him now. Go on in," the talkative one of the two directed. "And if for some reason you find Zach's not the trainer for you, don't hold it against us. The Body Shop's got a lot of trainers. Younger . . . nicer . . ."

"Duly noted."

I headed inside. Zach had grabbed a mammoth-size water bottle and was pouring the liquid down his throat. He saw me coming and put the bottle down, wiping his mouth with the back of a very hairy forearm. I wondered about little hairs catching in his teeth, but his smile of greeting seemed fur-free. "Hullo," he said. "Looking for me?"

"As a matter of fact, I am."

"You look in pretty good shape," he assessed. "Could use some upper arm development. What happened? Someone attack you?"

"No . . ."

He examined my face. "You look a little beat up."

Well, that was a bitch. Before lunch with Mom I'd applied makeup, done my darnedest to make myself look attractive, but my bruises apparently showed through. I couldn't wait for them to disappear. "You got a minute?" I asked. "I'm really interested in talking more than joining the club."

"Yeah? You want to interview me?" He was clearly puzzled.

We walked over to a stairway that led to an upper loft and a café. I snagged a menu, saw way too much healthy stuff, and was glad I'd had lunch with Mom. Zach ordered some kind of protein shake from a gal at the front counter. It came out looking like lavender goop.

"Hit me," he said, throwing away the straw and plastic top as we settled onto a bar-height table, the kind that make my feet dangle. He drank the shake like the water, lustily, with more energy than finesse. Again he wiped his mouth with his arm but this time a smear of protein goo caught in the hairs.

"Are you the same Zach Montrose who worked at Haven of Rest, now River Shores?"

He froze, his dark eyes boring holes into mine. "About a lifetime ago."

"Do you remember Lily Purcell?"

"Who are you? What do you want? I'm not talking to you." He got up abruptly and started striding downstairs.

"Wait. Wait a minute." I doggedly raced after him.

"Get lost," he told me, heading for the front doors. The guys behind the desk looked at me, eyebrows raised, as I charged after Zach into the late afternoon chill. "I'm not talking to you or anyone else about that. I'm done, okay? It's way over. It wasn't my fault then, it's not my fault now."

"Her death?"

"That, too. Jesus. You're not talking about the baby?"

"Well . . . I don't know."

To my shock he suddenly wrapped his hand around my neck and shoved me against the outside brick wall. To my right was the row of windows but no one could see us at this angle.

"I'm not the kid's father. Sure, we screwed around, but she screwed around with everybody. She was like stink, y'know? You couldn't get her off you. I was *seventeen*. What did I know? I just went for it. So sue me! I'm sick of having it ruin my life!"

His fingers tightened. I wondered briefly if he used steroids and was 'roiding out on me. I hadn't realized Lily was going to be such a hot button. We stayed that way for a moment or two. I counted my heartbeats and remained silent.

"And it wasn't my fault she died," he added a bit more calmly. "You wanna know about that? You talk to her sister. Got another flower name. I don't remember. But she's the one got her so upset that we had to hold her down. I said this at the time but that family of hers wasn't interested in the truth. You working for them?"

"Um . . . no."

"No? Why are you asking these questions?"

I cleared my throat. "Lily's son wants to know."

"Well, shit." That nonplussed him. He removed his hand from my neck and seemed to pull himself together. "The kid . . . ? Damn." He shook his head. "Look, she was something weird, okay? Doc Bergin called it hypersexuality. She came onto him, too."

"What?" I tried to give Zach a hard look, though I didn't really want to piss him off any further. "I've met Bergin. He's only thirty-something."

"Old Doc Bergin. Young Doc's his kid. His wife damn near divorced him and took the kid with her when he was fooling around with Lily, especially Lily being pregnant and all. It was . . . sick. When she started showing, I couldn't touch her no more. Turned me off, the idea of something growing inside her. But it wasn't mine, I swear."

"Would you take a DNA test to see?"

"I guess," he said without enthusiasm. "But I quit being with her as soon as it was obvious. That's when she turned to Old Doc. He was supposed to be treating her for all kinds of crazy stuff, but she got to him, too. Damn near got him fired, but they couldn't prove it. Lily wouldn't tell. He claimed she'd been abused as a little girl. Guess it comes out like that sometimes—hypersexuality. Whatever. She sure had it." He reminisced briefly, shaking his head. "She sure was a looker, though."

My knees were quaking a bit. He'd thoroughly scared me and it was hard to shake off.

He seemed to realize it and looked around as if to escape. "I got problems of my own. Leave me alone."

He turned and jogged to a black vintage Mustang.

It took me a couple of minutes more to get my legs in gear and give up the support of the wall. The whole drive back to Portland I could feel my insides clench with anxiety.

I stopped into the Nook before I went home. It was early evening and the grocery shoppers were swarming the parking lot. My mind was full of questions and my equilibrium was still off. Zach's attack had really gotten to me. Where was my bad ass attitude when I really needed it? I'd felt overpowered and small, like a vulnerable girl, and it was that niggling worry that kept me distracted as I told the high school girls behind the counter all I wanted was a cup of black coffee. I still wasn't sure I was meant for this business.

"You!" a woman's voice declared.

I didn't immediately look up because I sure didn't think she meant me. But then she crowded my space. Glancing around, my heart seized a bit. Miriam Westerly's pink collagen lips were right next to me. As I turned toward her, I had to be careful I didn't brush into them. Her red hair looked like it was on fire and so did her eyes.

She pointed an accusing finger at my nose. "You were at the spa!"

I smiled, pretending I didn't know what she was talking about though my pulse was beating rapidly. "Ummm . . . ?"

"My husband hired a *private investigator!*" She spat the term as if were dirty. "It was *you.*"

Okay, this was not one of those days where I could say I loved my job. Pretty much it sucked. I gave up pretending, mainly because I just didn't have the energy, and said to her, "You may not believe this, but I hope you get every cent of your money back from Trev. The guy scams women all the time. And you know what? You oughtta think about losing Spence, too. The guy doesn't deserve you. You have potential. Use it. Stop defining yourself by narcissistic men." The teenager behind the counter handed me an empty cup, so caught up in our conversation she didn't even ask me my name. "Jane Kelly," I told her, so she could mark on my prepaid coffee card that I was up to date. I walked over to the coffeepot and poured myself a steaming cup. My hand shook a little and I looked at it in a kind of wonder. Geez, Louise. I am such a friggin' wimp.

"Jane Kelly," Miriam repeated.

That's my name, don't wear it out. I headed out of the store, hoping Miriam would just evaporate. But she hung beside me, clearly needing to vent her feelings.

"I don't know how you can sleep at night," she volleyed at me.

Oh, puhleeze . . . I swung open my car door and said, "Miriam?" She lifted her chin and glared at me.

"Gain some self-respect."

"Just who do you think you are?"

"Your neighborhood Ann Landers. And FYI. Lose the lips. They frighten me." I slammed the door behind me. My last vision was of her sucking her lips between her teeth, a look of consternation on her face.

Jazz invited me over to his house for dinner, but I declined, using my mother as an excuse. It wasn't fair of me but I had a lot to digest after my "meeting" with Zach and my run-in with Miriam. That night I lay sleepless on the couch, staring up at the ceiling. I was alone as Binkster had chosen the bed and Mom over the couch and me. This was more than fine because with her neck cone, the couch can get really, really crowded.

When I got up the next morning I still felt tired. I ran through the shower early, trying to be quiet in order to not wake my mother, then scrutinized my face and added more makeup. I scribbled Mom a note that said I was working, then got in the Volvo and headed to Dwayne's.

I knocked on his door. Well, banged, actually, and when he didn't immediately answer I let myself in with my key.

Dwayne appeared from the bedroom in a pair of boxers and nothing else. I opened my mouth to say something but my mind simply shut off. I've always suspected the man goes commando style, but at least he apparently wears something to sleep in.

Unless he'd hastily pulled them on when he heard an intruder.

Seeing it was me, he raked a hand through his blond-brown hair and yawned, a surprisingly sexy move as it stretched out the muscles of his chest. "What the hell are you doing up so early?"

"Escaping my mother."

"Why aren't you at the Nook?"

I gave him a brief recap on Miriam which served to amuse him.

"Well, she probably won't be there in the morning," he assured me.

"Yeah, but Spence might. I'm taking a day off. Besides, I want to talk to you."

"Okay. Anything in particular?"

"The Purcells."

He groaned as if in pain. "Cammie hasn't called me in five days. Don't make me go there again."

"You might be done with Cammie, but I need your help."

"Oh, now you need my help." He headed into the kitchen, pulling a couple of mugs down and searching through a cupboard until he dragged out a bag of coffee. Nook coffee. I wondered how long it had been in his cupboard.

I told him about my meeting, such as it was, with Zach, then I went on to relate how Lily had been labeled hypersexual, how Old Doc Bergin had said it was probably brought on by sexual abuse, and how William DeForest said Percy thought she was a "hotpants." I laid it down in a straight narration, and when I was finished I waited for him to say something.

He was watching the coffee drip through the filter as if it were the greatest show on earth. Into the silence, he said, "So what do you want to do about it?"

"I don't know. That's what I'm asking you."

Dwayne poured us each a cup of coffee. I sniffed mine suspiciously, but it smelled all right. I'm not generally fussy about my coffee, but I don't trust Dwayne's pull-date skills. He asked, "You think she was abused?"

"Maybe," I said cautiously.

"By someone in the family?"

"That would be the likely assumption," I said.

"Okay, let's put that aside for a moment." He could tell he was icking me out. "You asked if I thought someone killed Orchid. You didn't think there was any reason. Do you think there's a reason now?" He gazed at me. Dwayne, mostly undressed and unshowered, looked rakish and very male. I stared at him, making sure I didn't telegraph the fact that I was picking up sexual signals he wasn't intending to send.

"I don't know," I said.

"Orchid was losing her grip on sanity. She was sad, crying, and she brought up things to you. You said there was a big secret. That it was eating away at them all. That you intended to find out what it was. You might not have been the only one picking those signals up."

I thought that over. "You think someone killed her to keep her from talking about Lily?"

"I'm just theorizing. Maybe Orchid knew about the abuse but has kept silent all these years. But with her mind starting to go, it was coming out in her behavior. Maybe someone got scared and gave her a shove into the mantel."

"That seems like a stretch," I said, though it was the train of thought that my mind had been following as well.

Dwayne inclined his head in agreement. "Lily's been gone a long time. Who can prove anything now? Where's the crime that someone would go to jail for?"

"These aren't people who necessarily make rational decisions."

"Good point." After a moment, he asked, "What was the deal with that doctor again? The one whose dad was supposedly doing Lily?"

"Cal Bergin."

"He has to know the Lily Purcell story if daddy was involved. But you said he acted like he'd never heard of her."

I shrugged. "He was just a kid at the time."

"Yeah, but he works there now . . . wasn't there talk of a lawsuit . . . something? Come on. It's got to be part of the River Shore's lore. He's not that out of it."

"He didn't mention it. Even when I brought up the fact that the Purcells recommended the place."

"He knows the Purcell name. I guarantee it. He didn't say something because he was waiting for you to give him some kind of signal about what you were really doing and what you wanted."

"I was acting like I was going to bring my sister there."

"You think he believed you?" Dwayne asked. "Come on. The Purcells would never recommend the place where Lily died."

"You're saying he knew I was a fake from the start."

"He's not an idiot. He told you he couldn't give out any information. Said it wasn't on the computer, right?"

"He told me the records were stored in the basement."

"He never figured you'd go that far. He thought he'd fobbed you off. He was just trying to get rid of you." Dwayne rinsed out his coffee cup. "You need to talk to him again. Tell him what the ex-employee said."

"Zach Montrose."

Dwayne nodded. "Find out what the young doc knows."

"I don't really want to," I admitted. I explained to Dwayne about using my alias and Jim Paine calling me Jane. "I bet Bergin rethought telling me about the records room. Probably went down there once everything died down with Gina and realized the file's gone. He'll know I stole it."

"Can't prove anything. Want me to go with you?"

I gazed at him in surprise. "Thought you were involved in that robbery case."

"We're kind of at an impasse. I've got this client who's loaded. His daughter got married about a month ago. Put up notices all over the place. Posted on the web. Date of the wedding. Their names. Pictures in the paper . . . the whole circus. So, all of the wedding gifts are sent to the house and guess what place gets hit the day of the wedding."

"Oh, no."

"It's like they laid out a treasure map with all the directions. The police haven't turned up a suspect, so my client called me. There have been some other robberies with the same MO, but this one was big. We don't have a lot to go on right now. I'm giving it some thought."

I loved the idea of having Dwayne work with me, but I always expect everyone to have a hidden agenda. "What's in this for you?" I asked.

"I seeketh the truth."

"Oh, sure." We smiled at each other, then a thought struck me. "There's something else. Something Zach said."

"What?"

"Lily was visited by her sister right before she had to be restrained that final time. She was really upset and out of control after Dahlia's visit."

"Maybe Dahlia said something, or knew something, that set Lily off?"

"Maybe . . ." I could feel something banging around in my head. I finally hit on it. "Oh. During one of her fretting episodes, Orchid was worrying about *both* of her daughters. Maybe she knew something was up between Dahlia and Lily?"

Dwayne frowned. "What are you thinking?"

"I don't know. Most of the women, Dahlia included, really missed out on the Purcell looks, but Lily didn't. Zach said she was a looker."

"So . . ."

"Two sisters. One's beautiful, and one's plain. It's the kind of thing gruesome fairy tales are written about."

"Hunh," Dwayne said. "Let's go talk to the doc."

* * *

Jazz called me as Dwayne and I were heading down the freeway toward River Shores. I was driving as I didn't want to spend more time than I had to in Dwayne's truck. It made me uncomfortable talking to Jazz while Dwayne was within earshot, but it couldn't be helped.

"What's up?" I asked by way of greeting.

"We're just going into the lawyer's office. I just wanted to check in."

"Okay. Let me know how that goes."

"What are you doing?" he asked curiously.

"Working with Dwayne."

"Oh."

"How about I call you this afternoon?"

"Sure," Jazz said, sounding like he wanted to keep me on the phone a little longer, but I managed to ease him off.

"The boyfriend checks in," Dwayne observed.

"He's not my boyfriend."

"He know that?"

"Yes," I said firmly, but I wasn't so sure.

Dwayne and I were both dressed in our usual garb: jeans and casual shirts. No Veronica Kellogg today. I'd called Doctor Bergin and explained that I was Jane Kelly and I'd been hired by the Purcell family. I did not reveal that Jane Kelly was Veronica Kellogg, but I suspected he knew by now. If by some chance he hadn't connected the dots, he soon would. He sounded less than thrilled to attend a meeting, but I was kind of insistent. I might have used the word "lawsuit" and the name "Gina" in one sentence.

The guard at the gate let us through when I invoked Dr. Bergin's name, but the fifty-something, cranky receptionist took one look at me and her hand shot for the phone. Dwayne leaned in and said in a soft drawl, "You might want to hold your horses, darlin'. We got ourselves an appointment."

She slowly pulled her hand away and checked the book. Then she buzzed us through.

"That shtick really works for you, doesn't it?"

"Seemed to today."

Doctor Bergin wasn't nearly as personally interested in Jane Kelly as he'd been in Veronica Kellogg. As we sat in front of his desk he studied the papers on his desk and didn't meet our eyes.

Dwayne acted as the intermediary between me and a possible lawsuit. He didn't look the part of a lawyer, but it didn't matter as he pointed out that I'd been attacked by one of the patients and all I'd heard were excuses about Gina "never having done anything like that before." Although my ear had healed and had mainly a scratch by now, it had been a horrifying experience.

While he laid out my story I adopted a long-suffering look accompanied by a lot of sighing.

"Just tell me what you want." Cal finally said, lifting his eyes. He wasn't fooled. "And I'll determine whether I can help you or not."

"We want the truth about Lily Purcell," I said.

"Funny thing about that. I went down to the records room. Lily Purcell's file is missing."

"Maybe you just didn't look hard enough," I said, meeting his gaze steadily.

"Maybe."

Dwayne asked, "Was your father the baby's father?"

Bergin hesitated briefly, then took a breath. "My father thought the baby's father was an employee who worked here when Lily was a patient, Zach Montrose."

I said, "I've spoken to Zach. He swears it wasn't him."

"From what I understand, Zach's not the most credible witness. There was a lawsuit at the time, which was settled. The family claimed undue force caused Lily's death. It was really just an unfortunate accident."

"And when was that? How long had she been here?"

"I believe the dates are in the file."

Touché, I thought. "If Zach is telling the truth, who's your best guess on the father?"

"I wouldn't know," he said tightly. "I think it was assumed she came to the Haven of Rest already pregnant."

"What makes you say that?"

"The family never accused anyone here. The truth is Lily Purcell really didn't belong here. Her problems weren't something to institutionalize over. She was hypersexual. She was pregnant. The general assumption was her father wanted to put her someplace where she wouldn't embarrass him any further."

"So, he sent her to a sanitarium?"

"I doubt he advertised the fact," Bergin said dryly. He gave me a cool glance. "You never intended to file suit about Gina, did you?"

I shook my head.

"Then we're done." He pushed himself back from his desk.

Dwayne asked casually, "How old was the baby when Lily died?"

"Again. It's in the file."

Dwayne and I were quiet on the way back, locked in our own thoughts. Finally, I said, "He's wrong. That information isn't in the file. I looked it over pretty carefully and there's not a lot there. I'm not saying anything's missing. I just think they were really careful about not writing anything down that could bite them in the ass."

"You find it kind of curious the family didn't ask about the baby's paternity?" Dwayne asked.

"They must have already known."

He nodded. "You thinking what I'm thinking?"

"What are you thinking?"

"I'm thinking unless Lily had some sweetheart we still haven't heard about, that Jazz's uncle or grandfather might also be his daddy."

I sighed. "How do you tell somebody that?"

"Maybe you don't. We're just talking out loud here."

"You're right. In fact, I'm going to forget it all. Orchid's death

was an accident. Lily's death was an accident. The secrets floating around in that family are best left alone."

I pulled up in front of Dwayne's cabana and dropped him off.

"You coming back to work then?" he asked, inclining his head
to his house. I hadn't spent a lot of time at his place recently. I
knew he was really asking if we could put things back on track,
work-wise.

"Mom's here for a few more days and Binks gets her stitches
out next week. Then I'll be back."

"All right, then." He headed out of sight. I watched the back
of him as he strode to the door. I've never been into that cowboy
thing. Not one of my personal fantasies, but Dwayne wore it so
well I was starting to come around.

Chapter Sixteen

"She left it all to Logan, just like she said . . ."

I stared through my windshield, my cell phone pressed to my ear, as Jazz's bemused voice gave me the outcome of the meeting with the lawyers. Though I really wasn't surprised, I kind of was, too. She'd really done it. She'd left everything to a twelve-year-old. "It's in trust, I hope," I said.

"Oh, yeah."

I relaxed a bit. The Purcells were a family who knew all about trusts.

"And there are some bequests to family members and a few other people, but the bulk of the estate is Logan's."

It was evening and Mom and the Binks were home while I was on my way to visit Jazz. He'd asked me to stop by and I'd been unable to come up with a reasonable excuse why not. He seemed so immersed in the aftermath of Orchid's death—the family was in the process of planning the funeral—that I believed he would not remember about our proposed trip back to River Shores. And I didn't want to admit that I'd gone without him. I hadn't learned anything I wanted to share, so there didn't seem to be any point.

I was following the directions he'd given me to his home in Portland Heights, an area of the West Hills located above the city.

Now I checked to see if I'd made a wrong turn as I'd lost concentration upon learning Logan was in charge of the purse strings.

"I bet that went over well," I told him, and he snorted his agreement.

Jazz's house wasn't nearly as imposing as I'd expected. A two-story colonial of modest proportions, it had the look of a property in need of serious attention. Not the moldy disuse of the Purcell mansion, but the scene of more recent neglect. I suspected Jennifer had paid more attention to home and hearth than Jazz, but then he'd been dealing with medical and family issues ever since the accident.

And maybe there was the matter of money involved. How much had Jazz been receiving from his grandmother's trust each month? And how much might he receive now? I could just see the rest of the Purcells aligning and realigning, figuring out how to wrest their fair share from Logan's control.

I hadn't dressed to stop by Jazz's. Truthfully, I was way over getting dressed up, and I was feeling a little prickly about even thinking I should. Who was I trying to impress? I'd told Dwayne that Jazz wasn't my boyfriend. The person I should be telling was Jazz.

"Hi," he greeted me warmly, ushering me into his living room. He switched on the gas fireplace and with the overstuffed furniture there was something homey and inviting that I hadn't expected from him. He was standing close to me and I wondered how to ease away.

"Where's Logan?" I asked.

"Upstairs. Go on up and say hello. I'll open a bottle of red."

"I can wait for you."

"No, no. Go ahead. I'll have your glass ready when you come back."

How had I suddenly become the person to go say hidey-ho to Logan? We weren't even friends. My feet dragged and I had to swallow back a certain resentment that was beyond childish. So, I didn't like him. He was just a kid, for God's sake.

I followed the electronic sound effects to the room at the end of the hall. Logan was squatting on the floor in front of a television the size of Paraguay, playing some game that involved animated females with Barbie figures dressed in camouflage and sporting Uzis, handguns, quivers full of arrows on their backs, and the rogue grenade or two. They seemed to be patrolling some burned out futuristic city.

"Hi, Logan, how's it going?" I said.

He didn't look up. "Did you hear about the will?"

"Sure did."

"I'm a multimillionaire. Maybe a billionaire."

"Yeah . . . well . . ."

"None of the kids are going to believe this!" He was grinning, his attention still on his pack of female killers. Maybe they wore the white hats. It was hard to tell.

That was pretty much the extent of our conversation. I headed back downstairs and accepted the glass of wine. Later, Jazz suggested we eat at a little café in the Pearl, so we spent a couple of hours alone where he kept reaching across the table to hold my hand, and I kept trying to figure out how to address our "non" relationship. Neither of us got what we wanted.

Back at his house, he tried to talk me into returning inside for a nightcap, but I begged off with my current favorite excuses: Mom and injured Binkster. I went home, crashed on the couch and slept like the dead.

I spent the next few days avoiding Jazz. Luckily, he was busy with funeral preparations, while I was trying to figure out how to completely extricate myself from all things Purcell without completely ruining my friendship with him. I liked Jazz. I wanted him as a friend. But I didn't want anything more.

Orchid's funeral was scheduled for Saturday, and though Jazz invited me, I graciously declined. I knew the rest of the Purcells would treat me like an interloper, and I didn't want to be there anyway.

Orchid's death had made the local news and her funeral became a minor media event. I resisted Jazz's continual pleas to have me be by his side, but I buckled for the post–funeral reception because Jazz was making me feel like a heel. He even went as far as saying he wouldn't go without me. This was an empty threat, but I'd spent so much time avoiding him that I couldn't say no again. I promised to meet him at the house.

Saturday afternoon I donned the black dress I save for these kinds of events, and drove myself over to the Purcells, joining the throng of about three hundred others who'd paid their respects and now were ready to partake of the food and drink. I recognized several Portland luminaries, members of families as influential as the Purcells who sang Orchid's praises and Percy's as well. I steered clear of Neusmeyer, who seemed to know everyone. William DeForest was there, too, looking sad and pissy that the attention wasn't on him. It was a little like a retiree convention: most of the seats were taken by people from Orchid's generation. I was introduced to Bonnie Chisholm, who eyed the appointments of the room enviously. I asked her how her son was and got an earful about how he'd been attacked by a person or persons unknown and it was a police matter now.

This both irked and worried me. I could picture myself getting dragged to jail in cuffs for taking him down. Stranger things have happened.

The hors d'oeuvres were enough to keep me hanging around: Ahi tuna with ginger sauce, tiny quiches with chopped mushrooms, olive tapenade, and glasses of soda water, fruity wines that made me gag, and coffee with or without a shot of bourbon.

Reyna was at the house but she was just kind of watching the catering staff. She told me she was quitting. The only Purcell she'd cared about was Orchid and now she was gone. With a faint smile she admitted none of them had shown much dismay when they'd learned she was leaving. Assuming the bulk of the Purcells were going back to their own homes, I asked Reyna what James was planning to do for meals. She just shrugged, so I said maybe he'd find a new interest in cooking—especially since he had such a thing for knives. It scared a smile out of Reyna but Dahlia overheard and her lips turned all tight and pruney.

As the crowd thinned I found Jazz at my side. The man was impossibly good looking and incredibly wealthy. He liked me. Kind of a lot, I was pretty sure. He could handle himself in social situations, even be clever upon occasion. Sharona had pointed out that he didn't have a lot of depth, but I asked myself if I needed depth. Was shallowness so bad?

Oh, Jane, you just don't want to face a messy breakup.

I went back to the coffee urn and tossed a bit of bourbon in my cup. Jazz followed me. He grabbed another glass of the fruity white wine. There was kind of a repressed excitement about him that I'd noticed vaguely. "What?" I asked.

"Look over at Logan," he said.

I gazed across the room. Logan was standing by the window, playing—big surprise—a handheld video game. His head tilted, he was listening to something Benjamin was saying to him. Benjamin did not look happy, but Logan was cock of the rock. He was grinning. Switching off the Game Boy, he looked over at Jazz, got down on one knee, gave an arm pump and said, "Yes!"

"That's what he did when he learned he was Nana's heir," Jazz told me, sounding a little embarrassed but also kind of proud.

I squinted at him. This was just not okay.

"It's almost funny," Jazz went on. "The family's in a state. Benjamin's pissed. Dahlia and Roderick are fit to be tied. I mean, Garrett can't even look at Logan and he won't talk to me. And James has suddenly become my new best friend."

"What about Cousin Cammie?" I asked, looking over at her. She had Rosalie on her lap and both of them had that set look around their mouths that speaks of bad temper.

"She's not happy, either."

An understatement, but I let it pass. "Logan's not exactly winning friends."

"He's a kid." Jazz shrugged. "Nothing's really changed. The trusts are still in place."

"But the bulk of the estate is still Logan's."

"Yes."

"What about the house? Is there a certain amount set aside for its upkeep?"

"I don't know," Jazz said, unconcerned. "Maybe we'll sell it."

I remembered Lorraine's comment about the Purcells owning a great deal of real estate all over the state. There were probably lots of places to sell.

"Logan gets control when he's eighteen," Jazz said. "Until then, I'm in charge to a certain point. It's all tied up in legal stuff."

But it's a hell of a lot of money, I thought, reading between the lines.

I looked over at Dahlia, whose color seemed to have left her face. I then glanced at Garrett, who was just the opposite of Dahlia; his skin was florid and blotchy. And James was just plain gray.

Jazz said, "When are we going to River Shores?"

My heart sank a bit. "You know, I've changed my mind about that. I don't think there's any big mystery to unravel down there."

"You don't?"

"No."

He thought about it a moment, then let it go. I expelled a breath, unaware I'd been holding it.

"I thought this was supposed to be a business arrangement," Roderick's amused voice sounded to my left, "but you two have gotten pretty cozy. Kissing on the landing." He made a *tsk, tsk, tsk* sound. "You must be a better private detective than I thought. You sure found where the money is."

I turned to him, expecting to see his usual satisfied expression. But today it was replaced by anxiety. He'd been smug and delighted when Dahlia had the Power of Attorney, but now things had taken a turn for the worse. He was really worried that I was edging my way in to the Purcell fortunes.

Cammie, overhearing, said, "Nana wasn't in her right mind. We all know that. The estate is going to be divided among all of us."

No one responded because it just wasn't true.

Cammie then glanced around in disbelief as Rosalie kicked herself out of her mother's arms. "You don't seriously believe

Logan will end up with everything. Oh, come on. That's ridiculous. We'll contest it and we'll win."

Benjamin said, "Well, it's not right. It's not what Nana wanted."

Oh, so now he called her Nana. Now, after she was gone and he could pretend that he cared about her more than he did. He met my gaze and I saw we had a momentary meeting of the minds. He blushed, his ears turning pink. Now, Benjamin wanted his share, the grasping shit heel.

"It's exactly what Nana wanted," Jazz disagreed. "She said so often enough."

"Easy for you to say, as Logan's father," Roderick murmured.

"Don't do us any favors, Jazz," Cammie snarked, throwing him a glare as she chased after Rosalie, who was about to tip over a tray full of glasses of wine.

Jazz shook his head. "Nana would hate this."

Logan, on the other hand, was loving it. We were all kind of watching him like an insect in a jar, and he was enjoying the attention. A smirky smile was stuck to his lips. If he'd been insufferable before, he was bound to be horrific from here on out.

I was feeling totally dissatisfied, so I did a quick internal check to find out what was really bothering me. Ah, yes. That bit about me being after the family money. Yes, I'm cheap. And I like getting paid. But siphoning off money that I haven't earned by virtue of just dating someone—that's not for me. There are strings attached I don't want pulled. And I really resented them placing their own suspect code of ethics on me.

I was bugged enough to do something about it. In fact, I felt like taking them on, one at a time, or all together. I was tired of their whiney, superior, snotty attitudes. I was tired of their secrets. I was tired of them. I might have actually said something biting and mean, but was diverted by a small commotion in the foyer. My back was to the open salon door so I turned to see what it was all about.

A beautiful blond woman strode into my line of vision. She looked about forty with a trim waist and breasts that were twenty-ish perky. She wore her hair shoulder length, cut into a contemporary style with shorter strands curving in to her chin. Her face was heart-shaped, and there was a hint of humor around some very red lips. In a short black skirt and a boat-neck sweater, she just oozed sex.

And her eyes were electric blue.

If I'd been a cartoon I would have had a question mark floating above my head. I glanced from her to Jazz who was gazing at her blankly. I looked past him to Dahlia and Roderick. Dahlia's already pale face had turned alabaster. My gaze next jumped to Garrett, who was poleaxed, then James, who appeared close to fainting. In the background Satin was carefully replacing her empty wineglass with a full one.

The vision stepped toward us, sweeping her gaze around the room. She said, Bette Davis style, "What a dump!" then laughed.

Her eyes, so like Orchid's, so like Jazz's, settled on me. Her red lips twisted into a smile, "Hi, I'm Violet. You are definitely not a Purcell."

"Violet?" I repeated. *Lily?* Wildly, I turned to Jazz. He was blinking rapidly.

"I'm Jazz. Jasper Purcell," he introduced himself, holding out his hand.

She shook it, her gaze perplexed as she sized him up. "How are you related?"

"I'm Lily's son?"

"Lily's son," she repeated.

I was really confused as was Jazz. Logan had left the room but everyone else stood in a semicircle around her. Cammie was clearly at sea as well.

Violet pushed between Roderick and Dahlia, who fell apart as if her touch burned. "The Ahi tuna canapes look great. These are kind of anemic though." She swept a hand over a tray that was mainly crumbs and contained one small hors d'oeuvre. "Got any more? It's been hellish getting here in time for the funeral, and I'm just starved!"

When no one moved, she added for clarification, "I'm the long

lost sister. The one no one wants to admit exists. Look at them."
She indicated Garrett, Dahlia and James. "They know." Then
she gazed at Jazz again, smiling a bit sadly. "You look a lot like
your mother," she said. "But then, so do I."

Bombshell was the word to describe her, I decided about an
hour later as things began to sort themselves out. Violet Purcell
sat in the fawn and green chair with a glass of wine in one hand
and a small cocktail plate full of hors d'oeuvres in the other. Her
legs were crossed and she was rocking one ankle seductively
without being fully aware of it. Dahlia, Garrett and James stared
at her soberly. She was their sister. Not Lily. Violet. Their young-
est sister. The fifth middle-ager, whom I'd unwittingly picked up
in my first background check. She'd disappeared when she was
fifteen; she claimed she'd been sent away by Orchid at the same
time Lily was sent away to Haven of Rest. The rest of the family
had acted as if she'd ceased to exist, though she'd kept up spo-
radic communication with Orchid.

"So, you don't tell me when Mom dies?" she accused, her
hand poised over her hors d'oeuvre plate. She threw her three
siblings a look but they couldn't meet her gaze. Cammie sat to
one side, mesmerized, Rosalie asleep in her arms. Benjamin
looked like a man who'd had too many blows in a row. Roderick's
arms were crossed. He stared at Violet, both bowled over and in-
trigued. Logan was upstairs, probably playing his Game Boy. No
one had seen fit to go alert him to the new arrival. We were using
all our energy to simply process.

"Mom wanted me to stay away so I did," she said conversationally. "Thought about coming back after dear old Dad died,
but she didn't think it was a good idea."

James slowly sank into a chair. He turned his eyes up to me, a
message in their tortured depths, but I couldn't pick it up.

"You left when you were fifteen?" Cammie asked, though this
had already been established. She couldn't quite get it. Neither
could I.

"You haven't talked to Mother in years," Garrett said through his teeth. "You're just here for the money."

"You can keep your stinking cash," she said, eyeing him darkly. "All I wanted is a few moments with Mom, but it's too late. And not one of you contacted me. I had to hear about her death from the lawyers."

"We didn't know you were alive," James said faintly.

"Bullshit."

I'd known there were secrets in the Purcell family, but this was a doozy. Now, some of Orchid's comments about her daughters made sense. She'd been fretting about Lily and Violet, not Lily and Dahlia. Or, maybe she'd been fretting about all of them.

Violet possessed all the Purcell good looks, and she had a strength of personality that was clear from the moment she entered anyone's air space. I would have said she was an anomaly as she looked like the men in the family, but Lily had apparently looked a great deal like her. She was the only Purcell who seemed straightforward. She wasn't warm, and after two seconds of being in her sphere you could tell she was completely self-centered, but I appreciated the way she didn't give a damn what anyone else thought.

"You wasted your energy, Violet," Garrett said. "Mother left the estate to Logan."

Her presence really got to Garrett. Violet could tell, and she was up for the challenge. She stared at him coldly, a faint smile on her lips. "I don't know who Logan is, yet. Hopefully Mom was a good judge of character and she left the money to the person most deserving."

"That's a joke!" Garrett sneered.

"Logan's my son," Jazz said.

That threw her. "You have a son?" She ran a hand through her hair. "Holy Mother of God. Lily's grandson. Hon, is there another bottle of wine somewhere?" she asked Benjamin. "And not that sweet shit. Something I can drink."

Benjamin said tightly, "The caterers have packed up everything."

"How about bourbon?" I suggested. The coffee urn had also been packed up, but there was an unopened bottle on the side buffet.

"Perfect. Who are you?"

"Jane Kelly."

I found some old-fashioned glasses in the buffet cupboard and splashed bourbon in the bottom of several. All faces turned my way, so I ended up serving everyone a drink except Satin, who pretended she didn't imbibe. Violet skewered her with a look and asked, "You're Garrett's wife?"

Satin nodded.

Violet stared at her oldest brother over the rim of her glass. Something passed between them. It was Garrett who turned away, though he pretended to fuss over getting Satin a soft drink.

"So, is there a room for me here, or should I get a hotel. My bags are in the hall."

"Where did you come from?" Cammie asked.

"L.A. . . . New York . . ." She uncrossed and recrossed her legs. "I lived in Portland for a while about two years ago. You didn't know that, did you? Mom never told you."

By the faces in the room, this was clearly news.

"Yep. I was married to my favorite ex-husband, then. A doctor. But I really wasn't into his cocaine habit, so I divorced him. But he's cleaned up now, so I'm seeing him tomorrow."

I excused myself, but they scarcely noticed as I headed out. In the entry hall I phoned Dwayne. "Come on, come on . . ." He didn't answer so I left him a short message that said if he wanted some big news he'd better call me *toute suite*.

While I was phoning Dwayne, Jazz headed upstairs to get Logan, who returned in poor humor. I reentered the salon just as Jazz was introducing his son to Violet. The two eyed each other like adversaries. I hadn't really paid much attention to Logan's looks. He was an obnoxious kid and I hadn't been able to get past that. Now, I saw he was going to possess his father and aunt's at-tractiveness. With the inheritance and his own physical attrib-utes, he was going to be the chick magnet of all chick magnets.

Violet was staring at Logan. "This is the keeper of the cash?" she asked.

Then she just started laughing.

Chapter Seventeen

It wasn't an auspicious beginning for Logan and his newly discovered aunt. I expected some kind of fireworks on his part, some bad behavior, but Violet, whose age I'd now upped to near fifty—though she looked a decade younger—seemed to reach Logan at some level the rest of us couldn't. Maybe it was because she was a breath of fresh air to the Purcell family. She was irrepressible, unafraid and seemed to think life was a joke. She asked Logan about himself, even though we were all dying to know more about her, and Logan actually responded like a real human being. The rest of the family was still in shock, as was I.

I listened to Logan wax rhapsodic about his current video game and saw how Violet appeared to hang on every word. Stealing a glance at Jazz, I witnessed a transformation there, too. His initial disbelief had changed to acceptance, maybe even joy. Violet was taking care with his son.

Of course reading the faces of the other Purcells showed something else entirely: suspicion. Violet had sashayed in, assessed the situation quickly and accurately, then aligned herself with Logan.

She was smart as a whip, lusciously attractive, fearless.

The whole fam-damily was in trouble.

"She's unbelievable," Jazz said. "Look at Logan."

I was actually looking at Jazz and thinking what Lily might have been like had she lived.

I really hated to leave but it was getting late. The last of the catering staff was long gone and it was only me and the family left. Before I departed Jazz took me into his arms for a kiss. I let it take me over.

When he pulled back he said, "Let's go on vacation together. We've got a place near Black Butte. There are a lot of hiking trails. We could try fishing. I've never done it, but the Metolius River is right there."

The idea struck me with horror. Stuck sharing living accommodations with him, and possibly Logan? I could see myself screaming and peeling off my face with my fingernails after a couple of days. "I don't know . . ."

"Think about it," he urged.

I kind of wanted to point out that he had a lot to deal with, but it seemed more prudent just to escape. Dwayne called as I drove home. "You're not going to believe what happened," I said, then proceeded to give him the dramatic blow-by-blow of Violet's unexpected appearance and everyone's reactions.

"Wow," Dwayne said when I finished.

Somehow that wasn't enough, especially since his "wow" wasn't imbued with the sort of amazement I expected to hear. He sounded mostly disinterested.

"Wow?" I repeated.

"Was Chris around?" he asked.

"Cammie's husband? No."

"Okay."

"Aren't they heading for divorce?" I questioned. "You would never guess Cammie even had a husband."

"She might be holding it together in front of the rest of her family, but all she thinks about is Denton and her daughter. Watch her. She wants Denton at all costs, though how he got with her in the first case is one of life's mysteries. I never got close enough to meet him, but I thought he was a decent enough guy. "

"With two families," I said mildly.

"Sometimes funerals bring families together. Even people who hate each other."

"Hunh," I said.

My relationship with Dwayne was almost back to what it had been. He, at least, had quit teasing me. I, however, hadn't been *completely* able to stop thinking about him. I was still getting caught off guard. I'd be doing something, something mundane, and then the thought of sex with Dwayne would hit me like lightning, sending a sizzle right through my center. The guy at the pet store gave me a strange look when I lost track of my purchase of lo-cal kiblets because my mind suddenly filled with an image of Dwayne's muscular abdomen and an orgasmic rush shot through me.

Note to self: *He can never know.*

As I pulled into my drive, I thought about my own family. I was fairly close to my mother, less to my brother even though we lived in the same city. I didn't have a father to speak of. We Kellys were dysfunctional in our own way, but we were pikers compared with the Purcells.

As this thought crossed my mind, I had a sudden realization. Before I entered the cottage, I placed a call to my brother and was surprised when he actually answered his cell phone on the second ring. I'd half expected him to be on duty. "Jane," he greeted me.

You can't hide anything from Caller ID anymore. "Hey, there. You know I'm taking Mom to the airport on Monday."

"We had dinner with her this evening," he said patiently.

"I know," I said, just as patiently. "I was at a funeral reception. I'm sure you and Sharona and Mom have been talking about your wedding nonstop."

"Ad nauseam."

"Has Mom mentioned inviting our father?"

A long, long silence ensued. "No . . . why? You *want* to ask him?"

"Not me. Mom just brought it up once, and it got me thinking. We don't even know the names of our half-brothers and sister, or really how many we've even got. I lost count at three. Years from now, they could show up on our doorstep and we wouldn't know who they were."

"What's your point?"

"That's what happened at the Purcells tonight. Jazz's aunt showed up, and half the family didn't even know she existed. I was thinking how weird it was, and then I thought about us."

"I really don't care if I ever meet any of 'em."

I felt a lot the same way, but it was eating at me a little. "Violet didn't see any of her siblings for over thirty years."

"Probably for the best."

The thing about Booth is, he says all the same things I would say. We're twins, and though I tend to think we're polar opposites, it's just not true.

"He's not invited to the wedding," Booth reiterated.

"Good," I said, and went inside to my mother and The Binkster.

Monday morning I took Mom to the airport, my eyes peeled for my nemesis, who must have been still patrolling arrivals because she was nowhere to be seen at departures. Mom wanted to pin me down about Jazz, but I dodged her questions. She despairs of me ever having a serious, lasting relationship and she'd zeroed in on Jazz for all the obvious reasons. I fobbed her off as best I could, but she got that look in her eye that says, "This isn't over yet." I managed to sidetrack her with some more Booth and Sharona's wedding talk, but she was not completely diverted.

"You need to come stay with me," she said, as I hauled her bag from the back of the Volvo, pulled out its handle and balanced it on its wheels. "I've got things for you to do on the Venice property."

"What kind of things? I'm not all that handy."

"Private investigator things."

"And what would that be?"

She smiled, gave me a hug and kiss, said, "I'll think of something," then waved at me as she wheeled her bag into the terminal.

I felt a pang of loneliness as soon as she was out of sight. I had the absurd notion to either call her back or jump on a plane and join her. I did neither, but it made me worry about my own state of mind.

That afternoon Binks had her stitches removed. I hardly recognized her as my dog without the cone. "She looks great," the vet decreed, and Binks actually jumped into the Volvo on her own power and curled herself into her bed in the passenger seat. This is a move she can only make if her weight's under a certain level. It's a fine balance we have as she's wont to put on weight with a concentration that's awe-inspiring.

On the ride back she panted like she'd run a marathon, her tongue lolling out the side of her mouth. It amazes me how damn long it is. Where does it fit when her mouth's closed? Her head's too short for it, I swear.

I recognized it as the sign of stress it was. She did not like the vet and who could blame her. From her point of view nothing good ever happened there. When I got her home I refilled her water bowl, from which she drank lustily, and we shared a mochi. That about did her in, so she toddled into her bed in the corner of my bedroom, sighed loudly, and burrowed herself into the cushions.

Most of the day I avoided Jazz's calls, as I'd avoided them the day before. I had thoughts of easing myself away from the Purcells and their problems. But the Monday calls kept escalating in their frequency. I marveled at this, wondering if Jazz had suddenly developed stalker-esque tendencies. Finally, I picked up the line with a distinctly formal, "Hello."

"There you are," Jazz said, sounding frantic.

"Right here." I was settling in to be all frigid and annoyed. I could tell I was in the first stages of relationship ending: give the soon-to-be ex zero encouragement. Sometimes this stage happens even if there is no relationship. My situation was a case in point.

"Logan's been in an accident. He's at Laurel Park Hospital. I'm there now. Can you come?"

"Is he all right?" I asked, seized by guilt.

"Head injury." Jazz sounded about to weep. "Car accident. God, I hope it's not like mine!"

I hung up and flew out the door to Laurel Park.

I called myself all kinds of names on the way over. I was in some strange daze over Dwayne and I'd simply checked out with Jazz, and it had made me rude and selfish and uncaring.

I asked at the front desk for Logan Purcell's room, but was saved from explaining further when Jazz phoned me again and said they were still in Emergency. I think he just wanted to keep human contact, and as soon as I found my way, Jazz gathered me into his arms and squeezed the breath from me. It made me feel worse.

The bed was empty.

"Where is Logan?" I asked.

"They're running tests. MRI? X-ray? I don't know. Checking. He was unconscious when they brought him in. He kind of woke up, but it's not good." His eyes glistened.

"What happened?" I asked. "Were you in the car?"

"No, Cammie was picking him up from school. I had another meeting with the lawyers. She's here somewhere . . ." He gazed around.

"She a patient, too?"

"No, no. She's okay. But she's shook up. She said someone ran her off the road."

"What?"

"Not far from our accident last Christmas."

I absorbed that. "What about Rosalie?"

"Rosalie was with her nanny."

"Okay . . . okay . . ." I needed a moment to think. I didn't like what I was hearing one bit.

Cammie herself showed up a few moments later, moving

slowly. She was white-faced and there were scratches down the side of her right cheek. I learned the windshield had broken and glass flew like shrapnel. The air bags deployed but Logan's head hit the side window, a potentially dangerous blow.

"The police were at the scene," Cammie said dully. "They asked me questions."

Jazz looked stricken. "Another hit and run."

"He didn't actually hit me," Cammie said on a sigh, lifting a hand wearily to the side of her head and closing her eyes. "He was behind me. I was trying to get away from him. I took the corner too fast and lost control."

"It's all right," Jazz said, but his words were distracted.

"How is Logan?" she asked tentatively.

"They're doing tests now."

We all waited. Jazz kept an arm around me and I didn't protest. The rest of the Purcell clan showed up at varying times. Everyone professed concern. Garrett and Satin were first. Satin was worried sick about Cammie, even more so than Logan, apparently, her mothering instinct on overload. It only pissed Cammie off, who clearly felt responsible and wanted to be left alone to cope.

James came into the room and I felt his gaze on me. I gazed back at him. He looked like a man with something on his mind, but I had no idea what he was thinking.

Dahlia hustled in with Benjamin and the room got really crowded. I headed toward the Emergency waiting room just as Logan was being wheeled back toward the room, his head bandaged, his blue eyes huge. They'd had to stitch a huge gash in the back of his head, but preliminary tests showed no further evidence of trauma.

I gave a last look inside before I left. Logan lay on the bed, unfocused and small. I watched the Purcells crowd around him. James, Benjamin, Garrett, Dahlia . . . what were they thinking? I wondered. How much did they really care?

Roderick was in the waiting room, thumbing through a magazine when I entered. I wanted to steer clear of him, and today he seemed to feel the same way about me. We sat in chairs at opposite ends of the room and pretended we didn't notice each other.

Violet breezed in with a paper cup of coffee. I looked at the cup and she said, "Coffee kiosk around the corner. Want some? I'll go with you."

"Let me just make a call."

I stepped outside to phone Dwayne. Laurel Park was a no-cell zone, which was just as well because I think I'd go crazy if I were waiting for life and death news on someone and there was a yakker loudly going off on his cell.

Dwayne answered, sounding busy. I gave him a quick recap of what had happened. "Do you want me to come?" he asked, and I said, "Yes," without thinking beyond the fact that yes, I wanted him. I wanted his support. Jazz was leaning on me, but I wanted Dwayne. "I'll be at a coffee kiosk near Emergency."

I followed Violet down a wide hallway to a rotunda where, against one curved wall, was a coffee bar. A smattering of chairs were clustered around postage-stamp size tables. "I don't really need any coffee," I said. It was late afternoon, almost evening. Through the rotunda windows I could see across the parking lot to a row of birches, leaves rustling in shades of silver and yellow. The sky was steel gray and looked like rain.

"Sure you do. Cream? Sugar?"

"Black."

She ordered herself another cup as well, handed me mine, then filled hers with skim milk. "I talked to Logan's doctor. He's going to be fine."

"When did you talk to him?" I asked curiously.

"At the desk. I told the nurses I was his aunt, and his doctor happened to be right there. I'm sure he's in the room telling them now." She blew across the top of her cup.

I had a feeling Violet could get any information she wanted without doing much more than smiling. I would never be able to get away with that.

"I'm glad he's going to be okay," I said.

"Me, too. So, you're a private investigator hired by my nephew, Jasper. He told me all about you after you left."

"I'm not working for him anymore."

"No, you're dating him. He's a doll, isn't he?"

"I'm not sure we're dating."

"What would you call it?"

I didn't have an answer for that. Violet gave me a knowing look, and I just let her think whatever she wanted. I was going to have to address this issue, and soon, but it felt like every time it felt like the thing to do, something came along to derail me.

"Jasper and I have been having some great talks," Violet said. "He and Logan are the only ones who're really glad I'm back. The rest would prefer if I crawled back under the rock that I crawled out of." She took a sip of her coffee. "So, Jasper said you were hired to look after my mother, to check her sanity."

"Sort of."

"And that she took off with her friend William—I actually remember him from when I was a girl. He was sweet on my mother, you could tell." She shook her head.

I think it was then that I realized Violet had a lot of the information I'd been seeking about the family. It wasn't important to any investigation any longer, but it could certainly answer some of my own questions.

"William mentioned your name to me," I told her. "I thought he meant Lily, and he let me believe he did, but he said Violet, clear as a bell. He was hiding your mother and toying with me. I think he's got a fantasy about he and Orchid, about how they had true love."

"Mom might have shared that same fantasy," she said, thinking about it. "My father was . . . not a good husband. He wasn't much of a father, either."

I waited, wondering if I was reading more into that than she meant. But she seemed lost in her own thoughts. Finally, I said, "You took off at fifteen. Orchid moved you to a new family."

"A friend of hers. She wanted me out of the house." She gave me an assessing look. "She didn't trust the men in our family."

"Oh."

"You know about Lily, don't you?" she asked.

"Meaning?"

"The way she was with men." I wasn't sure what to say about that so I just kind of nodded. It seemed to satisfy Violet, who went on, "I was skinny as a girl. Really skinny. I didn't have any shape at all until I was almost fifteen. But Lily developed early. And she was a girl's girl, y'know? Blond curly hair, wide blue eyes, innocent face. She was adorable. I always felt like I was in her shadow. Bony knees. Skinned elbows. My teeth were all over the place. And my hair . . . I have to pay a fortune to get it to look like this.

"I was in trouble with Dad a lot," Violet said, her eyes narrowing. "He wanted me to be more like Lily. Didn't want me turning out like Dahlia, who was bossy and overbearing."

That hadn't changed. I made a sound of encouragement.

"We were Daddy's flowers," Violet said. "But Lily was his favorite. If we did something wrong, he laid us over his knees, pulled down our panties and spanked us."

She watched my reaction. I tried to remain neutral. "I thought Orchid named all of you flowers."

"She did. My great-aunt's name was Lilac Grace, and her name was a flower, too, and I think she just went with it. But my father was all about his girls." She gazed at me meaningfully. "Mom didn't get it for quite a while. She didn't realize why Dahlia was eating so much, purposely making herself unattractive. She didn't understand what Dad was doing."

"Your father had sex with you and your sisters."

"Depends on your definition of sex. He spanked us, got erections over it, then fumbled around in his pants while we were still lying across his knees. When I was little, I didn't understand. I just wanted the spanking to be over. Dahlia tried to be the best little girl she could be, so she wouldn't get spanked, but what saved her was that Lily was so much more attractive."

I nodded. All signs had pointed to sexual abuse but Violet's narrative was still hard to hear.

"He was focused on her all the while my brothers were growing up. They were about six and seven years older than she was. They started taking Lily to the playhouse. I wasn't invited. And they did have sex with her," Violet said, her lips tightening in memory.

I thought of James's paintings and my heart felt heavy. His guilt clearly weighed on him and had for a long time. I could picture Garrett being the instigator and James going along.

"It went on for years," Violet said. "I think in the end my father blamed himself. He wasn't the type to admit it, but as Lily just got prettier and prettier, and more and more sexual, he couldn't help but see what he'd started. We all sensed it. And then boys started driving over to pick her up at all hours. She was quietly getting back at our father. I remember her standing in front of him in the entry hall one night, head bent, while he was screaming at her for being a 'fucking whore.' She said, 'I don't take money, Daddy. That would be wrong.'"

I drew a breath. "In the middle of this dressing down, she gives him a lesson in semantics?"

"I didn't know the term passive aggressive at the time, but that's what she was. And then she said, 'Are you going to spank me now?' and my father just went nuts. Got all red. The veins were popping out in his neck. He banged out of the house and we didn't see him for nearly a week.

"Mom didn't know what to do. She tried to pretend she didn't see because my father wouldn't admit to anything. It just imploded. He locked Lily in the house. Have you seen the room with all the dolls?"

"Yes."

"The dolls were my mother's from when she was a girl, kind of a collection, but it was creepy. Dad put Lily in there. His little doll. She escaped and went right back to the playhouse with my brothers. It was my mother who actually begged to send Lily to Haven of Rest, and meanwhile she was making arrangements for me. By that time, my father was ready to ship me away. I wish Lily had been able to come with me, but Dad was afraid to have her out in the world to shame him."

"And she was pregnant."

Violet nodded. She paused a moment, then asked, "Have you seen the playhouse?"

"Yes."

My tone caught her attention. "Have you been in the play-house?" I nodded, and she asked curiously, "What did you think of it?"

"What do you mean?"

"You know what I mean," she said, her tone suggesting I wasn't being truthful.

"This is your story," I sidestepped. "Why don't you tell me?"

She pressed her lips together, then studied me silently for several moments. I could almost see her come to some kind of conclusion. "Do you think that inanimate objects can have a psyche?"

I recalled Jazz asking if I believed in fate when we were at Hill Villa. This was another of those questions that if you answer with, "Not on your life, you nutcase," you aren't going to learn anything further. Besides, I'd been inside the playhouse and I'd sensed the vibes.

She took my silence for agreement. "I went to the playhouse this morning, just to check it out. It's just like it was, only mustier. But it felt . . . bad. It's like whatever happened there is now in the walls and floor, the marrow of the boards. I'm going to ask Logan to tear it down."

I stared across the polished linoleum floor that stretched across the rotunda and emptied into four different hallways. I told myself I didn't believe in Violet's whole ju-ju thing, but taking the playhouse down sounded like a brilliant idea all the same.

I wondered if Jazz's father was one of his uncles, or his grandfather, or if Lily had managed to be with someone outside the family. DNA testing would tell, but I wondered if suggesting it would be the best course of action.

"You told all this to Jazz?"

"Not yet. I'm debating on confronting my brothers. What do you think?"

"I don't know how you talk to any of them about it."

Violet crumpled her empty cup. "I've been through some pretty ugly divorces, but they're nothing, you know? This . . ." She let the sentence hang, then abruptly moved on to something else. "Anyway, what do you think about the way Dahlia and Cammie over-mother their kids?"

I think we were both relieved by the change of subject. "Don't all mothers do a little of that?"

"Maybe." She sounded unconvinced. "I haven't been around them that long, but I've seen those looks they give. Dahlia just stares at Benjamin, and Cammie can't leave Rosalie alone. Benjamin's already weird and Rosalie's bound to turn out the same."

Her harsh assessment wasn't that far off my own thoughts, but I somehow felt compelled to come to their defense. "Dahlia lost a baby to SIDS. Rhoda."

"I know." Violet shook her head. "The problem is Dahlia hasn't moved past any of it. She'd like to keep staying at the house with that sleazoid husband who wants to get in everybody's pants, and with Benjamin. This is a kid who needs to leave home *now*."

I nodded, then asked, "Has Roderick come on to you yet?"

"In his way. He talks to my breasts and plays with his willie." Violet made a face. "Maybe if Rhoda had lived Dahlia would have turned out differently. Having a daughter, maybe she would've related to women better. But maybe not. Dad screwed her up, too." She gave me a look. "If it sounds like I've had thirty-some years of therapy, it's because I have," she said. "I lived on a farm outside Bakersfield. I stayed till I was eighteen and then moved to L.A. Got married when I was nineteen, the first time. I did the usual modeling thing, and was a film extra for a while. A couple more marriages. Being a housewife never really worked for me. I tried work as an escort, but silly me, I thought you could get away with just being a pretty face. Guess what? My dates al-

ways wanted to have sex." She half-smiled. "Divorce settle-
ments have been my steadiest source of income."

Violet was about as screwed up as the rest of them, but at least
she was honest with herself. I liked that about her.

Suddenly, she sucked in a breath. "Oh, my God, hon, would
you look at that . . . !"

I glanced back. Dwayne was striding toward us.

Be careful what you wish for.

Truer words—as it turned out—were never spoken. The gods
were apparently listening when I wished for Dwayne's and my
relationship to get back to what is was—sidekicks. Punch in the
arm buddies. Good old Jane and good old Dwayne. In fact, they
were listening so well that they sent me Violet, whose hungry
blue eyes practically stripped off Dwayne's clothes.

Initially, I wasn't unduly alarmed, especially since Dwayne's
attention was focused on me. I told him it looked as if Logan was
going to be fine, which was echoed by Jazz who joined us shortly
after Dwayne's arrival. No brain damage. Nothing as extensive as
Jazz's own injuries from the hit and run the previous winter.

But then, as we all relaxed a bit, Violet switched into female
predatory mode. It was like she'd pulled on a second skin. You
could practically feel the heat, and Dwayne wasn't missing a bit
of it. I sensed when he became aware of Violet at a new level.
One moment he was all about being there for me, questioning
me about Logan's condition, dutifully shaking hands with Jazz,
politely greeting Violet. Then it was as if his ears started listening
to some new source of sound, something underneath the conversation, something that hummed *sex*. His eyes grew half-lidded
and his voice deepened into its drawl. I wanted to elbow him as
hard as I could. I wanted to thunk him on the side of the head
and pull his ears.

I did none of those things. Instead I went right for the age-old
trick of pretending I didn't care. I turned my attention to Jazz.

From that point on it was like I'd suddenly joined an acting
class. Watch Jane Kelly be as bright and clever as she can be.

Watch her joke and tell stories and generally be the life of the party. Jazz gazed at me in wonder and appreciation; he'd never seen this side of me, and no wonder. I hadn't known I possessed it myself.

But did it do any good? Not really. By the time my act was in full gear, the damage was already done. Violet had captivated Dwayne. Their eyes were locked on each other as if by magnets.

I wanted to say: *Now, wait. She's got to be fifteen years older than you. At least ten or twelve. She's been married and divorced three or four times, maybe more. She's not for you, Dwayne!*

But I didn't say a word because I knew he wouldn't care. It wasn't about that, anyway. It was attraction in its purest form. The kind where the rest of the world simply fades into the background and all the color and life is in that space between the two of you.

People have killed over lesser things.

I subsided into silence and reminded myself I was glad Dwayne and I were best friends. Beneath the table I tore my little cocktail napkin to shreds.

Logan was released from the hospital with a concussion, and everybody breathed a sigh of relief and headed to their respective homes. I learned that Violet's appearance had basically forced Dahlia, Roderick and Benjamin from their rooms at the Purcell mansion. Garrett and Satin had followed suit, leaving only James on the premises. Violet clearly thought it was all for the best, and I had to agree. It seemed a good idea for the Purcells to get back to their everyday lives.

As we were all getting ready to leave, Violet casually invited Dwayne out for a drink, and maybe . . . dinner?

Dwayne and I locked eyes. I tried for a noncommital expression while I telegraphed, *no, no, no!*

Jazz said to Violet, Dwayne and me, "Come over to my house. We'll get Logan settled and I'll order in Chinese." He was clearly thrilled about the attraction developing between Dwayne and Violet. I was struggling. These things seem to suddenly have a life of their own.

Dwayne said, "Sounds good to me."

Violet purred, "Well, if that's all I can get for tonight, all right." Her red lips parted over blinding white teeth. I had a mental image of her filing them down like a cannibal.

I'd come in my own car to the hospital and I left the same way, sick at heart. Dwayne called me on my cell, and I debated about even answering. When I did pick up, I said, "Hey, there," as if nothing had changed.

"You okay?" he asked.

"Of course. Why?"

"I don't know." Ah, yes, we unfathomable females. We're just so darn hard to read.

"So, what do you think about this car accident?" he asked.

"I think it's damn suspicious." I bit off the words.

"Did Cammie give a description of the car?"

"I didn't ask her. The police are involved."

"You make it sound like you're not interested."

"I'm not, Dwayne. I'm not interested. I'm over the whole damn thing."

A pause. "Okay."

"I'll see you later, okay?"

"Sure thing. Bye, darlin'."

I threw my cell phone across the car. It bounced off the seat and onto the floor.

Chapter
Eighteen

By the time I met them for dinner, I was in a better state of mind. I'd managed to push thoughts of Dwayne and Violet aside, at least for the moment. Instead I'd concentrated on Logan who'd managed to tug at my heart with his quiet stoicism as Jazz had helped him to his car.

I had the presence of mind to stop and pick him up a gift. After all, the kid had been through a lot recently. When I arrived at Jazz's I saw that I was the last one there. Jazz had made another fire and Logan was ensconced on the couch with his Game Boy in hand. He was having a slushy drink of some weird lavender color. "Grape juice, lemon juice, and vodka," Violet said, holding up hers in a daiquiri glass. "Logan's is a virgin, of course. It's my signature drink."

"It's violet-colored," Logan said. He looked far healthier. No more starey gaze and his color had returned. The white head wrap gave him a foreign look that somehow worked for him. Or, maybe it was his sudden soberness. A newly adult look around his eyes.

I declined a signature drink though I was really trying not to be a total drag.

Music was playing softly. More Sinatra. Violet was mouthing the words, looking happy. "Mom loved Frankie," she said.

Dwayne was leaning against the mantel, holding a long-necked beer loosely in a couple of fingers. I was pissed off to see that he'd changed into a really nice blue shirt and his jeans were pressed. He had his cowboy boots on, and tonight they added to his "outfit." His blue eyes met mine squarely. I felt like blowing a raspberry at him but I contained myself. Instead I said, "How do I get one of those?" pointing to his beer.

"Coming right up," Jazz said, sailing into the kitchen. His worry over Logan had been replaced by a kind of manic relief.

I handed Logan the sack with the video store's logo. "I didn't have time to wrap it."

He gazed at the bag, then up at me in dumb surprise. Opening the sack, he pulled out the video game I'd purchased. "Fissure," he said.

"It doesn't come for Game Boy, so I bought it for your system upstairs. A friend of mine recommended it."

"It's a great game!"

I could tell by the way he gazed at me I'd zoomed way up in his estimation. I told myself to be careful. I just might start liking the little creep.

Jazz handed me my beer, looking bemused by my gift. "I wouldn't know which one to buy."

Violet had sidled over to Dwayne. Her hips swayed to the music. "Wanna dance, cowboy?" she asked.

Logan ripped Fissure out of its wrapper. "I'm going upstairs to play." He looked at me. "Wanna come?"

It was the best invitation I'd had all night. "Sure."

Jazz beamed at me as I followed Logan up the steps. I was scoring points all over the place only it was for the wrong team. I tried not to look back at Dwayne and Violet, but I couldn't stop myself. She had her hands around the back of his neck, her whole body slithering against his. Dwayne wasn't moving, but then I'd never known him to dance.

I hurried to catch up with Logan.

I entered his room, expecting to see him already flopped in

front of the huge TV, but he was waiting to shut the door behind me.

"I wanted to talk to you alone," he said.

I looked at his taut expression. Another Purcell with secrets.

"I don't want you to think I'm crazy. I'm not crazy."

"Okay."

"Someone's trying to kill me. This is the second time they've tried. I don't want to worry my dad, but that's what it is."

I met his gaze. I didn't really want to break this tenuous olive branch he was holding out to me—the first sign of his being more than a noxious brat—but I also didn't want to legitimize his own self-absorption. "It may seem that way, but your accident today wasn't a hit and run. It could have been just an accident."

"*I* got Nana's money," Logan reminded me, as if I could forget. "The first accident? It was right after Nana told me she was leaving everything to me. And this one? After she *did* leave it to me. Somebody's trying to kill me," he repeated, enunciating each word. "I don't want the money anymore. I want them to take it back. I want you to help me convince them."

I sighed. Like Jazz was going to let that happen. Jazz's doorbell rang as I pondered a response. "That's our dinner. Let's go downstairs and think this through a little more."

"I'm not making this up."

"Okay." I headed for the stairs.

The assortment from Mr. Chin's almost made me forget my problems. Food can do that for me, sometimes. It was a mouthwatering array of little white boxes filled with sesame beef, General Tso's chicken, ten-ingredient lo-mein, sauteed string beans, white rice and various and sundry hot mustards, soy sauce, fortune cookies, napkins and chopsticks. Jazz handed me a fresh beer and we all sat down at the table and dug in. Even Violet seemed distracted for the few moments while we ate. Only Logan picked at his food, his gaze digging into me, but I studiously ignored him until I was finished. Only when I pushed my plate aside, drank lustily of my beer and leaned back in my chair, did I look over at him.

He clearly wanted me to do something now. I'd become his new voice, apparently. He'd been all about Violet until I showed up with the video game. Sometimes it doesn't pay to be nice.

I was avoiding Dwayne's eyes, although he probably didn't have a clue because Violet began sucking up his attention again. She was like a death ray, the kind that entraps its victim inside the cone of its beam.

As I was walking outside to my car, Jazz at my side, my cell phone, back on vibrate, buzzed inside my purse. I congratulated myself on how good I was getting on reprogramming the damn thing. Today, ring tones, tomorrow text messaging. I might not have noticed it except I could feel and hear it vibrating against something inside.

I whipped it out as Jazz was leaning in for a kiss. "Sorry," I said, and gave him a smack on the lips and a wink. Keep it light, Jane. Oh, yes. It seemed to satisfy him and he mouthed, "I'll call you later," as he headed back inside.

I turned my attention to my Caller ID as I climbed behind the wheel. No name. A local prefix that I didn't recognize. The phone was still buzzing, so I offered a cautious "Hello?" as I slipped into the driver's seat.

"Hello, Jane," a familiar, slightly nervous male voice greeted.

I screwed up my face. "James?" I asked. His call was so unexpected that it took me a moment to put it together.

"I asked Jazz for your number," he said.

"Okay." I was waiting for the reason he called.

He seemed hard pressed to come up with that himself. After a hesitation, he asked, "Can you come to the house?"

"*Tonight?*"

"I'd like to talk to you about something."

My earlier conversation with Violet was still fresh on my mind. I thought of young, pretty Lily Purcell with her brothers in the playhouse, and I also thought about James's spectacularly creepy knife paintings. Cynthia had suggested the knives represented power: the male anatomy as a weapon.

Like, oh, sure. That's just what I wanted to do. Race over to that moldering house and have a tête-à-tête alone with James.

"Can I get a preview?" I asked.

He hesitated. "I know who murdered my mother. I saw them go into her room."

I blinked. "You're siding with Garrett on this?" My disbelief couldn't quite be disguised.

"I haven't talked to the police about it. I wanted to talk to you first."

"James, you really believe your mother was murdered?"

But I was talking to air, as he'd already hung up.

I put my cell phone back in my purse and glanced back at Jazz's front door, the one he'd just reentered. Should I go back inside? Rejoin the party? I didn't really want to. I wanted to talk to Dwayne. I didn't get what James was trying to pull. It felt like some kind of setup, but I couldn't figure out what. Orchid murdered? Was he serious? James's conscience seemed to be working overtime.

Through the windshield I saw the front door open and Dwayne step out on the porch. The entry's interior light spilled out around him, leaving him in silhouette. I reached for my door handle, glad for the chance to catch him alone, but then Violet joined him, shivering a little as she closed the door behind them. She didn't play coy. She just swooped in on him and laid a kiss on his lips that caused my mouth to drop open. I watched Dwayne slide a hand around her back. The vision of his fingers splayed across her skin reminded me of how he'd held me and kissed me only days earlier.

"God . . . damn . . . it," I muttered through gritted teeth, twisting the ignition and revving the engine more than I meant to.

I backed out carefully. I would've liked to burn rubber, spray gravel, roar my engine. Instead I simply left. I headed back to Lake Chinook. I wasn't going to the Purcells. I wasn't dealing with James, or anyone else. I was going home to my dog and bed.

Period.

My cell phone buzzed again. I fumbled inside my purse with one hand till I grasped it. This time the phone accessed my contact list: *Dwayne's cell*.

I made a series of frustrated noises to myself, fragments of swear words combined with derogatory names like dickweed and jerkwad, then pushed the green button. "Okay, hot lips, what is it?"

He barked out a laugh. "Hey, *she* kissed *me*."

"Yeah, I could see you were hating it."

"You sound like a jealous girlfriend."

"Keep telling yourself that," I said. "So, why'd you call?"

"Violet said you talked with her about Lily."

I could hear the rattletrap noise of his truck. "Where are you?" I asked.

"I'm in my truck, darlin', and the passenger seat is empty."

Did I ask? *Did I?* It bugged me that he seemed to know exactly what I was thinking. "I told you before, I'm over it. All the Purcells."

"Thought you were going with Jazz to Black Butte."

"What? Hell, no. Who told you that? Jazz? I never said I was going."

"Violet told me. She invited me along, too."

Violet was going? And Dwayne? "Well, have a great time," I said. "I'm out of that one."

"So, you're out of all of it, but you're still talking to Violet about Purcell history."

"Okay, fine." I cut to the chase. "Listen, James just called me."

"James Purcell?"

"He said he wants me to come over to the house. He wants to talk to me about his mother's *murder*. Says he saw someone go into her room."

"Are you kidding me?" Dwayne responded skeptically. "He brings this up now? Calls you on your cell?"

"He asked Jazz for the number."

"What's with the timing? Something clicked and he just decided to unburden himself? I don't buy it. Something's off." He paused. "You didn't say you'd meet him, did you?"

"He hung up. He seemed . . ." I searched for the word. "Skittish. Worried."

"You're not talking yourself into going, are you?"

"No . . . I don't know . . . Where's Violet?"

"She's probably halfway to the house by now."

"So, if I did go, she'd be there."

"Soon." He sounded dubious about the whole plan. "I don't like it."

"Dwayne, what if he's right?" I asked suddenly. "What if she was killed by someone? I just dismissed that idea as farfetched, but what do I know?"

"Why would she be killed?"

"I don't know. Maybe because she was losing it? Maybe someone didn't want her bringing up what happened in the past? But now Violet's showed up, and she knows what happened, and she's not afraid to say what she remembers."

"So, you think Orchid was killed to hide a secret?"

"I'm just trying it out as a theory, Dwayne."

He grunted, which I took as a sign to continue. "Now Violet shows up," I went on. "Someone they've practically dropped out of their consciousness. Cammie, Jazz and probably Benjamin didn't even know she existed. Someone could be really nervous, wondering just what Violet could blab."

"Maybe." He didn't sound like he believed me, but he was trying to keep an open mind.

"Okay, I don't know. If Orchid was deliberately murdered, and I'm not saying she was, then maybe the motive was something other than the money. After all they had the POA. The money was safe. And maybe they figured they would still inherit, so killing Orchid wasn't going to change things anyway. They just needed to close her mouth."

"But then Logan inherited and Violet showed up."

"That's right. And it gummed up the grand plan." I added,

"And along with that, Logan thinks someone's trying to kill him for the money. Says they've tried twice already."

Dwayne made a disparaging sound. "Yeah, well the first accident was long before Orchid's death, and this one could just be because Cammie panicked."

"I don't believe him, either, but there have been a lot of 'accidents.'" We both were silent for a moment, digesting it all, then I suddenly decided, "I'm going to go, Dwayne. "I want to know what he says he saw."

"Give me fifteen minutes, and I'll meet you there."

"Much as I'd like that, it won't work," I said. "James sounds tentative, maybe scared. And I won't be alone with him. Violet's gotta be right behind me."

"You can't wait fifteen minutes?"

"Just be hanging by your cell phone," I said. "I've got you on speed dial. You see a call coming in from me, don't answer, just storm the castle." Seeing the turn for Military Road, I said, "I'm heading into Dunthorpe now."

"I'm right behind you," Dwayne clipped out. "I'll park in the exit drive. If I don't hear from you in half an hour, I'm coming in."

I smiled as I hung up. I kind of like when he sounds all male and protective. But I'd told him the truth. I didn't feel all that worried for my own safety. There was an ick factor with James which was totally off-putting, but I'd be more worried if I were Violet. She was the one blabbing now.

I headed up my usual route. It was practically second nature by now. I'd learned every twist and turn to Chrysanthemum Lane and the Purcells' entry drive. It had only been a couple of weeks since I'd first met Jazz but it felt like a lifetime since my world and the Purcells' had become intertwined.

It was a comfort to know that Dwayne had my back. I didn't really know what to expect when I met with James, but at least he'd contacted me so maybe he was finally prepared to open up. To date it had been like pulling teeth to get any of the Purcells to reveal anything pertinent about the family. It was also a comfort to know Violet would be showing up soon, too. I didn't relish being the first one on James's doorstep. It would have been nice to have Reyna around, but I wasn't sure she hadn't already quit the job, and anyway the staff only worked days.

I parked my car in the portico. Nana's vanilla convertible was in its usual space. The two sports cars were there, as well. I'd never learned whom they belonged to. One of them was James's probably. Maybe both.

I knocked on the back door, the one they used like a front door. The other door off the kitchen area was dark, but I could see a light from the upstairs landing.

James came to admit me. Unlocking the door, he mumbled a hello, and then we were standing in the entry hall together. He'd always looked used up and far older than his years, but in the uncertain light from the landing, he seemed almost withered, ancient, as if he'd been reanimated from some long ago time.

That smell of decay I'd first noticed when I'd arrived at the property came to me again: musty, dank, with a thread of something noxious and sour. I suspected it was more my imagination than reality. With no Reyna, Carlotta and Orchid, the heart of the house was gone and we were left with the dying remains.

Maybe Violet was right. This place had a psyche all right.

I sought for normalcy. "All right," I said conversationally. "I'm here now. Who did you see go into Orchid's rooms?" My voice seemed to reverberate against the walls.

"I called you because I needed to talk to you." He turned and headed for the stairs.

"So talk." I didn't move. The atmosphere of the place was getting to me. I figured Violet was due any second, and my cell phone was back in my pocket. I'd left my purse in the car. There was no reason to play Nancy Drew with these weirdos.

James hesitated when he realized I wasn't following, one foot on the bottom step. He cocked his head, but he didn't turn around. "You've been listening to Violet."

My view was the back of his graying head. His voice was almost disembodied as he was facing the window at the upstairs landing. I took a couple of steps closer to him. "That's right."

"She was only a kid when she left. She didn't know us."

"She told me about the playhouse," I said.

He seemed to clutch at the stairway rail, but it was hard to tell. "The playhouse was Lily's."

Was that what this was, then? A confession? Was that why he'd called me? I began to doubt he'd ever seen anyone stealing into Orchid's rooms. I moved a little closer to him and said, "I've seen your paintings."

"When?"

"I let myself into your rooms the day after Orchid disappeared."

"You searched them?"

"I just looked inside."

He headed upstairs without another word. This time, I followed. At the top of the gallery I glanced down into the entry hall, listening hard for an approaching engine. Where was Violet?

James was unlocking his door. I gingerly stepped in his direction. I would rather drink the algae-furred waters of Lake Chinook than follow him inside a room with those paintings.

"I'm working on another one," he said. "I think it might be my last." He gazed back at me. "Violet said she told you we had sex with Lily."

I was surprised he approached the subject so boldly, but he seemed weary of everything.

"You have to understand," he said. "It's not what you think. It wasn't like that."

"Okay."

"Lily would go to the playhouse to hide from my father," James said. "Garrett and I would try to sneak up on her. She got mad and hit Garrett, and he hit her back. Then they were on the floor and she was screaming and pulling out his hair. And then . . ."

I waited, frozen and mesmerized.

"And then she was rubbing on him and he said, 'You want it. You want it. You want it,' and she said yes, and she was *laughing*."

He shook his head, as if to eradicate the vision. "And Garrett was on her and she was letting him. But she was watching me the whole time. I tried to run, but they wouldn't let me. She started kissing me. She was like that. But it only happened *once. Just once.* I wouldn't go back even though she taunted me. Garrett did, but I didn't. I couldn't." His eyes were deep hollows. "But Violet thinks it was more than once. She called me a liar."

"You talked to Violet about this?" So, she had brought it up to him.

"She said I was Jazz's father." He shook his head slowly from side-to-side. "It was only one time!"

I could have pointed out that one time is all it takes, but that wasn't really the issue. "A DNA test would answer that question."

"No . . ."

"Is this really why you called me?" I asked.

He didn't answer for a moment, too lost in his own guilty hell. Then he said, "No . . . no . . . I want the truth out, that's all." He drew a shaking breath. "She's in my mother's suite already."

"She?"

He closed the door to his room in my face. I turned to look toward the north end of the hall. Orchid's doors were closed, but they'd never truly shut tightly and now I saw a slim column of light shining through the gap between them.

My instinct was to race-walk out of the house, but then fleeing is always my first reaction. Nerves of steel I do not possess. However, curiosity and a certain amount of misplaced pride in my ability as an information specialist drove my legs forward. At Orchid's doors I hesitated. Should I knock, or just barge in?

Who the hell was "she"?

With one hand inside my pocket, wrapped around my cell phone, I pushed open the door with my other.

Chapter Nineteen

At first I thought there was no one inside. Like downstairs, the room was illuminated only by one light, a table lamp whose wattage was in the forties or less. But then I saw a figure standing by the window and my heart leapt to my throat.

She turned around, her bulk giving her away before I actually recognized her. "Dahlia," I said, surprised.

"What are you doing here?" she demanded.

I remembered then that she'd been here that first day, when I'd originally noticed the two sports cars. They were hers and James's. She didn't seem the type somehow, but what did I know about her?

"I'm . . . waiting for Violet," I said.

"Well, she's not staying in my mother's rooms."

My gaze wandered toward the mantel and the hearth. I had an image of Orchid's crumpled form flash briefly across my mind.

"James called you, didn't he?" she said, a note of betrayal in her voice. "He told you he saw me come in here that afternoon."

I didn't see any reason to lie. "Yes."

"He's such an idiot."

"So, he was wrong?"

"I did not kill my mother." Her mouth clamped shut but I

could see her chin tremble with emotion. "I hate him for saying that."

"I think he's under a certain amount of pressure," I said lightly, checking my watch. Violet was long delayed. I wondered if I should call Dwayne and give him an update.

"You have somewhere to go?" she asked. "You barge in here, and now you have to just leave?"

"I could stay," I said, not sure where this was going. "I was just wondering where Violet was."

"Violet," she sneered. Then she closed her eyes and shuddered. "You think I killed her? You think it was intentional? I could tell by the way you sneaked in here, you thought you were going to find out all the secrets. You were the one who talked her out of signing the power of attorney. She was going to do it, and then you had to open your big mouth."

"But she signed it anyway," I pointed out.

Dahlia's mouth worked. "I'm the signer for the family. I've done it for years. I can sign Mother's name better than she can."

"Are you saying you faked the POA?"

"Yes, that's what I'm saying, smart ass. And if it hadn't have been for you, I wouldn't have had to. Then all of a sudden Mom's missing, and she hasn't signed the goddamn form! So, I took care of it." She went back to staring out the window. "But then she came back, and she remembered she hadn't signed. All those things she forgot . . . all those things . . ." She shook her head at the irony of it. "But she remembered that. So, we got in an argument. But I—did—not—kill—her."

"What happened?" I asked.

"She was going to tell everybody about the POA. And she was really mad at me. She actually swung at me! Her whole life she was a doormat. Like Satin. Just let Daddy do whatever he wanted." She pointed to her chest. "I was Daddy's flower. It was me, not Lily. We had something special, and my mother was *jealous*. All of a sudden it comes out how she blames me for everything, when it was Lily's fault! And then she just swung at me. What was I supposed to do? *What was I supposed to do?*"

"Push her away from you?" I guessed.

"That's right. I didn't push her very hard. But she just lost her balance and her head hit the mantel. I ran downstairs to the meeting." Dahlia clasped her hands together and brought them to her lips.

"What happened between you and Lily at River Shores, Haven of Rest?"

"What?" Her mind wasn't on that.

"When they had to restrain her . . . you'd seen her that day and she was upset."

"She was pregnant," Dahlia said. "Could be Garrett's, could be James's, could be anybody's."

"Your father's?"

That brought fury to her face. "No! Daddy wasn't like that. Aren't you listening? Lily was a liar, too. My baby died. Lily was going to keep hers. She was like that. Selfish. Mean." She stepped toward me and I backed up, but she was lost in the power of her own narration. "I lost my baby, and Lily kept hers. And there's Jasper, big as life. A big dumb idiot. And Logan . . ." Her voice lowered with loathing.

I wanted to keep her on track, but it was difficult. "You found out about her keeping the baby when you went to see her."

"Lily was six months pregnant and sleeping with every cock that crossed her path. It was pathological. It was killing Daddy. He thought putting her there would save her, but nothing was going to change her. I told her she'd ruined her baby already, that it was damaged. I knew even then. She went into a screaming rage and they had to restrain her."

"Jazz isn't damaged."

"Yes, he is."

"He's lost his short-term memory, but that was from the car accident. And Lily was nine months pregnant," I pointed out, wondering why I was even arguing with her. She'd definitely had some kind of break with reality.

"Six months," Dahlia insisted. "They held her down, cut off her air supply by mistake. Killed her brain. She went into a coma.

They kept her on a ventilator until the baby was born, but she died that day. He's damaged, and my mother spent the rest of her life trying to make up for it."

"They kept her alive for three months, so that the child could be born?"

"That's right. Nobody wanted to. Daddy sure didn't, but there was nothing to do."

I absorbed this, thinking about Lily, and the staff at the hospital, and the secrets of the Purcells. Pulling the plug, so to speak, would have killed the baby. They waited till after Jazz was born.

Downstairs I heard the back entry door open. Violet called, "You hoo! Jane? Are you here?"

"In Orchid's rooms."

Violet's footsteps *tip-tapped* up the stairs, along the hallway, then she entered the room. She looked from me to Dahlia and back again. "Did I miss something?"

Dahlia looked at her, said, "Lily," with serious loathing, then collapsed on the couch, crying noisily into her hands.

Three days later I found myself on a road trip to the Purcells' house in central Oregon, near Black Butte. Jazz, Logan, The Binkster and I were in my Volvo as Jazz's convertible BMW wasn't going to fill the bill. Dwayne and Violet were meeting us.

I'd done my jolly best to be dis-included. The Purcell secrets were aired. Everything was over. All that was left was to lay the ground rules out to Jazz concerning our non-relationship.

But Logan would have none of it and in a weak moment I'd ended up saying yes. Logan seemed to consider me his new best friend. He'd gotten the major head wrap off, and though he was a little self-conscious about the shaved section of his head and the stitches, it didn't seem to bother him pain-wise. I hadn't completely been won over by him, but I was beginning to think he was almost okay.

It was Jazz who was having trouble with head pain. Initially I thought it was just your usual garden variety headache until he admitted that he suffered from migraine-type pain, another by-product of the accident. Dahlia's "damaged" comments ran around my brain like the silver ball in a pinball machine, bouncing off one thing, hitting another, jumping back the other way. Not that Jazz's problems had anything to do with the circumstances of his birth—that I did not believe. Dahlia just had some desperate need to blame Lily for everything—dear old Dad being entirely blameless in the series of events that had caused the downward spiral for the whole family. No, Jazz's problems were more recent and I had a gut feeling they were far worse than he maintained. It also made it difficult for me to pass on to him the gist of Dahlia's big revelation. What purpose would it serve? Unfortunately, now I was the one with the secret, but since it was all half-baked assumptions, I couldn't figure out how to present the information or if I even should.

So, instead, I focused on the positive, or at least tried to. There was a part of me that congratulated myself on a job well done. This is the deluded part of myself that wanted to cheer the fact that all Purcell secrets were out in the open and that I, Jane Kelly, had been responsible for that fact. The other part of me, the reality-based part, had the audacity to ask what I'd really accomplished. Orchid was gone. Nobody had benefited from the information I'd uncovered in any positive way. James had squirreled himself away in his room to paint his last painting. Dahlia acted like we'd never had the conversation that, in some ways, had begged more questions than answered about who'd been with whom and whose child was whose. All I really knew was, there'd been a whole lotta lovin' going on, none of it what you'd call a healthy relationship.

Even Violet, who'd developed late and escaped most of the sexual abuse, hadn't been able to settle into her own life and put her energy into anything lasting. Four marriages and four divorces later, she wasn't the picture of romantic stability.

Not that it seemed to bother Dwayne.

When Violet walked in on the tail end of my conversation with Dahlia, Dwayne walked into the entry hall. He'd grown tired of waiting for my call. Violet, as it turns out, had stopped at a small diner on Macadam, worried that she may have consumed too many of her signature drinks to be within the legal blood alcohol level. She'd ordered french fries and coffee, consumed them, then resumed her drive home.

Dwayne didn't know she'd been delayed. He'd actually entered the Purcell mansion, gun drawn. I learned this later as it would have freaked me out a little. By the time he reached the north suite, he'd tucked the gun in the waistband of his jeans at the small of his back. I saw the weapon when we all turned to leave. It reminded me that I'd stepped into a job that required some means of self-protection. Dwayne had suggested more than once that I needed to get over my aversion to guns and get a license. He may be right. It just worries me that if I try to tuck my weapon down my own waistband at the small of my back, I could shoot my ass off. Yeah, yeah I know that's what safeties are for. It still sounds too possible to ignore.

As soon as I have my reckoning with Jazz, I'm going to rethink some of these things. The cool mace cans still sound pretty good. Or pepper spray. Or a stun gun.

We arrived at the lane that led to the ranch house around six PM. Like their residence in Dunthorpe, this one was down a long drive. Unlike the Dunthorpe home, however, this drive was a two-wheel track dug into the red central Oregon dust that led through skinny aspens and Ponderosa pines. No Douglas firs on this side of the Cascade Mountains. Not enough water. Yes, it rains in Oregon a lot, but that's mostly throughout the Willamette Valley. Those same rain clouds get hung up in the Cascade Mountains and never make it any further. It leaves central and eastern Oregon dry and cold in the winter, dry and hot in the summer.

The home itself was a huge lodge out of peeled logs. It had a wraparound porch and wide steps leading to massive front doors with wooden handles made from ax handles. Walking inside was like entering a theme park. I expected Paul Bunyan and Babe to be waiting in the dining room, but the room's space was filled with a huge table constructed out of several enormous tree rounds bolted together in three rings with some kind of inch-thick plastic material covering it. Twenty-some chairs were parked around the circles of the table.

I'd worried that Jazz expected me to share a room with him, but when I grabbed an empty one, proclaiming it for mine, he didn't try to bring his bags inside. Having Logan with us was probably the reason. Difficult to have wild, uninhibited sex with your child in the next room. I wasn't into the kind of yee-haw romping fun the house seemed to cry for anyway.

It did give me pause about Dwayne and Violet, however. I could picture the two of them whoopee-ki-ying all over the place.

As soon as I'd unpacked—which consisted of taking out my toothbrush and brushing my teeth—I moseyed downstairs to set a spell on the back porch. There was, by golly, a porch swing out of more barkless branches. I sat down and let the sun dapple my skin as it threaded its way through the pines that surrounded the entire property. A small deck jutted out from the back of the porch, which held a hot tub on a platform. You could sit in its depths under the hot sun or night stars.

I tried to get into thoughts of relaxation, but honestly I would have preferred to be back in Lake Chinook, working on another job.

Binkster had learned that Logan was a complete pushover for food. All she had to do was press her chin against his leg, if he was standing, or his arm, if he was sitting, and Logan would head for the chow. I'd given him a stern talking to, and Logan had taken to keeping bits of lo-cal kiblets in his pockets. Now and again he would give her one which she would wolf down with the speed of light. It wasn't much food and it kept them both happy. They were currently up in Logan's room where he'd hooked up his video system in record time, and they were deep into Fissure.

I'd put a call into Cynthia before we left, explaining with no enthusiasm about my trip to central Oregon. She cut off my whining with a recap: "You're going to a mountain retreat with a wealthy, handsome guy who's nice to you. You'll probably have good weather and good food. His son's there, but the son has accepted you, and you get to take your dog."

Okay, she was right, but I couldn't completely capitulate, so I told her about Dwayne and Violet. If I'd been expecting commiseration, I was sorely disappointed. She said, "What's the deal? You can have somebody but Dwayne can't?"

"That isn't what this is about."

"Then explain it to me."

I tried to. I really did. But the answer escaped me. Or, more accurately, I didn't want to dig too deeply into my own feelings and then relate them to Cynthia. It didn't matter in the end because she's often better at reading between the lines than what's written on the page. "You've got a thing for Dwayne," she marveled at the end of my recitation.

"No."

"That's why you can't get into Jazz."

"Cynthia—"

"Are you seriously going to deny this?"

I grimaced—and buckled. "It's just so messy. In fact this whole 'case' was messy, and I'm not usually so obsessive about tying up every last detail, but I live for a sense of completion."

"You're changing the subject. We're talking about Dwayne."

"I don't want him, Cynthia," I said. "But then, I don't *not* want him."

She snorted in amusement. "You are in so much trouble."

"Dwayne's with Violet, and if I go to the Purcell ranch, I'll be faced with it."

"I do not believe Dwayne is with this Violet person."

"You haven't met her."

"I've met Dwayne. I do know what you're feeling," she added in a side bar. "He just doesn't jump into relationships. You know that. If he's hanging around with Violet, it's either a temporary feel-good, or he's doing it for other reasons. So, ask yourself: do I want him, or do I *not* want him? And give yourself the right answer. I had to do that with Ernst. I did not want him. Not really."

Cynthia's words both encouraged and worried me. I wondered what was going through Dwayne's mind. The problem was every time I saw him with Violet I wanted to turn my eyes away and simply skeedaddle. It was too hard and took too much energy.

I took a stroll around the grounds just to relieve my own dissatisfaction. The trees had been cleared from a large area directly surrounding the house, and two-to-three inch chips of pine bark and small rocks had been arranged as a ground cover. Hardy wildflowers grew along the edges, and everything was overlaid with the red dust. There was a three-car garage angled off the side of the house, and farther back, where the drive continued around the back side of the house and led into the trees, was a building that looked like it could house large equipment. I could only see the building's west side; its north faced Black Butte—the small mountain, so thick and dark with trees that it appeared black. Not far from the Purcell home was Black Butte Ranch, a resort with several golf courses, swimming pools and horseback riding. No doubt about it, I was in cowboy country. Luckily, we were close to the town of Sisters, named for the nearby Three Sisters Mountains. About another hour farther was the city of Bend, which actually had strip malls and national fast-food restaurants. If I had to I could jump in the Volvo and make a run for it.

Dwayne and Violet arrived just as I was returning to the house. There was much oohing and ahhing over the house from Violet, more of a quiet visual inspection by Dwayne.

I made it my mission to cut Dwayne from the herd—please note the ranch parlance—and have a talk with him about Violet. Cynthia's words had made an impression and I wasn't feeling quite so distressed.

I caught up with him on the back porch as Violet went upstairs in search of rooms. He was still holding a duffel bag and he was drinking in the sight of the grounds, trees and sky as I let myself through the screen door.

"What are we doing here?" I whispered.

He slid me a look. "We're having fun."

"How will I know when it starts?"

And then Violet yelled from somewhere upstairs. "Hey! There's somebody living here."

Dwayne and I looked at each other and headed inside together.

We all stood inside the narrow bedroom at the end of the hall. It was the smallest and though I'd looked at all the rooms, mostly out of nosiness, it hadn't appealed to me because out of the six bedrooms along the upper floor, it was farthest from the bathroom. Violet, apparently, shared my nosiness, although she'd taken it a step farther and thrown open the closet. There were men's shirts and slacks lined up on hangers and a large suitcase on the floor filled with miscellaneous boxers, socks, shaving supplies, etc. Several pairs of shoes were tucked in the back.

Dwayne said to Jazz, "Know whose these are?"

He shook his head. "I didn't know anyone was staying here."

"Maybe they're not an invited guest," I suggested.

Violet said, "Whoever it is, they're pretty tidy about things. Not your average squatter."

"Maybe somebody just left the stuff here," Logan said, losing interest quickly. He headed back to his room and Binkster trotted after him.

I gingerly opened the shaving kit. There was moisture inside. "This has been used recently."

Dwayne examined the man's shoes. "Size ten." He took a look at the pants and shirts. "He's about my size."

"Not one of my brothers," Violet said. "Garrett's too fat, and James is too fragile. Possibly Roderick?"

"Or Benjamin?" I suggested dubiously.

We left the mystery for the moment. Violet made noise about trying out the hot tub and I left her to convince Dwayne, though it looked like it was going to be a hard sell. Jazz was still fighting his headache. He knocked back a couple of tablets of a prescription painkiller and apologized about having to lie down for a while. I told them I might run into Sisters.

We'd parked our cars to the side of the house in a gravel-filled area next to the garage. I was unlocking my car door when my attention snagged at the thought that there might be a vehicle parked inside. I went through the side door, the "man" door, and discovered two cars, a white sedan and a red Dodge truck. The third bay was empty.

Hunh, I thought. I tried the cars' doors but they were locked. I walked around them. They had current Oregon plates and they were washed and clean. I suspected one, or both, belonged to our mystery guest.

I left the garage and walked back to my car. I don't know what made me look, but I gazed down toward the large outbuilding. The man door was cracked open.

It hadn't been that way the last time I looked.

I walked down the dusty lane toward the building. Upon closer inspection, it was aluminum-sided with a metal roof. It was definitely some kind of utility building. I peeked inside the door and my gaze met tree trimmers, blowers, axes, gas cans and various and sundry clippers, hedgers and weed beaters. There was another car parked at the far side with a dust cover over it.

I'd barely absorbed this when a man suddenly stood up and looked at me. I squeaked in surprise and he was just as taken aback. He held a wrench in one hand. I realized he'd been tinkering with some equipment on the floor. I hadn't seen him because he'd been shielded by some waist-high shelving that had been erected in the center of the building. "Who are you?" he asked.

"Jane Kelly. We're staying at the house?" I hitched a thumb back in the direction I'd come.

He had to be our mystery guest, as he was about Dwayne's height and weight. He was nice looking with even white teeth and a comfortable way about him. His hair was light brown, his eyes anywhere from blue to brown; I couldn't tell from where I stood.

"Oh, yeah? You're a guest of the Purcells, huh," he said, setting down the wrench and wiping his hands on a rag he pulled

from a back pocket of his jeans. He walked toward me, hand out-
stretched. "I'm Chris."

I shook his hand. "You work here?"

"I'm actually staying here temporarily. Don't worry, the
Purcells know. I'm married to Camellia."

The penny dropped. "Chris Denton," I said.

"You've heard of me." He pulled back a little and made a face.
"All bad, I'm sure."

"I'm just surprised you're here."

"Well . . . if you know my name you probably know my circumstances. Cammie and I split up, although she wants to get
back together."

I thought about Chris's family Number Two and wondered if
he were seriously considering it. My brows lifted. "Is that a possibility?"

"Not really. Although Kayla and I had a fight. She kicked me
out." He half-laughed, sighed and ran a hand through his hair.
"So, Cammie said I could stay here awhile. Figured I might as
well get things running while I was at it." He gestured around
the room.

"I see."

"I can move my stuff out of the house. No problem."

"No, it's okay. We're just here for a few days." It didn't sound
like Cammie had cleared this decision with the rest of the family,
but it didn't matter to me. I wondered if she knew we were all
here.

"She said she's coming over, so I was thinking about leaving
anyway." Chris said. "I don't want another scene. She gets kinda
mad."

I nodded, not wanting to go into how Dwayne had said much
the same thing. "Is your car one of those in the garage?"

He glanced toward the vehicle under the tarp. "No, that's
Cammie's. She racked it up last winter in the snow and just
parked it." He snorted. "She's not much of a driver."

"I meant in the garage by the house."

"Oh, the truck's mine. I think they just leave the car here." He hooked a thumb in the direction of the house. "How many of you are there?"

"Five, and a dog."

"I think I might head into Bend," Chris said, putting his tools away.

"You don't have to."

"When Cammie starts screaming, it ruins it for everyone. She kinda thinks now that Kayla and I are fighting that she and I can just go back the way it was, but it's not that way. I was out of there before Rosalie came along. Cammie, she kept talking me into trying again and again. But as soon as I met Kayla, there was no going back. I'm not saying I haven't screwed up, I have, but Cammie planned on getting pregnant. She set that up."

"I understand you have two girls, Jasmine and Blossom."

"Yeah, that torqued Cammie but good. Jasmine's Kayla's middle name, so that's why we chose it. Didn't have anything to do with that flower thing the Purcells got going." He looked a little shamefaced as he added, "But, yeah, I suggested Blossom 'cause I was so pissed off over her setting me up for that pregnancy. I know." He lifted his hands. "It takes two. I was stupid. I just wanted her to calm down, y'know. So we slept together and then bam, Rosalie. She's a cute little bug, but I can't go back to that. I just can't."

I said lightly, "I was under the impression you were, well, living off some Purcell money."

"No, ma'am. Unless you count the money Cammie gave me originally to lure me back. But I sent her back every dime. Now, she's kinda given up on that. She's spending most of her energy getting a piece of the pie for Rosalie, which is fine by me. I made the mistake of telling her I was kicked out, so she offered up this place and I took it, even though I knew better. But she didn't come over right away so I thought maybe she's just being a friend after all, no strings attached. I didn't know then that Orchid had died and Cammie was just too busy to show."

He held the door for me and we walked into the late afternoon sunshine together. Chris was pretty easy to be around. It amazed me he'd ever hooked up with Cammie in the first place, but then there's no accounting for whom we pick for love.

Violet had apparently been unable to convince Dwayne to join her in the hot tub, but she was lying in the bubbling froth, her eyes closed, a satisfied look on her face. Opening one eye, she gave Chris the once over. "Our mystery man?"

"This is Chris Denton, Violet. Cammie's husband."

"Really. What are you doing here?"

I left him to fill her in on the details. Something was tugging at my brain but I couldn't put my finger on it. I went in search of Dwayne, thinking maybe talking to him would bring it to mind. I couldn't find him immediately, so I ducked my head into Logan's room. Binkster wagged her tail at me, panted, and came to circle around my legs. I petted her as I asked Logan, "Have you seen Dwayne?"

"I heard him say he was going for a walk."

That didn't really sound like him. "Okay."

"Want to play Fissure with me?" he asked eagerly.

"Maybe later."

I wandered back outside. Chris was standing by the hot tub and Violet had turned on the charm. It seemed to be second nature with her, though Chris didn't appear to be interested.

I finally caught up with Dwayne by the outbuilding. He looked like he'd come from a trail toward the back. "Hey," I called, jogging to catch up with him. "Chris Denton's here."

Dwayne's eyes shot past me. "Where?"

"Back at the house. Does he know you were the investigator Cammie hired?"

"Doubt it. He the one living in the house?"

"Yeah, Cammie gave him the okay. How long have she and Chris been split?"

"Probably from the day they said I do," Dwayne said with a snort. "That's been one long bad scene. She just decided she wanted him, and that's all she wrote."

"She's hardly mentioned him."

"Yeah, well, her brain's always working on a plan. Glad I don't have to deal with her anymore." Dwayne glanced at the out-building. "What's in there?"

"Equipment. Basic outdoor maintenance stuff. Oh, and Cammie's car. One she wrecked."

"Yeah?" Dwayne squinted. "What's it doing here?"

"I don't know, I guess she just hasn't fixed it yet."

I looked toward the house, hearing the sound of my own words still hanging in the air. That was what was bothering me, I realized. The car.

Dwayne said, "Someone's pulling in."

I heard the engine. From where we were the front drive was blocked by the house. "It's Cammie," I said, my voice sounding odd to my ears.

"Damn," Dwayne said, taking off at a fast clip toward the house. "If she sees me and Chris, she's bound to jump to some conclusion that'll set her off."

I let him go. Instead of following I reentered the equipment garage, walking briskly to the tarp-covered car. I folded back the heavy sailcloth from the front end. It was a Range Rover, similar to the one Cammie drove now. Same color. Maybe even the same year. Only this one's right headlight was broken out, the fender crumpled back to the tire. The hood was buckled and there was green paint along its bumper and streaked across the fender.

I looked inside the front window. On the floor was a box of candy canes, the peppermint sticks broken and crumpled.

I backed up as if burned. I reheard Logan's voice in my mind, telling me someone was trying to kill him.

It had been Christmas when Orchid first told Logan he would inherit . . . Christmas when Logan had bragged about being the one to inherit it all.

Cammie wanted everything for Rosalie and Logan stood in the way.

She attempted homicide twice.

Cammie . . .

I ran for the front of the house, the side door banging shut behind me. Cammie was just stepping out of her car, her face a dark cloud as she gazed at Dwayne, who was approaching to talk to her. Chris was standing in the open bay of the garage, next to his truck. Cammie gazed at him, then at Dwayne, then at me, running toward them.

She climbed back behind the wheel of her Range Rover and started it up. I could picture Cammie driving from the scene of the crime to the Black Butte house, then driving the white sedan "house" car back. It could be done in one night, if necessary. She'd then bought another Range Rover, just like her damaged one, and made the switch somewhere in the intervening months.

If anyone happened to go to Black Butte, the car was there, but that was a chance she had to take. She'd hidden the damaged vehicle in the equipment garage, and I doubted anyone knew it was there but Chris. She'd gambled that he might realize what it was, but she was desperate to reconnect with him as well. He was wrong. Cammie wanted everything for Rosalie, yes, but she also wanted everything for herself and that package included Chris. And so far she'd been right: she'd had to tell Chris the car was hers but he already thought she was a terrible driver, so she spun the plausible lie about slipping in the snow. It simply wouldn't occur to him that she'd run Jazz's car off the road to try and take out Logan. He might not believe it now, but I knew it as if she'd whispered the truth in my ear.

"Dwayne!" I yelled.

He'd stepped back as Cammie threw the Range Rover in reverse. I wondered for a moment if she was about to shoot out of the driveway backward.

Her face was grim through the windshield. She'd seen the direction from where Dwayne and I had come. She knew where we'd been. She had to know what I'd seen. She thought Dwayne knew, too.

I started running. My legs felt like ice.

Chris yelled something. He stepped forward, waving at her. He was puzzled by her actions, worried probably that he hadn't vamoosed before her arrival.

I stopped short at the front of the house, breathing hard.

"Dwayne," I called again, but I didn't have a lot of voice. He glanced over at me.

And then she threw the vehicle in drive and hit the gas. The back wheels spun for half a beat, then the Range Rover jumped forward, charging like a roaring beast straight at Dwayne.

"Dwayne!" I screamed as he dove to the right. Cammie twisted the wheel and came at him full bore.

He almost made it but she rammed forward. She caught him a glancing blow. His shoulder slammed into a tree. To my utter horror, she backed up to make another run at him. I was racing forward but I was too far away. Dwayne staggered a bit as Cammie punched the accelerator. The vehicle bumped forward over a stump. I screamed again as it burst forward, jamming him against the bole of a tree. His body jerked and fell over the hood.

"God, oh, God . . ." I ran toward him, ran toward Cammie, breathing his name. "Dwayne . . . Dwayne . . ." Behind me I was aware of Chris at my heels. Violet was yelling something from the house.

I skidded to a stop. Dwayne was splayed across her hood, his right leg crushed at the thigh.

He said, quietly, "I think it's broken."

Tears jumped to my eyes. "You're okay though? Okay? You're going to be okay?"

He glanced up, white-faced, then bent back on the hood of the Range Rover, restoring blood to his head.

"Jesus, Cammie," Chris whispered.

She sat in her car, hands gripped around the wheel, body taut as a bow string. Chris stared through the windshield at her through horror-stricken eyes.

Violet breathed heavily behind me. "I'll call nine-one-one," she said, and hurried back toward the house.

But Cammie suddenly pushed open her door, eyes wild, jaw set. She was breathing hard. To my shock she lunged at Dwayne, as if he were the cause of all her problems. Her fingernails raked at his face.

I scrambled around the vehicle, propelled by emotion. I

grabbed her by her hair. She turned on me like a wild thing, but I yanked as hard as I knew how, ripping some out by the roots. Inhuman noises were issuing from my throat. She shrieked and slapped at my hands. I hauled back with my right fist and punched her, hard, directly at her nose. I felt cartilage break beneath her skin. Blood flew in a spray. She gurgled and wailed. Her blue eyes were saucers.

"Get away from him," I growled. "Get away from him."

"You . . . You . . ." Her mouth opened in an O of shock and pain. She was crying, tears mixing with blood.

Rage consumed me. Something murderous moved through me. It must have showed on my face because Chris said, "Whoa . . ." in fear.

"Darlin', let it go," Dwayne's strained voice said somewhere through the red mist of fury that blinded me.

My one hand was still tangled in her hair; the other still in a fist. She was a pathetic quivering mass. I shook her hard. With an effort, I dropped her and backed away. I looked up and found Dwayne eyeing me with real concern.

"She broke your leg." I was outraged.

"You broke her nose," he pointed out.

Cammie sent up a piteous wail at this.

"Shut up," I said, and just managed to keep myself from kicking her.

We all ended up at the hospital in Bend. A couple of officers met us there and tried to ascertain what had come down. I think they thought we were all a bunch of meth addicts, high and crazed. When my tale about Cammie's murderous intent came out, they looked at each other in silent disbelief. I told them about the damaged car and explained it was linked to a hit-and-run in Portland, right around the previous Christmas. They left to check out my story.

Once Cammie's own rage subsided, she fell into hysterics, blaming anyone but herself. No one stood up for her. Chris was horrified when he learned the real reason the fender of her car was crumpled. Cammie cried for him, but he moved away from her as if she were acid.

Jazz was white-faced, both from shock and his own worsening headache. He started swaying on his feet, and the staff put him into a wheelchair. I explained about the headaches and he was put into another examining room.

The whole thing was a circus.

As for me, I wouldn't leave Dwayne. When they'd pushed the Range Rover away from him, I'd seen bone, blood, muscle and fat. It was like a view beneath Dwayne's skin. I'd had to duck my head between my knees and hang onto my stomach contents with an effort as the EMTs got him moved to a gurney and into the ambulance.

"I've got surgery ahead of me," Dwayne said, sounding more pissed than concerned as they prepared to take him to the operating room. "The bone's split. There's some blood vessel repair, too."

"I know," I said, fighting back another wave of sissy wooziness. "I heard."

"She blamed me," he said, in a totally conversational tone. I knew an IV was feeding him a soothing cocktail of drugs, but he sounded so normal it was eerie. "She blamed me for her breakup with her husband. Can you get that? She blamed me."

"She saw you coming from the direction of the equipment garage. She thought you knew she was responsible for the hit-and-run. And Chris was standing there. She probably believed you told him. It all just mixed together and she snapped."

"She's crazy," he said. His voice was taking on a slurred edge. "They're all crazy."

"Yes, Dwayne. They are."

Epilogue

I look back on the whole thing and what keeps bothering me is the fact that I was never really on a case. I was more of an investigator for the Spence/Miriam/Janice love triangle and for the First Addition vandal than I ever was for the Purcell fiasco.

Nevertheless, I wrote up the paperwork as if it were a major case file. I wrote everything down, all the data I'd learned and all my suppositions. I debated on handing the report over to Jazz but decided against it. He didn't ask for it, so I didn't offer. Besides, he's got more pressing issues. The accident that took his wife's life and left him with short-term memory loss created a slow-building blood clot. Unnoticed these many months, said clot had been slowly cutting off vital blood flow. It's been two weeks since Jazz underwent surgery to correct the problem. By all accounts, he's doing very well. I've been to see him several times but he doesn't really recognize me. Like before, he knows who he is and he knows Logan and the rest of the Purcells, sans Violet, of course, but Jane Kelly's association with the Purcells is a foggy sea. Logan desperately wants to think Jazz will remember me as soon as he recovers. He's got this lame-brained idea that we could be this little nuclear family, but I kind of think it's okay to be a missing piece. What a way to avoid a messy breakup.

As we all pulled our lives together, one more remarkable event occurred: James Purcell the Fourth walked onto the railroad bridge that spans the Willamette River between Lake Chinook and Milwaukie and stepped off to this death, an echo of his great-uncle Garrett I's suicide from the Steel Bridge on his twenty-first birthday over a hundred years earlier. James did manage to paint one more picture before he died. It was discovered in the playhouse the other day when Violet brought in a contractor to have it demolished.

It was a woman lying on a bed of thorns with three knifelike serpents aimed at her as if to bite.

Now, I glanced at my watch as I pulled to a stop in front of Dwayne's cabana. I was late from a trip to Lou's and the purchase of a couple of seriously saucy chili dogs. Dwayne's right leg is in a cast up to his hip. He's been spending most of his time on his back deck, but that may change as it's now the first week of November and the weather's gray and blustery with icy, shooting winds that whip your hair and nearly stop your breath. Hasn't fazed Dwayne yet. He just wraps himself in a down jacket, stocking cap and blankets and watches the world go by. I know the inactivity is making him stir crazy, but hey, as I keep telling him, he's lucky to be alive.

Unlocking his door, I stepped into the kitchen, balancing the dogs and looking for plates. These suckers were messy. Once I got them arranged, I headed to the back door, peering out at Dwayne for a moment while he still couldn't see me.

It's ironic that Logan was right all along: someone was trying to kill him. We now know that someone was Cammie. She detested him and reacted with murderous rage when she overheard him brag that Nana was leaving everything to him. But unfortunately for Cammie, though Jennifer was killed in that first accident and Jazz was seriously injured, her real target escaped harm. Logan was alive and well and free to inherit, which he did. The first chance she could, Cammie got him in her car and smashed it on purpose, trying to kill him, risking her own life in the process. There was never anyone following them. Hyped up on rage and a sense of injustice, Cammie used any means that would cross her daring, twisted mind to gain control of the money. She wanted it for Rosalie. She wanted it to buy back Chris's affections. She wanted it because she believed it was her due.

And when it all started to unravel she zeroed in on Dwayne and went after him like a crazed hunter.

Jesus. Sometimes I get a shiver all over when I think what could have happened to Dwayne. Now I took a moment before I opened the sliding door.

Dwayne looked up. At the same moment he picked up the thin metal rod with its small hook on the end that he uses as a scratcher and shoved it down inside his cast.

"Aren't you worried you'll rip something apart you shouldn't?" I asked.

"What are you? My mother?" He must be getting better because he's certainly getting grouchy.

I set the plates down on the table between our two chairs. "Chili dogs?" he said in surprise. "From Lou's?"

"Uh huh. Don't say I never do anything for you. Holy moley it's cold out here."

"You just need the proper attire."

We ate in companionable silence. Whatever romance had been brewing between Violet and Dwayne ended at Black Butte. Violet still hangs around a bit. She's taken their non-relationship in stride, apparently, but she likes Dwayne enough to keep in touch. I've started thinking she's okay again now that she isn't all over Dwayne. And no, I don't *even* want to consider what that means. I know better than to get involved with Dwayne. I do. And one of these days I'm going to really convince myself of that fact.

Finishing his chili dog, Dwayne wiped his hands and mouth on a paper towel, then grabbed up a pair of binoculars to gaze across Lakewood Bay. "You gotta see this," he said. "The house over there with the brick and wrought iron fence. The one with the black Mastercraft and the little flag thing on the boathouse?"

"Uh huh."

"They're like exhibitionists. Right in front of the bedroom

window. You can see her legs in a V. And he's right there between them."

"You're spying on them?" I was getting a Jimmy Stewart, *Rear Window* hit, but I took the binoculars anyway. I watched for a few seconds, said, "Ick," watched some more.

"When are you going to let me see that rule book?" he asked lazily.

"Which one?" I asked, though I knew.

"The one with the no Dwayne rule."

"You'd have a better chance of me singing that camp song to you again." I passed back the binoculars.

He shrugged and grinned at me. "I got the time."

"I don't. One of us has to work otherwise the landlord'll be at the door."

A noise sounded from inside the cabana: the front door opening and closing.

"Violet," Dwayne said.

Sure, enough. I glanced through Dwayne's sliding glass and saw her approaching. "Sorry, the chili dogs are gone," I said, though I wasn't really sorry at all. I mean, okay, I don't *love* her.

She sat down in the one extra chair, hard.

Dwayne and I both looked at her.

"My ex-husband's dead," she said, sounding like she was struggling to process.

"The one in Portland?" I asked.

She nodded. I was kind of thinking she was Typhoid Mary, the way people she came in contact with had been checking out the past few weeks.

"He was killed yesterday. On his daughter's wedding day. He was still at the house, and these robbers showed up thinking he was gone, and he wasn't, and they killed him."

"Wedding robbers?" I asked, looking at Dwayne, whose focus had sharpened on Violet.

"The police came to see me today." Violet's eyes were huge. "God, I don't believe this. They seem to think *I* did it."

"You said the robbers killed him," I reminded.

"Why do the police think you're responsible?" Dwayne asked.

Violet swallowed. "Because he was killed with a heavy metal platter that has my fingerprints on it."

"Did you kill him?" Dwayne asked in the moment that followed.

"I don't think so."

Dwayne reached for the binoculars and focused on the house across the bay. "Well . . ." he said, "the Purcell penchant for secrets and death continues."

"I need your help," Violet said, alarmed at the way Dwayne appeared to have checked out.

Dwayne shot me a look and lifted his brows. "Jane's the lead investigator now."

Violet turned to me, all the bravado I'd come to expect from her completely missing. "Will you help me?" she asked in a small voice.

I looked at her. I thought about how much money I might be able to make. Smiling, I asked her, "What's it to ya?"